That Time I Got Reincarnated as a SLIME

6

FUSE

Illustration by **Mitz Vah**

YEN ON

NEW YORK

That Time I Got Reincarnated as a SLIME 6

FUSE

Translation by Kevin Gifford
Cover art by Mitz Vah

TENSEI SHITARA SLIME DATTA KEN volume 6
© Fuse / Mitz Vah
All rights reserved.
First published in Japan in 2015 by MICROMAGAZINE PUBLISHING Co.
English translation rights-arranged with MICROMAGAZINE PUBLISHING Co.
through Tuttle-Mori Agency, Inc., Tokyo.

English translation © 2019 by Yen Press, LLC

Yen On
150 West 30th Street, 19th Floor
New York, NY 10001

Visit us at yenpress.com
facebook.com/yenpress
twitter.com/yenpress
yenpress.tumblr.com
instagram.com/yenpress

First Yen On Edition: August 2019

Yen On is an imprint of Yen Press, LLC.
The Yen On name and logo are trademarks of Yen Press, LLC.

Library of Congress Cataloging-in-Publication Data
Names: Fuse, author. | Mitz Vah, illustrator. | Gifford, Kevin, translator.
Title: That time I got reincarnated as a slime / Fuse ; illustration by Mitz Vah ; translation by Kevin Gifford.
Other titles: Tensei Shitara Slime datta ken. English
Description: First Yen On edition. | New York : Yen ON, 2017–
Identifiers: LCCN 2017043646 | ISBN 9780316414203 (v. 1 : pbk.) | ISBN 9781975301118 (v. 2 : pbk.) |
    ISBN 9781975301132 (v. 3 : pbk.) | ISBN 9781975301149 (v. 4 : pbk.) | ISBN 9781975301163 (v. 5 : pbk.) |
    ISBN 9781975301187 (v. 6 : pbk.)
Subjects: GSAFD: Fantasy fiction.
Classification: LCC PL870.S4 T4613 2017 | DDC 895.63/6—dc23
LC record available at https://lccn.loc.gov/2017043646

ISBNs: 978-1-9753-0118-7 (paperback)
        978-1-9753-0119-4 (ebook)

10 9 8 7 6 5 4 3 2

LSC-C

Printed in the United States of America

That Time I Got Reincarnated as a SLIME

6

CONTENTS | THE OCTAGRAM RISING

THE MAGIC-BORN'S RUSE

That Time I Got Reincarnated as a Slime

"Hoo dear, nearly bit it for good back there..."

Laplace was muttering to himself as he appeared before his master. He clearly had the injuries to back that assessment up.

"Tough, huh?" casually replied his lord, a boy with black hair and a powerful presence.

"Well, hang on there, lad," Laplace whined. "*Tough* hardly even begins to describe what I had to wade through back there, yeah? Getting inside was painful enough, but getting *out*—oh, dear, who can say how many times I toed the line?"

"Oh, I think someone like you would work it out. Even if someone killed you, I'm not sure you'd even know *how* to die."

"Oof. You're a mean one, you know that?"

"So," the boy aloofly continued as Laplace cried the best fake tears he could, "did you find out what lies behind the Western Holy Church?"

"...Um. I know this ain't the kind of report I should be giving, but... Well, no. Nobody can. It's bloody impossible, is what it is."

This stone-faced admission didn't faze the boy at all. He gave a soft smile, as if he expected that reply the whole time.

"Hmm. Ever the liar, aren't you? You had to have uncovered a hint or two, at least?"

Laplace shrugged and sighed. "Sheesh. After all I went through for my info, I figured I could name my price with ya. But you just see right through me, don'tcha? There's no beating ya."

"Hee-hee-hee. Thanks for the compliment, but my prices remain firm, all right?"

"There's no beating ya," Laplace repeated.

"Oh, no need for complaints. I'll pay your full asking price. And in fact, our demon lord friend's consciousness has taken root for a while now. He's done a wonderful job transferring over to his homunculus."

The boy gave Laplace an amused smile as he rang a small bell to call for the woman stationed outside the door.

"Yes, sir?"

Into the room strode a beautiful woman—graceful, polite, the epitome of the classic executive secretary. Her skin was smooth, light in color, and her well-defined facial features suited the bun her blond hair was tied back in. She had blue eyes that shined like a pair of mystical lapis lazuli—but no matter how mesmerizing the light from them was, they still couldn't hide a vague sense of evil lurking inside.

"Huh? Ah, you don't mean…?"

The sight of the woman startled Laplace, but he could spot a familiar glint in her eyes. Then he erupted into laughter, realizing who she truly was.

"Well, what's with *that* getup, huh? Didja make a gender swap while I didn't notice? It looks good on you, I ain't gonna lie, but it couldn't be much *more* different from before, eh?"

"Enough from you," countered the woman, ignoring Laplace's bait. "It took me ten years to obtain a body I could freely move around in. I am not going to complain about minor grievances."

"Polite" was no longer the way to describe her. She stood boldly, sporting an undefeatable grin. She gave Laplace a friendly pat on the shoulder before sitting down.

"So if you're introducing me to this man, I suppose there's not much need to keep the act going?"

"No," replied the boy, "but I'd like you to maintain the facade in public, please. If it's just between us, I suppose there's no great need, no."

"Oh? Well, if that's what you want, boss, I'll do it. Is it all right if I ask why?"

"Because you're weak, Kazalim. Your powers still aren't complete yet, are they? Just watch over Clayman until your full Curse Lord force is back with you."

Kazalim, the woman posing as his secretary, gave this reply a sullen nod. She had the name of a very old demon lord—the one who attempted to punish a human named Leon for declaring himself a demon lord of some faraway backwater area and paid for it with his life. Once, he was head of the Moderate Jesters; now, she was a lord both Clayman and Laplace were attempting to resurrect.

Her overpowering strength was long gone. All that remained was a prim, graceful young woman. Just before she could be obliterated from existence, Kazalim experienced a rather unlikely series of coincidences that caused her to possess the body of this boy—and just the other day, they had finally managed to transfer her astral body into a replacement homunculus. The boy was her "boss" for now, the power from her glory days long gone. That was the way their pact worked, and Kazalim had no quarrel with it. Over the past ten years of dealing with this acquaintance, she had fully accepted her place in the power hierarchy.

"Fair enough. My power *is* incomplete. I let that demon lord Leon defeat me, and I lost my body in the most unsightly of fashions. I know my soul's settled in this homunculus, but it's so fragile, I'd tear it apart if I unleashed my full force. I can't really call this a *complete* resurrection…"

"Ah, is *that* the issue with ya? Well, if our president is callin' this guy boss, then I guess you're *my* boss, too. Sure ain't just another client by this point, no! So hopefully you don't mind if I clear the air with you guys a bit."

"You never change," the boy said. "After all this time, and after you helped us revive our fallen president, you still don't trust me?"

"Ha-ha-ha! Nah, nah, *that's* a different story. But I gotta laugh at how you look now, sir. You're this crazy beautiful woman now!"

"…Am I? What do my looks matter?"

"Nah, I mean, the dichotomy between your speech and your looks... It's funny, that's all."

"I *know* that, you... Or 'I am aware of that,' perhaps? If I am going to keep up the charade, I had best sound more like the lady I am."

"Uh, *that's* what you're concerned about? Because, I mean... Ba-ha-ha-ha!"

"Silence," Kazalim spat at the guffawing Laplace. "I'll have you know this body wasn't my choice. The boss here provided a homunculus modified with special technology from the Sorcerous Dynasty of Thalion."

"Yeah, I sure did. And that didn't come cheap, either. We needed a vessel without any soul at all, or else they'd get all mixed up, and the transplant probably wouldn't have worked." The boy sneered. "For that matter, if you had fled into anyone besides me, Kazalim, *you'd* probably be too tangled up to split off at all, I don't think. All right? So I really don't want to hear any complaints about how you look."

"I appreciate it, boss," said Kazalim.

The boy still didn't seem pleased, not until Laplace offered his own thanks.

"Sure. So can we move this along? I know it's great we're all back together again, but I want to get down to business. Tell me what you've found, Laplace."

The smile disappeared from Kazalim's face as she turned her eyes toward Laplace. He nodded, taking a more serious demeanor.

"Yeah, you kept yer promise and made my dream come true. I better show you a little sincerity, too, eh? So I infiltrated the Western Holy Church to find out what's behind it, but I tell you, I just don't have any idea."

He then began to describe his findings.

Laplace's mission was to find out what made the Holy Church tick. It remained an independent religion, headquartered in the Holy Empire of Lubelius, but much of its internal workings remained a mystery. It positioned itself as an advocate for justice and for the weak, enjoying tremendous influence on the Western

Nations—a very inconvenient truth for the boy. That was why he employed Laplace from the fixer team of the Moderate Jesters to find who they *really* were—and exploit any potential weaknesses for later.

The boy was fairly convinced there was another side to them. If the Western Holy Church was *really* an advocate for truth, he'd have to undertake whatever scheme it took to rip them away from that pedestal, but that was strictly a last resort. Now simply wasn't the time for it. The Church, after all, enjoyed the services of Hinata Sakaguchi, head of the Western Nation's crusaders and the most powerful paladin the world knew.

"So," Laplace continued, "thanks to Hinata's absence, I managed to make it into the Church all right, but there was nothin' suspicious about anything I saw inside. So I headed over to Lubelius's holy lands—to be exact, the Inner Cloister, at the peak of their holiest mountain."

He began to gesture excitedly as he spoke. It was there, after all, where he saw the fearsome truth.

"And the most amazing thing, you know... The entire land was just filled with this kind of sacred presence!"

"Why wouldn't it be?" the boy asked. "It's a holy land."

"What're you, stupid?" Kazalim added. "Did someone erase your brain since last we met?"

"No, no, listen to me! And you're falling back in to non-lady mode again, President."

"I don't need your— I mean, don't worry about little old me! Just keep going."

So Laplace kept going, a little resentful at this treatment.

....

......

...

A little ways from Western Holy Church headquarters was the religion's Holy Temple. This was where the Papacy was located, the political arm of the Church that worked at the behest of the Holy Emperor, spokesperson for the heavens.

It wasn't until he entered this Temple that Laplace began to feel something was off. Within its chambers, he could detect a faint amount of magic that applied itself to his nervous system. It was a very ingenious spell, one he noticed only because it was automatically blocked by Falsifier, his unique skill.

There's a surprise, ain't it? Must mean somebody here can wield spiritual magic as strong as mine...

Laplace braced himself as he walked toward the cathedral.

He already had some knowledge of the enemy's organizational structure—and from what he could see, the relationship between the Church and Lubelius was very tangled indeed.

The Church was built to worship Luminus, the one and only god in the world (as they defined it). Lubelius was the same way, which meant one could say they were allies when it came to religious issues. In terms of the balance of power, however, the Church held nearly all the cards.

The reason? Simple: Hinata. The Church had its knights deployed at points across the Western Nations, providing an effective bulwark to protect the weak—and it was Hinata Sakaguchi who built them, and by extension the Church, into the powerful group it was today. Technically speaking, the Church worked under the patronage of Lubelius, charged exclusively with spreading the good word about Luminism. Now that their mission had extended out into "doing good" for the weak at large, the relationship was no longer as simple as that.

More than anything, though, the real problem lay with the knights Hinata herself had trained. Even Laplace couldn't help but fear them a little, for their allegiance was not at all with Lubelius but solely with the one god, Luminus—and with Hinata, who devoted herself fully to Luminism. That was what enabled the Western Holy Church to exist independently from Lubelius.

And this brought up another problem—Lubelius's war power resided in more than just its crusaders. Even the Holy Emperor kept an official Lubelian force, the Imperial Guard that answered to nothing but the Papacy below it, and this was another group to be reckoned with. Founded on the ideal that everyone is equal under the name of Luminus, it was a motley collection of soldiers in assorted clothing and equipment. The qualifications for joining were straightforward—be a devoted follower of Luminism and be at least an A-ranked fighter. Thanks to these clear but fiendishly difficult requirements, the Imperial Guard was small and exclusive, packed with the best of the best in warriors and magicians, along with their servants. This force was underestimated at one's own peril.

Hinata was listed as head knight in this Guard as well, and the Papacy listed Cardinal Nicolaus Speltus, a dedicated admirer of Hinata, as its chief counsel. Hinata could almost claim the whole of the Church for herself, and this was the main reason why. She had control over both wings of the Holy Emperor's main force and yet was exempt from having to swear her allegiance to that leader. It was thanks to this inscrutable woman, Hinata, that relations between the Holy Church and Holy Empire were as twisted as they had become.

And simply recalling all this advance knowledge he had procured made Laplace sigh in frustration.

What a crazy lady…

The cathedral was full of spiritual force, more than enough to call forth the greatest of holy spirits. To a magic-born like Laplace, this spiritual presence was supremely difficult to deal with. It dulled his senses, making him want to flee the site as quickly as possible.

He took a moment to gather himself before deciding which way to go. Heading toward the peak of this holy mount would reportedly lead him to the Inner Cloister, where one could communicate with Luminus. His senses were telling him there was something to be found here in the cathedral as well.

"So, ah, now what…?"

He wavered, but for only a moment. Then he strode out of the cathedral and straight for the Cloister. Spend too much time in this building, and Hinata could come back at any moment. Now, while she was gone, was his best chance to find a hint as to what Luminus, the central doctrine of the Western Holy Church, really *was*.

I'll just hop on up, he thought as he traversed the mountain path, *and take a quick li'l peek around.*

It was his choice—and it was a mistake. No, it wasn't fruitless; he certainly learned much from the experience. But to Laplace, the danger that resulted proved far beyond his comfort level.

Proceeding up the stone steps, Laplace finally reached the shrine at the peak of the mountain. This was notably smaller than the cathedral down below, but in terms of grandeur, the two were incomparable. This small structure was, in the true meaning of the term, the god's domain.

Now, it was divine in its silence, putting pressure upon Laplace's mind. But even amid that solemnity, he could detect the familiar feel of magic.

...The heck? Magic, in this supposedly holiest of places? That's weird. Don't like that too much, no...

He could tell that Hinata, the most formidable obstacle in his way, was not here. If the magic belonged to someone else, that someone couldn't be ignored, but—in Laplace's mind—it was no threat to him, either.

But was that the right appraisal to make? Now Laplace, deep down in his heart, wasn't so sure. *Come on, man. You know you're completely hiding your presence here. Everything's perfect. If some ruffian shows up, just run.*

Bracing himself, Laplace reactivated his Stealth Mode and attempted to slip into the shrine. Then he rolled right back out, barely maintaining his balance, stymied by the vision of a beam of light piercing straight through his body.

"You insect, you mere cockroach, dirtying the throne of your *god*!!"

All of a sudden, the shrine was filled with an overwhelming presence, dressed in luxuriant garb that covered a chiseled, muscular figure. His short, curly blond hair shined brightly, exhibiting the full force of his will. This was a ruler—an absolute ruler—and what Laplace couldn't help but notice first about him were the two large fangs jutting out from his lips.

"A-a vampire...?!"

"Silence, insect. I will judge you myself. Consider it an honor to die here!"

The next moment, beams of crimson light danced across the peak. His path of escape cut off, Laplace stood there helplessly as his body was torn to shreds.

....

......

...

Laplace took a moment to quiver as he retold the story.

"I tell you, it was downright scary. I thought that was it for me!"

"Um, yeah," the boy replied, "but why wasn't it?"

Kazalim merely smiled. "Like I told you. He doesn't know *how* to die."

"Oh, stop phrasing it that way. Anyone should have an escape plan and a decent amount of security backup during an op like that, y'know? But I'm telling you, I've just been dragged across the coals lately. Wish I could have something to brag about for a change!"

"Yeah, yeah. You know you're a covert operative. If you're fixin' to be the hero in shining armor, maybe look for another line of work?"

"He's right," the boy agreed. "Laplace, the key to your job is completing your missions. How...*gallant* you look doing it hardly matters, does it?"

"No, true enough. It's just, if I keep this up, I'm gonna start getting *used* to being a loser..."

"What's the problem with that?"

"He said it. As long as you survive and win in the end, we have nothing to complain about." Kazalim hardened her expression. "So what happened?"

Laplace nodded at her. "Right. There's the rub. If this guy can overwhelm me *that* much, there's no mistakin' that he's one strong dude. The question is, who is he? What's a magic-born of *that* caliber doin' in this supposedly high holy place? That's the key to all this, and it could be enough to shake the very foundation of the Western Holy Church, huh?"

"A magic-born, huh...? And a high-level one, a vampire, conspiring with the Church..."

The boy nodded his agreement, unable to hide his surprise at this unexpected development.

"Whoever he is," commented Kazalim, "he is dangerous. A man capable of defeating Laplace, to the best of my knowledge, would have to be far more than *merely* magic-born."

"Yeah. I'm with ya there."

"What do you mean?" the boy asked.

"Well, not to brag, but I'm not exactly a wimp, y'know? Even with the dryad I faced down before, if I seriously duked it out, I woulda won, y'know? I just fled 'cause I was on their home turf in the forest, and I didn't want 'em callin' for reinforcements on me. No real point going all out to try to kill 'er, either. But *this* foe was on another level, I tell you. It didn't feel like some sub-demon lord to me—it felt like a *full* one, through 'n' through. Someone like me, all I could do was run."

Dryads were extremely powerful foes in forest lands, intrinsically capable of instant teleportation through the trees. The Plant Whisper skill let them "share" any and all information with others of their species, sending friends over to help their brethren anytime it was needed. This made them enough of a threat that Laplace opted to run away the last time he saw one, even though he could likely conquer one in a duel.

This guy, however, was different. "That was a monster," Laplace declared. "Stronger than me, no doubt about it."

The atmosphere in the room grew heavy.

"A demon lord, huh…? What do you think, Kazalim?"

Kazalim snorted. "I told you. He is dangerous. As far as I am aware, only one man could match that description."

"Oh? Who's that?"

"…The demon lord Valentine. One of the old guard, a man on par with myself during my glory years."

"For real? 'Cause if he's a match for *you*, I see I was totally right to flee. Lucky thing I trusted my instincts."

Laplace shrugged. He had taken pains to break in when Hinata was away, only to stumble right up to a demon lord. The irony of it made him wince.

"...Hmm. A demon lord within the Church, huh? D'you think this Valentine's actually the Holy Emperor, then?"

"Ooh, I dunno about that! You think a demon lord would raise a finger to protect humanity? President, what kind of guy was Valentine when you knew 'im?"

Kazalim closed her eyes and searched through her memories, tapping a graceful finger against her forehead as she recalled the vivid images of the past.

"This body may not show it," she said, "but I've lived through three of the Great Wars that occur every five hundred years. Three of them. You can call *me* one of the old guard as well, but by the time I joined that club, there were already six demon lords ahead of me..."

As she put it, the demon lord Valentine had attained the title before Kazalim herself. His force was massive, more than worthy of the term *vampire* and the connotations of immortality weaved into it. To Kazalim, who had evolved from an elf (similarly known for longevity) to a walking dead, the thought of a vampire, the symbol of eternal life, also serving as a demon lord gave her pause.

"...To tell you the truth, Valentine and I have dueled to the death a few different times. It never reached a definitive conclusion, though. Once you reach our level, you can lay waste to an entire landscape without hurting yourselves at all. So instead, we adopted the tradition of talking over things and deciding by majority vote... and that led to the Walpurgis system. The fact that it takes three votes to convene one is a throwback to when there were still only seven demon lords in existence. Guess nobody cared enough to change it."

She let out an elegant, ladylike chuckle. The juxtaposition between this and her other, masculine mannerisms was starting to unnerve the other two people in the room, not that she noticed. Then her face turned stony once more.

"And that's why I feel safe in telling you this. That man, Valentine; he sees humans and demi-humans as nothing more than chattel. Even if the entire world was turned on its end, the idea of him serving as guardian is simply impossible."

Laplace nodded his agreement as the boy thought over Kazalim's assessment.

"All right. So maybe they forced some kind of agreement?"

"Are you listening to me, Laplace? Promises and agreements only work between two parties with equal force behind them."

"Yeah..."

He didn't seem too married to the idea himself.

"Plus," the boy said, "I find it hard to believe that someone as closed-minded as Hinata would team up with a demon lord. I wonder if what Laplace ran into wasn't a demon lord at all, but some magic-born whose name we are not aware of yet?"

"No," Kazalim replied, "I do think that was Valentine. Those dancing beams of crimson light? That's the giveaway. Valentine also goes by the name of Bloody Lord, and he can take blood and vaporize it into beams of magicules known as Bloodrays."

As she put it, a Bloodray was a type of spread-fire particle cannon. By converting his own blood into magical particles, he was capable of firing it off in concentrated rays of force. The amount of magical power that process required meant it had to be a demon lord working it.

"So you're saying that Laplace ran into the demon lord Valentine, and that Valentine would never willingly cooperate with human kingdoms. Wouldn't that lend more credence to the theory that the Holy Emperor is Valentine?"

"Yeah," muttered Laplace, "that would explain matters. I'd sincerely wonder how he managed to pull the wool over Hinata's eyes, though."

"Well," Kazalim stated, "I suppose it remains the most convincing explanation we have. I do have my doubts and concerns about that... But the important thing is, we now know for a fact that Valentine, a demon lord, was lurking inside a domain that only the Holy Emperor has access to."

"And you're *sure* it's him?" the boy pressed.

"I'm fully convinced. Laplace's description matches my own memory, and from what I know about him, Valentine would never willfully serve under someone else..."

"Yeah, there ain't that many magic-born who could whip me, I don't think. But if I'm dealin' with the likes of *this*, well, I dunno how much more reconnaissance I'm capable of here."

"Well," the boy said, apparently convinced, "this is still pretty useful intelligence. Expertly done, Laplace."

His face shined now, revealing traces of the joy he felt now that he had a tool powerful enough to potentially take down the Holy Church. There was a powerful demon lord among his enemy's forces, but that didn't seem to concern him at all. He was too busy thinking about what to do next with this intel to care. For him, formulating his next plan of action came as easily as figuring out the next epic prank to pull off on the kids next door.

∗

"So that's all the info I have for ya. But speakin' of demon lords, what's Clayman up to these days?"

The boy scowled at Laplace's apparently unwelcome question, pulling his dark, shiny hair back with one hand. "Well," he complained, "*that* wound up being a total failure."

"Failure?"

"Yeah. Everything went fine up until we had Rimuru, that slime you mentioned, fight against Hinata. Then it all fell apart, pretty much..."

The boy briefed the others on how things unfolded. First, Clayman won over the demon lord Milim, thanks to the Orb of Domination the boy provided him. Once he did, they needed to test her out, to see just how deep the orb had put Milim in their thrall.

"So we tried to find a decent opponent to test her strength on. But instead of demon lords that we didn't have much intel or even a location on, we picked Carillon, since he seemed to be the least intelligent out of them all."

"Along the way," Kazalim continued, "we thought we could have her destroy the capital of the Beast Kingdom of Eurazania. The city would've been packed with former enslaved humans, souls to harvest so I can become a true demon lord once more..."

He and the boy exchanged glances and sighed.

"We figured those souls would energize Clayman, too. Two birds with one stone."

"But then Milim went out of control and declared war on the guy..."

And thanks to that, Carillon and the other targets had a weeklong head start to prepare for the battle—more than enough time to evacuate the capital.

"You know," the boy reflected, "looking back at it, I guess it's pretty hard to enthrall a demon lord with a magical item like that. You have to apply all these conditions to it, or else it'll get all messed up."

"I hope you would trust me more than that. They don't call me the Curse Lord for show, I'll have you know. That Orb of Domination was a perfectly crafted Artifact, one of my best pieces of work. It was Clayman who ruined everything."

"Ah, no point dredging that up any longer. Anyway, we couldn't collect any souls in the Beast Kingdom, so we decided to check things out in Farmus next."

"Farmus? That kingdom?"

"Right. Thanks to that summoning ritual they invented, Farmus had a ton of otherworlders living there. I figured now was as good a time as any to pare down their forces a little. So I used a few back channels to give them intelligence on Tempest and whet the appetites of their greedy king and his advisers."

"You wouldn't believe how quickly they bit, either."

That idea grew from Laplace's previous report, back when their operation to make an orc lord into a malleable demon lord ran into setbacks. The idea was to whip Farmus up into enough of a frenzy to make them declare war on the Jura-Tempest Federation. With all the high-level magic-born in their ranks, Tempest surely had what it took to take out at least a few of Farmus's otherworlders before going down for the count.

What's more, Rimuru, lord of the monsters, was traveling abroad on his own business, and Clayman's own minions had infiltrated Tempest lands. The boy had planned to use Rimuru as bait for

Hinata; as far as he was concerned, this plan offered the best of both worlds.

"But then, well, nothing went according to plan. I mean, that slime Rimuru actually fled Hinata with his life intact. You can't let your guard down around him for a moment. Kind of like you, Laplace."

"Thanks for the compliment."

"And as if *that* wasn't bad enough..."

"By my prediction," Kazalim continued, "that still wouldn't be have been enough to keep Farmus from winning the war. If the monsters' lord joined the battle, that would be another matter, but honestly speaking, it didn't matter who won. We'd just work with the victors. The purpose of the war was to generate dead people—more souls to harvest. Then we could finally awaken our beloved Clayman to his true self. And then..."

And then it all fell apart. The entire Farmus force was wiped off the face of the earth by a single slime.

"It's hard to believe, but it's the truth," the boy grumbled.

"In all the many times I've used my unique skill Schemer to formulate a plan," the clearly angry Kazalim added, "I've never seen it go quite *this* far awry."

"H-hang on a second! Just *one* slime? You pullin' my leg? Did Farmus get caught *that* off guard, man?"

"I told you, you wouldn't believe how quickly they bit. With a snap of the fingers, they had a force of twenty thousand knights and magicians on the ground. And just like that, they were all gone. We couldn't confirm any survivors at all."

"Whaa?! That's ridiculous..."

The unlikeliness of it all had even Laplace at a loss for words.

"Oh, it hasn't even *begun* to be ridiculous. Clayman surveyed the battlefield after it was over, and according to his report, there were absolutely no corpses left to be found. That could only mean a monster was summoned, or created, using the bodies as an offering."

"If I cast Creation: Golem with *that* number of corpses," Kazalim said, "I couldn't even begin to guess what kind of monster would result. And not just corpses—the corpses of strong, well-trained fighters, in a battlefield laden with anguish and despair. The perfect casting environment! I would expect a sub-demon lord to result from it, at the very least."

"Sounds like it. Although it's the fact *we* couldn't retrieve those souls that's the worst of all. Clayman said there wasn't a single one left floating around. So once again, we've failed to awaken him to the next level."

The boy sighed in regret. He began to wonder whether conducting all these plans in parallel was coming back to bite him. He had focused on efficiency, only to put too many things into action at once—and once one tactic came undone, it affected everything else. *Maybe*, he thought, *I was too greedy myself.*

"So you're sayin' that this slime Rimuru sucked up all those souls for 'imself?"

"Is that some kind of joke, Laplace? No magic-born could do that! Not unless he is the seed of a demon lord."

Kazalim was right. Even the most seasoned of wizards would have a hard time gathering twenty thousand souls and keeping them all under their control. Recklessly attempting that would cause the souls' latent energies to unravel, quickly falling out of control. And even if it worked—

"Ha-ha-ha! No, I know what you mean, Laplace," the boy said. "If he *did* snatch up twenty thousand souls, then he'll have turned into one hell of a monster by now, eh? Was that what you were thinking?"

"Pretty much, yeah. Just a passing thought, really. Better not overthink it."

Laplace's mere suggestion caused them both to laugh at him. The concept was simply beyond comprehension.

Not even Kazalim knew the exact conditions required for making a potential demon lord into a "true" demon lord, although she could at least guess that it required a tremendous number of souls. They were currently limited to having Clayman experiment to see what results they got. Clayman had tried to experiment on the orc lord, of course, and everybody in the room knew how *that* turned out. And given that knowledge, the idea of something like a *slime* appearing out of nowhere and becoming a "true" demon lord was beyond even Kazalim's imagination.

Laplace, of course, was absolutely correct, even if none of them knew it at the time. He began to wonder what kind of odyssey Clayman had been on while he was running for dear life from Valentine.

"So, ah, what's Clayman up to right now?"

"Awaiting further orders," said the boy. "At this point, we can't do anything bolder than what we're doing now. Luckily, Milim kept her end of the promise—she waited a week, and then she turned the Beast Kingdom into a field of ash. So we're pulling back for now, to reconsider our strategy."

"Oh? So things haven't been a total failure, then?"

"Underestimate me at your peril, Laplace. I may have lost most of my force, but trickery remains my core asset."

"It sure is. If *everything* went awry, even I would blow my top a little about that! So maybe things have been delayed a bit, but we did weaken the kingdom of Farmus tremendously. That pretty much puts the Western Nations in order, so it'll be simple to seize them all."

"And once that happens," reflected Kazalim, "the Forest of Jura should provide a fine breakwater against the Eastern Empire."

"Ah, I see, President. Negotiate with whichever side wins. Ain't no need to destroy the monster nation at all, huh?"

That, in a way, was the true worth of the demon lord Kazalim's Schemer ability. No matter how things turned out, she had a knack for concocting plans where her side wound up on top. Recalling that, Laplace was relieved to see Kazalim was still herself after all.

"Plus," the boy continued, "with Milim defeating Carillon, we've proven that the Orb of Domination is an effective tool against this caliber of enemy. That's all the force we'll need to show. Beyond that, all we need to do is see how the other demon lords fall into place."

"Precisely. That's why I ordered Clayman to refrain from taking further action. The Eastern Empire's going to do something either way—and with that comes our opportunity to recover some souls for ourselves."

"Uh-huh. And as long as the eyes of the Western Holy Church are on the monster nation, it's more convenient for us to keep that federation around anyway."

Laplace could see the logic in this. No need for panic. Just keep your eyes on the Church and avoid conflict with any of the other forces.

"So for now, at least, we're targetin' the Church?"

"That's the plan."

"Not that it'll be easy," cautioned Kazalim. "We have to consider the possibility of Hinata and Valentine working as a team. Needlessly prodding them would be dangerous."

As she and the boy saw it, as long as the Western Nations were in their hands, the monster nation didn't have to be considered an obstacle. Plus, considering the mistakes they made, they now thought it wiser to fully gauge the enemy forces, avoiding a dual-pronged operation for the time being. For now, they were gunning for the Western Holy Church—and the Holy Empire of Lubelius behind it. Those two would be struck first—carefully this time, making sure none of their activities were noticed on the surface. In that scenario, the monster nation was actually helpful to them. As long as they kept fanning the flames of Church doctrine, it'd be child's play to keep the eyes of Hinata and her force squarely upon Tempest.

"The Church can hardly afford to ignore the presence of the magic-born Rimuru, either. With Farmus thoroughly defeated, I doubt the other nations will be so willing to take on the mantle of waging holy war. They'll need to perform some kind of action to reaffirm their authority."

"Yeah." The boy grinned. "If we can parry them and keep both sides engaged, they might even destroy each other. All we have to do is wait for an opportunity to weaken the both of them."

They were talking about a magic-born capable of single-handedly sweeping a force of twenty thousand into the afterlife. Without Hinata on the scene, taking him on was patently impossible. So they would wait for the right moment and come up with the perfect scheme for it—and the way it sounded to Laplace, they already had a pretty solid idea what they'd do. Neither sounded irresolute at all about it.

"But the problem, Laplace, is that your report was a little... unexpected," said the boy.

"Very much so," agreed Kazalim, also a tad indignant. "Valentine being involved in this... Assuming he truly *is* involved with anything at all. I find it hard to believe Hinata would ever cooperate with him, judging by her personality."

It was clear from the way they phrased it that conquering the Western Holy Church would be far easier without Valentine around. It made Laplace feel awkward, despite it being no fault of his.

"Well," he attempted, "we don't know about that yet. But if you'd just want to lure the demon lord out into public so he wouldn't get in the way of our investigations, we could pull that off, couldn't we?"

"Mm? What do you mean, Laplace?"

"I mean, why not just ask Clayman to convene Walpurgis? Frey's bound to join us on that, and her along with Milim gives us the three signatories we need, yeah?"

Convening the Walpurgis Council would bring all the demon lords together.

The boy smiled a bit. "...I see. That *would* drag Valentine out of his holy domain, I think."

"Well, well! Your eyes are sharper than I thought, Laplace. If we can just find the right timing to keep Hinata away from the mountain as well, your inquiry should advance by leaps and bounds."

"Huh? You want *me* going back there?!"

"Why wouldn't we?"

"Yes, why wouldn't we?"

Oh, brother, Laplace thought. But the boy and Kazalim weren't interested in his feedback. They had the outline of a plan, and now it was time to work out the details.

BETWEEN
MONSTER
AND MAN

That Time I Got Reincarnated as a Slime

Clayman was never one to place too much trust in his strength.

He was the demon lord who took over all of Kazalim's lands. Once Kazalim was defeated at the hands of the demon lord Leon, all the people who served him came to rely upon Clayman for guidance. The domains of the two lords wound up being merged under Clayman's rule, something none of the other demon lords voiced any complaint over. It all happened fairly quickly, thanks to the ever-careful Kazalim's preparations in case the worst came to pass.

This resulted in a large war chest for Clayman to work with, allowing him to build a first-class force despite being a relatively new member of the club. Financially speaking, he was number one in the group—or to put it another way, Clayman was the demon lord who best knew how to manage his money. He engaged in under-the-table trade with the Eastern Empire and had a roaring business going with the Dwarven Kingdom as well. Taking advantage of both trade connections allowed him access to the newest weapons and armor from both east and west.

He took advantage of his access to past relics and magical armor to boost his war power. It proved to be useful bait to make power-hungry magic-born do his bidding. His riches attracted them right to him, ripe for using and abusing. That was how Clayman preferred to do business, and it didn't mean he was stingy with his earnings. He lavished his forces with gifts, carefully meting them out so he could establish a vast network of coconspirators in nations across the world—none of whom even knew one another's faces.

Everything was going the way he planned it. His ultimate mission, to gain access to every piece of information and place the entire world under his rule, was already halfway complete.

The only thing Clayman lacked, he knew, was power. War, in the end, was ultimately a game of numbers—that was his reasoning and also the rationale for why he never overestimated his capabilities. No matter how much power he had built up, he knew all too well that he could still falter in the end. That was how much of a shock the demon lord Kazalim's defeat was to him, although Clayman *did* feel he was a little too unprepared for it.

So he established roots at the core of each geopolitical force and gradually, carefully, expanded on them. And now, Clayman had new strength to tap, truly decisive strength. That was the demon lord Milim—capable of enough overwhelming violence to stand head and shoulders above the other nine. Carillon, whom Clayman appraised as stronger than him, barely put up a fight. She destroyed his nation completely by herself.

And now that he had the power he lacked within himself, Clayman could feel his mood soaring to the skies. He had always wanted to defeat Leon, and now he believed that desire was within sight.

Before that, however...

Heh-heh-heh. How nice to see that boy came to the same conclusion that I did. Have the hated Holy Church fight against the magic-born Rimuru—that's the best way to sap the strength of both sides.

Have them crush each other. No need to go through any pain themselves.

To make that happen, we need more information on the Holy Church's internal workings. Could they truly be connected with the demon lord Valentine...? If we can convene Walpurgis right when we send Laplace back in, there's little doubt that security will be lighter. A fine plan of action!

He brought a glass of wine to his lips, savoring the taste and basking in euphoria.

The wine was a hundred-year-old vintage, old enough that one could almost taste the time and labor put into it, to say nothing of the aroma. Only the most carefully picked examples reached his cellar, carefully stored to ensure only the highest of quality, waiting ever so patiently to be served—all this, just for the sake of Clayman. To him, all of this was a given. It was perfectly natural for him to believe that, for a mighty king like him, only the best would be appropriate.

He let the aroma settle in his nose as he began to think.

"So what should be the pretext of this Walpurgis...?"

It was set for one week from now, at night. It would be a new moon that night, the time of the month when the power of vampires was at its weakest. Every measure had to be taken to ensure Valentine couldn't flex his full muscle. The main question to figure out was the motivation—the reason why all these demon lords were coming together. He squinted, staring into thin air.

"...If we are going to attack," he whispered lightly, "now is the time. We could take this chance to seize Carillon's territory as well."

"Sure, Clayman, but ya just got ordered to sit tight for a spell, didn'tcha?"

Clayman smirked at the voice that apparently came from nowhere. "You're here, Laplace? Just as rude as always, I see."

"Don't tell me you didn't notice me. You were *that* lost in thought?"

"Heh-heh-heh. Can you blame me? I have been granted the opportunity twice to awaken to my full demon lord self, and I lost it both times out of my failures."

"Ah, no need to stew over it. The way the president sees it, the Eastern Empire's gonna go on the move soon enough either way."

"I'm sure they will. But you see, Laplace, I've come up with a wonderful idea. The Beast Kingdom's capital might be gone, but there are still a plethora of weaker races residing in its hinterlands. Perhaps I could swallow up Carillon's territory before the other demon lords can, gather the survivors together, and kill them. That should be enough to trigger my awakening. A smart plan of action, don't you think?"

"Whoa, whoa, kinda pushing it a bit too far, eh? I mean, killing innocent people when we still don't really know what sets off the whole thing?"

Clayman winced. It was not the enthusiastic agreement he was expecting.

"That's rather out of character for you, Laplace. Do you sympathize for them? The weak are there to be exploited. What could make them happier than dying for my sake?"

"Maybe, but you already killed thousands of human slaves, and *that* didn't amount to nothin', either. How's this gonna be any different? I tell ya, it's not a good idea to push it right now. You needa think a little more and take your time with this!"

Laplace was right. Clayman had a history of purchasing slaves, then murdering them. The number had indeed grown to several thousand, but the effort had yet to make Clayman a true demon lord. Having this pointed out to him did little to change Clayman's mind.

"Don't be silly, Laplace. I was their owner, and I am free to handle my purchases any way I like. If killing a thousand isn't enough, we'll go with ten thousand next. We know that human souls are required for the awakening. There is no need to restrain ourselves with the weak!"

He paused, letting his arrogant theory sink in Laplace's mind.

"Besides, this plan of action is good for *him*, too. I'm planning to launch this Walpurgis on the pretext that there's a new force in the Forest of Jura whose leader has declared himself a demon lord."

"Right, that's fine and all, but that ain't gonna be any reason to invade the Beast Kingdom, is it?"

"Oh, but it will be, Laplace. One of my agents, Mjurran, was killed by someone while on a covert mission. I plan to declare that it was then when I realized the demon lord Carillon had turned on me. No one should have any complaint about me taking over Carillon's territory to gather the evidence I need to prove it. After all, I was the one who suffered the loss."

Laplace scrutinized Clayman's words. Eurazania was adjacent to the lands ruled by Milim—hardly a ruler who cared much about things like "gathering evidence." The fact that Milim had defeated Carillon was really all Clayman needed to back up his alibi. He could even say he sent Milim over to investigate, for that matter. That way, Clayman's forces could go through Milim's land to reach the Beast Kingdom, and no one would have any reason to object. And once things were at *that* point, fabricating some evidence would be the easy part.

There was nothing unnatural about any of this plan. But Laplace still didn't think now was the time to act.

Aren'tcha panicking a little too much, Clayman? Not that I'm gonna change your mind anytime soon, but...

"Yeah, what you're saying all makes sense..."

Then Laplace recalled something that had nearly slipped past him. "...but hang on, she's been *killed*?"

He knew full well that Clayman thought extremely little of Mjurran, but Laplace thought of her as a decent, trustworthy magic-born. In Clayman's bureaucracy, she was one of the five fingers, the highest echelons of leadership. She wasn't too good in a fight, but as a wizard who could handle almost any situation, she was highly valued as rearguard support. Plus, she often had handy advice for Laplace and the rest of the Moderate Jesters, even if she acted like she hated it.

More than anything, though, Mjurran had common sense. Laplace gave her top marks for that.

"Ah yes," the unmoved Clayman replied. "I don't know what that disappointed tone in your voice is, but yes, she's dead."

"Huh. She died, eh...? You're sure about that?"

"Mm? The Marionette Heart I implanted in her broke. Her real heart, which I kept here, crumbled into ash and disappeared. So yes, I'm quite sure, thank you. Her role in my outfit was over anyway, so you could say it was good timing."

The flatness of Clayman's report saddened Laplace a little. "C'mon, Clayman," he chided, "would it really hurt ya to be a little sadder when one of yer best people passes away?"

He used to be a better man that that. Ever since he reached the demon lord ranks, it's like he's grown more and more twisted...

And this wasn't a phenomenon limited to Clayman. Well near everyone in the Moderate Jesters—the group that Laplace called home—seemed to begin warping a bit personality-wise, as he saw it. Laplace himself was the same. He certainly had no business criticizing Clayman for it, but he still couldn't shake the feeling that Clayman had fundamentally changed.

"Ha-ha-ha! Oh, you're too kind, Laplace. Did you know that Teare said the same thing earlier? 'You need to treat your tools right,' she told me, 'or else they'll fall apart.' I believe she learned that from you, Laplace? But that is exactly why, if a tool falls apart on you, you have to make the perpetrator pay for it. I can atone for the tool as well, then, can't I?"

The sight of Clayman's artificial smile made Laplace give up pursuing the question any further. "...Yeah. I'd like to keep her death from going to waste, at least."

"Of course you do. I thought you would say that."

Another smile.

Not quite how I meant it, Clayman...

It generated a wealth of mixed emotions in Laplace's mind. He shook it off, wondering if there were any cracks in Clayman's plan he had failed to notice.

"But y'know, Clayman, about that Walpurgis... Isn't anyone else gonna complain atcha about it?"

"Oh, they may." The smile disappeared from Clayman's face. Now it was twisted in unwavering confidence and warped desire. "But now that I have Milim at my beck and call, I can just toss her in their direction, and that's it."

Laplace turned pale. "Now wait a minute! That's dangerous talk, there! *He* said there's a chance Milim could go berserk, too, didn't he? Just because the president built that Artifact doesn't mean you can get away with relying on it for everything."

"It's going to be all right, Laplace. Milim fully followed my orders."

"So I heard. But she also went off script and made that crazy war declaration, didn't she? She's ancient by demon lord standards; she's got to have a hell of a lot of resistance against outside influence. If you come to rely on that lady too much, I think it's your neck on the line, y'know?"

But Clayman had little interest in the impassioned warning. "Are you envious, Laplace, that Milim is under my full control?"

"No! I'm saying that they call it a 'trump card' 'cause you save it until the final deal!"

"Enough from you. You have nothing to worry about. *He* wishes to see me awaken as a true demon lord. To do that, I will overrun the Beast Kingdom. If anyone stands in my way, I will show you just how easily I will mow them down."

"Hang on a sec! He and the president just told you to sit tight, didn't they? What you needa be thinkin' about right now is how we'll navigate this Walpurgis thing!"

"Trust in me, Laplace. If I merely sit here and do whatever Lord Kazalim tells me to do, that will not fulfill *his* goals for me. Now is the time to go on the attack!"

That was enough to fully shut down Laplace's desperate protests.

In the end, Laplace was unable to stop Clayman. They were in agreement on some things, and it wasn't that Clayman was wildly diverging from his orders. But Laplace just couldn't shake the premonition that something was up with the demon lord. So he spoke once more.

"Listen, Clayman. Lemme ask you one more thing: Did you really decide on this plan of action on yer own free will?"

"What are you talking about, Laplace? There are two people in the world who can give me orders: Lord Kazalim and the one who resurrected him. You should be more aware of that than anyone."

He was right. If Clayman saw nothing wrong with his scheme, Laplace had no authority to intervene. He had his own work to do, infiltrating the Western Holy Church a second time.

"All right. No worries, then. I need to get goin', but you be careful, too, okay, Clayman? Now's not the time to be too reckless. Whatever ya do, don't letcher guard down."

With that final warning, Laplace took his leave, allowing Clayman to refocus on his own thoughts.

Did he mean to accuse me of being under the influence of another? Ridiculous. Or perhaps...is he worried that I will reap all the spoils of victory for myself, because I have Milim's powers to use as I please? Hardly like him to be jealous...

Clayman never overestimated his own strength. The self-confidence that controlling Milim gave him, however, had emboldened him. And now, it had made him take the words of Laplace, his most trustworthy of confidants, and dismiss them as mere jealousy against him.

It was with some disappointment in his friend that he took another sip of his wine. Now, however, it was bitter. The mellow sweetness from before was nowhere to be found.

...Curse it all!

Suddenly, Clayman threw the glass in his hand against the wall. His anger was making him act out, following orders given from emotions not even he could understand.

The force of the outburst made the bottle of first-rate wine on the table shatter. But Clayman didn't care. Instead, to calm his nerves, he took something out from his pocket—a mask molded into a smiling face.

"Don't you worry, Laplace. I'm going to make this awakening work, and then I will have the world in my grasp. All right, Laplace? I'm not going to lose this again! So this time, at least, let's all be one happy family together..."

There, by himself in that room, Clayman reminded himself of the hopes hidden in his heart—rubbing the mask softly, as if running his hand over a precious treasure.

Right. First decision: defeat the demon lord Clayman. That's set in stone. If you got someone lurking around in the darkness, trying to pull off some grand scheme, better to rub him out ahead of anything else. Plus, now that I've declared myself to be a demon lord, I need ways to keep the other demon lords from taking action against me. Sacrificing Clayman should be a fine way to do that. There's the other reason.

As long as we don't know why Milim decided to pick a fight with Carillon, we can't really rely on what she says. Time to throw my weight around a little and keep things from getting any gloomier going forward. Besides, Clayman just went too far. He needs to feel the retribution. To pay for what he did.

Moving on, our future direction. Yohm was a popular guy in Farmus, hailed as a hero by most. We'll take advantage of this to have the current king of Farmus released from imprisonment and forced to come to the negotiating table. I want the kingdom to be a thing of the past by the time we're done. Beyond that, we need to figure out how to deal with the Western Holy Church, as well as send out declarations to the nations we've signed pacts with so they'll know our take on matters.

We had a lot to talk about. Something told me it was going to be kind of a long meeting.

I kicked things off by taking a report from Soei. Clayman was on the move, apparently, and we needed to hear all the details and confer over what to do. Thus, I was on my way to our main meeting hall, expecting to meet with Tempest leadership and the Three Lycanthropeers.

As I did, my Universal Detect sniffed out a group of fifty or so approaching town. *Huh? Oh, it's Fuze, guild master from the kingdom of Blumund.* Before long, our security team had us all face-to-face. He pushed through his own soldiers to see me, his face grim.

"It has been much too long, Sir Rimuru. I am only glad that I made it here in time! We have come to satisfy our duty under the terms of the security agreement signed between Blumund and Tempest, and I feared I was already too late."

He smiled as he spoke, but he still looked at me intensely, and the soldiers surrounding him looked ready to face death at any moment. Each was fully equipped, heavily armored, and prepared for war.

"Whoa. The guild master himself? What on…?"

"Ha-ha! No need to put it like that. Thegis is ready to take over my post, should it come to it. I've heard many things about this town from our merchants, that sneak Mjöllmile in particular. You've been engaged with the Kingdom of Farmus, it seems…"

Huh? Ummm…?

Come to think of it, I suppose it had been about ten days since we brought our visitors from Blumund back home. Did they immediately suit up and come running to our aid the moment they heard the news? Great if they did, but…

"…Even if we lack the time to erect a defensive wall," Fuze feverishly continued, "it would be best to build a circle of personnel around the city to beef up our defenses. It doesn't look like Farmus's main force has arrived yet, but there is no telling when their vanguard troops may reach us. We've passed the date of their war ultimatum, yes?"

The steely resolve in his eyes seemed clear to me as he said his piece. Well, not just "seemed." They *were* clear to me. He had already willed his guild master's seat to Thegis. I guess he really *was* here to fight to the death for Tempest.

But um…you know… It's all kinda over already. And with the way Fuze and his soldiers were all decked out in their finest equipment, ready to fan out the moment I said the word, I wasn't too sure how to give the news.

"Or perhaps you actually intend to seize the initiative and attack first? I have to tell you, Sir Rimuru, that could be a brash move. According to our intelligence, we have confirmed sightings of an army nearly twenty thousand strong. We lack the numbers to defeat them in a frontal assault. Over the past few days, I have been working my connections—I now have a team of three hundred adventurers on standby. They may be few in number, but I assure you they are at your beck and call. This may be a protracted war; our best bet might be to use the forest landscape to wage a guerrilla campaign…"

Fuze was wholeheartedly devoted to us. Almost to the point where I wondered if he *should* be, really.

"Still," he confidently concluded, "it gladdens my heart to be able to fight alongside the beasts and creatures who call this forest home."

Now it was even harder to tell him. The Tempest leaders around me were stone silent, and the contingent from Eurazania was visibly confused. This stuff was already in the past for us all. Like, I wasn't expecting them to actually lend us support! I know we had that treaty, but it had more than enough loopholes in its interpretation to let them weasel out of this stuff. But, however few, Fuze still got a bunch of fighters together and zoomed right over here. I was kinda happy to see that, but—

"...Ah, what a fine town this is. Beautiful buildings, well-designed houses, paved roads... It pains me to admit it, but it is far more splendid than anything one could find in Blumund. I can understand your reluctance against turning it into a battlefield. But we must hold out and await reinforcements! Our king has promised to deploy our knights, and while it will take them time to prepare—"

"Ahhh, Fuzie, one moment?"

I hated to do it, but I had to stop him, or else we were gonna be here all day.

"Yes, Sir Rimuru? Did you have a suggestion for our strategy?"

"Um, yeah, our, our strategy... Like, if you wanna call it that..."

"Is this something to be kept secret from us? Certainly, I can understand your suspicion, but I hope you can place your trust in—"

"N-no, no, Fuzie! I really appreciate what you've done, but it's all over now!"

"Huh? Over? How do you mean?"

"Um, how to put it...? Well, to sum up, I kind of killed 'em all!"

"...Um? Them all? Them all, who? What are you talking about?"

I could understand his confusion.

"I mean, um, the army from Farmus you were talking about? I killed 'em all!"

"Wh-*whaaa*?!"

That was about all the utterly shocked Fuze could choke out. Yohm stepped up to give him a pat on the shoulder, while Kabal offered a few condolences of his own.

"No, I bet he wouldn't believe it," commented Elen.

"Nope," Gido added.

Nope, indeed. It hadn't even been two weeks since that war declaration. I suppose Fuze figured their main force would reach Tempest in a week, so we'd buy two or three days of time in open-field combat and prepare for a siege in the worst case. Considering how the war should've started days ago, and we were totally serene about it, I figured he had to think it was at least a *bit* weird by now—but seeing all of us assembled like this, he must've assumed we were about to sally forth and attack, or something.

In his eyes, we went from dealing with a delayed Farmus force to the war being in the books. That *was* a lot to take in at once, wasn't it?

"The other day," Rigurd finally began, "we sent my son Rigur out to you to give the news. You two must have missed each other along the way, I fear. But it is just as Sir Rimuru says. The war is already over."

Between his and Kabal's and Elen's supplemental commentary, we managed in a little over a few minutes to convince Fuze that we weren't pulling an elaborate prank.

"You must be joking," I heard him whisper under his breath, but time heals all wounds and all that.

The fifty fighters accompanying him weren't too enthused about it, either, so I ordered our soldiers to take them to our barracks and let them rest up. They looked exhausted enough to collapse on the spot, limp and lifeless. *Hearing that there wasn't any war to fight would cut the tension in pretty short order*, I thought. They had apparently been relying on natural trails in the forest instead of the highway, in order to avoid encountering Farmus forces, and all that bushwhacking in full armor couldn't have been fun.

So the fighters all muttered their thanks to us as they marched off to their quarters. All that remained was the hangdog-looking Fuze.

"Why don't you get some rest, too, Fuzie?"

"Yes..." He nodded at me. "Yes, this has put my mind in quite a state of disorder. If I could lie down for a bit..."

But just as he was about to walk toward the barracks, another guest interrupted him with (im)perfect timing.

"Oops. Here's someone else. And who could it be but…"

"But?" Fuze asked, stopping as he heard me mutter. He should've kept going. Once he saw who it was, resting was the last thing on his mind—because standing right there was Gazel Dwargo, king of the dwarves himself.

✳

Something I had noticed a while ago: Having my Magic Sense skill evolve into Universal Detect had made my ability to grasp my surroundings far more accurate across a much wider range. Despite how far away they were from town, I could spot the squadron of Pegasus Knights flying in remarkably fast.

Report. Thirty knights incoming. The individual Gazel Dwargo is confirmed to be in the vanguard position.

The ultimate skill Raphael, Lord of Wisdom, gave the report as if nothing could be more trivial.

With this upgrade in accuracy, I was now able to detect and identify people I had met before. *That's incredibly convenient. Convenient…but with this range, easily enough to cover the whole town and a great deal beyond, I'm starting to think this is literally too much information. To be frank, I'm getting sick of all these reports, every single time.*

So could you keep 'em a bit more on the brief side, Sage…um, I mean, Raphael? To be exact, you can report in when someone's approaching only if they're malicious or harmful to me or whatever.

……Understood.

It felt like Raphael really wanted to say something back there, but nothing to get worked up about. It's always best to assign all the dirty work to someone else, if you can. Leave it to Raphael! That's my motto.

So I turned my skill down to the minimum setting as I awaited our guests. Since it was the skill performing the ID for me, I could rest assured that these were no impostors. But before I could even tell Fuze, the Pegasus Knights flitted down in front of us. King Gazel dismounted first.

He smiled the moment he spotted me. "Ah, Rimuru, nice to see you again! So I hear you've become a demon lord?"

Oh, *that*. I thought he'd want a word about that. Didn't expect him to fly on over himself, though.

"Ah, yeah, kinda. There's been a lot of stuff going on around here, Gazel, so I figured I'd become a demon lord." I gave him an awkward grin. "Not to make you feel unwelcome or anything, but we were just about to all meet up and discuss our future strategy."

"Well, perfect! I would be happy to join this conference," he declared, like it was his god-given right.

It was right about then that Fuze, exhausted and ready to cry, came up to me.

"Demon lord...? What in heavens is *that* all about?!"

He had heard our conversation from the side, and I could tell he wasn't about to let it slide. Yeah, I didn't really talk about *that*, either... Going in depth right now would just be a pain in the ass, but Fuze wasn't going to accept a polite no, I could tell.

"Sir Rimuru, I find it hard to ignore what you just said! Because it sounded very much to me that you have become a demon lord—or something to that effect...?"

He was shaking from head to toe, about ready to pee his pants.

"Um, if you needed a bathroom, it's down this street and—"

"I do *not* need a bathroom! I never said anything about a bathroom! This 'demon lord' business... Tell me what you mean by it!"

I suppose that feint didn't work. Fuze was clearly starting to lose his temper, and his real personality was starting to show itself.

"Oh. Um, yeah, demon lord. Well," I replied as breezily as possible, "I'm one of 'em now."

This, sadly, didn't end the topic.

"Ha-ha-ha! Rather poor taste for a joke, wouldn't you think? I was hoping for a more serious answer from you…"

Ugghh, this is such a pain. Do I have to start from the very beginning before you'll get off my back? And now I could see Gazel looking curiously at me, too. So as much as I hated going through all this in the middle of the street, I gave them both a quick recap.

Once I wrapped up, I noticed Fuze was muttering to nobody in particular, eyes glazed over. His mind must've shut off in an attempt to avoid the reality of it all. At least he wasn't lecturing me or anything. Leaving him to his own ranting, I turned to King Gazel again.

"By the way, Gazel, are you sure it's all right for a king to slip out of his own kingdom that easily?"

It was a sincere concern of mine. Not that I'm one to talk, but the king was being allowed *way* too long a leash, wasn't he? The Armed Nation of Dwargon, in terms of national power, had to be several dozen times stronger a nation than ours. Wasn't the king going out on trips whenever he pleased kind of a problem?

"Pfft. What is the issue? I have a decoy fully serving for me!"

Huh? I thought decoys were meant for, like, drawing the attention of assassins away from the real thing or something? Or were they meant for playing hooky like this? I wasn't too sure either way, but whatever. Gazel had Pegasus Knight captain Dolph with him, along with quite a number of his trusted companions. For a security detail, it was almost too extensive.

"Regardless, Rimuru…" He turned his now-kingly eyes toward me. "The report Vester sent me three days ago—that was no mistake, then?"

"Oh, you mean the twenty thousand—"

"Wait, Rimuru. I had heard the Farmus force had gone missing under mysterious circumstances. Do you know something about that?"

"Uh, missing?"

Huh? What was he talking about?

"The way Vester phrased it," he slowly continued, "a force of some twenty thousand troops simply vanished before they could reach this town. Do you have any idea what may have happened to them?"

He gave Vester a sidelong glance out the corner of his eye, the silent pressure he emitted almost making his subject collapse to the ground. I joined his gaze. Vester vigorously shook his head at me.

"I received the report as well, Vester."

This was Vaughn speaking, admiral paladin for the dwarven army and sworn friend to King Gazel; and to Vester right now, a source of terror.

"At the time, I believe you told us that the Farmus force had disappeared, and you were investigating why. The report was curious enough to us that we decided to venture over ourselves, but is *this* the explanation?"

His annoyance might be understandable. I had just brutally massacred a force of twenty thousand, and Gazel and Vester were trying to kind of gloss over it.

"Well, yes, um, the cause still isn't quite known yet..."

Vester began choosing his words carefully, trying to guess at the intentions of his dwarven friends. He was a quick thinker like that, already trying to bury the lede on what I had done.

"Fool!" I heard Gazel whisper to me. "If you tell the truth here, you'll become an enemy to all humanity—or if not the enemy, a symbol of terror worldwide."

Yeah, I guess so, come to think of it. Someone who can kill in the five figures on one go was scarier than a nuclear bomb, really. The fewer people who knew about this, the better—and certainly, nations and people who weren't directly involved at all didn't need to hear the story. The Kingdom of Farmus attempted to invade monster lands, only to go completely missing due to an unknown incident or incidents. That much was the truth, decent enough to spread across the land.

There's Gazel for you. Far more shrewd than I would ever be. Which means I now have to walk back what I just said a moment ago. Ugh.

I didn't mind if the townspeople knew; that wasn't the problem, and it was too late now anyway. Nobody was about to go blabbing it to the general public regardless. The main issue was Fuze. I gave him a glance; he was still in a state of panicked confusion.

"Ummm, Fuzie?"

"Sir Rimuruuu..."

So now what? I just declared to him that I wiped out the entire Farmus military by myself. Should I laugh it off as a lie?

But as I thought about it, Fuze sighed and raised his arms up. "I heard nothing. And of course, I don't think my fighters in the barracks will remember anything by tomorrow morning. We're all so exhausted right now, we must be hearing voices in our heads."

Guess he's staying mum for me. He seemed remarkably more aged to me now, sorrowful. I suppose he found this the most convenient way to solve the problem—and certainly, the best way to tie up all the strings here right now.

"Hee-hee-hee-hee... In that case, allow me to visit them to make sure," Diablo offered. He had sidled up next to me out of nowhere with that smile on his face again. Funny guy. The perfect butler. You could ask pretty much anything of him, and he'd do it. At the moment, he was gleefully taking care of the assorted errands I asked him to do. I think I might have heard him whisper "I am quite gifted at altering memories" to me just now, but let's pretend I didn't.

Fuze had mixed feelings about it, I could tell, but he was willing to deal with it as long as his people were safe. He understood King Gazel's take—the fewer people who knew, the better. When politics get involved like this, governments might not be afraid to shut witnesses up permanently, after all. Maybe it's smarter to shut your eyes now and again.

Still...

"I will not question how my fighters are handled, but I insist on joining this conference of yours."

It sounded to me like this was one point Fuze refused to negotiate on. His eyes were resolute—he must've figured the topic of our meeting wasn't something he could afford to be in the dark on.

"All right." I shrugged. "I want you to believe that I'm not hostile to humanity. I won't keep you out."

*

And so, Rigurd guided Fuze to a waiting room. Since we now had a dwarven contingent participating, we needed to set up a larger meeting hall for everybody, and in the meantime, they could all probably use some rest.

"Hmph," grumbled Gazel as we saw them go off. "You trust that man, Rimuru?"

"Yeah, he's safe."

Fuze was a trustworthy man. I was confident enough in that.

"Mm. Then I suppose the problem is *those* people."

He turned his attention toward the empty space behind us. Um, or *was* it empty? I turned around, surprised, only to find an unfamiliar group watching us. There was a well-dressed gentleman at the lead, his face well-defined; he must have been very popular with the opposite sex when he was younger. His eyes were notably sharp, and he was flanked on both sides by five or so guards, all outfitted in similarly fine gear; perhaps high-ranked military officers or the like.

The group was clearly well trained, and…man, they were right behind me this whole time, and I never noticed? What the hell happened to Universal Detect, man?!

However, I was the only concerned witness, it turned out.

Report. No clear hostility detected among the group.

If that's what the somewhat pouty Raphael had to say, I could believe it. Maybe this was my fault. I *did* just tell it to stop giving me reports all the time. I suppose "malicious or harmful" is a bit too vague to make much sense of. Raphael had a right to be angry, perhaps.

Sorry, I said to myself. *Go ahead and give the full reports from now on.* It seemed kind of lame, really, apologizing to one of my own skills, but I at least wanted to express my feelings.

As I underwent this internal conflict, Gazel and the mystery group were already engaging each other.

"And *you* people are…?"

"Ah, I see it's the emperor who enjoys hiding in his underground burrow! Very impressive, to see a coward like you provide backing to the 'demon lord' like this…"

The stern greeting did nothing to break the man's easygoing style. He was clearly trying to goad the dwarven king while the officers rolled their eyes at him in exasperation.

Gazel, recognizing them all, flashed a bold smile. "Aha. You, then. The elf descendants whose heads are always in the clouds. Did you descend from that fancy tree city of yours, then?"

I suppose they all knew each other. Raphael was right—no malice to speak of; these two just didn't get along too well, is all. Or more like they enjoyed arguing for the sake of arguing.

"Sir Rimuru, I believe these to be envoys from the Sorcerous Dynasty of Thalion," stated Soka, one of Soei's operatives. She had apparently brought these people here—and once the man recognized King Gazel, he immediately started giving him crap.

"You never change, do you, Erald?"

"Neither do you, Gazel."

This was the way the two decided to greet each other, looks of sheer contempt on their faces.

"And that girl there is…?"

"Oh, hello there. My name's Rimuru, and I run things around the forest alliance we have here."

Erald, the squinty-eyed guy, had his eyes turned to me, so I gave him a casual hello. Any visitors from Thalion needed to be treated with the utmost courtesy—not that I really knew anything about manners or diplomatic customs or anything. Becoming a demon lord's great and all, but it's not like there's an instruction manual for it. Hopefully I'll track someone down who can teach me the finer points sometime.

Upon hearing my name, Erald suddenly tensed up—then opened his eyes as wide as he could. "*You!*" he bellowed. "The demon lord who seduced my daughter! I hope you are prepared to atone for that!"

He immediately began to cast what even I could tell was a vastly overpowered flame spell. Yikes. Chill out, dude.

Based on the knowledge I gathered, a flame spell on such a high level was one of the most difficult pieces of magic to pull off. The whole family of fire magic occupied its own branch in the tree of aspectual magic, starting with your garden-variety puff of Fire and moving on from there to Fireball and the more difficult Fire Wall and Fire Storm. The harder it is to pull off, the more of a boom it makes.

At the very peak of this scale lies what, for the sake of simplicity, I call "compounding" magic. Combining the burning nature of flame spells with the shock-wave effects of explosive spells, for example, can provide magic on a scale beyond either of the original two types. That was just the type of compounding Shizu was gifted at, come to think of it. The main difference was that she relied on an elemental spirit to power her casting. That's not easy, not unless you're as talented a caster as Shizu was, but once you have that relationship in place, the elemental will do most of the fine-tuning for you.

Compounded spells on the very tippy top of the scale like this were quite hazardous, because they required you to control the magic manually. But since they were not a part of any "official" magic family, they offered a great deal of freedom. You had full control, juggling aspects of the spell like launch speed, targeting accuracy, size and scope of the effect, and duration. If brute strength was all you wanted, you could level a town easily enough with one.

This, of course, came at some danger to the caster. You needed enough spiritual force to gather the required magicules together to keep the spell under control, or else it wouldn't work, letting that energy run amok instead of being consumed—and potentially raze the entire area around you. It goes without saying that this sort of magic wasn't something the general public saw much of—we're talking literally military-grade stuff. You had to be at least an accredited wizard to be allowed to touch it.

It was absolutely *not* the kind of thing I wanted in my city, and now Erald was casting it. What was he thinking? It made no sense to me. And what's he mean *seduced*?

The whole thing left me confused for a moment, but again, I

shouldn't have worried. From the side came a loud *bang*, like someone fired off a shotgun, and then Elen's distressed shouting.

"Dad, come onnnn! What are *you* here for?!"

She barged in, looking livid, and immediately gave Erald a bop on the head before he could react. It was enough for him to come back to his senses. I suppose he was her father, then? And judging by the chewing out Elen was giving him, he must've been a bit regretful by now. Scary, isn't it, seeing someone fly into a rage without warning like that? He seemed like such an intellectual gentleman, like Gazel. So much for that.

"Ah… Ha-ha-ha. Sorry about that," he said with a cheerful smile. "I was informed that a demon lord had kidnapped my daughter, and I suppose I lost my cool for a moment."

Yeah, but that doesn't mean you get to cast maximum-force fire magic in my town. What a loony dad.

"No, my lord," one of his men, a timid-looking assistant, coolly observed. "Our reports involved far more than that, but you jumped to a hasty conclusion."

"See? I knew it! This is *totally* your fault, Daddd!"

I felt a little bad for Dad, visibly withering on the spot, but he had it coming. If anything, I wanted him to regret it even more.

"…You always were too overprotective a father," Gazel said once things calmed down.

"I am not," Erald fired back unapologetically. "How can I help it? Elen is simply too precious to me."

"Yes, all children are to their parents, but… Ah, this is pointless."

The way Gazel rolled his eyes told me that Erald was known for this. You can't fix the fatherly instinct, I guess.

Once things had simmered down between Gazel and Erald, Elen stepped up to say hello, an elegant air surrounding her despite her rough adventurer's garb.

"I am sorry I have been out of contact, King Gazel."

"Ah, Ellwyn? I hardly recognized you! How grand it is to see you in good health. I see the years have been very kind to your beauty!"

"Keep your hands off her, Gazel!" Erald interjected, earning him another slap from Elen and round of admonishment from his assistant. Gazel just shrugged, apparently used to this act. *If Elen's on the scene, her father just loses all sense of self, doesn't he? Not exactly the member of the intelligentsia I took him for at first. Better watch out for that.*

"Sir Rimuru, this is Erald Grimwald, my father and archduke of Thalion."

"It is an honor to meet you, leader of Jura and master of the monsters. As my daughter just said, I am Archduke Erald Grimwald. Please, just Erald is fine."

So this guy's an archduke in the Sorcerous Dynasty? That's pretty high up there, isn't it? Dwargon isn't the only kingdom sending their big guns over to see us. I would later learn that he was closely related to the Thalion royal family—the current emperor's uncle, in fact. That explained why he was acting so familiar and casual around Gazel. To put it simply, he was one of three most powerful people from his native country.

I could hardly hide my surprise. *Does that mean...? Wow, is Elen some kind of crazy-influential fairy-tale princess?! I knew she was of noble blood, but not that much! She's not far from the throne at all, lineage-wise, and she's working as an adventurer? Talk about being given a lot of freedom! And I can't be the only one to think it'd be better to put a stop to that, not that Elen herself would likely care. I imagined she probably had people keeping an eye on her, given how sure she was that the advice she gave me on becoming a demon lord would come back to haunt her. And all that trouble she gives Kabal and Gido, too. I really ought to reward them for that next time.*

But for now...

"So did you travel here just to inquire about Elen?"

I doubted it, as I sized up Erald.

"Hee-hee-hee! No, of course not. As we consider how we should interact with your nation, I wanted a chance to see you with my own eyes—this leader that my daughter seems so fond of. Given the sense of authority you appear to bring to your people, I find it hard to believe you are a slime at all... But still, I feel I have a much more complete picture of your strengths now."

He accentuated this with a nefarious-sounding laugh. I suppose that overpowered flame strike was his way of testing me as well. Me—and Benimaru, Shuna, and Shion adjacent; none demonstrated a hint of panic—it wouldn't have; they had already seen he had no intention of actually launching it. Given how hotheaded they all were not long ago, that was some palpable growth.

"It was clear," Shuna explained, "that you had far less than the required energy needed for the spell you were casting, once I read what it was."

Erald grinned at this, a bit ashamed that his act was spotted for what it was.

"Well, I suppose I have quite a while to go, if you can see through me *that* clearly!"

"Not at all," she calmly replied. "Between the speed at which you deployed it and the skill you showed at making it look real, it was an impressive sight to see. Considering the artificial body you possess, that level of accuracy is remarkable."

"Oh? You noticed I was using a homunculus? Color me surprised."

"Yes. It seemed to me you had fused your spiritual body into it. *Very* impressive. It would certainly take a nation of magic-users such as yours to pull that off."

I used Analyze and Assess at Shuna's suggestion. She was right; Erald had borrowed this body from somewhere else. His officers were all "real," but once you reach the higher ranks of nobility, I suppose it paid to be careful. I had *thought* he was rather lightly outfitted for a summit with a self-styled demon lord. Maybe the dwarven King Gazel over there was the crazy one.

Still, it was really something. An elaborately fine-tuned homunculus, indistinguishable from a human being. *Once things calm down, I'd love to learn how that works.*

So Erald was here to size up our nation and its leaders. That and a few other things, too, I'm sure, but we can tackle that later. No need to force it out of him right this moment.

Since he's here and all, I figured I might as well have him join the conference, so he'd have more stuff to judge us with. I wanted his take on our future direction as well, and this would be a good opportunity for that. It might result in us and the Sorcerous Dynasty becoming enemies, of course, but we'd just have to cross that bridge when we came to it.

Gobta ran up to inform me that the meeting hall was ready.

I was planning to have this be a more informal confab between Jura buddies, but things had changed. This really *was* a summit. Usually, with things like these, you'd have lower-level diplomats meet up first and agree in advance on questions to ask and topics to tackle, figuring out where there was room for compromise once both sides were aware of each other's stakes. Here, though, there was no greasing the gears in advance. We'd be giving frank opinions to each other, and in the end, we'd pin down our federation's future. It wouldn't be going too far to call it a war of words.

Steeling my resolve, I headed for the meeting hall, ready to emcee one of the most important gatherings I—and Tempest—had ever experienced.

In later years, the event would come to be known as the Monster-and-Man Summit.

*

In the hall, I found everyone standing upright, awaiting our arrival. All the main powerbrokers in the event—the Three Lycanthropeers, Fuze, King Gazel, and Archduke Erald—were shown to their guest seats. Once I took my own at the far end of the hall, everyone else sat down.

The air was heavy when the talks began.

We began by having each side introduce themselves, given the multiple large nations now involved. Some already knew one another, but I thought it best for politeness' sake that everybody was on the same page.

"So. Let's begin by having our guests introduced."

I turned to Shuna, who promptly began reading off names.

*　　*　　*

The Beast Kingdom of Eurazania, represented by the Three Lycanthropeers from the Beast Master's Warrior Alliance. Given that Phobio and Sufia had a slight—all right, serious—tendency to think with their sword-swingin' muscles instead of their brains, I figured we'd mostly be focused on Alvis's feedback.

The Armed Nation of Dwargon, land of the dwarves, represented by their kin himself, Gazel Dwargo. He seemed perfectly content with me trying to cover up the whole twenty-thousand-dead thing. He undoubtedly had his own motivations for it, so I suppose I ought to keep that under consideration. It seemed like I'd be able to rely on him quite a bit going forward.

The kingdom of Blumund, represented by…no one, officially, although having the nation's guild master in Fuze wasn't a bad substitute. Fuze was intimately connected with Baron Veryard, one of the kingdom's top ministers, so he did have enough authority to be here and provide some valuable advice.

The Sorcerous Dynasty of Thalion, very suddenly represented by Archduke Erald—a sharp-minded, noble-looking, powerful figure, even if he was near powerless to defy his beloved daughter. If he was here to gauge the worth of our nation, I presumed he wasn't foolish enough to let Elen sway his judgment. He wasn't someone to neglect—and definitely not someone to drop my guard around.

Besides…Thalion was powerful enough to take on the entire Council by itself, on the same level as Dwargon. If all went well, we could establish formal ties with them, perhaps. I didn't want to be greedy, though, so baby steps would be key in dealing with him.

Sizing them all up like this, we had a fairly prestigious lineup here. In a way, I was glad all these humans were here for it. If it was just us Forest of Jura denizens, our deliberations might've drifted off the rails entirely.

Next came introductions from the Tempest side. One by one, I had my top brass talk about themselves a little bit. Rigurd and the hobgoblin elders practically oozed authority by this point, decked out in befittingly regal-ish clothing and not losing out at all to their counterparts in foreign lands. More regal than myself, really. The bedrock of our whole nation.

Once every department in town checked in, we next heard from Treyni, dryad and caretaker of the forest. Having such a lofty local presence around seemed to surprise Erald at first, but he bottled it up and nodded a greeting to her. Gazel found this more than a little amusing, even though I'm sure he and his crew were just as surprised about the whole damn thing when *they* first met her. Ah well.

Finally, there was the contingent from Farmus—Yohm, Mjurran, and Gruecith as well. I wanted to have them build a new nation for me, something I was planning to suggest at this summit. Would people be open to it? That was a vital part of the whole thing, something that'd augur the ultimate success of this event.

Once Shion and Diablo behind me gave a couple of quick hellos, the meet-and-greet part of the summit was over. Oh, wait. Forgot someone.

"Shuna, do we have a change of clothes for Veldora?"

"Yes, Sir Veldora is…"

Before Shuna could finish, a loud, hearty *Gwaaah-ha-ha-ha!* filled the hall. I wanted some clothing for him since being in the buff probably wouldn't impress too many visitors, and it looks like we were just in time. The doors opened to reveal Veldora, taking in the sight curiously. I stood up to greet him and explain things to our visitors.

"I have one more friend to introduce, one whose name should be familiar to you all. I know this may sound surprising, but…"

The Tempestians in the audience nervously gulped. They already knew Veldora well enough, but having a legendary, villainous dragon in their presence still unnerved them more than a little bit. I could feel the electricity in the air as silence began to take hold.

"This is the Jura-Tempest Federation's friend, Veldora."

"Yes, Veldora! Some also refer to me as the Storm Dragon!

Although, so few have an encounter with me and live to tell the tale, so perhaps you all should consider yourselves lucky. Lucky and *honored* to be in my lofty presence!!"

Pompous as always, I could see, although it suited him well. But could I really trust him to behave at a summit like this? All I could picture was him growing bored in five minutes and attempting to butt in.

"For today's summit, I was kinda hoping you could join in as an adviser and maybe try to stay on good behavior. Or you can leave, if you want?"

"Gah-ha-ha-ha! Why the cold shoulder, Rimuru? Don't leave me out of the party!"

"Well, look, we're trying to have a serious conversation here, so just try not to get in the way, all right?"

"Trust me! There is no way I would ever interfere with you!"

If that's how he saw it, I had to be content with that. If worse came to worst, I could give him some of that beloved manga he took from my mind to keep him quiet.

The hall remained quiet as Veldora and I spoke, nobody moving an inch.

Well… Hmm? Actually, Fuze and Elen had passed out on the floor. Rigurd and the other hob-gobs were prostrating themselves before us for some reason, while Gazel was shouting "A moment, Rimuru, please! We must discuss this at once!!" and order was generally falling apart all over the place. The whole thing was pandemonium, and it goes without saying that the summit had to go into recess for a bit. Not that we had started yet.

∗

There was panic in the aisles, a lot more than I was expecting. You would think the apocalypse was here. Man… That Veldora. Guess that Storm Dragon stuff wasn't just a nickname after all. I suppose I should've expected it. Having a catastrophe-rated monster, the highest level of danger there was, stroll into the meeting hall without warning was bound to lead to chaos. They were treated as stronger than demon lords, even.

But think about it. If that guy's gonna sow chaos sooner or later, might as well get his intro out of the way quickly. Considering my plans, I couldn't leave Veldora and his motivations out of the picture. So I wanted him here, even if it left the other guests limp and pale with terror.

As much as Veldora was keeping his aura bottled up, some of it might've been hitting them all anyway. Benimaru, Shion, and my other leaders shut off their auras as a habit, something we were all used to now that weaker monsters and humans were frequent visitors. Diablo, despite being the new guy, could fully switch it off without me having to ask. I was honestly impressed. He was a good model for the others to follow.

So Veldora was still a problem in that aspect, but thanks to our intensive training, he could now adjust his aura on the fly. He proudly proclaimed it was like child's play to him, but it was really more thanks to the ultimate skill Faust, Lord of Investigation.

With that, I figured he'd be fine to bring out. Was that too optimistic, maybe? After all, even when sealed away, his aura was still daunting enough to keep any monster ranked B or below at bay. I ran Analyze and Assess on the magicules that filled the hall. No problems there. So the cause would have to be—

"Rimuru? We need to talk."

Gazel was there, giving me a pat on the shoulder and a threatening smile. "Let's delay this summit, so I may have some time."

He must have been serious about it, given his shouting earlier. My instincts told me not to defy him. So I declared recess and stood up. I didn't hear any complaints from the gallery (not that all of them were conscious enough to voice them).

Leaving the hall to my assistants, we moved into the reception area. I left Veldora behind at Gazel's request, which I figured wouldn't be a problem. Some of the attendees, the Three Lycanthropeers included, were so keen on currying favor with the Storm Dragon that I was sure he'd be occupied for a least a little while.

....

......

...

I was alone in the room with Gazel and Erald. Shuna was off brewing tea for the whole conference while Benimaru and Shion fought to calm things down.

"Let me just say this first," Erald began. "I have been given full freedom of action by Her Excellency, the Heavenly Emperor. It is my word that will decide the position of the Sorcerous Dynasty of Thalion, and I would advise you to keep that in mind as you explain all this to me."

The doting-father Erald was a distant memory. Here was the Thalion statesman, the face of an all-powerful nobility, and even I had to admire the dignity he held himself with. So Thalion wouldn't be willing to sweep this incident under the rug? He didn't voice any intention of hostilities against us, but depending on what I decided to do, we might become foes regardless. At the same time, I figured, he also had to clean up after Elen, what with everything she's been doing around here.

Which meant, hey, if we aren't enemies, it couldn't be a problem to ask for an alliance.

"All right. I promise I'll be honest with you as well."

He seemed to be speaking frankly with me. I should be just as serious with him. So our confidential talks began.

We kicked off with Gazel.

"So what did you want to talk about?"

"Certainly not the weather, you fool!" Not even the dwarven king could hide his shock as he excitedly half shouted at me. "Why has the Storm Dragon been resurrected?!"

That was a rare sight from the normally coolheaded Gazel. He must've really flipped his lid. I thought about talking my way out of this, but there was no point to it. So I decided to summarize things—at least, the part about how I ran into Veldora in the cave and agreed to help him out of his prison.

Once I wrapped up, Gazel groaned, a hand covering his face. "This is beyond all expectation. You becoming a demon lord is a problem in itself without this to contend with..."

I thought about lightening the mood by saying "Oh, no need to compliment me *that* much" but opted against it. If I was wrong, it'd send Gazel flying into a rage.

"So, Sir Rimuru, is that really, truly…?"

I nodded at Erald. Veldora was in human form and hiding his aura, perhaps making it a tad hard to swallow.

"…I suppose it would have to be," he observed. "No one, man or monster, would be foolish enough to pretend to be that terrible dragon."

I suppose not. That must be why Elen and Fuze were so readily accepting. Names held particular importance for monsters, but even a human would earn no advantage whatsoever from pretending to be the Storm Dragon. And Gazel never doubted it from the start. I asked him why later, and his reply was simple: "Because I couldn't read him." Which implied that Gazel has some kind of intrinsic mind-reading ability. Strong in more ways than one, I guess. But I digress.

"What should we do with this, though…?"

"Indeed," Erald said to his fellow king. "And here I am, already frantic enough attempting to clean up after all my daughter's misdeeds…"

I suppose the two were much closer friends than they seemed at first glance.

"Do we announce this, or do we cover it up? There's the problem."

"The Western Nations are not a concern," Erald said. "Even in Thalion, I see no issue with reporting this to Her Excellency the Emperor and no one else. But…"

"But the Western Holy Church, yes? Secrecy will earn us nothing with them. The Church has made it clear the Storm Dragon is the one dragon type they are most hostile to. If it's resurrected, they would know immediately."

"And if we tried to hide it, we would need to feign ignorance, which would be impossible to back up. Either way, he would be branded an 'enemy of god' in short order."

The two pondered what to do. Me? Oh, I was just saying "mm-hmm" or "yeah" now and then. Not a bad gig.

"Are you listening, Rimuru?"

"Yes. You're the one who roped us into this crisis, one that puts a great deal of trouble upon all of us. We need you to think more seriously about matters, or…or I don't know *what* we'll do!"

Oops. Guess they're pissed off. Let's just be a bit more apologetic and give my side of the story.

"Well, there's no way to fully hide Veldora, so my intention's to let the word out to the public. There's no way my nation's going to avoid the Church's eyes anyway, so…you know. I'll figure something out."

"Hmm." Gazel nodded at me. "If that is your decision, I have no qualms with it."

"A demon lord and dragon joining hands is not at all a laughing matter. This has become a more pressing issue than even I had thought at first. But looking at it another way, this is also a stroke of good luck, being able to participate in this summit. I have obtained exactly the information we need to decide how our country will stand…"

Erald, meanwhile, was discussing his country's standpoint more than his own, with another one of his eerie smiles. His take: It would be foolish to pick a fight against a nation with both a disaster-class demon lord and a catastrophe-class dragon. Gazel agreed with him, solemnly nodding. In terms of international pedigree, Tempest couldn't hold a candle to superpowers like Dwargon and Thalion, but if you focused solely on military strength, we didn't just match these guys; we surpassed them. Gazel and Erald, in their own ways, were admitting to that.

"Should I take that to mean," I ventured, "that should hostilities break out between us and the Western Church, you will take our side?"

"*That* is what you ask?" Gazel bitterly countered. "Rimuru, you truly must learn how to express these things better. Thank heavens this is a confidential talk…"

As he explained, just because he had no reason for Dwargon to see Tempest as a foe didn't mean he was obligated to expose his own nation to danger. That was doubly true in the case of the Western Holy Church, which the Dwarven Kingdom was not particularly connected to. Instead, all he could promise was that we could retain current relations, with neutrality being the word of the day.

That left Erald, archduke of a nation I hadn't even begun to try establishing relations with. Despite the circumstances, he seemed oddly willing to see things my way...so far, at least.

"I'm glad to have your support, Gazel. So, um, mister...um, Sir Erald, could I ask why you are being so kind to me with this...?"

Erald looked similarly reluctant to put it into words. "...You know you can call me whatever you like here, 'sir' or not. Just please be sure to include my name and appellation in public, Sir Rimuru. As the leader of a nation, there is absolutely no reason to place yourself below other leaders on the record—not unless you are eager to become the vassal territory of another nation. But to answer your question..."

Funny how he's taking pains to save me from embarrassment. I guess he's got a kinder side as well. I thanked him for that, only to be greeted with a stare and a long sigh before he began to explain why he was here and what he wanted.

It all started with Elen, his daughter. Her leaking info about how to awaken as a demon lord had led to an investigation as to who should be held responsible. It *was* kind of like she had created a new one, I suppose, and no nation could afford to ignore that. But then the archduke sprang into action. Someone like Erald had enough strength to kill the whole affair, and he did, making sure only the emperor knew the truth. All that remained was for him to gauge the situation and take action as necessary.

Keeping tabs on us magically was apparently quite a strenuous feat for him, but he still managed to confirm that I had indeed become a demon lord. He could've just played dumb if I had failed, but once I did, I could no longer be ignored. So he was here to size me up and potentially send a force over to suppress me should things go awry.

"So," he said in closing, "I wanted as few people to be aware of those facts as possible. Thus, I came out here myself."

In other words, I supposed, if he thought I was an evil presence, he would've destroyed us all and pretended nothing had ever happened.

"And what's your decision, then?"

"Well, as I said before, my decision for today is friendship over hostility."

Aha. That makes sense. And being seen as non-evil made me kind of happy, too.

"A fairly obvious choice," Gazel retorted.

"Of course. Our nation enjoys freedom of religion. Our people adhere to more than only the monotheistic Luminus faith. I seek to prioritize the fortunes of our nation, rather than sacrifice myself for the sake of religion."

"Pfft. I never did like you, Erald, but we keep agreeing on these matters. My nation and the Western Holy Church do not share a common motive, either. From the very beginning, I intended to support our friends in Tempest."

They shared a smile.

"But this doesn't mean we're without problems of our own. For example, the Farmus force that Sir Rimuru destroyed. Whether it was war or not, the death toll is simply too high." Erald scowled. "And to think it was my daughter who planted that seed..."

So that was his real motivation, then. The problem wasn't whether I was evil or not—it lay in whether the circumstances of the battle was known to the Western Holy Church. A demon lord who killed twenty thousand was going to look pretty damn evil to just about any sane person. It would lend valuable credence to the Church's declarations, and I'd be named an enemy of god in short order.

Now I see. The fallout from forging friendly ties with such an evil presence—i.e., me—could be uncomfortable for any nation to deal with. Sounded rough. I began wondering what we could do about that, before Gazel grinned at me.

"Don't worry. I've got an idea."

Oh, could it be...? The way Gazel went on about how the Farmus army went "missing" earlier?

"All the bodies are gone. There is no evidence. And scarily

enough, there are no survivors, either, are there?" He smiled. "Then why not change the plot to whatever we damn well want it to be?"

The common people, along with the rest of the world? They didn't need the truth. Just give 'em a nice-sounding story, and everyone will be happy.

"Hohh, a fascinating offer," Erald said, eyes shining as he went back into statesman mode. "Would you mind if I contributed to that, Gazel?"

He must've intended to fabricate a convenient story, one that ensured none of our hands were dirty. That'd help out Elen, he no doubt believed, and somewhere down the line, it'd even help Thalion's fortunes. Better go all in on this, then. Besides, I had already decided to keep my nation safe, even if it meant massacring twenty thousand. Even if I have to shoulder heavier crimes, that faith of mine wasn't going anywhere.

"I suppose you have the broadness of mind to deal with whatever may come, Rimuru? Very well. A king must never live with regrets."

Yeah, no point ruing the past. That was part of the Initiation, and I needed it.

"I'm ready for anything. But what's the story you have in mind, Gazel?"

"Heh-heh. Well said."

Gazel's eyes on me softened. We had little time left and a great number of details to work out.

....
......
...

The chaos had subsided by the time we were back in the meeting hall. Cooler heads had prevailed, and the unconscious had been attended to. I wasn't expecting this kind of furor, but ah well. What's past is past. Gotta focus on what's ahead. I got to discuss things with Gazel and Erald, too, and if you think about it, that was a golden opportunity.

Fuze and Elen and the others were sprawled out on their chairs, all but lifeless.

"Are you all right? How are you feeling?"

"I…I heard nothing about this devastating news…"

"You, you're just awful, Rimuru! I didn't hear anything about that. V-Veldora was your friend? Did, did you ever mention that?"

They had a lot of, shall we say, negative feedback. I mean, what do you want from me? I couldn't really say "Well, I had swallowed him into my Stomach" and even if I did, they'd never believe me.

"Oh, didn't I? I think I did, maybe…? Well, there's no point dwelling on the past. Come on! We got a summit to run!"

I tried to give them as breezy a smile as possible. It didn't work.

""""Don't gloss over it!!"""" they all shouted in unison.

"Ha, ha-ha-ha, yeah…"

I did what I could to soothe them, smiling as I kept chattering away. Why're they acting so *mean* with me, though? I'm a demon lord now, and they're treating me the exact same way. Which I was glad for; I didn't want things to get all distant and weird. But maybe a little more respect?

"Are you even listening to me?" Elen protested. "You could at least try to be a little more apologetic!"

"Yeah, she's right, pal!"

"This has been hard on the ol' ticker," commented Gido.

Respect seemed like a distant dream at the moment. Of course, it's totally in character for them all.

Fuze hadn't changed, either. "Ah, I just… How am I going to report this to my boss…? Wait! I'm a guild master, aren't I?!" He had already accepted the situation, just as bold and brazen as before. I couldn't believe this was the guy who let Veldora freak him out a moment ago. If I hadn't advised him to use the bathroom earlier, I'm sure he would've peed his pants.

I congratulated him on that. He glared back at me.

"As if none of this is *your* fault… I'm going to report this in detail to my bosses, then bill you for the mental distress you're putting me through!"

And here I was expecting him to thank me for my timely advice. Now he's angrier than ever. Well, whatever. At least my joking around helped Fuze find his voice again.

*　　*　　*

So everyone had now accepted Veldora, more or less. It was another hour before we finally got the summit rolling again.

*

Now we were starting for real.

Our conflict with Clayman remained an internal affair for the moment; that could wait. Soei gave me a quick report, but apparently, they couldn't discover Clayman's main base of operations. The fact that he had an army on the move was concerning, but Soei was keeping up his watch.

Nothing new was going to happen with that immediately, so I decided to get this summit wrapped up first.

I decided to begin with a recap, as annoying as it was to me. We had all been through a lot, but laying out everything in detail to everyone at once should save us time later. I wanted everyone to be on the same page.

So I began by relating how I met Veldora, dropping in my status as an otherworlder along the way. Hiding my origins seemed meaningless at this point. All of my people in Tempest knew, and I had no vested interest in keeping it from Gazel or Erald. It's not like a demon lord also being an ex-otherworlder would give them anything new to work with against me. Leon was one himself, after all.

I gave a quick summary of the orc lord fight and how it led to us building the town here. Sharing information was important, even if doing so led people to react in different ways.

Moving on, I shifted to my voluntary journeys in Englesia. This involved a lot of glossing over of my life there, along with the request I received from Yuuki, but I did go into detail about my fight with Hinata. *Man*, she was rough. If it had been anyone besides me, they probably would've been killed—Benimaru or Soei, even. Her skills were on par with or beyond Hakuro's, and she could cast magic the likes of which I never saw before. That Holy Field one was particularly nasty. I used Thought Communication to let everyone else experience my memory and recognition of it. She might have a smaller version of that in her pocket, ready to spring on single targets. I didn't think anyone in the room could do much against it, but it was better than going on nothing. The more they knew about the threat Hinata posed, the better. They might be able to escape, at least.

"Hinata Sakaguchi?"

It was Fuze who reacted first.

"She may seem cruel at first. I suppose she gives the impression of a crazed murderer to most. But according to the information we have, she's actually a little different from all that. For one thing, she's always willing to extend a helping hand to anyone who depends on her, and anyone willing to accept her help is sure to receive it—but if you *don't* listen to her advice, she'll never deal with you again. Whatever her motivations, though, I am assured she is a rational leader."

He seemed to know a lot about her—and was willing to come to her defense, too. I didn't want to fight her, either… It's just that she didn't want to listen to my story one bit, you know? If she refuses to help people who ignore her own background and situation, that describes my interactions with her pretty well. She must have a ton of people seeking favors from her, and I can see how she'd want to ignore them after a while. Pragmatic would be the way to describe it. Yuuki described her as a realist, too. I'm sure Fuze's intelligence was valid. He sure seems well-informed, doesn't he?

Gazel nodded at this. "Mm. The guild master of Blumund clearly has a finger in every pie, as they say. The accuracy of your information is equal only to that of my own dark agents. I will gladly testify that what you heard is exactly what we have heard."

Nice to have the confirmation. But:

"Maybe so, but she didn't listen to *me* at all."

She didn't. From the get-go, I was her target. Even if someone was feeding her a line about me beforehand, it was like she was deaf to me.

"Well," Erald said, "that would be because one core tenet of Luminism is that you are never allowed to bargain with monsters." I was surprised to hear that from him. Hinata was enough of a celebrity to even be known in Thalion, it seemed. She had a rep in places I never dreamed of… Although, I suppose any nation's intelligence agency would keep tabs on the most powerful knight in the Western Holy Church. *Is she famous because she's beautiful?* I thought for a moment but decided it best to keep that secret.

Following their guidance, I began to build a picture of Hinata in my mind. She was notorious for her cruel words and coldhearted actions, but apparently she had never actually broken a single tenet of her religion. She was the model soldier in every way, an unblemished guardian of law and order. So why didn't she put an end to the summoning rituals taking place worldwide? The kind of rapid-fire summons favored by certain lands bore a very high chance of bringing children over. It was evil, really, on a national level.

"On the other hand," Fuze countered, "do we really know for sure Hinata is aware of all of this summoning and willfully ignoring it?"

A fair point, but...

"Summoning magic powerful enough to produce an otherworlder is a forbidden, secret Art, not the kind of magic you'll see in public. The Council of the West has criminalized it, and I'm sure you won't find a lot of nations who'll voluntarily admit to it. They'll just say 'No, we don't do that' and then make it impossibly difficult to pursue the issue any further. The Western Holy Church holds a lot of sway in their region, yes, but if we're talking about getting to the point of freely meddling in internal government politics, then no, it's not *that* deep."

Even if a kingdom like Farmus used otherworlders as military weapons, I'm sure they'd just explain it away as, you know, discovering an otherworlder on their doorstep and giving them shelter. Without solid evidence, not even the Church could investigate. You couldn't really complain that Hinata was negligent, per se.

And that brought to mind something else Yuuki had mentioned:

"If something seems the most effective way to her, she'll do it, I guess you could say, but...but it makes no sense to me, no."

Maybe Hinata really *was* working to stop this, in her own way. If so, there was no point stewing about it here.

"The point is," I reflected, "Hinata's a serious threat. If I could at least get her to talk to me, we could set something up where we don't have to be dueling to the death..."

But if the Church labeled me a foe of all divinity, a duel would be unavoidable. I wanted to avoid that if possible, but if it happens, it happens.

"Heh-heh-heh-heh-heh. Perhaps I could go out and take care of her, then? There is no better way to quell your anxieties for the future than eliminating the problem from the start, no?"

Wow, Diablo. Confident much? Being the new guy on the team must've made him hungry for work. I really wish he would think more before he opened his mouth.

"Whoa, man, you realize that even I lost to— Um, I mean, fought to an even tie with Hinata, right? Just because *you're* on the scene won't make it some open-and-shut case!"

"He's right, Diablo," Shion added. "If someone like *you* wants to face him down, then I'll go over and finish her off first. I await your order, Sir Rimuru!"

See? First Diablo starts mouthing off, then Shion joins the fray and goes all battle crazy again.

"Now, now, Lady Shion. I do owe you a debt for teaching me the ins and outs of assisting Sir Rimuru, so I hardly wish to berate you...but I sadly cannot believe that you could defeat Hinata."

"Oh, really? So you think you're stronger than I am? Well, fine. Let's go out and settle this for—"

"We will settle *nothing*!" I shouted to distract them.

Diablo might have acted all calm and collected, but I guess he enjoyed egging people into a fight, too. He was polite to me, but that didn't seem to extend to the rest of his superiors. Pretty brazen for a new guy. And the way he provoked potential opponents was downright dangerous with the hyper-impulsive Shion.

"Gwah-ha-ha-ha-ha! So it's time for *me* to take action, is it? Very well! Allow me to just step out for a moment—"

"You're not going anywhere, Veldora! If she targets us, we'll deal with it then, but there's no need to take a fight to her right now. Let me just repeat, I don't want to antagonize the Western Holy Church!"

I had forgotten Veldora was seated next to me. He was ready to fly out the door before I stopped him.

Man, all these problem children... They're growing fast, but still, education's so important for them. Come to think of it, Benimaru

and Soei weren't itching to start fights at all anymore, and Geld had enough common sense that I could rely on him. Gabil got carried away a lot, but he still knew his place, so he never caused me many headaches. Plus, the way Ranga practically resided in my shadow, ears perked up for my command—he was almost cute compared to the others.

The big issue was with Shion, Diablo, and Veldora. Any mixture of the three was dangerous. I could feel my anxieties ramping up. *Better be more careful dealing with them.*

"Either way, that's enough debate about Hinata and the Church. We may fight them depending on how matters unfold, but I intend to proceed with caution and watch what happens!"

So that was settled. But one thing I couldn't forget was the presence of someone maneuvering behind the scenes. Hinata knew about me—she had an "informant," she said, but there weren't many people out there who knew I killed Shizu. It'd be hard to identify the mole, but it had to be someone I knew. The Kabal-Elen-Gido trio; Fuze and a few other Blumundians; and Yuuki. Beyond that, the only ones who knew all lived in this forest.

But that would mean...

Raphael was busy deriving a list of suspects for me. I appreciated his logic, but it could be someone, or something, we had no knowledge of at all. I didn't want to work with the wrong impression, and I didn't want to suspect anyone without real evidence. Better just lock that in my mind and keep my eyes open.

What was the point behind having Hinata and me fight each other anyway?

Was someone hoping I would dispatch her?

Did they want to obstruct me from returning to town?

Or did they want to lure Hinata out into the open?

...Or all of those things.

Seriously, Raphael? Talk about greedy. There were too many unknowns, and I couldn't shake the impression that I was being played like a fiddle. *Let's just be patient for now. It can wait.*

*   *   *

Getting back on track, I told the assembled group about how our town was attacked once I escaped Hinata—a wild, bloody conflict, engineered by a clutch of Farmus otherworlders. I wanted to do something for the victims, so I elected to make myself a demon lord...but before I could continue, Elen made the confession herself.

"And my dad already knows, doesn't he? Like, that's the whole reason you're here, isn't it?"

Wow. The way she looked at Erald with those upturned eyes. Dangerously cute. The poor guy's like putty in her hands with that act.

"Elen..." He sighed, resigned. "It doesn't matter if I know or not. There's no need for other nations to know, too..."

I could guess how he felt. This really was Elen's fault. What she did went beyond rocking the boat—it totally ignored the balance in this world. But Erald had guessed this would happen. *"I'm sure,"* he had said in our earlier secret talk, *"my daughter Elen will reveal she gave you the demon lord suggestion. The only way to stop her would be to drag her back home, and she'd hate me for it. It would be a terrible plan."*

He might've tried sounding like an expert strategist when he said it, although he sounded more like an idiot to me. Hard to tell, really. But Erald's prediction was right, so maybe the former.

I turned my eyes toward Gazel, a bit conflicted about all this. Seeing him nod back, I decided to proceed with this discussion the way we had planned.

"All right. And thanks to that, I used the assembled Farmus forces as a sacrifice, and one thing led to another, and I successfully became a demon lord."

∗

That wrapped up the basic story I had. Now for the real work.

"So... Right. Everything I just discussed with you is the truth, but what we'll announce to the public will be adjusted somewhat."

The Tempestians in the audience seemed pretty thrown by this. To the monsters, brute strength meant everything. Something like fudging the details for the story we'd give other nations must've seemed pointless to them. But lies and deceit are what politics are all about, really.

"What is the reason for this?" Benimaru asked for the group. "And in what way would you change it?"

I was ready for this question. We worked that one out in advance, too.

The way we'll do this is that I'll declare myself to be a demon lord, but we *won't* reveal that I've actually awakened.

This is based on the assumption that other nations have no idea what actually went on around here. There's no way for them to investigate the facts. Every potential eyewitness is dead, and apart from those of us in the room, only three humans know the truth. Everybody knew that the king of Farmus was a greedy tyrant, so it would be easy to frame our actions as justifiable self-defense.

By our logic, it'd sound far more credible if Farmus lost following a fully engaged battle, rather than being annihilated by a single demon lord. We'll also say that all those many piles of dead had unwittingly opened up an awful, dreadful seal. Yes, the blood that they shed as they lay there seeped its way underground, opening the eyes of the dragon that stirred below—in other words, resurrecting Veldora.

Luckily, the champion Yohm, accompanied by me (the plucky Jura-Tempest Federation leader who's angling to become a recognized demon lord), worked together to coax the dragon to our side, at the cost of many sacrifices. Quelling the beast's anger, we agreed to worship Veldora as our guardian. Setting things up this way would establish my claim to the demon lord name and neatly pin all the blame on Farmus while establishing us as the good guys.

"Think about it," Gazel commented. "People fear what they do not understand; they will never willfully accept it. A monster who singlehandedly destroyed an army of twenty thousand will find no one willing to believe his claims about peace and friendship."

Fuze and Yohm seemed to understand, as much as they groaned about it. And these guys were two of my closest confidants. Someone who didn't know me? They'd react just like Gazel said they would. I could wind up at war with all the Western Nations the next day.

"But," he continued, "if we claim the Storm Dragon is behind the twenty thousand missing soldiers, that would be easier for the masses to grasp. The Storm Dragon is already a living catastrophe, after all, a mastermind of all types of destruction."

This seemed to convince the crowd. Only Veldora stayed in his seat, snickering "Heh-heh-heh, call me a mastermind, will you? You are a smart man, indeed" and completely missing the point. Well, if he's happy, I'm happy.

"I support this plan of action as well," Erald said. "Stating that my daughter helped Sir Rimuru become a demon lord would inspire nothing but fear and disdain. Much better for him to have been able to negotiate successfully with the Storm Dragon *because* he became a demon lord. He'll be much more appreciated that way, I think you'll find."

He smiled, his eyes looming over the meeting hall in search of dissent. I swear, he's the kind of guy who would do anything for Elen.

"Oh, Dad... That's exactly the kind of nefarious scheme I would've expected from a noble as crafty as you..."

I couldn't tell if Elen was praising him or making fun of him, really. It made me feel bad for Erald a bit, as I waited for the audience to quiet down.

"And that's not the only advantage for me," I said. "It's important that the human race doesn't needlessly fear us, but this might also fool the other demon lords eyeing me into thinking that Veldora's the only threat, right?"

And *that* would give me some breathing room to work with.

After I thrashed Farmus, the demon lord Clayman must be on the lookout for me, at least. If we spread the rumor that it was actually Veldora providing the big guns, I think that'd make me less of a worry to him. Gazel, king of an allied nation, wanted to have Dwargon come out of this looking good. Me, I wanted the Western Nations to think nicely of me, while making anyone hostile to me underestimate my abilities and put their guards down a little. For now, it was much more helpful if they thought I was a whiny pushover than someone worth fearing.

"Besides, if word gets out that we've got the authority to negotiate with Veldora, that's gonna keep a lot of nations from messin' with us, don't you think? No matter what the Western Holy Church says, I think there's a good chance they'll have trouble finding anyone to carry out their orders."

That might be the biggest advantage of all. Even before Gazel's suggestion, we needed to reveal Veldora's presence sooner or later—and if we did, we might as well do it when he's at his most useful. We were planning to tango with Clayman soon, so deliberately antagonizing the Church right now was nothing short of idiotic. Waging a two-front war would just spread us out too thin; we had to avoid that as best we could.

The trick here was to keep our foes as unworried about *me* as possible but as worried about *Tempest* as we could manage. I tell you, Raphael made some choice edits to what was already a killer scheme from Gazel. Sensing his, my, and Erald's motivations, he weaved them all together to get the most use out of them in this plan. Amazing work. Ever since that ultimate-skill evolution, his mind's been sharper than ever before.

"I see," Veldora said, nodding his satisfaction. "So now you have a reason to take care of me, then?"

Oh, great. He only listened to the parts of this story he liked, didn't he? That wasn't quite what I meant...but ah well.

Apart from him, the rest of my government seemed to enjoy the idea. "I understand the merits of this," Rigurd said, looking a tad relieved as he vigorously nodded. "In this case, we can continue negotiating in much the same way we have before."

That must have been a worry for him; how this would affect future trade with other nations. He was developing a keen eye for Tempest's economic development that I appreciated.

"Brilliantly done, Sir Rimuru! A truly ingenious plan!"

"No, Shion," I admonished, relieved that at least she understood the gist of it. "King Gazel thought it up. I just made sure all our feedback was included."

"My thanks to you, King Gazel," Sufia commented, baring a fanged grin. "Now when we make our move, we can expect great things from Sir Rimuru's forces!"

Phobio and Alvis seemed just as eager for the idea. The Three Lycanthropeers were on our side.

Benimaru's mind, meanwhile, was already elsewhere. "Heh-heh-heh... Very well. So now we can focus entirely on Clayman? If we can't win this, it will just prove we were talentless from the start."

Good to hear. I'd need him on the field. Soei, Geld, and Benimaru were of a similar mind, ready to roll out this very moment.

Now I had dozens of passion-filled eyes fixed upon me. I nodded back at them. *I need you to wait a bit longer, guys. You can go hog wild once this summit is over.*

*

We had a backstory—and now that we had somewhere to start, we needed to decide what we'd do next.

I told the audience about how we had the king of Farmus and a Church archbishop in our custody. In their place, we would support Yohm as the land's new king and launch a plan to build a new nation for its people.

Now Fuze was groaning again. After falling silent for a while, I guess he had finally worked everything out in his mind.

Gazel was similarly quiet, eyes closed. His friends were bouncing ideas off one another, but opinions seemed to be split, without any clear consensus. Even Erald offered no words, no doubt coldly considering how the Sorcerous Dynasty should react to this.

I watched them all closely as I continued my guidance.

First off, we would release the current king, then force him to pay reparations for invading our country. This would be a pretext, of course; the actual aim was to throw Farmus itself into a state of civil war. If the king managed to gather his nobility again and attempt a resistance, his life was as good as gone. I was dealing with a king here. I wasn't about to let him off the hook twice.

Now, if this king meekly agreed to our demands at this point, we'd delay the whole Yohm-as-king thing for a while. By Raphael's estimation, however, the chances of this were practically nil. Even if he suddenly became a king who lived up to his promises, fulfilling his obligations would be punishingly difficult. His nation had just lost twenty thousand men and women of working age, and he needed money to rebuild his power. He'd be forced to claim it from the nation's noble families, but they were all far too greedy to cooperate.

No, the king would find some excuse or another to ignore the reparations entirely. Then Yohm would raise the flag of resistance, staging a coup to help restore good faith in the government. It was the duty of the survivors to take responsibility for a lost war. What if the king didn't do that? What if he ordered his government to de facto shake down the nobility for money instead? He'd lose any authority he had.

The whole reparations thing was a wedge to rip the king apart from the nobility. Once he had lost all influence with them, the internal factions of their government would undoubtedly fall apart. The king's sons were not of adult age yet, reportedly; it was easy to imagine them becoming puppets of the nobility. That, in turn, would certainly lead into battles over succession.

Either way, whenever things descended into physical combat, Yohm would step forward, and the exhausted masses would hail him as their champion. No matter which way it shook out, it all meant that the current kingdom of Farmus was about to meet its downfall. Tempest, of course, would announce its support for Yohm, a champion they had been on good terms with for a while now. Once Yohm declared the establishment of a new kingdom, we would be the first to officially recognize it and open sanctioned relations.

The nobility, the source of current ruling power, would no doubt form an alliance to fight back, but we'd already factored that into the equation. We'd simply exile them all, except for those who offered to cooperate from an early stage. If they insisted upon meddling with us, then they'd have to just disappear, sadly. We would serve as a deterrent to any such alliance, preventing any direct military activity while we sorted out who was friend and who was foe.

In the midst of this, we would take the time to announce new policies that would win the trust of the people, boosting Yohm's popularity. Once this happened, the plan was to destroy the opposing forces.

A nation couldn't be built overnight. Even at breakneck speed, it'd have to extend to two, maybe three years. Of course, Yohm might be on the throne even quicker than that, if the current king made some particularly ill-advised decisions…

That was the basic outline. It meant that, however the timeline wound up actually working out, Yohm was ultimately all but guaranteed to become king.

"Personally," I explained, "I have no interest in oppressing the people of Farmus. In terms of allowing their own ruler to go around like he owned the whole world, however, I'm not absolving them of guilt. They will have to put up with some tight times for a while, and I'd like them to put in a solid effort at rebuilding once it's all said and done."

Everyone thought silently for a moment before Gazel spoke up. "I like this. I have no objections to the plan itself. However, Rimuru, the idea of Yohm becoming king is another issue altogether."

He stood up, putting the full force of his gaze upon Yohm. It was powerfully withering, even from far away. Having experienced it myself, I knew exactly how the man was feeling right then.

"…Ngh?!"

Yohm let out a grunt and clenched his teeth in the process, but he met Gazel eye to eye.

"Hmph. Well, he has great willpower, at least. But what of his character? Is he prepared to feel for his people, to take up their pain and stand before them?"

A hush fell upon the meeting hall.

"Heh. How the hell should I know? I'm not here to be a king 'cause I want to. But if I turn down this role after he's put his full trust in me, what kinda man would I be, huh?!"

"Hmm?"

"I'm just sayin', I don't wanna convince myself I can't do it and give up before I even try. I also wanna impress the woman I love, too, I'll grant ya that, but if I'm going in, I'm going in at full power."

There was no waver to Yohm's voice. He was speaking a heap of nonsense, but his determination made it all oddly convincing.

"...Fool," Mjurran whispered.

"But so much like Yohm, eh?" the beastman Gruecith replied, grinning. "You have my word on this, Dwarven King. This guy's an idiot, but he's not an irresponsible idiot. Once he takes something on, he'll carry it out all the way to the end. And I, Gruecith, promise I'll be there with him the whole time!"

Mjurran nodded her agreement as all three sized up Gazel.

"...Is that the case? Very well, then. If you need anything, call upon me."

Like a light switch, Gazel turned off all his intimidation, nodding at them good-naturedly. I guess they all passed his final exam—and if they have the Armed Nation of Dwargon backing them up, that was huge.

"I have to say, though, you found quite an interesting man here," the king added with a smile.

"He seeks the throne to impress a woman?" a shocked Erald stammered.

"Nice going, Gruecith. I sure wasn't expecting you to stand up here and abandon Lord Carillon in front of us all!" chided Phobio.

It felt like a circus, really.

"Yohm," intoned Gazel once everyone was done laughing, "what we seek from your nation is agricultural production. I don't want to meddle in your political affairs, but listen to this: I know Farmus can keep itself afloat through its black-market trade in my nation's manufactured goods, but I think we've recently proven that this won't last forever, hmm?"

It was true. The exorbitant taxes Farmus placed on imported goods before reselling them had made it into one of the world's most notorious price-gouging outfits. They were not exactly one of the Dwarven Kingdom's favored customers. Now, with a new highway linking Dwargon to a vast, fresh market, Farmus was losing its previous advantage. If the kingdom wanted to survive, it needed to have something new—and instead of a field where it'd be competing with other nations, it'd be easier to coexist if they blazed a trail into unexplored markets.

I had heard before that the Dwarven Kingdom faced issues with self-sufficiency in their food supply, so I could easily tell what Gazel was hinting at. I was just thinking that I wanted a new import supplier of grain for our nation, something that wasn't so dependent on what naturally grew in the forest. In short, the idea made sense.

"I'd like to be in on this, too. Add new grain varieties for us to your list!"

"Who woulda guessed *you'd* jump on the train, too, huh, pal? ...Well, I'll get on it. We're pretty developed agriculturally over in Farmus. I think it'll be easier for folks to accept than you'd think."

Thus, with Gazel and me sharing common goals, we made a preliminary agricultural agreement for whenever Yohm was crowned.

We agreed to take a break at this point while Shuna passed out tea to everyone. Once we were done, I dove right back in to the summit, reenergized. With Yohm formally accepted by the summit, our mission to build a new Farmus was now under way. That was really the trickiest part of this whole meet; the rest was much smoother sailing.

"So as a representative of Blumund," Fuze stated, "I have a proposal. Listening to King Gazel and Sir Rimuru speak, I believe we might have something to offer this plan as well. In Farmus, there are two noblemen—the Marquis of Muller and Count Hellman—who share an intimate relationship with Blumund. If we could negotiate with them to join our side on this matter, I think they could do much for our cause, don't you think? I believe they will provide staunch support when it is time for Yohm to take action."

Whether he's a Guild branch leader or not, does Fuze really have that kind of power? Fuze, perhaps sensing my disbelief, gave me an awkward grin.

"As I stated, I represent Blumund here, and you may consider me to be a part of the Blumund government. I make this proposal not as a guild master but as a public servant."

As he explained, Fuze apparently had a seat in Blumund's intelligence department—not as a member of staff but as kind of an assistant supervisor to the whole outfit. Which was fine and all, but this was kind of a huge offer he was making, wasn't he? Could he really decide on this solo?

I asked him about this, and then he gave me an even more startling revelation. While I was meeting with Gazel and Erald earlier, he had already tipped off the king of Blumund about events here and had him draw up a document providing him full representational rights. That's the kind of quick footwork I suppose I should expect from a tiny kingdom like that—not to mention a sign of just how much Fuze was trusted.

As he put it, Fuze had "several pieces of info that would sink the whole kingdom if they were released." Secretly, I considered making him tell me somehow. I couldn't help it.

So Fuze had been taking advantage of his position to divert all kinds of information his way—anything he thought might be necessary, even before he heard about our plans.

The way he described it, the Marquis of Muller and Count Hellman could basically enjoy the Blumund king's personal support. Being a powerful noble in Farmus, the marquis was in no position to offer any public kindness to Blumund, but he and their king were close friends behind closed doors. Muller, in fact, was distantly related to the Blumundian royal family, and they had gotten along well for many years. Count Hellman, meanwhile, owed a great debt of gratitude to the marquis, making it extremely unlikely he would betray him.

"Wow, you sure you want to reveal all these secrets to us?"

"Ha-ha-ha! Oh, it's fine. I am sure the Dwarven King was well aware of it all before I came here. The dark agents of Dwargon are just as talented in their jobs as our own intelligence group."

As neighbor states, Fuze must have figured the dwarves would have known a thing or two about them already. Gazel simply twitched one of his shoulders upward a bit, offering no further reply. Henrietta, the beautiful night assassin poised behind him, blinked a bit as well. Soei praised her as a talented agent, and I could believe it.

"Hoh-hoh-hoh! Oh, you are being too humble," she said. "The kingdom of Blumund's bread and butter lies in intelligence. If you are posted in the center of a spy agency for a nation that treats information as salable goods, I'm sure you must be far more talented than my own team, no?"

The voice was friendly enough, but her expression indicated she didn't actually believe what she was saying.

"Ha-ha! No need to be so harsh on yourself. Our fighting forces would have nothing on your dark agents, I don't think! In terms of intelligence gathering, of course, I do believe we enjoy some useful advantages."

Fuze was just as headstrong, it seemed. But Blumund's small size allowed it to cover intel from every nation in the world, no doubt. That was the most powerful weapon it had to defend its borders with. But regardless, if Fuze said it, it had to be true. Those two Farmus nobles definitely need to be recruited—and fast.

"Did you hear all that, Yohm?"

"Yep. I'll add it to the list."

We'd sell Yohm to them first. He'd enjoy a true champion's welcome, and it'd be an epic event. But we could work out the details at another time. Yohm's team could handle that at their leisure.

✳

"Great! So that's how Yohm the champion will gain a country of his own soon."

Everyone murmured their agreement, Yohm bringing a hand to his head in bashful embarrassment. *I'll pretend I didn't see that and declare this topic well and truly settled. Next up—*

Just as I was about to proceed to the next topic, Erald apparently finished processing our discussion and burst out into hysterical laughter.

"Pff! Ah-ha-ha-ha-ha! This is so entertaining! The leaders and representatives of entire nations, expressing their minds freely without doubting one another for a moment... I feel almost like a fool for staying on the alert around you all!"

He couldn't help but chuckle at the ridiculousness of it all, even though the light remained sharp in his eyes. This was absolutely the face of a high nobleman, not Erald the helplessly devoted father. Archduke Erald of Thalion, a man whose position made speaking his mind virtually impossible.

Without warning, he stood up, overwhelming the air around him. The sudden change in atmosphere turned all eyes silently toward him. We nervously awaited whatever he might say next.

The meeting hall was silent, save for the turning of the pages as Veldora read some manga... *Whoa! What the hell, man?! I didn't even give that to you yet! Where'd you pluck that out from?! ...Ah well.* He had no interest in listening to anyone here anyway. As long as he's shutting up, I have no complaints. He certainly helped relieve my tension just now. *Let's just see what Erald has to say.*

The archduke cleared his throat to return the attention to himself, then solemnly opened his mouth. That's resilience, there.

"...Allow me to ask. The man over there... Fuze. Do you truly place your trust in this monster, Rimuru?"

"That... How do you mean, sir?"

"I mean, even if a bunch of monsters decide to go and start a country, did you have to officially recognize them? And was there any need to establish official trade relations, for that matter? In terms of your relative locations, you certainly could have acted with less haste."

"We..."

It seemed like an honest question, not one hurled out of spite. That was why Fuze found himself without words, having trouble finding his reply.

"What I am saying is this. If I were in your position, I would engage them in trade, yes, but I would also see how the Western Holy Church reacted. Give them confidential reports, you see, and leave matters to them if there are any problems. That way, you enjoy all the profit, but you aren't beholden entirely to one side should issues crop up later. Isn't that the way any smaller nation should handle matters?"

The words, and his gaze, were sharper than any sword. And Erald wasn't the only one—it seemed like everyone's eyes were upon Fuze now.

"Ugh, why me?" he whispered to himself, and then: "All right! All right! In that case, allow me to be honest!"

Resigned to his fate, Fuze tore at his hair and began speaking loudly. His usual brazen personality was back—he was facing the Archduke of Thalion, and he had had enough of all this formal, ceremonial speech.

"Duke Erald, I was of the exact same opinion as you. I stated the same case to my superior as well, not to mention a nobleman friend. But I was brushed off..."

As Fuze went on to explain, when he tried to convince his boss of this, his concerns were immediately dismissed. The reasoning: "What if Tempest decides to declare war on us?" This was before I visited Blumund but after the battle with Charybdis ended.

To them, we were this nation packed with high-level magic-born, powerful enough to take out both Charybdis and an orc lord. Waging war with them, Fuze was told, would result in instant annihilation. Luminism was not widespread in Blumund; the Western Holy Church would provide little serious backup. Any unwise moves, and the country would cease to exist. Resistance, they concluded, was futile.

—So what to do, then?

"We'd earn their trust, build a mutual friendship, and find a way to coexist. We wouldn't be afraid to cooperate with them as much as possible. That was the conclusion the highest levels of Blumund government made. And I mean, your nation and the Dwarven Kingdom are powerful enough that you have all kinds of choices available...but with us, one misstep, and it's over. And if we're wagering our fates here, better to trust in the monster lord than the Church. That's basically it," Fuze explained with some chagrin.

Thinking about it, having his exact thoughts pointed out to him made me feel kind of sorry for Fuze. It was basically admitting that the kingdom of Blumund was too puny to take up Erald's common-sense suggestion. Not that it was wrong, but...still, good or bad, right or wrong; that wasn't important. They had decided to fully trust me.

It was beyond reckless... Or was it, really? If it blew up in their face, that was it, but they had concluded that there was no other way for them to survive. I was as powerful as an entire army; no wonder they saw me as a threat. Better to fight with us, not against us. For a small nation dealing in intelligence and living in the shadows of superpowers, maybe that was an effective strategy. Definitely reckless, but in a way, effective, maybe. Effective against me anyway.

Regardless, I was sure I could trust in Blumund as well—and Erald must have come to the same conclusion.

"...Still, that is quite the brash decision. And if I could change the subject for a moment, I understand you came here to provide military assistance to Sir Rimuru? Was that the decision of your, ah, superior as well?"

"Exactly. We've ratified a common security agreement, and I've been ordered to follow it to the letter. Of course, even if the government broke its promise, I would have come here anyway. I'm a free man, I'll have you know. The Guild is unaffiliated with any nation by design—normally, you see, it'd be crazy for someone like me to be here. You could say my luck ran out the moment I was appointed to Blumund's intelligence team..."

He sounded like he had no idea why he took the job in the first place. Almost too honest of him, not that he could do much about it now. I had no idea his king was so dedicated to keeping his word, though. Complying with that agreement and bracing themselves for war with Farmus... And here I thought that treaty didn't earn us much of anything. Now, I was glad for it. I had real insight into how they thought of us at present.

Sticking to promises lies at the core of any human relationship. That applies to nations as well; any nation that doesn't follow its promises, or treaties, can't really be trusted. This whole incident had proved to me that Blumund is *eminently* trustworthy. They risked their necks because they believed we would win, not that even *they* thought I'd wipe out the enemy by myself.

"Can I guess who this superior is? He sounds like quite the gambling man."

Fuze nodded, seemingly fighting back tears of frustration as he smiled. "...As you've probably surmised, it is His Majesty the King."

You know, he did seem like a pretty nice guy when I met him. Guess he's more of an expert at this whole nation-leading thing than I thought. You need the guts to go all in when you're running a country, sometimes.

"...So," he continued with a sigh, "that's what was going on, and his choice wound up being the right one. Never in my life would I have imagined you defeating a force of twenty thousand, Sir Rimuru. And resurrecting the Storm Dragon? It's no longer a question of trust at all, I'd say. And that document giving me negotiation rights here? I think the higher-ups may've set a new record drawing it up."

It was like he was the sole bulwark keeping his homeland from collapsing. I could understand why he was a tad overwrought.

"...Ah. I see now." The tension disappeared from Erald's face as he lowered his head a bit toward Fuze. "I apologize, Sir Fuze. Thanks to you, however, I fully understand the kingdom of Blumund's intentions, here."

"Sly as always, aren't you, Erald?" interjected Gazel. "You know I trust Rimuru. There's no need to go feeling out other nations to satisfy your doubts."

"You may say that, Gazel, but it's not going to be that easy for us to forge a new pact with a nation of monsters. I have a new, and healthy, respect for the king of Blumund."

"Ha. Enough of that rot. You came here because you had the decision made beforehand, did you not? So what is your conclusion, master strategist Erald?"

Erald reacted stonily to Gazel's provocation—not because he was relatively safe in his homunculus, but because he really did just have that much nerve.

"You could say I have...made my own conclusions, yes. But before I answer you, can I ask one more question?"

He turned to me next—

"Dad, come *onnnnn*! Stop acting all stuck-up and just answer!"

"Whoa! Hey, lady, pipe down!"

"Yeah! The archduke's trying his hardest to look all cool for you, okay?!"

The tension in the air was thoroughly ruined by Elen and her two cohorts. "So much for the master strategist," mused Gazel.

I felt a little bad for Erald, so I decided to bring some solemnity to the environment. Meaning I unleashed a bit of Lord's Ambition.

"...Let me hear it, Erald."

I could hear my government stir in their seats, even as Gazel and his friends groaned in astonishment, and Yohm, Fuze, and the Eurazania contingent began sweating. I set it to run as long as possible, but it was even fiercer than I gave it credit for. This was, after all, the merger of skills like Coercion and Magic Aura, something I could use as an attack. Misuse would be dangerous.

Still, I thought I had gotten pretty good at acting all kingly like this. The trick was to erase all expression from your face as you spoke. Hiding your emotions and taking a dispassionate tone was enough to freak your audience out, really. Between Shizu's good looks and the wispy, transparent feel of a slime, the mix gave me this perfect sort of mystique. Add Lord's Ambition to the picture, and it was perfect. I didn't need anything else. If I let my emotions bubble to the surface and started acting more like myself, that mystique vanished in short order. You had to train at this, really, so as a former middle-class schmo, I think I was doing pretty well.

Either way, it was enough to take in Erald.

"...Heh. Impressive. In that case, Demon Lord Rimuru, let me ask you: How do you intend to wield your powers as demon lord?"

Oh. That? Simple. I wanted to create a world that's easy to live in, the way I picture it. A bountiful world where people could be as content as possible. No bluffing, no dodging it; that's what I really thought. So that's what I told him.

"...That kind of thing, I guess. And I'm sure I'll have some stumbles along the way. It's not going to be that easy, I imagine."

"You—you seriously believe you can build that kind of fantasy world?!"

Oops. That sounds like real surprise, there. I've successfully managed to shock a high noble who almost never reveals his emotions.

"Well, you know, that's what my power is for. Ideals are just a bunch of raving without power to back them up, and power is just kind of a vacant void without ideals to back it up, isn't it? And I know I'm pretty greedy, but I'm not into seeking pure power for power's sake with no other particular goals in mind."

I was rephrasing a famous line or two in my mind, and I think I managed to get my point across. I mean, doesn't this go without saying? You work at something because you want to accomplish something. That's the essence of humanity, I think.

"Ha, ha-ha-ha, ha-ha-ha-ha-ha! Hilarious! That is hilarious, Demon Lord Rimuru! A demon lord versed in the concept of karma! I think I understand why you managed to awaken yourself now!"

I didn't stop him from laughing at me. Let him have his fun. And once he settled down, he stood up and kneeled before me.

"My pardons. Demon Lord Rimuru, as the envoy of the Sorcerous Dynasty of Thalion, I hereby request the establishment of formal relations with your nation, the Jura-Tempest Federation. I hope to hear a positive reply from you..."

The hall fell quiet again...except for that page flipping. Better not let that bother me. If I turned toward him right now, it'd ruin the entire atmosphere. The sight of a Storm Dragon lying on a bench, reading manga while sipping some iced tea he had someone make for him, would just scramble my brain.

"...I was hoping we could build a positive relationship myself. I will gladly accept the offer."

Cheers erupted, and everyone leaped out of their seats to celebrate this memorable new bond.

Today, we welcomed another faithful ally.

So we now had the beginnings of diplomatic relations with Thalion, our third human nation. Soon, Farmus would be no more, and Yohm would be at the helm of a new nation. Slowly but surely, the map was being redrawn. Things were moving, and accelerating, faster than I had pictured at first.

WORD FROM RAMIRIS

That Time I Got Reincarnated as a Slime

Just as the summit was winding down, and I felt it was time to wrap things up:

Bwaaam!!

The doors flew open as someone stormed in.

"I heard all that! Tempest shall fall to ruin!!"

There was a tiny winged girl—and while it was hard to believe from looks, it was Ramiris of the Labyrinth, one of the world's ten demon lords.

I wasn't exactly sure how to take this. Should I open my eyes wide and go "Wha-*what* was that?!"? I didn't have much time to react, because Ramiris was flying straight for me, while Beretta was kindly closing the front door behind her. *Long-suffering* is the way I'd describe that demon's body language, and I bet I was right. Getting bossed around by Ramiris all day would do that to anyone.

Now Diablo was standing in front of her, dressed to the nines in his butler-y outfit. He had been stationed behind me, quietly listening to the proceedings, but he wasn't willing to let this interloper barge in. And really, he made capturing Ramiris look as easy as grabbing a dragonfly out of the air.

"H-hey!" she shouted, flailing around. "What're you doing to

me?!" I just love her. She doesn't act the part of a demon lord one bit, and it's just adorable.

"Sir Rimuru," Diablo said, walking back to me, "I have captured an intruder. What should we do with her? She raved about this town falling to ruin, but how should we address this insolence?"

I looked at Ramiris. She was batting her wings helplessly, trying to escape Diablo's grasp. "Gehhh! I'm using my full magic force, and I still can't escape him?! This, this can't be any kind of regular bodyguard! Who *are* you? What did I ever do to you?!"

She never was very quiet. And no offense, but given the incomparable difference in power, I didn't think Diablo would lose her anytime soon. And this was a demon lord? See, *this* is why I sometimes wonder if being a demon lord is anything special at all.

"Do you know this fairy, Sir Rimuru?" Fuze asked. Oh, right, we were in the middle of a summit. Right toward the end, in fact. If she had only come in a couple minutes later... She never was good at taking social cues like that, either.

"Yeah, I do. This is Ramiris, and she might not show it, but I guess she's a demon lord, too?"

"Hey! What d'you *mean*, I don't show it?! I am feared as the strongest out of all ten demon lords, I'll have you know!"

She flashed me the most arrogant smile possible, still stuck in Diablo's grasp and oblivious to how nonthreatening she looked. The audience was nonplussed, a few giving comments like "Huh? A demon lord...?" and "Someone like *that*?"

"...What? Like, *whaaaat*? Come on, what's your problem? You're supposed to act more surprised! I'm kind of a demon lord, guys! Ramiris of the Labyrinth, in the flesh, all right?! Why is everyone acting so uninterested?"

I mean, demon lord or not, you're kind of caught between two fingers right now. If I had to guess, everyone thinks you must be some kind of poseur, you know? I'm too kind to actually voice this, of course, but...

"...Well, as a demon lord himself, it's only fair that Sir Rimuru would be acquainted with other demon lords, I suppose..."

"If anything, the Storm Dragon's resurrection was such a shock, I don't think anything could surprise me at this point..."

Our audience was nodding at one another. I suppose that makes sense, actually.

Ramiris, on the other hand, was less than satisfied with that.

"Huh? The Storm Dragon? Veldora's been revived? You guys are being tricked! I beat Veldora into the ground with a single punch! That guy was all roar and no bite. Besides, his era's over now. If you want someone to fear, you can start being horrified around *my* presence today!"

She punctuated this with a high, haughty laugh. If anything, she had an even bigger mouth than Veldora. I had Diablo hand her over to me and took her to see him.

"Veldora, you mind entertaining this girl for me? She's a demon lord, too, more or less, so maybe she'll wanna be friends with you."

"Mm? I am busy unraveling a grand riddle at the moment."

I didn't have time for his sulking.

"Oh, *that* manga? The murderer was [REDACTED]. You're good now, right? Thanks."

With that bout of mercilessness, I returned to my seat. Veldora looked shocked, eyes wide open. Maybe it wasn't the nicest thing to do, but we're in the middle of a summit. I wanted him to think about his actions a little, not let him do whatever he wants.

Besides, the sight of Veldora had already made Ramiris faint on the spot. Two problem children taken care of in one stroke.

✳

So wrapping up, I wanted to go over everything we had to do.

"Benimaru, our next target is Clayman. I want him taken down!"

"Just what I've been waiting to hear!" Benimaru gave me a fearless smile, flames dancing eerily in his eyes. The rest of the Tempestians in the audience were similarly elated; I guess they'd all become would-be warriors over time. *Didn't they all just have a huge battle in town a few days ago? Ah well. High morale's never a bad thing.*

"As for the Three Lycanthropeers and the beastmen under them…"

"No need to say it," Alvis growled. "We are under your command,

Sir Rimuru." Phobio and Sufia seemed just as enthused. I shouldn't have bothered asking.

"And you think you can beat him with this team, Rimuru?"

"I will. He's riled me."

"I see…" Gazel gave me a wry grin. "I will trust you in your word, then." And in a smaller voice that I figured only I could hear: "Here I thought you were my junior training partner. You've grown far too much…"

"But I do not believe you can afford to think lightly of Clayman," observed a concerned Erald. "He holds sway over a vast army of magic-born, and rumors tell of close connections with the Eastern Empire…"

"That doesn't matter. War is about quality, not quantity!"

"Heavens, I think I can hear my common sense collapsing as we speak…"

It was, indeed, totally lacking in common sense, but it was enough to quiet him. I could tell he was interested in what I had now. I knew it was crazy, too, but I also knew I was right. The larger army usually wins the battle, but that didn't apply to this world. The orc lord was a good example of that. As long as you can decapitate the leader, it was always the more adept fighters that dictated the results.

Besides, this time, we didn't lose out in numbers, either. I had cut it out from the summit for brevity, but Soei had already briefed me on Clayman's movements. Soei was still pinning down an exact number, but they were moving sluggishly and still stuck inside Milim's domain. His Replication would be back here soon, though, and I could save my final decision for then.

That strategic meeting could come later, but for now, we needed to make sure we had the script down for conquering Farmus. We'd release the king, then have the Marquis of Muller and Count Hellman pursue his blame, beseeching him to take responsibility for his failure. Depending on how he reacted, Yohm would then spring into action.

"Regarding any actual war with them, that will be our issue to tackle. For now, I want all of you to trust in me and leave Farmus for us to worry about. It shouldn't be long before I'll ask you to help us make Yohm into the champion king of a new generation."

The audience nodded their approval. When it came to human affairs, we'd make a lot fewer mistakes relying on them instead of trying to go it alone. I was looking forward to their support.

"Now, Fuze, I want you to contact Muller and Hellman confidentially."

"Sure thing," he replied.

Again, we'd likely work out the details in a later meeting, but we had a plan of action now. First, we'd portray things so it was Yohm and his forces reclaiming the king from us. We'd then have the Marquis of Muller put the king under his protection, providing backup for Yohm the whole way. And about those three POWs, actually:

"By the way, Shion, how are those three dealing with your questioning? Did they give us anything useful?"

I had forgotten about that—it didn't really matter, in the grand scheme of things—but I had left our prisoners in the care of Shion this whole time.

"Heh-heh-heh... Of course they did, Sir Rimuru!"

Ooh. Somebody sure is confident. I had a bad feeling about that. I turned toward Yohm and Mjurran, who were supposed to be present during all the questioning. They awkwardly turned their eyes away.

"Um," Yohm began. "Yeah, um, questioning? Interrogation? Either way, they talked a lot, pal."

"That they did," agreed Mjurran. "But that was no questioning. It was something surreal. I'm not sure you could even call it interrogation."

I really don't want to hear anything else, thanks. Shion overdid it, no doubt about it—but then, I let her. It'd be unreasonable for me to complain about it, and I had no intention to. Even if I wanted to stop her violent rage, I guess I was cooped up in the cave and beyond contact range anyway. In a way, it's my fault for not being there. Let's just assume I never noticed.

Sorry, people of Farmus. But then again, you guys struck first. Hopefully, you'll consider yourselves lucky for surviving at all.

Either way, we had three prisoners in custody, and following Shion's interro—um, *questioning*, they seemed fairly willing to talk.

"First off," Shion began, "Ed, Ednoyol? Ed…"

"…King Edmaris?" whispered Shuna into her ear. *Thanks for that. But really, Shion? You couldn't even come up with the king's name? I know it's kind of a weird one, but…*

"King Edmaris had apparently made contact with a merchant, one who brought him silken fabrics from our nation and whetted his appetite for conquest. The king also feared that trade would drift over to our nation in the future, which also led to those moves on his part…"

Shion's rundown continued, the content of which didn't surprise me much. The only thing it made me wonder about was whether that merchant deliberately spurred Edmaris to action.

"Do we know who this merchant is? Some black-market dealer?"

"I apologize, my lord. That much we do not know."

She looked so sad about it that I felt the need to hurriedly console her. The question wasn't that important anyway. Let's switch subjects to Archbishop Reyhiem.

"That's fine. What about the Church?"

"Ah yes! He revealed who was pushing him behind the scenes. The name was—"

It's a long one, Shion. You think you got that one remembered at all?

"…The core of it all was Cardinal Nicolaus Speltus," Mjurran said after Shion shot her a pleading look. Shion was great at extracting information from people, but anything else? Forget it. She had some kind of mental block keeping her from remembering proper names. Better give her some other assignment next time. Good thing Mjurran was around. I can't really expect much in the critical-analysis department from Yohm, either, so she no doubt provided some handy backup.

According to her, Nicolaus stated that they planned to take us all down, as a nation clearly against the will of their god. *Planned* to anyway.

"I see," Fuze muttered. "So Archbishop Reyhiem wanted all the glory of defeating a godless enemy, so he could earn extra clout with the central authorities?"

Everyone seemed to agree with this.

"Either way, we still have some wiggle room. The Western Holy Church hasn't made a definitive decision yet. Perhaps there's a way to negotiate ourselves out of being designated hostile."

"In that case," Fuze said, "let me handle that."

His approach involved taking advantage of the Council's presence. They would release a statement declaring that the nation of Tempest should be recognized, putting pressure on the Church to act. Appealing to the Council would also place the spotlight further on Tempest as a waypoint along a series of new trade routes. The fact that monsters lived there was an issue, but they were all both kind to strangers and fully capable of speech. If anything, they'd gladly be your friend.

That much, of course, we had already proven. Or really, we'd made it happen through all this astonishing evolution. In so many words, our aim was to earn treatment from the humans similar to what dwarves, elves, and other demi-human races enjoyed. King Gazel would back us up as well, keeping up a lively trade relationship with us and advertising the benefits of Tempest with more energy than ever.

This, I imagined, would likely not be enough to make the Western Holy Church abandon their core tenets. But Dwargon and Blumund already had formal trade relations with Tempest. Not even the Church had the kind of power to annul those agreements. And with us having such deep ties with a small group of human nations like this, other countries were bound to grow curious soon. Plus, we now had the Sorcerous Dynasty of Thalion declaring their allegiance. That put even more pressure on the Church to settle matters.

"Not that this is for me to say," Fuze added, "but recognizing Tempest is a double-edged sword. We all need to be careful to make sure we don't accidentally stab ourselves in the process."

He was right. Blumund was in the tightest spot out of them all.

Dwargon and Thalion were essentially beyond the range of Holy Church influence. Both were powerful enough that they could give the united Western Nations a run for their money. Blumund, meanwhile, was a blip, all too susceptible to pressure from outside its borders.

—Except all that was a thing of the past.

"Heh-heh… Fuze, was it? No need to fret. We dwarves can make runs through Tempest to access your markets as well. And with the stronger position that will put your nation in, the Council will find it prudent to tread lightly with you."

Gazel's right, I thought. Two nations, Dwargon and Thalion, both with different cultures and technical expertise, were interacting with each other through Tempest. This town was going to grow exponentially, I was sure of it—and then, a new culture would bloom. Culture and technology. The sorcerous science Thalion boasted and the spirit engineering Dwargon cultivated would connect on our doorstep, two different families of tech rolled into one. It could create an industrial revolution straight out of fantasy, and the kingdom of Blumund would have dibs on enjoying it first. Even in terms of pure accounting numbers, the potential profits were enormous.

Meanwhile, the new kingdom of Farmus created by Yohm would be reborn as a breadbasket to the entire region, filling the people's stomachs and planting the seeds for an entirely new food culture. We'd need to spread the wealth around, to make sure none of us was competing with another member of the alliance in each specialty—but I was planning to attend to that anyway, on the sly. Raphael, Lord of Wisdom, had calculation skills that went beyond what even quantum computing could manage. Calculating global economic effects was no sweat—and at accuracies far greater than even the Earth Simulator supercomputer in Japan could manage. That kind of made me sound like the "man behind the curtain" ruling the world, but I *am* a demon lord, so at least it'd be in character.

I could understand Fuze's concern, too. Blumund was so tiny, it might wind up being exploited by its bigger neighbors without any recourse to turn to. That's why it was so hard for them turn away from the Council, as friendly as that alliance was to smaller nations like theirs. Of course he's worried.

Maybe, in the short term, it would've been better for them to keep dealing with the Council. Pool all their intelligence skills together, and Blumund might've even been able to force the Western Holy Church into all-out war against us. If that was the choice they made when they first met us, I might've been slain by now. But the Blumundians didn't opt for that. They trusted me and decided to walk down the same path.

You do the deed, and then you get rewarded for it.

Blumund had already picked me. I didn't see any reason not to take the hint. Living together in harmony was right at the crux of my ideal, besides.

"Fuze, when you return home, I want you to tell the king that I have a favor to ask."

"A favor? Not another painful one, I trust?"

"Kinda rude, wouldn't you say? It'll take a while to explain, and I'll probably fail to get the point across to you, so I'll visit later to go over it in detail with him."

"Hoh! And *I'm* the rude one? You make me sound like some kind of dullard!"

"No, no, I didn't mean it like that. I just mean, you know, do you know much of anything about economics, Fuze?"

"I… All right. I will give word to the king and arrange a time."

"Great." I nodded.

Blumund's role here would be to keep statistics on the amount of trade in all the main manufactured goods of the region. I'd have them examine the products imported and exported from each nation, then make sure that the necessary items were shipped to the necessary place. To put it another way, I would have Blumund become the first large-scale trading company in the world. Get it right, and there'd be nothing "small" about this nation any longer. They'd be a financial superpower, wielding influence beyond comprehension.

Considering Blumund's geographical location, I wanted them to be a trade hub going forward. But that would wait until everything else wrapped up. I needed to defeat Clayman. Yohm needed to build a new nation; Fuze and Blumund needed to use their information access to check on the movements of the Western Council and Church—until we won, at least.

My main concern was the Church. I didn't *think* they'd make any sudden moves, but they still needed to be kept in place. Neither they nor the Holy Empire of Lubelius were willing to recognize our nation. I wanted to postpone any conflict for as long as I could, giving us time to prove our effectiveness and devotion to common harmony. If we had to fight, I'd like to keep it peaceful...but judging by Hinata's reaction to me, that might be tough.

None of these problems would be wiped up that easily. Everything depended on what we did from here on out.

※

So about those three prisoners—hmm? There's King Edmaris, Archbishop Reyhiem, and...who was the other guy? Oh, right! The dude who survived my attack. Were we safe letting *him* go?

"Shion, we had three POWs, right? The one who survived all the killing? That guy has to be pretty bad news, right?"

"Huh? Oh, um, yes. That terribly frightened man."

Frightened? Hmm. Maybe he was just some wimp who managed to survive through sheer luck.

"Hoh? The final survivor? If I had to guess, perhaps Folgen, captain of their knights?"

If Gazel knew someone on that force by name, he must've been at least a half-decent military officer. So maybe it'd be risky to free him? I turned to Diablo.

"What kind of guy was he like? Pretty strong, right? You think it'd be all right to let him off the hook?"

"No, Sir Rimuru," he replied, smile still on his face. "He is a minnow, incapable of being a problem at all. By human standards, however, he does seem rather well-versed in magic."

He's a magician? Maybe not a knight captain like Folgen, then.

"Do you know the name, Shion?"

"Yes! It's Ramen, sir!"

Ramen. Hmm. I haven't had ramen in years, actually. Nothing like a steaming cup of instant noodles during an all-night deadline crunch at work. I miss that. Maybe I'll try to fashion some later.

"Ramen?" Fuze asked as I basked in fond memories of my past life. "Was there someone named that in Farmus?"

"It does not ring a bell," replied Erald. "And a magician, you say? I am aware of a magic-born named Razen who should still live there..."

"Razen the champion? Mm, a man who should never be omitted from the story."

"I know that name," Phobio chimed in. "It is well-known even within the Beast Kingdom. The guardian of the great land of Farmus and among the most intelligent of magic-born!"

"Yeah, I know him, too. A human who's mastered magic up to the wizard level and beyond. I've always wanted a chance to challenge him!"

"I'm sure we'd win in close-quarter combat, but he is not one to trifle with, no..."

All the Lycanthropeers knew him, which surprised me. There was someone like *that* still left in Farmus? This Ramen guy didn't matter to me, but Razen certainly needed some attending to.

"You're sure the man we have is named Ramen, Shion?"

"Y-yes, er... Probably. But he's just a young man! One of the people who attacked this town. Certainly not the master magician you all are talking about!"

She sounded a lot more assertive on the second half of that statement than the first. But hang on, didn't Diablo just describe our prisoner Ramen as a magic-user? Curious, I decided to get the story from a few more witnesses.

What we knew for sure is that our captive was a young man, an otherworlder, who had participated in the attack. Everyone was in agreement on that.

"Diablo, are you making up stories in an attempt to earn Sir Rimuru's praise?" Shion goaded him.

"Not at all. I would hardly expect to be heaped with adulation for having defeated someone of such low caliber. I simply seek recognition that I have carried out the work provided by the master I serve."

That's true. Diablo wanted me to know he was a good servant, but he didn't say anything about his opponent being tough at all. He was dissing the guy every chance he had. So…

"…Come to think of it," Hakuro mused, "when Geld and I cornered that otherworlder, a fairly powerful magic wielder interfered. I believe that man was named Razen, actually. He had prepared a type of nuclear magic he was ready to unleash at any moment. So we let the otherworlder go, since this wizard was much more of an imminent threat."

So it *is* Razen, not Ramen? Razen, this guy I wanted to keep an eye on, was involved in the battle after all?

Report. Using certain secret rituals in the realm of spiritual magic would allow one to leap between physical bodies.

Oh, right. That.

"D'you think maybe that Razen guy took over the body of the younger dude?"

"Wha?!"

Shion was floored. She never seemed all that sure about our prisoner's name. I was fairly certain my theory was correct.

"Heh-heh-heh-heh-heh… And I am sure we will discover our ward's true name shortly."

Diablo pounded the final nail into Shion's coffin. It almost drove her to tears.

Our man turned out to be Razen, in the end. Nobody named Ramen out there after all. *All right? So enough bullying Shion over this. What do you want from her? She's Shion. Asking any kind of brainwork out of Shion is a mistake in the first place.*

But:

"You dispatched Razen himself *that* easily?!"

"I cannot believe it. The champion who supported Farmus for centuries..."

"He was one of the rare humans who was equal to me as a wizard. Superior, even..."

All the shocked eyes in the room turned to Diablo. *If you think about it, he is kind of a mystery. Why's he so keen on being my servant? He claimed to be willing to work for free, so I had no real reason to turn him down. The guy describing this amazing wizard as a "minnow" kind of confirms how strong he is. And this was before I named him, too...*

And right now, this guy was choosing to lord it over Shion. She gritted her teeth, no doubt frustrated over how she brought this fight to him and lost big. Ah well. Nothing should come of it, as long as Shion doesn't go and start acting like they're bitter rivals. Having both a talented secretary and a ditzy one on board is going to lead to a *lot* of jealousy, I'm sure.

Right! So let's do this:

"Yohm, I want you to take the three prisoners and do something with them for me. Diablo, I want you to join him."

Now Diablo was looking panicked at me. I could see Shion sneer back at him, but that order wasn't for her sake. This was the result of more serious thought. I was just thinking about who I could have help out Yohm's team, assuming I left Veldora to keep the town safe. Someone who was reasonably intelligent, strong enough to handle anything that came his way, and could move fast if needed.

Soei would've been the best choice, but I needed him on the battlefield. Benimaru was my general field commander. Shion was out of the question. Hakuro couldn't use Shadow or Spatial Motion, so it'd take time for him to travel anywhere. Geld and Gabil would stand out too much in human society.

Meaning Diablo fulfilled all my conditions. He said he'd lend a hand when it came time to take Farmus down, so I doubted he'd have any complaints. He'd have no problem guarding someone as potentially harmful as Razen, either.

"I will leave this to you, Diablo!"

"Ah, I understand, Sir Rimuru!"

He gave me a delighted smile. Something didn't seem quite right about it to me, but if he said yes, then no complaints. Right now, Diablo was probably third in strength after Veldora and me. No matter what happened, he'd have it handled in a flash.

"This job might take several years, so I hope you'll be patient with it. Contact me with Thought Communication if anything comes up."

"Not a problem, sir. I will be happy to handle this mission well before the allotted time."

He sure had a lot of confidence. This was an entire nation I was asking 'em to take down...but again, that's another reason I felt safe giving him this assignment. Now, with all the plans settled, we could end this summit between nations—and now I could focus my full attention on all-out war with Clayman without any regrets.

To finish off, I asked if anyone else had something to say.

A hand shot up. It belonged to Erald, who was looking expectantly at me.

"Yes?" I asked.

Erald had been waiting for this. "Our nation and yours are separated from each other by extremely treacherous forests and mountains. If we could connect ourselves directly through that region, that would allow us to cut the travel distance by quite a margin. A highway, in particular, would make the trek far easier..."

He shot me a glance. Ah-*ha*. I knew what he was getting at. If we were gonna be building a formal relationship with Thalion, of course we'd want a direct link between us. We'd have to do that, of course. Products that used to require long detours to deliver would naturally be more attractive once we had a better road. That was a part of my plan from the start.

Of course, it'd also mean we'd have a lot of civil engineering to do—cutting down trees, building tunnels, paving the roads. The budget would be huge, and maybe they were a superpower, but it wouldn't be *that* easy to procure a budget like that. No doubt Erald already had some ballpark figures he composed himself, in hopes of forcing the whole job upon us.

"Erald," Gazel commented, "you are asking for too much. Not even Rimuru can accept such a massive undertaking so lightly."

Well, hang on. I'm pretty sure we covered all the work and expenses for the highway to the Dwarven Kingdom, didn't we?!

"Don't be ridiculous, Gazel! If it was Sir Rimuru saying that, I would accept it, but not from *you* of all people!"

Ah. Guess Erald knew, too.

So if I'd already accepted the job from Gazel, would it be wrong to say no to Thalion? In my honest opinion, I had no problem being left to the task. A highway was a small price to pay for their recognition, really. But if I kept taking these low-paying jobs, so to speak, every country we ran into going forward might expect a similar handout. Humans are sly like that, something I was sure reminded of by my experience in Blumund. They had me right where they wanted me.

Let's get a thing or two straight before we go any further.

"I understand your suggestion, Duke Erald. We would be willing to accept your request for a highway. However…"

"However?" Erald nervously swallowed as he looked at me. *Don't worry, man. I'm not gonna ask for much.*

"However, I want you to let us handle the highway's security and lodging facilities. Of course, we would take payment for this, in the form of a small transport tax on top of operating expenses for those services."

It would be like running a toll road. We'd set up stops at decently sized regular intervals where people would have to pay fees to advance. That would provide us with permanent funding. We might start in the red, but over the long term, it'd probably lead to profit. Our special interests at work, you could say. On top of all that, we'd keep the highway maintained for them. A bargain, really.

"…I see. Impressive. And only natural to demand that much. However, I would like to have the right to negotiate this transport tax, perhaps once every few years."

Hohh? Erald's pretty impressive himself. He immediately saw what I was trying to accomplish. Of course, none of this would happen without both sides coming to an agreement. No point setting that tax too high. *I'll take the offer.*

"All right. Let's go with that!"

"That's *it*?!"

Fuze seemed flabbergasted, but I let it slide. In diplomacy, the power to make a decision trumps all else.

"Geld! We got a new job for you!"

"Yes sir! It gladdens me to hear. We have the teamwork to handle every step of the operation, the supply lines to transport the needed materials, and people with skills that knead and control the earth. The work you provide us is our very nourishment, Sir Rimuru, the best military training ground we could ever hope for!"

Huh?! Oh, uh, yeah… That's the motivation they go with, huh? And here I thought Geld had some common sense. Maybe not so much? It was so surprising, I didn't know how to react for a moment.

"Um, yeah. Well, in *that* case, we better get this war finished up so you can get to work."

"Indeed. Soon you will enjoy the results of our daily training regimen!"

Geld was really up for a fight. *I'm sure he'll be an asset in the one against Clayman.*

That was the last of the feedback I received—and thus, after several twists and turns, our summit was finally over.

A wealth of nations came to the bargaining table today, each with their own motivations, duking it out with words in search of a world where man and monster live hand in hand. It might have come out of nowhere, but this so-called Monster-and-Man Summit would later wind up becoming a turning point in history.

I had once again taken a major step toward my ideal.

∗

With our talks between national leaders complete, it was finally time for our anti-Clayman strategy conference. I figured we all needed to hear Soei's report first, so I ordered the meeting hall to be set up once more.

As I did, I had the nagging feeling I was forgetting something. And it just so happened that I was. Ramiris. What was that noisy little pixie going on about? Was she still unconscious?

Worried, I headed over to Veldora, only to find... Well, take a guess. It was Ramiris, entranced by the manga she was reading! I was concerned she'd start bawling unless I gave her some attention, but I had nothing to worry about.

"...Hey. Hey, what're you doing?"

"Shut up a second. I'm just getting to the good part."

She didn't even look up at me. Why was she here again? That manga had her full attention right now, but she had *something* important to do here, right?!

I suppose she must've woken up, set off to yell at me again, and then noticed the manga volumes strewn all over the sofa. They must've captured her imagination so thoroughly she didn't even realize the summit was over. She must've made amends with Veldora as well, because now he was happily being served by Beretta, as if that whole fainting spell never took place. Eesh.

I turned toward Beretta.

"Congratulations on your evolution to demon lord," it said with a polite bow. "Allow me to thank you, grand master, for letting me share in the benefits of said evolution. Thanks to you, I have transformed from an arch-golem into a chaos golem."

This evolution had imparted elements of both holy and demonic force into it. That was mainly thanks to the skill Reverser, which allowed the user to obtain two diametrically opposed essences at once—in Beretta's case, aspects of both demonic and angelic power, I suppose. A new spirit core was born inside it, fusing with its older, demonic one to create a new chaos core. This let it handle holy-element attacks, something it was weaker against before.

I couldn't have been the only one who saw that as incredibly unfair. That rock-solid magisteel body, already impervious to most physical attacks and magic, and now it was even covered for what few weaknesses it had. You couldn't ask for a better upgrade than that.

This unique skill Reverser was something involved with me, it seemed. A lot of the panic I felt at the time must've come across to Beretta. When I was encased in that Holy Field, my emotions when I was left powerless by the sealed-off magicules must've affected how this power manifested itself, I think. Given that an arch-golem runs on magicules, it must've feared that it, too, would stop in its tracks. So it came up with this countermeasure.

Between Reverser and that chaos chore, Beretta was turning into one extremely interesting research subject.

Report. The unique skill Reverser is already integrated into the ultimate skill Uriel, Lord of Vows. Its effect can be re-created by applying Control Laws to metallic elements. Creating a new chaos core requires providing the correct conditions and materials to...

What?!

Raphael just chucked that out offhand, but I couldn't believe how useful he was. *That's it—Food Chain! I have Food Chain as part of the ultimate skill Belzebuth, Lord of Gluttony, so I can obtain the original model for any skills owned by my friends.*

Beretta had it, too, so we talked about it for a little bit. It seemed rather satisfied with the skill and the fun it had experimenting in the labyrinth. Following its evolution, it figured something similar must've happened to me as well, too.

"In any case," I said, "I'm glad you're still doing well. Once this is all settled down, we should talk a little more in-depth."

"Ha-ha! I appreciate you saying that. Now I have something to look forward to."

"Yeah. I'm also glad you're still listening to Ramiris. Keep that up, unless she gives you any orders that're *too* crazy."

"I will be happy to. I promise I will not betray your expectations!"

"Great. Hang in there. By the way, what're you guys here for?"

I shot a glance at Ramiris, still enthralled by her manga.

"We…"

Beretta must've forgotten, too. It made a beeline for Ramiris, bringing her out of her trancelike state.

"Lady Ramiris, now is not the time for this. We must inform Sir Rimuru of the news…"

"Shut up! I'm really busy right now!"

"Please, my lady, recall your goals traveling here."

"I *told* you! Fate has brought me and this wonderful thing they call manga together! Oh, which suitor will she choose in the end…?"

You can't argue with that impassioned logic. Literally, you can't. Oh, the pains Beretta must go through. I couldn't let this go on. I had a general idea of what she was reading, so—with a sigh—I decided to threaten her a little. If I didn't, we'd all be forced to wait until she was done with the series, and *that* one was an epic running over forty volumes, so even someone as calm and Buddha-like in his patience as I couldn't hold out that long.

"Hey, Ramiris? If you don't want me to spoil it for you on who she goes with, then tell me why you're here already!"

The threat produced immediate results. "Right!" she shouted, saluting to me and hurriedly flying into the air, not a care in the world. It couldn't have been anything serious—just her overreacting and carrying on as always. The rest of our visitors had stopped their chatting as they prepared to leave, also remembering that Ramiris was still there. I guess they all wanted to satisfy their curiosities before going.

The fairy noticed the attention and proudly puffed out her chest (or lack thereof), crossed her arms, and gave me the boldest nod she could.

"I'll say it one more time! Tempest shall fall to ruin!!"

"Wh-what did you say?!" I replied without enthusiasm, following the script. She took the bait.

"Hmph! You know," she said patronizingly, "that isn't something I want to happen, of course. So I came all the way over here to tell you. You better thank me!"

I tried my best to avoid all her little jabs at me. Giving them attention would just prolong the conversation.

"So why're we falling to ruin?"

"Well, before I tell you…" She stopped, turning serious as she looked around to size up the dignitaries around her. Then she nodded to herself. "Ah, I suppose this has a lot to do with you humans, too. All right—listen up, all of you. Clayman's just proposed that we launch a Walpurgis Council!"

"A Walpurgis what?"

"Right, a Walpurgis Council. A special meeting of all the demon lords!"

Oh. She said "launch," so I thought it was some kinda huge magic spell at first. I was planning to storm Clayman's domain, so if she told me that Clayman was attacking first, I would've freaked out.

Pressing her for more details, Ramiris stated that staging Walpurgis required the consent of at least three demon lords, and once convened, attendance was very much mandatory. Absence was never forgiven. It was one of the very few things the capricious, self-serving demon lords had agreed to on paper (although this still didn't prevent some extremely lazy demon lords from sending a representative with full rights to the Council instead).

"…I think I have read about this," Erald said. "Once, all the demon lords came together to wage an epic battle, one that the Western Holy Church named Walpurgis, or the feast of demons."

This was something he had apparently read in some records dating back a thousand years ago. The war was a costly one, causing serious damage and disasters across the land. *Walpurgis*, the term coined by the Holy Church for it, had the connotation of not just a demonic feast but one attended by those who spread chaos and destruction worldwide. These were worldwide affairs, I supposed.

So if demon lords gathered together like this, did it mean war among themselves, or them teaming up against some other enemy?

"So are the demon lords about to declare war on something?"

"No! I'm a busy woman! I don't have time for wars and other annoying stuff like that!"

Ramiris looked like she had a *lot* of free time, but never mind. She *was* a demon lord, one who had been around for a long time to boot. Maybe she was part of those conferences of a millennium ago; it wasn't out of the question.

Erald nodded at her. "I believe the demon lord Ramiris is telling the truth. The war in the records I read was officially called the Temma War, the War Between Heaven and Demon. It was fought by multiple factions, all vying for power. Of course…"

As he put it, these Temma Wars (or Great Wars) were triggered every five hundred years. There was a reason for that. It was because the forces of heaven—in other words, the angels—came down to earth at around that cycle. These angels were kind of natural enemies to demons, I suppose, but oddly enough, they would attack pretty much everyone indiscriminately. Developed cities and towns, for some reason, were a particularly favored target. Nobody knew why, but there you go.

"That is the reason why we never left the underground," Gazel said—and maybe they had the right idea. As advanced as they were, they'd stick out like a sore thumb. The Sorcerous Dynasty of Thalion took the same tactic, building a city in the hollow of a gigantic divine tree—that "fancy tree city," as Gazel had mockingly called it. As superpowers, both nations spared no expense in keeping their lands safe.

So what about the Western Nations? The Council of the West was established to protect themselves against monsters, but also so they could survive an upcoming Great War. Member nations worked together, while Dwargon and Thalion basically hunkered down.

But the angels weren't the only enemy to worry about. As if responding to their descent, the monsters on the ground would suddenly explode into action—in this case, the magic-born, knowledge-bearing monsters. Some demon lords would use Temma Wars to stage invasions of human nations as well. The Great War of a millennium ago saw that happen, which led to a lot of tragedy for everyone involved.

The humans, to their credit, weren't anyone to be trifled with. That could be seen in what was likely to be the largest antagonist of the next war—the Nasca Namrium Ulmeria United Eastern Empire. The Empire's thirst for power could strike anytime, anyplace. If the Western Nations showed any sign of weakness, the eastern power could bare their fangs at a moment's notice.

Thus, you would have these wild, frantic world wars, with angel and demon and human brutally slaughtering one another. That was your typical Temma War.

So I guess it was kind of slander to accuse the demon lords of triggering them. Not that *I* wanted one of those, either. And what's with angels setting their sights on the bigger cities? I wanted *my* city to be the richest one in the land, incomparable to anything else—but maybe I ought to wait a bit. Maybe it's smarter not to develop the most important facilities we needed until we had the resources to defend them. But this was all in the future anyway. Let's just put it in the file for now.

Back to this Walpurgis.

"So what *is* Walpurgis, though? What do all the demon lords assemble for?"

If it didn't have anything to do with a Great War, there had to be some other motivation.

Wait. Is it that, maybe? Like, what Milim was talking about, how they punished anyone else who declared themselves to be a demon king? Are they gonna decide who'll do me in?

"Um, well, first, I think you have kinda the wrong idea, so lemme start with this."

What Ramiris had to say hadn't occurred to me at all.

"These Walpurgis Councils, y'know; we hold a lot of them. All you need is three demon lords to agree to one, which is pretty darn easy. Back in the day, it'd just be this informal chat over tea with me, Guy, and Milim… But Walpurgis is just a place where demon lords come together, catch up on news, and talk about whatever's happened lately. It's really not a huge deal; it's just that humans don't know about it."

This sounded like quite a revelation. Maybe *she* saw it as nothing, but it was almost scary how lightly she treated the demon lord job sometimes. Maybe I should take what she said with a grain of salt. If I accepted it as the unvarnished truth, it might come back to bite me in the ass sometime.

"Okay, then, stupid, if it's just high tea with your friends, then why's this nation gonna fall to ruin?!"

Even someone as kind as I am felt the need to yell at her a little. This kid just has no idea what's going on.

"Look, no, all right?!" She waved her arms up and down. "The problem isn't that they're holding Walpurgis; it's what they're gonna talk about!"

What they'll talk about? If they're all meeting together, it's gonna be about killing me, isn't it…?

As Ramiris put it, two people agreed to Clayman's initial Walpurgis request—the demon lords Frey and Milim. That triggered it—and the topic of discussion: "The new force born in the Forest of Jura and their leader assuming the title of demon lord." So me, then.

"So you… You declared yourself a demon lord?"

I nodded. "Yep. And I don't regret it one bit."

"Mm, well, that's not so weird coming from you. You might have to deal with a few tricky spots, but with all the power you've got, it oughtta work out, huh?"

Ramiris made it all sound like it wasn't her problem at all. Which I guess it wasn't. I mean, I was prepared for this, but still.

"You think they wanna punish me for it?"

"That's how they're phrasing it," she replied, "but one of the unwritten rules in our line of work is that if you wanna punish someone, go do it yourself, if you care that much. They're holding Walpurgis this time because they were betrayed by the demon lord Carillon. Plus, Clayman was going on and on about how Mjurran, one of his underlings, was killed."

"What kind of 'line of work' is demon lord anyway?"

She ignored the question.

But apparently Clayman had already fingered "Rimuru, so-called new demon lord" as Mjurran's killer. Which meant his goal was—

Report. It is believed to be the takeover of the demon lord Carillon's territory and the suppression of the Forest of Jura.

Yeah. I think so, too. So that's why his army's en route. I guess he made the first move before we even realized it. Shrewder than I thought, I guess…

"Hey! Are you listening to me?" Now Ramiris was giving me an uncharacteristically stern look. "You're acting like this no big deal, but it's huge! Milim's already taken down Carillon, I heard, and Clayman's ready to send an entire army of magic-born someone's way. Punishment, heck—this is war! Clayman's come up with an excuse to take each and every one of you down, all right?!"

The summit attendees began to stir. Having one of the demon lords "taken down" was serious news to the superpower nations. I suppose it would be. It could totally disrupt the balance of power between them. And while it had already happened, the news was a total bolt from the blue for everyone else. Pretty heady stuff.

That, and:

"Lord Carillon, a betrayer? How dare that brute accuse him!"

"Clayman will pay for this. I'll crush that upstart with my own two hands!"

"Whether Lord Carillon is there to lead it or not, our armies are unhurt and in full fighting shape. We'll never let Clayman's minions seize our land!"

It goes without saying that the Lycanthropeers had the most visceral reaction to it all. Nobody likes their master being called a backstabber, I suppose. Plus, from what Ramiris said, apparently Clayman was gunning for his whole territory.

Man, we really got a late start, didn't we? I had no idea he'd be moving this fast. Better dispatch him quick—he can't be up to anything good.

"Calm down a sec, Ramiris. Yes, it's true I declared myself demon lord, but I didn't kill Mjurran."

"What do you mean?"

"I mean that Clayman's telling you a pack of lies. I expected him to come out against me with that accusation."

Plus...

"Wh-what?! You got any evidence to show for that?"

...either way...

"...Um, demon lord Ramiris? Pardon me for speaking me out of turn. I am Mjurran, the magic-born servant of Clayman who was allegedly killed..."

...I'm gonna crush Clayman.

The moment I made him think Mjurran was dead, I knew he was going to react sooner or later. I didn't take the bait—Clayman was just hooked by my lure. The rest of the demon lords weren't involved.

The sight of Mjurran threw Ramiris for a loop.

"Huh? Wha?! Wait, so... Now I get it! The demon lord Clayman's the real culprit now, isn't he?! I *knew* it!"

Good thing she recovered so fast. Too bad that was incredibly obvious to anyone else in the room. I felt bad for her, so I decided to follow up on something else I'd wondered about.

"Yeah, I agree with you there, but I wanted to ask you something."

"Mm? What? Just ask Detective Ramiris here, and she'll crack the case!"

Uh-oh. I wound up just egging her on, didn't I? "Detective?" *Seriously? She must've been peeking at whatever Veldora was reading, huh?* I opted not to pursue that for now.

"How do you think the other demon lords will react to this?"

I wasn't expecting much, but figured I had to ask. She had been a demon lord for ages, so I couldn't deny the possibility that she had something to go on. The room went quiet, awaiting her response. It was a question of deep interest to everyone else, too. Too bad Ramiris was so indifferent to that.

"Huh? Well, I dunno. It was just, like, 'Here's what we'll talk about during the party, so join in,' okay?"

So nonchalant with it. I shouldn't have expected anything else. Just a kid. I should be glad she came over to tell me at all.

Next question.

"Okay, so when *is* this Walpurgis, Ramiris? Do you know the exact date and time?"

I'd want to know that before we formulate our anti-Clayman strategy.

"Oh, didn't I mention it? Um, it's gonna be three days from now, on the night of the new moon."

Three days? That's sooner than I thought. Gonna be kind of hard to finish him off in just three days.

So…is this showdown gonna have to wait until after Walpurgis?
Another issue to bring up with the gang, I guess.

That was about all I wanted to ask Ramiris. That was all she was here for, it turned out, and it wasn't like I'd be able to glean anything else useful from her.

Then a sudden thought came to mind.

"So why'd you come all the way here to tell me?"

"Mm? Well, really, it's like, if you get killed, what's gonna happen to my Beretta here? So I decided to take your side on this, and that's why I'm here. That kinda thing. And I'm gonna build a labyrinth entrance here, but is that okay?"

"No, it's *not* okay! Where'd *that* come from?! What kind of entrance anyway?!"

I appreciated her bringing the news, but this came right out of nowhere.

"Huhhh?! What's the big deal? Don't sweat the small stuff!"

She never was one for listening. No, she was much more for talking—and arguing her point until she got it. As far as she was concerned, this conversation was already over. *She's one of the most free 'n' wild fairies I've ever met.*

"I *am* sweating the small stuff, and you should, too! And don't go around thinking that Beretta is all yours, either!"

I held my ground, refusing to let her get her way. Any "entrance to the labyrinth" built around here could never possibly bode well for us. And Beretta's fate wasn't just in my hands—it had a lot to do with the golem, as well. It wasn't something she had any right to dictate. A simple question on my part led to what I could only call an outrageous proposal.

We argued vehemently about it for a while, to no effect, before the crowd finally broke up. I was too busy to deal with her any longer, and Ramiris, her business apparently done, went back to her manga.

As they left, I promised all the attendees that I'd inform them of whatever new information I found. They all agreed to this before they went their separate ways.

Fuze planned to stay the night at the inn before heading home. "I hope you're prepared for what lies ahead," he warned. "It's your country being targeted this time. A demon lord is a very dangerous thing. I think I know how strong you are, Sir Rimuru, but…"

I understood what he meant. At worst, I could wind up making enemies out of several demon lords at once. Out of the ten of 'em, who could I count on as nonhostile? Carillon was AWOL. *Ramiris promised to back me up, so there's one. Milim… Milim's my biggest worry. I'm pretty sure she's just being tricked, but I'd still need to prepare myself for the worst.*

So if I managed to completely screw up everything, I could have eight demon lords wanting me dead. Of course, if it looked like I was gonna lose Milim before that, it was probably best to run for the hills immediately at that point.

"Oh, I'll figure something out," I reassured Fuze.

Erald and Elen also whined at me about wanting some time to talk to each other. I agreed to have them stay for several nights before leaving—not at the inn but at our luxury *ryokan*-style hotel. All of Tempest was proud of that place, and if we could earn the duke's praise for it, he was welcome anytime.

It was funny, though, seeing how different Erald the statesman was from Erald the person. He was so preoccupied with his daughter that I was worried she'd run off on him—I just had to pray he wouldn't do anything to make her even angrier.

Gazel also opted to stay a few extra days, so I lodged him in the *ryokan* as well. As I guessed from seeing them speak, they had known each other for ages, even fighting in battles together. Erald must've really been a hell of a wizard. And now, funnily enough, they were using Tempest as a new channel to build geopolitical ties with. It's always better to get along, of course.

We really enjoyed a celebrity lineup at this summit, though, didn't we? Leaders who'd hold major sway over human nations in the future. And—if you think about it—I was standing on equal footing with them. Having that selfish fairy crash it at the very end made for a less-than-snappy ending, but I think it's safe to say I gained a lot from it all.

＊

We would've liked to rest up as well, but that wasn't happening. I didn't want demon lords breathing down my neck, and we needed some countermeasures.

After a meal, we all gathered again in the meeting hall. The Three Lycanthropeers and Mjurran were our only guests this time. Yohm and Gruecith were already preparing to depart—Gruecith really wanted a seat in the conference but relented after Phobio screamed at him. They had an important job to do, so I really wanted them to focus their full attention on that. I was hoping Mjurran would join in the preparations as well, but she was the one with concrete intelligence on Clayman, so I had to ask her to join.

And for some reason, Diablo was joining us. "Heh-heh-heh-heh… I hardly have any need to prepare," he declared, and really, I had to assume he was right. There wasn't any reason to kick him out, so I gave him permission.

The moment I entered the hall:

"Oh! You! You! What're you doing? What's the meaning of this?!"

Ramiris accosted me yet again.

"What do you mean?" I asked. Then she began yelling at me, her face turning red.

Here was the basic story: During this break period, she was called into the dining hall. I had totally forgotten about this, but Ramiris had a long history with Treyni and the other dryads, who served her back when she was still Spirit Queen. Treyni recognized her at once, of course, and it wasn't long before they were all giving her the royal treatment, answering her every beck and call.

"That's pretty great, huh?"

"Yes! Yes, it *is* great! *Really* great! So I've decided to live here, too, Rimuru!"

Guess Ramiris really likes this town. And as a lonely demon lord with no minions to serve her, I'm sure the dryad kindness lifted her spirits sky-high. Between that and being guided around town, soaking up all the sights, she decided to take the plunge.

"I told you to stop making all these unilateral decisions! Plus, remember, Treyni and the dryads are kind of busy managing things in the forest. They don't live with you anymore! They can't spend all day dealing with you here."

I gave the three doting dryad sisters waiting behind her some serious side-eye as I lectured Ramiris. She wasn't interested in listening.

"Oh, don't be so stingy! What's the big deal? If anything happens, I'll help you out of it! Ol' Ramiris is the strongest gal you'll ever find!"

With your help, I'm headed straight for the— No. Never mind. If I said that out loud, it'd make her cry.

"Sir Rimuru," Treyni said, "we promise to take care of Lady Ramiris. I do hope you will be forward-thinking in your decision."

""""Do it for us, please!"""" her sisters said in chorus. *I dunno. She's gonna be such a troublemaker. We'll be dealing with even more humans here before long, and Ramiris flitting around will be hard to ignore.*

Hmm... Another issue for the back burner, then.

"All right. I'll think about it."

"You will?! Oh, Rimuru, I knew you'd see things my way!"

Let's give some thought later to how Ramiris's presence would impact the town. I had other issues to take care of before that.

With Ramiris suitably placated, it was time to start the conference.

"Right. I know it's tough, having all these discussions at once, but bear with me. We have two items on the agenda here: fighting Clayman and the Walpurgis Council. Ramiris here has just informed me that I am being targeted. First, I'd like you all to hear Soei's report and discuss our strategy. Soei, give us your briefing on Clayman's forces."

"Sir!"

He began right after my introduction.

While we were holding our summits, Clayman's army had been busy. They had stopped in Milim's domain to rest and organize their troops.

"They do not appear to be led by Clayman himself," Soei stated. "Their leader is accompanied by a slew of magic-born and boasts a great deal more magicule energy than the rest of them, but even then, his force is along the lines of the Three Lycanthropeers. If *that* is the demon lord Clayman, he is far too feeble a threat."

Man, he's brimming with confidence, too, huh?

"In terms of Lycanthropeer-level strength, I can think of three magic-born serving Clayman who would fit that description…"

That many, huh? Yep. He's sure a demon lord, I gotta admit. These three were three of Clayman's five fingers, his most favored of assistants: Yamza, the middle finger; Adalmann, the pointer finger; and Nine-Head, the thumb. Mjurran, by the way, was the ring finger. The final little finger was named Pironé but was mostly involved in intelligence gathering and rarely appeared in public.

I had been wondering about the Moderate Jesters group and their relation to Clayman, but Mjurran apparently knew nothing about them. "Clayman was never one to trust in his underlings," she explained, "so it wouldn't be strange at all for him to put observers in place to keep tabs on us during missions."

You could call them the audience for his puppet shows, I suppose. They might've been active without any of Clayman's forces knowing, like in the orc lord battle. *Better make sure I don't forget that.*

"So who's their commander, Mjurran?"

The leader Soei had spotted was a thin, frail-looking magic-born. His Thought Communication broadcast a perfect image of him to all of us.

"This is Yamza. Yamza, the Frozen Swordmage. He is a cruel, unfair, merciless lowlife but a regrettably talented one. He willingly swore his loyalty to Clayman, and we never did get on well after that."

So the army was led by Yamza, a magic-born and (according to Mjurran) the strongest of the five fingers. Clayman had granted him an ornate, expensive magic sword with the power to freeze its targets, earning him the nickname. In other words, there was no guessing what his latent skills were without that weapon.

Yamza was commanding an army of some thirty thousand magic-born, all with varying levels of power. By Soei's estimation, around four-fifths were a solid B rank, the rest mostly an A-minus.

There were a few solid A's at the top, but we're still talking Gelmud level at best. That made them stronger and dicier than the Farmus army I annihilated but still nothing to really break a sweat over.

"A little too weak, aren't they?"

Right now, the number of refugees we had taken in from the Beast Kingdom of Eurazania had surpassed twenty thousand. Around half, ten thousand, were in fighting shape, each averaging a B rank—which went up to A-minus after their beast transformation. It was a surprisingly powerful force. Even Farmus's most elite knight corps were lucky to average a B, and that was with assorted magical enhancements placed on them, so it said a lot about how strong Eurazania's fighters were.

Humans and beastmen were just different, down to the foundation. We had a big force of them, but Carillon's domain still had more on reserves. These were beastmen that the army recruited from nearby villages during the capital evacuation, only to have them spread out across the countryside. The most powerful officers of the Beast Master's Warrior Alliance had brought them back together, regrouped them, and sent them off to hide out at strategic points. Add their numbers up, and they, conservatively, amounted to over ten thousand themselves.

Thus, we had a total of twenty thousand A-minus fighters on hand. Carillon really *was* a demon lord. What a force he'd had on him.

"It is strange, yes," Alvis said. "Yamza is undoubtedly a powerful magic-born, but we Three Lycanthropeers would never lose to him. And while his force outnumbers ours, we hold an overwhelming advantage in training and fighting ability."

"Yeah," agreed Phobio, "if you want leadership, we've got loads of it!"

"Do they think that Lord Carillon died, and we'll just fall over like trees to them?" Sufia sniffed. "No, Clayman can't be that much of a fool..."

All seemed to believe that Clayman's force wasn't much of a threat.

Benimaru wasn't as sure. "One moment, though... Could Clayman be aiming at something besides this town?"

Ah yes. Maybe we had the wrong idea. Everyone was always trying to hit this town first, so Ramiris sort of assumed Clayman was after me once more and flew on over. And here I was hoping we'd get to strike them from both sides once the army left Eurazania. The best-laid plans and all that.

"So are they marching for the Beast Kingdom?! There are nothing but refugees left there, plus over ten thousand fighters. They may be better in combat, but Clayman's numbers could overwhelm them!"

Right. Soei reported that they were camped in Milim's domain for now, but they had already reorganized and were ready to head into Eurazania territory tomorrow or the next day. I didn't think they'd attempt a night march, but we'd need to factor that possibility into the equation, too.

"I wonder if they are aware at all that we are on the lookout for Clayman," Geld gravely stated. I wasn't so optimistic about that. Better to assume the worst; then we can take action when it happens.

"But even if they are marching for this town," observed Mjurran, "Clayman would never ignore danger from the rear. He would snuff out the source of that first before proceeding."

Yeah. So would I, actually. But..."snuff it out"?!

"Wait, so you mean...Clayman's intending to kill off all the fighters in the Beast Kingdom?!"

And who can say if it was *just* the fighters...

Understood. I have predicted the actions of the demon lord Clayman. There is a 100 percent likelihood that he seeks to awaken himself to become a "true" demon lord. I do not believe this town factors into his plans. However, to achieve this, he is likely taking the crude and uncertain tactic of hunting down all remaining life in the Beast Kingdom of Eurazania.

Ah. So genocide, then. I'm a total hypocrite for saying this, but I can't say I'm a fan of his any-means-necessary approach.

Clayman never left any stone unturned. I was sure he'd been

observing the highway leading out from this town. The moment we sent out reinforcements, he would know. And even before that—

"Clayman is a master of intelligence gathering. I imagine he's aware that we Lycanthropeers and the main Carillon force have evacuated here. Even if we marched for home right now, it would take two days, at least..."

We've totally been given the slip. Just as Alvis said, Clayman had read through it all. An army composed of what're normally B ranks wouldn't make it in time, even if they never stopped to rest. I was intending to invest all my troops in the fight as well, but by the time we reached the battle, the Beast Kingdom would be massacred already, I'm sure...

But would that genocide be enough to make Clayman awaken?

Understood. Despite the lack of efficiency, he would be able to obtain a vast number of souls. Clayman's chances of awakening are...78 percent. This probability would rise if he was able to obtain more souls shortly afterward.

That's bad. We gotta stop him—if not for all those imperiled beastmen, then at least for my own ass. That being said, Eurazania's people were on friendly terms with us, and trust is worth a lot more than money. Sometimes, compassion can help you as much as the other person. There's no need to refrain from being fully involved.

"Benimaru, stop them."

He grinned at my fairly reckless order. "You got it—or I should say, leave it to me!"

Nice to see he's a man of integrity, too. Get him heated up, and he can't help but drop the formal speech. He always treats me with so much respect in public, seeking to draw a line between personal and political life, but I wish he wouldn't go through so much effort. I don't want him openly sneering at me, so at least I don't have to worry about that...not that public derision of me is a problem in this nation.

I suppose it's kind of like if you get promoted beyond your former boss in your workplace, and it gets all awkward between you two.

It's just the way society works—deal with it. So I decided to deal with it and act the part of the boss.

"Great. We will now design a defense line for the Beast Kingdom of Eurazania. I want to hear suggestions for a way to win, with Benimaru taking the helm!"

My leaders all bowed at me.

""""Yes sir!""""

Even the Three Lycanthropeers joined them. I guess my dignity was more than intact.

Still, that Clayman's even sneakier than I thought. Scheduling Walpurgis in the evening three days from now must've all been part of the plan. He'd stage his Eurazania genocide before any other demon lord could intervene, then gleefully report on it during the event.

It would take time to unite the scattered forces across the land; right now, any fighters in the Beast Kingdom would just be picked off, one by one. It'd be impossible to resist. And then you have all those powerless civilians being killed without a second thought…

Now that we'd decided to block that, the meeting hall was buzzing with ideas. Everyone wanted to assemble a force at once and head on over—but nobody verbally brought it up. Everyone here was deeply acquainted with the importance of starting with intel. I didn't move immediately after declaring we'd defeat Clayman, precisely because I was awaiting Soei's report.

Even now, we were having supplies gathered in the town's main square and refreshing our soldiers' equipment. Kaijin, Garm, and Dold were all crafting new weapons and armor, using their respective technical skills, and all our fighters were changing into them and preparing for the battle ahead.

No point in panicking. You had to know the enemy's location, army formation, numbers, and mission. Running into the fray without at least that much won't earn you any results to be proud of.

Now our deliberations were nearing their climax.

"So that's about the war power we have on hand. If we can have them be there in time, we can win. The problem is transport, isn't it? There's no way to make it, so we need a way to buy time."

"Why not send the goblin riders and Gabil's force in first to stage a guerrilla resistance?" Hakuro suggested.

"No, it would mean nothing," Benimaru calmly stated. "I've examined the geography of the Beast Kingdom, and much of it is either flat or features low hills. There are few natural elements to conceal oneself in. A surprise attack from the air would be effective, but a guerrilla force of a hundred or so simply wouldn't be adequate."

The best place to hide a force like this would be the fruit orchards lining rivers, but these were spread out across hilly areas with good drainage, so not as subtle as we'd want. The terrain wasn't suitable for concealing large numbers of troops.

"Since when were you looking into our geography?" Sufia quietly groused. I was actually kind of wondering that myself. Benimaru probably did some research when I sent him to lead our first envoy team into the Beast Kingdom. I guess I really *can* rely on him to be thorough. Sufia didn't seem genuinely offended, at least.

"We have a team of approximately four hundred beastmen who are geared for speed," Alvis advised. "Bird types are rare among us—no more than a hundred. Sending them out in advance would be a death sentence."

Simply being able to fly didn't shield them from fatigue, after all. If they plus Gabil's team couldn't even reach two hundred, there was little point deploying them first. With the high visibility of the terrain, too, small squadrons couldn't accomplish much.

So for our strategy, we would have to go back to basics. Plow everything into doing what we could, as accurately as possible. That's it. We'd send messages out to the fighters across the land, gather up as many civilians as we could, and evacuate them out. Once they were in Tempest, the dryads' protection should do a lot for their survival rate. We'd then have our speedier forces to use guerrilla tactics to aid in their escape. The slower armies would march as well, swallowing up the refugees as they prepared to face off against Clayman's force.

That was the basic wrap-up. It was a battle against time and relied a fair bit on luck, but we didn't have any better ideas. Thus, to prevent the worst, we decided that all of us should go out on the field to fight as well.

Our top leaders—Benimaru, Shuna, Soei, Shion, Geld, and Ranga—had all learned the Spatial Motion extra skill, giving them control over "transport gates" linking two locations together. Diablo was "born" with that ability, too, but he was with Yohm's team at the moment. I could call him back if things got bad, but I wanted to handle this with us seven if possible, myself included. Each of us may've had the power of a whole army, but we couldn't afford to push ourselves too far. Shuna, in particular, wasn't too suited for on-the-ground combat; I wanted to have Gabil and Hakuro covering for her, if possible.

"Guess it's the only way," I reasoned. "If we can help earn our forces some time, I think we can pull this off with a minimum of casualties. Would've been nice if we could just bring 'em all over there with regular transport magic, but…"

I brought up that idea mainly so I could publicly shoot it down. Our problems would be solved if we had magic that could instantly transport an entire army from one point to another, but not even my Spatial Motion worked on ten thousand troops at once.

But:

Understood. Transportation magic allows for the transferal of materials at a low cost. It works by using a separate dimension to link two points together, but it is not effective for handling organic matter, due to heavy magicule irradiation. However, anyone protected by a Barrier would not be affected by the transport. Those are the fundamental rules of transportation magic.

Ummm… So that's the difference between teleport and transport magic? It's just that teleport costs more magicules to cast, since it includes spells to protect who you're teleporting? Wait, so…

In other words, since magic-born and monsters have natural magicule resistance, anyone capable of erecting a Barrier over themselves can be transported successfully without issue. A full-transportation spell that included measures to protect the target would also be possible.

So if you're strong enough not to die when exposed to a ton of magicules, you can go across this "separate dimension" or whatever. I guess that's the way the Spatial Motion skill works. I should've noticed that. What's more, if you can fully protect whoever you're transporting, it's no problem to send 'em over. I suppose that's a sort of teleportation, really, but wouldn't that just waste a lot of magical energy? Besides, trying to adapt that into a legion magic you could deploy on tens of thousands of troops is far beyond what I could do right now...

Understood. The spell has already been developed. I have also succeeded in pairing it with the extra skill Dominate Space to greatly reduce the magical force required.

Well, look at that! I can't believe how much Raphael has grown, developing new skills and magic without me even having to ask. I mean, my skills must've evolved a huge amount when I awoke into demon lord form, but I still didn't have a grasp of them all. They would've just been going to waste without Raphael. If I had to guess, this was Ability Adjust at work—but either way, I couldn't ask for anything better. Right here, right now, it had just provided me the exact spell I wanted more than anything in the world. No complaints here!

"Sir Rimuru," Shuna warned me, aware of the danger, "it's too hazardous to attempt transport magic on an army..."

"Yeah, you're right, Shuna. But just now, I've successfully developed a new spell!"

All our problems were cleared away. I felt bad for Clayman, kinda. He would've won if it wasn't for my evolution.

"Ohhh...!"

"What on...?!"

"Just now?!"

Everyone gave me surprised looks. I nodded back at them. "The question is: Are you prepared for this? If we use this spell, we can send our entire army over there at once. But it'll be the first time I've ever used it, and we haven't tested its safety at all. There's no time to experiment with it. But do you still trust me?"

I, at least, trusted Raphael. *If Raphael says we can do it, then there's no room for doubt. But what about everyone else? Do they trust me enough to stake their lives on this?*

"No need to worry," Benimaru said with a brazen smile. "I have given you my loyalty—and as your loyal retainer, I would gladly die if ordered to do so. I know all too well by now that you'd never give us a meaningless order."

The rest of my leaders agreed—even Diablo, the new guy, was nodding with that eerie grin on his face.

The Lycanthropeers joined them. "You got my trust," Sufia declared. "We can't start getting suspicious of someone whose help we're askin' for."

"He's already saved me once. Our fighters know that, so I ain't about to start whining now."

"Oh dear, Phobio, you're making it sound like I have no choice but to agree. But we're the slowest force, and as long as we are, I'll want to rely on Sir Rimuru's power to help us out." Alvis seemed a tad dubious still but not enough to turn us down.

I nodded at them all. "I hear you loud and clear! Time to turn the tables on Clayman's schemes. It's all up to you men and women now. Let me see some victory!"

"""Rahhh!!"""

I was starting to see some wild, ferocious smiles. *If we can all make it in time, we're sure to win. Plus, no matter how closely Clayman's surveilling the highways, he'll never notice our troops get transported in. It's practically in the bag.* No wonder everyone seemed so confident again.

So I left reworking our strategy to Benimaru. While he was doing that, Soei gave another report—that a group of one hundred "Dragon Faithful" had merged with Clayman's force.

"One hundred? That much shouldn't be a problem," said Benimaru.

Did Benimaru know about this group already, or…?

"Soei," I meekly asked, "what are these Dragon Faithful?"

"The name for those who worship the dragon—in other words, Lady Milim, the Dragon Princess."

Oh, Milim's people? I thought Milim said she didn't *have* anyone working under her. So kind of like her fans, then? Her domain, which didn't really have an official name, featured a population of under a hundred thousand, mostly people living off the land in harmony with nature. Maybe they were acting as bodyguards to Clayman's force as they proceeded through their domain.

Soei didn't have any more information yet, so we dropped the subject. For now, I ordered him to continue monitoring the Clayman army, as well as search for a suitable area to deploy our own forces.

$$*$$

That wrapped up how we'd handle the battle. Next came the Walpurgis Council Ramiris had warned me about. The Three Lycanthropeers were already gone, relaying our strategy to their troops and convincing them my transport magic would work.

Mjurran left as well, since Walpurgis was my problem, and she wouldn't have any feedback for that. Her job was to assist Yohm.

This meant it was just the usual Tempest gang and me, which put me quite a bit at ease. There was no need to hold anything back for politeness' sake now.

"If we only knew where Clayman was, I could just teleport right on over and put an end to this pronto, but…"

If his military was in motion, that meant his headquarters had to be more lightly guarded. My leaders and I could've zoomed right over and finished him off without having to worry about a counterattack. Of course, I couldn't afford to laze out on this town's defenses while I was away, either. Better keep that in mind.

"I apologize," Soei said. "There is an area in the region surrounded by a thick fog of magicules. I found it too dangerous to proceed inside."

No need for him to be sorry. He needed to be careful in every-thing he does, even with a Replication of himself. It'd be a lot worse if he screwed up and the enemy found out what we were up to. Clayman's HQ ought to be beyond that cloud—this was already enough of a lead to go on.

"Should several of us explore the area while it is unguarded?" Benimaru suggested.

"Isn't Clayman holding Walpurgis shortly?" Shuna coldly countered. "I fear we may miss him entirely."

"True, true," added Hakuro as Benimaru winced. "It would reflect quite poorly on us if we underestimated the enemy force and tasted defeat. We need Sir Benimaru to keep our forces together."

"All right. Any other suggestions?"

Shion's hand shot up.

"Yes?"

"Why don't we storm that Walpurgis thing and slash up both Clayman and any other demon lords who have a problem with us?"

Her eyes were gleaming as she said it. It was my fault for letting that idiot talk in the first place. I could feel the veins throbbing around my temples, but I held it all back. This wasn't the first time I had to deal with something like this.

"Shion, how are you going to 'slash them up'? Can you give me something more realistic to work with?"

Clayman solo was one thing, but picking a fight with yet more demon lords would never work. We needed to handle them one at a time, something Shion would have to learn sooner rather than later.

My scolding made her visibly depressed. *Eesh. Let's try to soften the blow a bit.* I may not act it all the time, but I like being kind to her.

"But crashing their Council might be a good idea."

Her face rose, full of expectant joy. She was never willing to let a bit of praise go unnoticed.

"Listen, Ramiris. You have experience with them. Do you think I could join in this thing, too?"

"Uweh?! You want to participate, Rimuru?"

"No, I just wanted to ask. Clayman's gonna be there, so I thought it would be interesting if I paid a visit as well."

If I'm being targeted, showing up somewhere Clayman didn't expect me ought to rock him a little bit. Resorting to violence during a Council might not be too apropos, but I could consider my options once I'm there.

"Hmm… I think it's probably okay. But you can only have two attendants along with you!"

Any more than that would lead to trouble that all the demon lords preferred to avoid. Once, one of the newer demon lords brought along a hundred or so warriors to the Council as a show of force. This stoked the ire of another demon lord whose nation had just been razed and was looking for someone—anyone—to serve as a little stress relief. That newer lord wound up killed, along with all the magic-born for dessert. Ever since, it was forbidden for relatively powerless magic-born to participate, and only two guests per demon lord were allowed.

In other words, Walpurgis Councils *had* ended in violence before. Which meant it wouldn't be, you know, unprecedented if I did it. Maybe I should seriously consider trying to rile Clayman into a fight over there.

"Well, what do you think, guys? Think it'd be fun to join in?"

"Heh-heh-heh-heh. A wonderful suggestion. I would be happy to join you at—"

"Diablo, you fool! I will be by his side, and I refuse to allow anyone else!"

There they go. Shion and Diablo, back at it again. Bringing those two along would be suicide, so I crossed them off the list from the start…

"…But either way," Diablo said, "if we go into battle with the demon lords, as long as we can defeat them, all is well. What need do we have for a demon lord besides yourself, Sir Rimuru?"

Shion briskly nodded her total agreement. "Exactly! I had thought you were an idiot, but for a new recruit, you seem to have much potential! You stated exactly what I was trying to say!"

Are they friends, or foes, or what? Whatever they were, I used to think Shion was the only one who didn't think. But no, they both agreed that killing all the other demon lords was a fine idea.

Why'd it turn out like this? Looking around the room, I could see a few other people nodding their agreement. A few were more conservative, but a lot of them seemed more interested in spilling blood than securing a victory. The flock of war hawks in my leadership seemed to be growing. But that was just way too reckless. Better hit the brakes on this conversation.

"Whoa, whoa. No need to go crazy. We haven't decided on anything yet. Besides, Diablo, I put you in charge of Farmus, so I'm not bringing you along either way."

"Ah, true. I understand."

Diablo seemed to think of conquering Farmus as a children's pastime. I liked that confidence, but hopefully it didn't cause him to miss something and mess up the whole thing. His emotions appeared mixed to me—disappointed but glad to be assigned work.

"Isn't that dangerous, though?" Shuna asked. There we go. *That's* the kind of opinion I wanted to hear.

"It is," replied Geld. "Besides, even if we don't join the Council, wouldn't it be more effective to seize Clayman's headquarters while he is away?"

He was absolutely right. It was better to proceed with a battle we could win without exposing ourselves to danger. Geld was as much a hawk as any of them, but he wasn't that impulsive. I was glad to hear that from him—but I had my reasons to contemplate attending Walpurgis, too. Something concerned me about it.

"No," Benimaru said, "what Sir Rimuru is most concerned about is what move the demon lord Milim will make. It is hard to imagine Lady Milim betraying us, but we cannot deny the possibility that Clayman is controlling her. Perhaps she has her own motivations, but at the very least, we are sure she has defeated Lord Carillon. I think it is not a bad idea to pursue the truth of that matter at the Council."

"Exactly," agreed Soei. "I wonder why Lady Milim signed on to convene the event. Perhaps she has some kind of plot in mind?"

Great to see they were of the same mind—sharing both my ideas and the issues they presented.

"Yeah, it'd be crazy to think that Milim would just do whatever Clayman wants. I mean, Milim is *so* self-centered!"

Are you really one to talk, Ramiris? Maybe not, but I couldn't help but agree with her.

"I find it impossible to believe that Lady Milim betrayed us," Shion concluded. "I have no evidence to back it up, but that's absolutely how I feel!"

Right. No evidence. And I didn't think she stabbed me in the back, either, really. Raphael complained about a lack of data to work with, but even I thought that scenario unlikely, unless there was some vast change in the state of things. *I've decided to believe in Milim—but that doesn't mean I'm letting her do whatever she wants.*

"I agree with all of you. Milim hasn't betrayed us—which means something else must've happened to her. Like Ramiris suggested, I think it's a good idea to consider Clayman the culprit—or at least the cause of this. That's why I'd like to take up Benimaru's suggestion. I'm thinking about joining the Walpurgis Council and seeing what I can find out in there..."

Something definitely must've happened. At the very worst, Milim might attack us the moment Walpurgis ended. *That* was the real cause of my anxieties, the reason why I couldn't let her be. Clayman alone, I could handle. Him *plus* Milim, I really wanted to avoid. *Well, at least I've steered this in the right direction, and we won't resort to violence as our first—*

"Right? Right, right! Looks like Detective Ramiris had the right hunch the whole time. So how about we just kick Clayman's butt?"

Oops. Maybe not. Not as long as Ramiris was here.

"Besides, what the heck is *with* all you guys? You have this, like, treasure trove of powerful magic-born at your beck and call, Rimuru! If you had *this* many, what's the big deal about just handing Beretta over to me for good, huh?!"

She was getting carried away. The strength she saw in us was giving her a swelled head—and she *still* hadn't given up on Beretta. Which, as I noted, Beretta has a say in, too, so her selfishness isn't gonna get her anywhere.

But she had her allies in the meeting hall.

"I see. She makes a very good point. Right—perhaps I could come over and do a little killing?"

"Whoa, chill out, Shion! And Benimaru and Soei, I see you guys packing up to leave town! You're not going anywhere yet!"

Here we go again. Just when I was ready to RSVP for Walpurgis.

I needed Benimaru and Soei to fight Clayman's forces. We'd be carrying out these plans at the same time, so I had to select the two attendants joining me carefully.

Who should it be…? I could physically feel the pressure from behind my back. It was from Shion, of course. She might go nuts if I didn't take her. It was getting harder for Benimaru to keep her calm, so maybe I should babysit her instead. Besides, Clayman's schemes almost killed Shion—they *did* kill her, in fact. She might have a chance to take revenge for that, which was another reason to take her along.

All right. She's in.

I wavered a bit on the second choice before settling on Ranga. I thought about having him stand by in my shadow, but that'd put us in trouble if a Holy Field or other special barrier was thrown over us. I could feel him perking his ears up toward me. *Let's go with him. He'd make a great bodyguard.*

So that was the two. They both knew Spatial Motion, so it'd also be easy for them to flee if it came to that. If I tried deploying the new barrier I devised based on Holy Field, I was pretty sure that'd get us out of there safe, at worst. That was something we could rely on as we joined the Council, at least.

But what if Milim really *was* being controlled? In that case, it was likely that our town was next on the list for destruction. I had to do everything I could to prevent that. I had no interest in seeing this town be scarred again.

"All right. I'm gonna join in. I'm taking Shion and Ranga with me. Ramiris, can you send word that I'll be at the Council?"

"Sure thing!" she casually replied, before immediately opening up some kind of special demon lord–only line and informing the others about my presence. It was powered by this ridiculously complex-looking spell, using spatial interference to allow for synchronous communication. I looked at it, curious about how it worked—and then I heard loud, haughty laughter coming my way.

"Gwah-ha-ha-ha-ha! So! Finally thirsty for some action, are you?

No need to hold back now, Rimuru! Why don't you and I come along together? I will tag along with you! Those demon lords aren't worth fearing for a single moment!"

Come to think of it, I had totally forgotten I had this guy, too. I appreciated his confidence, but Veldora wouldn't work, no.

"Well, hear me out, Veldora. I want you to stay here in town so you can defend it."

"What?!" He looked genuinely shocked. "I said I will tag along with you. With me, you will stand taller than all the demon lords combined!"

Hey, defending this town's really important work, too. Like, the most important work. We'd have all available forces tackling Clayman's armies. That just left a few of Rigur's security platoons and Shion's team. Defending the town only worked with Veldora's presence. With him around, even if the Western Holy Church stopped by to attack, we'd have nothing to worry about.

I tried explaining all this to him.

"...So you see? You need to hold down the fort."

"Mmgh..."

He seemed less than convinced. *Right. Maybe I should give him the real reason.* But just as I was about to open my mouth, Ramiris started shouting again.

"Hey! Rimuru! I just got off the line! They said it was okay, but aren't you being really mean to Master Veldora? He could just be one of *my* guests, then. That'd make *me* feel a lot safer, too!"

That seemed reasonable, at first glance. But I could tell Ramiris just wanted Beretta and Veldora by her side so she could look super-cool around her colleagues. Veldora probably thought along the same lines, too.

"...Hmm? No, I wasn't interested in coming so I could serve as *your* guardian, no."

"Uwehh?! Oh, you're so cold, wise teacher!"

What's with that *teacher* stuff? Ramiris and Veldora had become manga buddies in record time, I guess. They definitely got along, but in terms of the power balance between them, I'd say this was all Ramiris trying to curry Veldora's favor.

…Well, fine. The most important thing was that my presence at Walpurgis had been recognized. That was helpful for me, although it probably had more to do with how the other demon lords didn't want to venture near human lands just to deal with me.

"We're actually planning to start spreading rumors about you, Veldora. We discussed that at the summit earlier, but you knew that, right?"

Having him be Ramiris's attendant *was* an idea. Personally, though, I wanted the other lords to think he wasn't coming, since it'd put them off guard for me.

"Mm. Yes. Of course."

Nope. Sounds like he wasn't paying attention. He was way too enthralled in his manga to notice any of our proceedings. In that case, it'd be easy to trick him.

"Well, it's like this: If I brought you along, it'd probably make Clayman think, like, 'Oh, that Rimuru, he's a wimp just bringing Veldora along as a ringer.'"

"What?! Curse that Clayman! I'll make him pay for that!" Shion cried.

"Heh. That insect doesn't know what he's waded into," added Diablo. "Perhaps I should come over and kill him after all."

"Shion, Diablo, calm *down* already," Benimaru chided, looking a little angered himself. "That was just an example."

Man, it's *so* easy to tick those two guys off.

"Yeah, like Benimaru said, that's just what I'm picturing him saying. So I mean, if we bring Veldora to the Council, people will be so wary of us that it'd mess up the whole point of us being there, right?"

Veldora blinked. "Hohh? Ah, I see."

Shion beamed, though I wasn't sure she had thought about my words at all. "A fine idea! Well said, Sir Rimuru!"

"Heh-heh-heh-heh-heh… Still, he will pay for making light of you. I'd love to make him atone with my own two hands, but perhaps I should let Shion do the honors?"

"So you'll throw the enemy off their guard in order to make your negotiations easier?"

Benimaru, at least, had the right idea.

"But shouldn't we be avoiding danger as much as possible?" asked Shuna. She had a point, and Geld and Gabil nodded their agreement.

"If the enemy is going to be wary of us anyway," added Hakuro, "would it not be best to focus more on our own safety?"

Soei gave this a silent nod of his own.

I could understand everyone's worries, sure. But I could cover for that.

"It's all right. I can actually call for Veldora anytime I want with the Summon Storm Dragon skill. That doesn't count as an attendant, right? So if things go bad, I can ask for his help then. Until that happens, *if* it does, I want him protecting this town."

I smiled triumphantly at the audience, asking them to defy me.

My leadership seemed impressed, at least, as did Veldora: "Gwaaaaahhhh-ha-ha-ha! I see! I'll be the great hero who swoops in to the rescue at the last moment!"

Great. If you're fine with that, so am I.

"Isn't that kinda unfair...?"

"Don't be stupid, Ramiris. I was hoping you'd call it smart."

Ramiris may not have liked it much, but Veldora was already murmuring his agreement. Just one more push...

"Besides, that gives you one more slot to fill for Walpurgis, doesn't it?"

This visibly excited her, as it did the rest of my government.

"Oh, that totally makes sense, Rimuru! So who're you gonna match me with?"

I guess she had no complaints. Really, I think all she wanted was a chance to show off to the other demon lords. But at least she was on my side.

Now for that last one. I could feel all the unpicked holding their breath, but sadly for them, I needed someone strong in that position. Benimaru would've been great, but he'd kinda be handling a war in my absence, so I went with someone else:

"Sorry to disappoint you all, but I'd like Haku—"

"A moment, please!"

I was stopped by the woman standing behind Ramiris—Treyni.

"Sir Rimuru, I hope you will give me this assignment!"

"Oh, Treyni! Just look at you!"

Ramiris was already tearfully accepting the offer. Well, so be it.

"All right. I'll let you go along, Treyni."

Now we had our member assignments for the Walpurgis Council. Me, with Shion and Ranga as my attendants, and Ramiris, with Beretta and Treyni under her. Then, if we needed it, Veldora was a quick summon away.

Lucky thing, indeed, that I was accepted.

Me and Leon Cromwell also kind of had some issues to tackle, but I'd settle with just meeting him in person this time. I had Shizu's request to fulfill, and I didn't want to ignore that forever, but my target right now was Clayman. I hadn't forgotten about the orc lord chaos or about Mjurran.

But most of all, I was concerned about Milim. One slipup, and I might be forced to fight her next. I was prepared to face down Clayman, but the idea of a life-and-death struggle with Milim made me singularly unenthusiastic. It'd be great if I could get all that worked out at Walpurgis. If not, I'll think of something then.

Clayman, you've made an enemy out of me. And I'm not lenient enough to easily forgive someone I've identified as such. You better be ready for me. And if you lay a hand on any of my people, you can expect to pay for everything you dish out.

Dahh… Now I'm starting to adopt Shion's way of thinking. Still, I couldn't help but feel a little happy about it. The time for fretting in darkened rooms was over. Now we had a clear, concrete goal to reach out to.

ALVIS

SUFIA

CHAPTER
3

THE EVE OF
BATTLE

That Time I Got Reincarnated as a Slime

It turned out to be unusually easy for Clayman to convene a Walpurgis Council.

The use of Carillon's "betrayal" as the topic was important to him. The way it was explained to the demon lords was basically that Carillon violated their nonaggression agreement by invading the Forest of Jura, and Milim punished him for it. That was clearly a screen, but none of the other demon lords protested. It would all be coming out during the Council—but by then, it'd be over. That was Clayman's aim. Walpurgis would earn him valuable time toward awakening himself, becoming a true demon lord, and obtaining immense powers. And Milim would be there, too. If she acted subservient to him in front of the other demon lords, that'd just prove to them all that Clayman was not willing to accept any back talk.

That was his plan, and to make it reality, he needed his military operation to succeed. It had to wrap up quickly, before the other demon lords could interfere. He also had the perfect excuse—to punish Carillon for violating that treaty, just like how the Council was convened. He just had to produce the evidence he needed to prove it.

With everything in place, Clayman immediately took action. Passing through the demon lord Milim's domain, his forces pressed on into the Beast Kingdom of Eurazania. Yamza, a man faithful to Clayman from his very heart, was chosen to be their leader. He was the only one who knew his master's true aims—to drive his army of thirty thousand into Eurazania and claim the over ten thousand souls inside before the Council began.

●

"These people drive me up the wall! How dare they propose that we work together?!"

The man yelling angrily was Middray, head priest of the temple built for the Dragon Faithful in their domain's largest city. This made him leader of those who worshiped Milim as a goddess.

"But, Father Middray, failing to follow this order would put us in serious trouble. Yamza, their commander... He bore an imperial edict from Lady Milim herself, did he not?"

The simpering associate pleading his case before Middray was Hermes, a member of the priests who served this temple. He had a transcendental air about him, which most people mistook as him being spaced out and insincere. It grated on Middray's nerves.

"Silence, Hermes. I don't need you telling me that! I *know* it!"

Hermes couldn't help but roll his eyes at the enraged head priest, even though he understood too well what irked him. It was those magic-born who had been camped out since yesterday. They had come here, to the City of the Forgotten Dragon, without warning and promptly occupied it like it was theirs all along. Apparently, they were a force from the demon lord Clayman, heading for the demon lord Carillon's domain to investigate an agreement he had broken.

Refusing them simply wasn't an option. Middray could rant and rave all he wanted; it wouldn't have changed a thing. There was a pretty good reason for this—the demon lord who toppled Carillon's Beast Kingdom of Eurazania was none other than Milim, the object of Hermes's and his fellow priests' worship. If their supreme being was involved, it was only natural for Clayman's forces to ask them for help in collecting evidence against Carillon. In fact, if they *didn't* find anything, that would put Milim in an embarrassing position. Milim herself wouldn't care, but Hermes and the others would.

"Ah, Lady Milim can be such a handful sometimes..."

Her selfishness could be forgiven, Hermes reasoned, but just a little—really, a *tiny* amount would be fine—he wished that she gave them a moment's worth of consideration.

"How *dare* you, Hermes! You will *never* cast doubt upon Lady Milim's actions!"

"No, I know that, but..."

But it's getting harder and harder for us because we're always spoiling her. He didn't say it. It'd just spark another wave of anger from Middray. *This is quite a handful*, he thought, sighing.

He recalled how things had spiraled downward since yesterday. The army had requested permission to pass through in advance, and even then, their high-pressure tactics rubbed the priests the wrong way. This force clearly looked down upon the Dragon Faithful; it was obvious that their requests for "support" weren't really requests at all. They were orders, through and through.

The Dragon Faithful that resided here, in the City of the Forgotten Dragon, numbered less than a hundred thousand in total. They all worked together in their daily lives, there being no central government to speak of. As a result, none were particularly gifted in battle—they relied on Milim's protection to keep the peace.

That, at least, was how it appeared to outside observers. But this was only half right.

Yes, there was no government. All the crops and other goods produced were collected at the Central Temple, where it was distributed equally by the head priest. It might seem like this system would fail, encouraging people to grow unproductive and lazy, but that wasn't the case. Everyone, workers and nonworkers, was guaranteed at least a certain amount of the wealth—and the more hardworking would also be provided with additional supplies.

This was similar to the "universal basic income" idea that had gained traction around modern Japan. The main issue was who got to decide how much of a contribution each individual made to society... and that was Middray's job, granted exclusively to him by Milim.

That right afforded Middray all but absolute power in this city, but he never abused that power. Why? Simple: Because the other priests who served him had the right to dismiss him from office. If he got too selfish with his decisions, he'd lose his post. That understanding was what kept Middray from becoming a tyrant. (Of course, they already *had* a tyrant on hand in Milim, and nobody was stupid enough to try to imitate her game, but still.)

Thus, these tens of thousands of people were far better led and organized than one would expect at first. While some may think the city was lacking in military strength, that was completely untrue. The Dragon Faithful, thanks to certain local conditions, all had very strong physical skills. In addition to their organizational acumen, each adult was strong enough to almost reach C rank. Their pacifism didn't make it clear at first, but this was actually quite a formidable group of warriors.

The priests, in particular, were in a class of their own. There were only a hundred or so of these guys, handpicked from the best the region had to offer, and they could definitely mess you up. Their daily "prayer sessions" to Milim (i.e. battle training) gave them superior combat skills, and once you got up to the level of Middray or Hermes, they were even strong enough to give Milim a run for her money. That's why Middray was so enraged that Clayman's forces were treating them like dirt.

And that wasn't this people's only secret. The second one was the clincher.

Another day passed. Clayman's army was now freely raiding the city's storehouses for food supplies. The veins throbbed on Middray's forehead as he was asked to remain patient with them.

"But why has Lady Milim not returned?" he asked, trying to adjust the target of his rage.

"Well, who knows?" Hermes distractedly replied. They had gone through this back-and-forth a dozen times or so, and it was getting on his nerves more and more.

"We prepared this wonderful meal for her... I hope Lady Milim is not hungry somewhere out there, you see..."

"I doubt it," Hermes countered. In fact, he was sure about it. The wonderful meal Middray mentioned was a "plate of nature's bounties," which in fact was a bunch of raw vegetables on a plate. The last time he had a meal with Milim, Hermes stole a glance at her, only to find her lamely chewing away, all expression drained from her face.

I could tell she wasn't enjoying it, he thought. *She was just trying her best to power through it.* Judging by her joy when some roasted meat was brought out, there was no doubt in his mind.

He had suggested to Middray that actually cooking the food might please Lady Milim more, but that fell on deaf ears. It was the head priest's firm belief that providing all the glories of nature, in their most natural form, was the best possible way to pamper her. *That's exactly why Lady Milim hardly comes around any longer,* he wanted to say, but it'd be his neck on the line if he did.

Hermes had traveled extensively across the land, giving him insight into the cuisines of many nations. The other priests, meanwhile, didn't have that experience. They were too closed-minded to think that anything apart from "pure nature" would be right, so Hermes just gave up eventually.

"Perhaps, perhaps not," mused Middray. "But just imagine. That villain Clayman, thinking he's king of the world, making Lady Milim write that edict..."

It was definitely written in Milim's sloppy— Er, *unique* handwriting. They had no choice but to carry it out, but they could only go so far with it.

"Yeah, true. We can't do much if it's Lady Milim's orders...but they've emptied out Food Storehouse Number Three, too. We've only got seven left. That's going to make things lean until the next harvest..."

"Dammit all!!"

Veins swelled across Middray's bald head like the skin of a melon. It was rather clear just how angry he was. And given how he had to work hard to keep from laughing at it, Hermes was a pretty shameless priest, too.

As they spoke, the very source of all their troubles came walking up—the general manager of the Clayman force.

"Feh! Keep your cool, Hermes."

"I hear you."

You first, Hermes thought. He was hoping the man would walk on past, but sadly, he was headed straight toward them. They closed their mouths and waited for the man, Yamza, to arrive.

Yamza was the general commander of Clayman's forces, a man seen as one of the demon lord's most trusted confidants. Slender in size and build, he looked light enough to float into the air, making him a fighter built for speed. Or perhaps, not a fighter so much as a swordsman. A first-class swordsman with arms as fast as a passing gale. The Ice Blade, a Unique weapon gifted to him by Clayman, allowed him to use the aspectual magic Ice Blizzard. Between that and his latent sword skills, the Frozen Swordmage was an A-plus magic-born in rank.

"Well, hello there, Father Middray. We do appreciate the provisions you're supporting us with. With an army of thirty thousand, there's just never enough to go around."

He flashed a friendly grin at them, but his eyes weren't smiling. He silently, carefully gauged Middray's response. He didn't give Hermes a glance. It was a common thing to see, magic-born treating humans like second-class citizens. Hermes wasn't a fan, but he sucked it up, just as Middray told him to. There was no point starting a fight. He saw it as just a temporary affront.

"Ha-ha-ha! It's an honor to be in your service. However, sadly, it is difficult to provide you with much more than we already have. Lady Milim would be saddened if our people don't have enough to eat."

"What are you saying?!" Even that little retort was enough to set Yamza off. "*Your* Milim was the one who stepped out of line. We're trying to clean up the mess she made, so the least you could do is show us all the respect you can!"

It was an act, of course. He was pretending to be mad so that he could see how Middray reacted. If the head priest retaliated, he clearly intended to use that as a pretext to sack the city.

"Ah, my pardons," Middray modestly began. "We were thinking only about ourselves there, for a moment. We will provide you with all the cooperation we can, so please feel free to ask."

Hermes was thoroughly impressed. All that haughty elitism, and Middray didn't let any of his anger reach his face. He kept the smile going the whole time.

Well done, Father Middray. Your head didn't go all melon-like at all. I would've snapped at him long ago.

Yamza returned his smile. "I see, I see. I was hoping to hear that. We have enough people to sweep up the Beast Kingdom, but allow me to give you the opportunity to help us out. You should be able to support us with material transport, shouldn't you?"

"W-wait just a minute! First you take our food, then you take our people from—"

Hermes hadn't intended to resist him. He just let his mouth run off. The next instant, Hermes felt an intense pain in what used to be his left arm.

"Ah?!"

"Silence, you piece of trash!"

The slitted eyes of Yamza, placed upon Hermes for the first time, were cold as ice. Holding his severed arm in place, Hermes gritted his teeth and glared at him.

"...So you don't know your place. You appear in a hurry to die."

Now his smile was brutal in its chill, as Yamza pointed his blood-stained sword at Hermes.

Bastard. Thinks he can tell me what to do—

Just as Hermes was about to lose his temper, he was thrown back by a force like a wild animal butting against him. This was a kick, from Middray, hard enough to nearly break the skin.

"Ah, no, my apologies for all of this, Sir Yamza. I'll teach this fool how to behave correctly, so please, by my name, I hope you will forgive him."

Middray bowed his head toward the magic-born.

"Pfft. Always a pain, isn't it, when the people below you are such idiots? I will forgive him just this once. We will depart tomorrow morning, so I want all of you priests to prepare immediately!"

Middray's mediation was enough to make Yamza sheathe his sword. But it came at a heavy price. The Dragon Faithful's priests, the leaders of their people, had just been forcibly conscripted.

Yamza promptly left with nothing more to say. He wasn't expecting fighters among the Faithful; he just wanted the priests and their healing magic. And thanks to Hermes's needless meddling, Yamza had everything he wanted.

After he left, Middray sighed and healed Hermes's wound.

"You utter fool. I warned you about that."

"I'm sorry—I just couldn't help myself..."

Hermes held his arm in place as Middray began his work, casting the holy magic Recovery on it. In a few moments, the amputated limb was good as new. The blood loss made him a little light-headed, but he could use his own Healing skill to tackle that.

"All right. Well, even if the priests are gone, our people won't be affected right away. But that man..."

The anger he held back was now clear on his face as Middray glared in the direction Yamza walked off to.

"...He is damaging Lady Milim's own assets."

He was referring to his attack on Hermes. It was an unforgivable act of aggression, although he was now trying to sweep that kick he landed under the rug.

That kick hurt like hell, too, y'know...

But Hermes didn't bring it up. He knew Middray didn't mean ill of him. As befitting someone who worshiped Milim, Middray tended to fly into violent rages all too easily. Something you could say about everyone in this domain, really...

"No, but really... Do you mind if I kill him?"

"Fool," the head priest promptly replied. "You don't stand a chance."

He wasn't wrong. Hermes probably couldn't even scratch him.

"Yeah. That sword's unbeatable, and I think he's hiding something else, too."

"Indeed. He is the confidant of that scheming sneak Clayman; he won't reveal his true powers that easily. A real man would put it all on the table to secure victory, but not them..."

I wouldn't call that *approach very smart*, Hermes thought, but again, Hermes didn't agree too often with the way people thought in this domain. So he pretended to agree and went back to work. With the new deadline of tomorrow morning coming out of nowhere, he had a mountain of business to settle.

The next morning, with two days left until the Walpurgis Council, the Clayman force continued their forward march.

It was the morning after the summit. I had been working all night, and my body was giving me a lot of guff for it. Or my mind was, anyway. In reality, I couldn't have been healthier. Not needing to sleep helps a lot at times like these.

Last night, after our conference, Soei contacted me again. He participated in the meeting in the flesh, but one of his Replications reported in this time, after collecting information from across the Beast Kingdom. Soka, and the other four people on his team, were contributing as well, providing a few more solid leads.

The Clayman force, ever on the lookout, still had not moved.

In the midst of this, they all searched for someplace to deploy our own forces, but a problem arose. The fleeing residents of the Beast Kingdom were spread out all over the place. If we wanted to rescue them, then no matter where we transported our army to, we might have some areas left unevacuated before time ran out. Thanks to the Clayman force's invasion route, we were lagging behind schedule.

Suggestion. It would be more effective to transport the citizens to a single location.

Hmm. I see. Yeah, I suppose it would be. No reason why that kind of transport is military only. Dominate Space allowed me to smoothly travel wherever I wanted, including to Soei, his Replications, or Soka and the others. I could then use the new type of transport spell we devised to collect all the evacuees together.

Thanks to that, things got very busy after the conference. First, I had Geld's army go on ahead to build a field base that could accept these refugees. I transported them over to the former location of Eurazania's capital, which Milim had turned into a vacant lot. Being a wide-open field, it stuck out like a sore thumb, but there'd be no better place to deploy a large force in.

Then I personally went from village to village, transporting the refugees out. This we wrapped up before the end of last night, which was why I was so exhausted—mentally speaking, that is.

Phobio was with me, which thankfully kept us from dealing with any resistance, although it exhausted him as well. "Performing all this teleportation," he marveled before he left, looking at me like I was some kind of fiend. "How can you keep yourself together...? And such elaborate transport magic, over and over again... It seems absurd."

Well, that's rude of him, isn't it? Of course I'm tired.

By now, Phobio should have been asleep in a room inside one of the field tents Geld's force built. But that didn't matter. Our main force would be ready soon, so I needed to perform one really *big* transport shortly.

I headed for an empty field just outside town. Rigurd was there, having spent the night preparing for this. Unlike me, he was running and hopping around, a bottomless well of energy. Rigur was called back as well, and he was pitching in all he could to help Rigurd. Once they were done, it was my job to transport all the people gathered here to our Beast Kingdom field camp. Once that was over, I planned to start preparing for the Walpurgis Council two days from now.

Upon reaching the field, I found lines of Tempestian soldiers waiting for me—including ten thousand beastmen, led by Sufia and Alvis. Their armor was piecemeal, nothing unified about it, but that was unavoidable. We had simply provided them whatever armor we didn't need, and since many were capable of transformation anyway, this was better than confining them in full uniform.

Next to them were my leaders, ready to serve as reinforcements. Even compared to the Charybdis battle, our size—and our power to wage war—had grown tremendously.

Benimaru, noticing, stood next to me and took this opportunity to explain the evolutions that had taken place.

Following my own demon lord evolution, everyone else in Tempest had some change of their own. The World Language said something about everyone in my "genealogy" receiving "gifts," and I assumed that meant everyone I had named.

"Based on what we heard from the townspeople," he said as we faced the ranks of soldiers, "the men now enjoy enhanced stamina. The women report that their skin is glossier and more beautiful than before. None of that mattered to me—or I should say, it was beyond my comprehension, but I suppose you could say their spiritual strength has risen."

Some, he reported, looked like they turned back the clock a few years. Everyone appreciated it. But these were the townspeople. They were holding down the fort back home. Let's see what our fighters are packing.

Among our platoons, as well, there was a litany of changes. Some soldiers learned new skills for themselves; others gained the same skill in groups, based on the unique nature of their squad. I couldn't wait to dive in and see for myself.

We first visited a group that had been with me almost from the start—Gobta's goblin riders, a legion of hobgoblins led by starwolves that almost never naturally appeared unless the right conditions were in place. But were they really hobgoblins? That's their species, perhaps, but their essence was something wholly different now.

Astoundingly, they had all learned the extra skill Unify. This was a rare one that let man and mount quite literally become one, turning them into mobile, high-speed, four-legged warriors. They were awarded an A-minus rank in this form—they didn't manage a solid A since they were geared mainly for one-on-one combat, but they were killers in battle. A few working together could probably beat an A-ranked magic-born.

That was the whole gimmick with them, of course. The goblin riders were a team, guaranteed to work rapidly with one another's thoughts and remain steadily in formation. They were keeping up with Hakuro's training, after all—and if you imagine a hundred moving in tandem, you can see what made these Riders so fearsome.

I definitely felt like the human-invented ranking system was doing these guys a disservice. I could expect a lot more from them than that, even.

Next, we visited some of Benimaru's personal trainees.

Once I became leader of the Forest of Jura, we started enjoying a lot more combat-ready monsters in our midst. This included three hundred ogres, the most powerful of which were young men and women from the village that sought my help early on. They looked up to Benimaru a lot, which affected the "gifts" they received.

It was really a crazy sight to see. Some had volunteered for the force, making them named warriors from the start. They were strong enough to be considered low-level magic-born, which made them a tremendously reliable asset. Even a wild, non-sentient ogre ranked a B—and these guys were both fully equipped and had learned some Arts. These were never gonna be wimpy kids.

These ogres had formed a sort of elite personal guard for Benimaru, and each was A-minus in rank. I named them Team Kurenai, or *red flame*.

Now, for the fighters assigned to Benimaru's main force.

This was around four thousand hobgoblins, and their evolution was really fascinating to me. They had more or less taken on the flame element, learning skills like Control Flame and Resist Temperature Change. Kind of a surprise. Each soldier ranked a B equivalent, and you could call them a specialized assault team.

By the way, these hobgoblins all had a reference to the color "green" in their names, since their skin was green. I don't know who named them, but I really wish he thought a little more about the long-term effect with that.

Report. They were named by you, Master.

I know!!
Eesh, I wasn't expecting to get dissed by my own skill here. Talk about unwanted sarcasm. Like, I can't read *that* far into every single thing, guys. These monster evolutions just made no sense.

Since everybody was named "green" something, I named this army the Green Numbers. Might as well go with it. I wanted to go with "red" something since these were Benimaru's forces, but I kinda liked the feel of this, too. It'd be a nice little surprise, this green force unleashing all these flame attacks. I think I'll have their equipment repainted green for the battlefield sometime.

Next up was Geld's force, a sort of complement to the Green Numbers.

The high orcs all evolved in the same way, earning power-up skills like Steel Strength and Iron Wall. Their officer class also had the extra skill Control Earth, letting them mold and sculpt the land around them. Good for digging trenches in a hurry, as Geld put it.

In addition, everyone in the army had earned the extra skill Armorize Body, making them into much more of a defense-oriented tank unit. They had also taken on a lot of my personal resistances—Resist Melee Attack to start with, followed by Pain, Rot, Electricity, and Paralysis. Kabal's Charus Shield, the completed version of the one I gave him as a present, was now a Unique piece of equipment that boosted his magic resistance. Basically, whether it was melee or magic, they could deal with it. I gave half a thought to exposing them to Shion's cuisine so they could gain poison resistance but quickly banished the thought.

Still, obtaining all those shield-like scales from Charybdis was really a stroke of luck. Kurobe had made lots of copies of the items Garm had created from them, and I really have those craftsmen to thank for that.

Now, this unit was sturdy enough that each member ranked a solid B. That, plus the Unique equipment on each one, made them impervious to any normal force. It was almost unfair how defensively able they were, and they numbered five thousand, their ranks beefed up by a constant stream of volunteers. Normally, they were involved in construction work, but when they received the call, they transformed into a powerhouse, an iron wall that no attack could pierce.

Their official name was now the Yellow Numbers.

Close behind them were the hundred dragonewts under Gabil's command.

Dragonewts were naturally gifted with a pretty decent array of skills, and they had all but breezed into the A-minus ranks. Now, with my gifts, the dragon in their blood had awakened to an even stronger degree. Each of them now had the intrinsic skill Dragon Body, along with either Flame Breath or Thunder Breath, giving them some much-needed long-range attacks. Gabil could use them both, which meant he really *was* an exceptional dragonewt, I guess.

What I still didn't really get was Dragon Body.

Report. The intrinsic skill Dragon Body is—

Oh, um, I didn't need the full documentation. I know now that I can't use it, so there's not much point in hearing it. I'm sure Gabil and the rest will take the time to figure out how to use it best, if they want. What's the point of having power if you never earned it for yourself? That's what I think.

Huh? What about me? Well, I have the ultimate skill Raphael, Lord of Wisdom. If I have a problem, Raphael will help me out. No issue there. That's *my* power, so in a way, it's like *I'm* the one making the effort there. I don't think it's going too far to say that.

So! Hopefully Gabil and his team can learn how to use that Dragon Body thing before it's too late! Not to throw it all on you, but good luck.

Still, in a way, it was almost like this squad's talents were going to waste with Gabil. They could fly; they could breathe fire and lightning from the air... It's nuts. And thanks to their intrinsic species aspects, they were resistant to pretty much everything—scales of steel, breastplate armor of magisteel. Whether by sword or by magic, no halfhearted strike was going to break their skin. Flight alone was enough to give them an overwhelming advantage, but look at that defense! Speed, offense, defense—the complete surprise-assault package, all in one.

I named them Team Hiryu, or *flying dragon*. They only numbered a hundred, but they were the strongest unit in our forces.

Last but not least, we had a brand-new unit, one positioned as my personal elite guard. Led by Shion, they were also a hundred strong, composed of the victims I revived after the battle in Tempest. There were some children, age-wise, among them, but apparently they had grown up to—and beyond—the point of maturity. I guess their frustration at not being able to fight encouraged that kind of evolution? Who knows?

As far as skills go, they all earned the extra skills Complete Memory and Self-Regeneration. Those two complemented each other. Complete Memory meant that even if their heads were blown off, their memories remained in their astral bodies. They could then use Self-Regeneration to recover fully instead of dying instantly. This meant they had basically gained the astonishing healing skills of the Orc Disaster of yore.

If Self-Regeneration ever evolved into Ultraspeed Regeneration, they'd be pretty much immortal. And I had a hundred of these guys. I couldn't even deal. And thanks to that regeneration, they were durable enough to take Shion's ultra-intense training and deal with it just fine. As a female member put it, one who was just a little girl not long ago: "We don't die or anything!" I didn't have much of an answer to that, no. I wasn't sure if this was the best thing for 'em, but hey, have fun! Break a leg!

Their strength was at around a rank C for now, but I had a feeling that, over time, they'd become the strongest unit in our forces. With that expectation, I decided to name them Team Reborn. They all had a whole new life ahead of them, after all.

That rounded out the briefing.

It felt like the effects of my evolution dovetailed well with everybody's personal efforts to bear some major fruit for us. My first impression was *Wow, we're more damaging than ever.* The total force was under ten thousand, but we could whip pretty much any army out there. Their numbers weren't as strong as the Farmus military I wiped out, but in terms of war power, we would've totally overwhelmed them.

All this stuff came as a total surprise to me. Being outnumbered is still a weakness, but we'd just have to gradually build that up, between strengthening our country and negotiating with others. I think a standing force of around ten thousand would be the number to shoot for.

Plus, we still had our reserve forces protecting the Forest of Jura. They weren't part of this campaign—the difference in training was just too much—but if we could work 'em up, they'd serve us well enough in battle, too. That's something to tackle in the future.

$$*$$

Still, after Benimaru finished his report, I couldn't help but be amazed by the sight of ten thousand of my soldiers in formation. That, plus ten thousand beastman soldiers—an army of twenty thousand, all lined up and waiting for the order to march.

Shion's Team Reborn, as my personal guard, was on standby away from the crowd. They were holding down the fort back home this time, so they'd just get in the way among these ranks.

"Sir Rimuru," Rigurd reported, "everything is ready." I thanked him for his long hours of frantic work. "Oh, I hardly deserve it," he said, smiling.

So if we're all set, it's time to get transporting.

"Oh, um, Lady Alvis...?"

"Alvis is fine, Sir Rimuru."

I was trying to be polite, but I guess I made things worse. Let's just bulldoze right over that.

"All right, Alvis. We have all your friends assembled on the other side, so I want you to relay what we talked about to them. I think Phobio should be organizing them into units, so you take care of the rest!"

"Understood. I promise I will not forget your kindness."

She bowed deeply at me, followed by Sufia and the rest of the beastmen. It felt almost oppressive, but I didn't react. That was how they wanted to show their appreciation.

"You really saved us," a smiling Sufia told me. "Now we can smash up Clayman's forces without a second thought. We'll let you have him, Sir Rimuru, so take out all our anger on him for me!"

Pretty scary face, considering that smile. Alvis was similarly glaring at me, in apparent agreement. Everything was set for them; now all they had to do was go wild on the battlefield. We'd enjoy a force of twenty thousand beastmen alone, so I'm not sure we needed the reinforcements, but the more the merrier. If it was just them, we'd still be outnumbered anyway.

With these extra fighters, we now had a unified force of thirty thousand to go against Clayman's own thirty thousand. We were even now, and we were the better-quality army. Victory was as good as ours. The only problem...

"Benimaru, any issues with our operation?"

While I was rounding up beastmen last night, I had Benimaru and his team shake down our plan of action once more. The gist of it hadn't changed, but since we weren't spreading out our forces to collect the refugees any longer, a few details needed to be changed.

"We're all set, sir." He shot me a crafty smile. "If Clayman is targeting the citizens of the Beast Kingdom, then retreat is certainly an effective option as well."

Yes. I agreed with him. No need to smash right against his front line and get people killed.

"I discussed it with Sir Benimaru as well," Alvis said, excitedly playing with the staff in her hand. "We've got enough leeway now to move the site of battle, so it'll be a little while before we begin..."

All systems go, then. Failing to complete his mission before Walpurgis would make for one angry Clayman, no doubt. At the very least, he'd treat his underlings even worse than usual. If their army's commander fears that and starts freaking out, the ball's on our side.

"...We will deploy the force at the entrance to the Forest of Jura. The wasteland that was once our home, the now-toppled orcish kingdom of Orbic—now, it shall be their grave."

There was something close to sheer malice in Geld's voice. Clayman's scheming cost him his home nation, and now it would be the site of the decisive battle. I suppose anyone would've felt the hand of fate at play here.

The strategy, as it was, is pretty simple. We'd make it look like we had the refugees evacuate into the Forest of Jura, then strike at the enemy forces trying to pursue them. That's about it.

Raphael provided the perfect simulation of it in my brain. Obtaining and replaying the information Soei and his gang gave me, I had a picture of the future that was almost as vivid as reality. I then Thought Communication'ed that to everyone else, so we could all equally grasp it.

Our original plan called for us to keep the refugees secure as we lured the enemy over, eventually surrounding and destroying the force. With this change, the faster units would serve as bait instead. That reduced the danger to the individual forces involved, which greatly boosted the chances of this working.

The key to this was making sure they were all inside the forest before crushing them. I didn't intend to kill them all, but I didn't like the idea of them running away and attacking again later. We had to be thorough.

"You got all that, Benimaru?"

"Of course. Let's give them enough hell that they never dare defy us again!"

Ooh, he's got his no-mercy face on. I like that.

"Let's wipe 'em out, Benimaru!" Shion added, cheering him on.

"Heh-heh-heh-heh-heh... You need to take out the garbage fast, you see, before it rots."

Diablo was...also cheering him on? I'm not so sure, but whatever. They both wanted to join in, of course—they just *loooove* fighting. But Shion would stay with me to prepare, and Diablo would be stepping into Farmus land soon. They were out of the picture. Now to just leave things to Benimaru and wait for the good news.

"Right! No matter what happens, I want you to report back immediately. I'm sending you off now. Win this one, guys!!"

"""Rahhh! Victory shall be yours!!"""

And now they were *all* looking at me, all those many, many eyes. As I regarded them with my own golden pair, I deployed a square of magic. I spent ages practicing this last night, so I had it down pat. Beneath the feet of all twenty thousand, a giant square drew itself in layers, from the bottom to the top. A complex array of geometrical shapes built themselves up inside, too intricate for me to figure out. Something this size, of course, required a lot of magic and concentration. My energy rapidly drained, but based on my figures, I should manage to hold out. (Not to brag, but my magicule stores had risen exponentially, too.)

It took around five minutes in all. Everyone stood there, bolt upright, waiting for the transport spell to complete. And then, the moment the mélange of shapes within the square stacked up above the heads of everyone inside—the entire army was gone, in the blink of an eye.

Transport complete. Looks like we got them out of there.

Back when I was practicing last night, I was a little concerned Clayman had noticed all the light this was generating in the darkness. So I combined it with a blindness bomb to sap all the light away from the magic square. You never know where you may mess up—diligence is key. There was no need for that now, though, and the sight that unfolded before me could only be described as magnificent.

"Well done, Sir Rimuru. Such a beautiful spell."

"Indeed. It was so charming!"

I had earned high marks from Diablo and Shion. Diablo must've really liked magic. *Once things calm down, I'd like to talk shop with him a little. Maybe he's got a spell or two I don't know about.* And I've got to help Shion stop being jealous of everyone around her. I can't afford any weird drama around here.

Such were my thoughts as I nodded at them, and we went on our way.

After everyone left, we were greeted by a clearly bored Veldora. "Rimuru," he asked, "can I go and beat 'em all up, too?"

I knew it. He hadn't listened to a single word I told him.

"What are you, deaf? I'm *trying* to keep you a secret until the Walpurgis Council begins! If you go crazy out there, the secret's gonna be out in two seconds!"

"Gwaaaah-ha-ha-ha! Yes, yes, of course. I almost forgot!"

"Almost," my ass. I don't know what to do with this old coot. I gave him a whole bunch of manga volumes I had stored up, but will that be enough? Because I'm really worried he's gonna try to pull something stupid. Better keep a very close eye on him.

Yohm and his squad also set off that afternoon. I look forward to having them tell everyone they run into along the way that Veldora is back—I told them to make sure and phrase it so it spreads as quickly from village to village as possible.

The purpose for this, of course, was so Clayman would hear about it as he keeps snooping on us. *Hopefully the news will reach him sooner than later,* I thought as I saw them off. Diablo told me to "expect us back very, very soon," but how much of a pushover does he think Farmus is anyway? It almost made me worried, but I still left things up to them anyway. Everybody makes mistakes, after all, and if something came up, we could think about it then.

It wasn't long after when Gazel set off toward the Dwarven Kingdom. His assorted ministers were livid, which made his departure a bit more hurried than I think he would've liked. Guess that decoy he hired wasn't up to the job, and I could guess why. I definitely shouldn't be taking any lessons from him on *that* front. Nobody likes being found out.

Another day passed—and while Benimaru reported that things were moving along well, we weren't without our problems.

Naturally, a group of thirty thousand soldiers and refugees is a little restricted in where it can go. These were stout beastmen, however, not humans, so I was told that they should reach their destination without too much delay. I wasn't too worried, though. I had something to deal with that.

"Right," I said, patting Benimaru's shoulder. "We're all ready to take in the refugees here, so I'm gonna transport all the noncombatants over to Tempest."

"Oh... There *is* that, yes..."

Benimaru groaned, chiding himself for not coming up with it first.

You know, though, that transport spell costs a *lot* of magicules. The more people you're transporting, the more it adds up. At this point yesterday, I was fresh off moving a force of twenty thousand around; I didn't really have much free energy left. I couldn't go shooting that off rapid-fire, so it wasn't like I was deliberately wasting time. Besides, this was a completely new sort of magic, one that flew in the face of conventional approaches, so we'd be able to weave this into future tactics with a lot more frequency. I mean, I don't think too many people could cast that spell anyway, so that should help preserve our unique superiority.

Regardless, Rigurd had set up the required camping quarters after I sent everyone off yesterday, so I figured we could transport the refugees alone into here. So I did it all in a snap. And none of them were nervous about it, either. I guess they were all adaptable enough that they got used to it quick.

I let Rigurd guide them around, since that work I started yesterday was still calling my name. I really wanted to finish it up in time for Walpurgis, so I just had to hope no more issues arose.

∗

In the end, the day of the Walpurgis Council began without any major crisis. My work was done before lunch, allowing me to dive into the final stages that afternoon. *Looks like I'll be on time. That's a relief.*

"Rimuru, is this…?"

"What do you think? Pretty neat, huh?"

"What're you, some kind of genius?!"

I had enough of dealing with Ramiris's yelling at me. I didn't want to engage any longer. I had to save my mental acuity for this evening, so I'd just ignore her rantings for now.

After lunch, I worked on the final touches, then placed the finished item in my Stomach and headed over to the treant village where Treyni lived. Veldora wanted to join me, but he'd have to wait. I didn't want anyone attacking town, not that I thought they would. Right now, the whole urban area was being protected by a Barrier that Veldora put over it. That prevented any potential eavesdropping from Clayman as well, so him abandoning town at the moment was a bad idea.

So I promised him "next time" and set off with Ramiris and Treyni. I assigned Beretta to deal with him, as much as it hurt my conscience. *He'll probably be used and abused, I'm sure. I'll have to reward him later.*

With a quick casting of Dominate Space, we were on our way. Once we reached the village, we quickly spotted the insectoids Apito and Zegion. When I first saved his life, Apito was maybe around a foot long, but now he had grown to nearly twenty inches. It was great to see that guy in good health. Zegion, meanwhile, was at well over two feet and strong enough that a lot of monsters knew better than to pick a fight. Of course, there weren't any monsters around here that were hostile to Zegion anyway, so there's no real way to gauge his power. I told it not to do anything too risky, so it probably hasn't. Unlike Gobta and Gabil, it knew its limits and didn't get all carried away over everything.

Apito flitted right up once it spotted me, happily providing me with some honey. *Ah, thanks! The perfect medicine. Let's have a li'l taste of that… Mm. Yep. That most rare of cure-alls—and it tastes real good, too.*

"Hey, whoa, um, Rimuru— Er, Sir Rimuru? I wanted to ask you something."

I looked toward Ramiris. She looked freaked out.

"What?"

"Those insects… Are those army wasps?"

"Hmm? I dunno."

"You don't *know*?!"

Ramiris gave me the most exaggerated double take I ever saw. So what if they're army wasps?

(Sir Rimuru,) Apito telepathically said to me, (it is as that person says. I am a queen wasp, the highest of the army wasp order. Would you like me to summon my queendom?)

Whoa, that sounds pretty fancy. I think we can go without that for now, though.

(You can save it for when this village is under attack. If you want your friends around here, I'm sure you can talk that over with the treants.)

(I'll refrain for now, then,) Apito said, wings thrumming in what sounded like a happy buzz as it flew off. It sounded quite pretty, if a bit chainsaw-like and lethal. *Are army wasps pretty dangerous beasts, then? I doubt it.* Apito, collecting honey for me and everything, hardly seemed hostile at all.

Plus, Zegion was there, too, giving me a shy salute as it followed after Apito. Maybe that guy was the king of the insects or something—it certainly *felt* kind of regal. I was pretty sure it'd only grow in strength. Maybe evolve, even. If so, I'd love to have that guy join my team.

Turning around, I saw Ramiris with her mouth agape, while Treyni was doing her best to console her.

"Yeah, you're right. I guess they *are* army wasps. Plus, one's a queen."

"I heard them! I mean, you… Ugh. Never mind. You can do just about anything, can't you? And that other one… I mean, I really don't think it could be, but…"

She wasn't making much coherent sense. I ignored her. No time to deal with it, and besides, if it was Ramiris, it couldn't be that important.

We had reached our destination—a dryas, the holy tree that was Treyni's "main" body.

I took out my completed project from my Stomach. It was an orb, dull in color. No sheen, no glow to it—but you could absolutely feel the power.

What was I going to use it for? Well, Treyni—and all dryads—were descendants of fairies, a form of spiritual life that could take on physical form by combining themselves with plants. They could freely release their spiritual bodies and use magicules to create temporary corpuses to live in. Their "real" bodies, however, were these dryas trees.

The Walpurgis Council was going to be held in some kind of special dimension, so Treyni might not be able to get in. So I decided to conduct a bit of large-scale surgery on her so she'd be able to move around in her "real" body. Unlike Beretta, which had no physical form in this world, Treyni had a corpus. As a result, we needed to transfer the "core" within her from her current body to the new one, much like a golem becoming established in its own form.

I had an idea of what this new core could be. It was a chaos core, one that can only be made with certain materials under certain conditions, and that orb I just took out would be the vessel for this core. In a way, it was like extracting magicules from the magic stones that can be taken from the cores of monsters. It's hard to make these retain no element at all, so I went through many failures before I created this. I also needed several other materials to make this orb, so I spent nearly all of yesterday gathering them.

Making a chaos core required an equal mixture of spiritual and mystical force inside this vessel. With Beretta I could've just filled them with both in equal quantities and densities, but it wasn't so simple with Treyni. She would have to inject the orb with her own spiritual energy herself, while I put in mystical force that had been mixed to an exactly proportionate density and size.

Now it was time to get to work, and that meant it was time for Raphael to shine. With my signal, Treyni began to turn her body into spiritual matter and let it flow into the orb, without a moment's hesitation. I injected the mystical force alongside her, not missing a beat. This was precision work, but it proceeded with no calculation errors.

The dryas lost its life force, visibly withering before me. Alongside that, the orb began to blink on and off, almost like a pulse. Light and darkness traced a spiral inside it—and then, the orb began to shine a light shade of green. The flickering of life was thriving inside.

Report. The individual Treyni's element has mixed into it, but construction of the chaos core is successful.

It had all gone as planned.

"Okay, it worked. This orb is now Treyni's main body."

(Thank you so much, Sir Rimuru!)

"Yeah, thanks, Rimuru! Now I can take Treyni here along with me!"

"You should be safe with that, yeah. But... Hmm..."

Treyni would no longer be separate from her main body, so she wouldn't have issues traveling across dimensions anymore. But something still seemed missing.

"Treyni, do you mind if I take this tree that used to be your body?"

"Of course not. Use it however you like."

I thanked her, then got straight to work.

"What're you gonna use it for?"

"You'll see!"

I cut down the tree, working the wood, creating precision parts with it to form a human shape.

(Oh! Ohhhhh! Is this...? Are you gonna...?!)

Ramiris quickly understood what I was up to. She was right—I thought I would make a replacement body for Treyni, using the dryas that was imbued with her magical force.

Three hours later, the doll-like figure I had been working on all afternoon was complete. Its core was reinforced with magisteel, the surface made of fully polished wood. It felt remarkably comfortable to the touch—a very fine piece of work.

"Oh, is this...?"

Even Treyni, who rarely expressed surprise at anything, couldn't hide her excitement.

"What do you think? Pretty good, huh? You can use this as your body if you want."

I didn't need to ask. Ramiris was overjoyed, but Treyni needed no encouragement from her. She thanked me profusely and installed herself in her new body. From that moment, the wooden doll became Treyni's new corpus. It was the world's first fully mobile dryad.

From the moment the chaos core—the heart of any monster, you could say—entered the doll, magic force surged out of it, penetrating and filling every grain on the surface. Then, amazingly, the white grains faded, no longer standing out, turning as intricate and detailed as human skin. Perhaps more beautiful, even. A beauty that goes beyond humanity.

Unlike with Beretta, I didn't work from a skeletal frame for the face. I simply carved the head to look the way Treyni looked. But once her orb was in there, its expression grew as soft as anyone you met on the street. It was wood, but the mouth still moved, and the eyes blinked. I have no idea what was driving that. "Because she's a monster" was my only real guess. This body *was* kind of herself, once, so maybe it was more compatible than most cases.

Either way, that pie-in-the-sky surgery of mine was a greater success than I ever could've guessed.

And for some reason, she was stronger now, too.

My mystical aura, injected into the orb so perfectly by Raphael's fine-tuned work, had produced a chaos orb that worked in exact harmony with Treyni's spiritual force. It was the equivalent of doubling her magicule stores. I think taking in the holy and demon elements earned her some new skills, too. She struck a greater presence than Shion, who boasted the most magical force out of us all. Definitely stronger than the Orc Disaster. Not up to the demon lord Carillon, but I could feel a different type of sheer awesomeness from her.

I think it could bring her to disaster level, the venerable S rank. Of course, she'd still be Special A for now, a calamity-level threat, due to not actually being a demon lord. The Guild-crafted ranking system really couldn't deal with special-case magic-born like this. Personally I'd feel safe calling her a sub-demon lord.

Between the dryas, the doll, and the dryad, we had here a creature that was worthy of awakening into a demon lord someday. That's the kind of powerful magic-born Treyni was now—and among other things, it let her join Ramiris on the trip.

I'll bet even Raphael was surprised by that one!

Understood. It was all according to plan.

See? Totally surprised. *No need to be a sore loser about it.*

…

Raphael had nothing to counter me with.

With that mental victory in hand, we all said good-bye to Treyni's sisters, Traya and Doreth. They had been watching the whole surgery, looking incredibly jealous. I suppose I should do the same thing for them, as thanks for all their work watching over the Forest of Jura…but that would have to wait. We could consider that after we were all back safe from Walpurgis. I didn't want to lose Jura's guardians because they were too busy doting on Ramiris, besides.

Well, we were now on our way back to town, and I'd now done all the preparing I could. Looking up, I realized there was no moon in the sky, the stars twinkling at me. Today *was* a new moon, wasn't it? And soon, under this beautiful night sky, the bell for the first round would ring out.

With the stars behind me, I set off for my battlefield.

INTERLUDE

THE DEMON LORDS

That Time I Got Reincarnated as a Slime

The demon lord Clayman awaited the appointed hour, a glass of wine in his hand. The Walpurgis Council was tonight, and as a mixture of anger and happiness danced across his face, he thought over a few things.

First, the bad news.

Ignoring the warnings of his friend Laplace, he had advanced his forces into the Beast Kingdom of Eurazania. But they had failed to discover even a single citizen left there. The effort had gone to waste.

The briefing from his commander Yamza drove him into a fit of rage. But until they knew why this happened, giving further orders would be careless. Instead, Clayman decided to gather his forces together and carefully continue the search.

What they found was a group of stragglers, frantically attempting to flee the kingdom. Upon being advised of them, Clayman immediately ordered an attack, sending scouts to the area to search for anyone else hidden nearby. They eventually found several hundred civilians in hiding, but as they attempted to dispatch them all, they immediately ran away.

Finding this suspect, the army conducted further investigation, only to discover that a larger group of some several thousand refugees was fleeing toward the Forest of Jura. The small group of several hundred was just bait to help the rest of them flee.

Those insolent…!

Now Clayman knew why there was nobody left living in the Beast Kingdom. They had undergone a mass emigration to Tempest, relying upon Rimuru for their continued survival. The stragglers were also on to the Clayman force's activity, fleeing the area once the bait was taken.

He wanted to have those souls safely hunted and collected before Walpurgis, but it just wasn't going to happen. He had to admit that now, and it made him deeply unhappy.

"Yamza, the Council is about to begin. I want your entire force to chase them down before I return. Kill every last one of them and bring the survivors before me!"

"I swear to you it shall happen, sir!"

He nodded, but it did nothing to overturn the fact that he wouldn't be awakening tonight. It annoyed Clayman terribly as he closed the magical link.

Meanwhile, there was good news to be had.

Using his feelers in the ground—electric signals and natural geomagnetism—he was constantly gathering information. Nobody had been fully aware of this power yet, giving Clayman free rein over a vast array of data. It was what allowed him to enjoy the alias of Marionette Master.

At the time he gained this skill, it permitted him to interact only with people or things within his line of vision. Now, however, thanks to ceaseless training and effort, it had become the keystone force of his entire empire. This unique skill—Manipulator, it was called—converted information into encrypted communications as it conducted surveillance over a wide area. Deploying a member of his team to an area allowed them to function as his eyes and ears to gather intelligence.

It was this vast network that informed him that Veldora, the Storm Dragon, had revived. This, in itself, was not welcome news—but the human beings who had spoken with the Storm Dragon and apparently survived the experience had some very fascinating things to say.

According to conversations surreptitiously heard from adventurer types leaving the monster town, Rimuru, self-styled leader of the forest, hadn't defeated the Farmus force at all. The missing army was the result of the Storm Dragon's resurrection—and since he had only just been reborn, the dragon's stores of magicules were largely lost, emptied out as it raged upon Farmus's army. That explained why there was no massive onrush of magicules around the Forest of Jura, as one would expect from such a cataclysmic event. That these adventurers lived to tell the tale was another sure indicator.

If the Storm Dragon Veldora was alive once more, there was no way Clayman, a demon lord, wouldn't have picked up on that. The rumors must have been true, then—he lost his magic force during the battle with Farmus.

These two pieces of news conflicted Clayman.

It would be a simple matter to slay that dragon right now. I may even be able to add him to my cache of pawns...

A tantalizing fantasy. The dragon has been using the town the monsters built as his personal den, it seemed, and it was hard to gather information in that area...but he felt no need for concern. Those empty stores of magicules wouldn't rebuild themselves in two or three days. After Walpurgis, he'd have all the time in the world to snare him.

And if all else fails, I can simply send Milim after him. For now, though...

It was time to concentrate on the Council.

Or perhaps, if Clayman hadn't been over-reliant upon Milim's strength...he might have noticed all the points that didn't quite add up.

The fact that there wasn't a single enemy casualty yet. The force, reportedly scattered all across the Beast Kingdom, was now gathered together. Both pieces of information were too important for someone as careful as Clayman to overlook. But it wasn't Clayman on the ground—it was Yamza. And Clayman's mind was too full of the upcoming Council to notice. That was how vital this Wal-purgis was.

Out of nowhere, Ramiris—a demon lord who preferred to remain incognito, cooped up in her labyrinth, most of the time—asked for Rimuru, the subject of the meeting, to be extended an invite as a supplementary condition. Clayman hadn't accounted for that possibility; it prevented him from making a snap judgment. But as he groused over it, the others quickly agreed to the suggestion, making it impossible to stage any resistance.

Still, this could lead to good things for him.

It's better this way. Now we've unmasked Rimuru's true nature. I was almost fooled into believing that he leveled the Farmus military by himself…but there's no hiding the truth.

Clayman grinned. If Rimuru was joining the Council, he should consider himself welcome. There, before all the other demon lords, he'd know exactly how powerless he really is.

A mere slime, borrowing the majesty of a dragon for his boasts! I hope you consider it an honor to be crushed by my own hands!

He went back to fantasizing about his own future glories. And that was why he missed it. Those small yet glaring inconsistencies out on the battlefield.

"…You be careful, too, okay, Clayman? Now's not the time to be too reckless."

His friend's words flashed across his mind. Now, a small sense of unease was taking root. The nagging feeling that he had missed something. But he laughed it off.

Don't you worry, Laplace. I will win this…

He drained his wineglass, as if to wash the anxiety away.

●

It was with a somber gloom that Frey prepared for the Council. Things were in a constant state of flux. The original plan had all but gone by the wayside. She didn't expect any of this, and now it was all too unclear how things would shake out.

But she wasn't nervous. She was aware of her limits, and she always made decisions based on cold, hard facts. That was how the Sky Queen always acted. If all went well, then fine. If not...she would have to prepare to make the right move herself.

It all began with a certain promise. In order to defeat Charybdis, she had accepted an offer from Clayman. In exchange, she agreed to take one request from him.

....

......

...

Several months ago, Milim visited Frey's domain. She didn't exactly slip in unnoticed. There was a loud *bang!* as she shoved the doors open and ran into the room.

Frey didn't bat an eye. Milim always acted like this. When she felt that massive aura—one Milim never bothered to hide—she knew it had to be her.

"Hey, Frey! Beautiful day out, huh?!"

She beamed at her, playing around with her beautiful platinum-pink hair to show it off. Was Frey busy at the moment? Who cares?

On Milim's hand, however, was something new. Not a ring—a brass knuckle covering her four fingers. It was something far too boorish for most young women, but on Milim, it couldn't have been more perfect. It had a relief of a dragon carved into it, half aglow in magical aura, and it fit snugly in her clenched little hand.

"Mmmm, maybe a little too hot, though?" she said as she fanned her face with one hand. It was obvious what she was doing. She never gave a crap about the weather.

"Oh, Milim. Haven't seen you in a while. You look like you're doing well. Did something nice happen to you?"

Frey had to take the bait. Otherwise, she'd have to put up with this act for the next hour.

"Ooh, you could tell? Well, just look at this!"

She thrust her Dragon Knuckle–equipped hand in front of Frey's face, giving her a proud little *eh-hem!*

Frey glumly sighed. "Oh, wow," she said, giving Milim what she thought the girl wanted. "It looks great on you. Where'd it come from?"

"Oh, you wanna know?" came the bashful reply. "Oooh, I dunno if I can tell you or not… Hmm, ohhh, what should I doooo?"

This I'm-the-best act was grating on Frey. Despite all the years they had known each other, it still rankled her.

"Well, aren't we *friends*, Milim? It's all right to tell me, isn't it?"

Milim's eyes sparkled. "Ooh! Oh yeah, we sure are friends, huh?! Okay, I'll tell you! To tell the truth—"

Now that Milim finally had the invitation she wanted, she burst into a long story about the town of monsters she visited. The self-aggrandizing tale went on for a while, accompanied by several wardrobe changes from the new clothes she picked up there. It gave Frey some pause. Milim loved carrying on about herself all the time, but rarely to *this* level.

Once the conversation died down a little, Frey realized that now was the time to do the favor she promised Clayman.

"Oh, right. You know, Milim, I actually have a present for you, too. From friend to friend. Would you like to see it?"

She signaled to her attendants. They quickly brought over a tray bearing a beautiful, shining pendant, perched on top of purple satin cloth. An orb had been installed on the pendant, a jewel that even someone who knew nothing about precious stones could tell was worth a fabulous amount of money.

"Mm? A pendant, huh? Can I have it? But that doesn't mean you can have my knuckle, okay?"

Frey chuckled. "That's fine, Milim. Consider it a symbol of our friendship. And as a friend, I hope you won't be too shy to wear it around."

Milim gave a bright nod to Frey's soft smile. "You got it!" she chirped as she attached it to her clothing.

Forbidden magic: Demon Marionette launching… Activated.

At that instant, the expression on Milim's face changed. Her eyes glazed over; the light of consciousness faded away from them. With the magic in the pendant released, a forbidden spell wormed its way into her.

This jewel was the Orb of Domination provided by Clayman to Frey—and having Milim put it on was the promised favor Clayman asked of her.

So there's my promise. That takes care of my duty, but what will Milim do...?

Frey observed the girl. She stood there motionless, face a total blank. Then, for just a single moment, she felt like Milim's blue eyes looked at her.

There, at that moment, Milim knew something weird was happening. *Maybe... Yes. Indeed. I suppose it is, Milim...*

The Dragon Knuckle fell out of her fingers, clunking on the ground. Frey looked at her and sighed.

"I'm done, Clayman," she called out to an empty corner of the room. "Are you happy?"

"I am," the Marionette Master replied, emerging from the corner. "Well done, Frey. Now I've obtained the strongest puppet there is! Ha-ha-ha-ha! This is what she gets for picking on me, calling me a young upstart. Pathetic, isn't it, Milim?!"

He punched her as he laughed his nasal laugh. Her face reddened, a cut appearing on her lips. The multiple layers of Barrier protecting her were gone, meaning that even she could be hurt now—especially if it was a demon lord like Clayman doing the hurting.

"Shouldn't you stop that?" Frey coldly commented as the half-giggling Clayman prepared to land another blow. It wasn't a pretty sight to see, and besides—

"Pfft! This isn't the sort of weak curse that'll undo itself after a punch or two. This is *forbidden* magic. It includes all the magic force I can muster from my body. Don't you resent her at all, after the way she acted around all of us? *That's* why you joined me on this plan, is it not?"

"It's not. I just fulfilled my promise to you."

"No need to lie to her face like that, you know. This girl is nothing more than a doll to us now. A pointlessly sturdily made doll, I should add. We can just fix her before she falls completely apart."

The veins were visible in his eyes as he kicked Milim away, Frey coldly watching the whole time. *Such an impertinent man. This is how you really are...?*

It was at that moment when Frey abandoned Clayman for good. Thus, she decided to act on her own instincts for a change.

"Listen, Clayman. Maybe you don't know, but Milim comes with a self-defense mechanism, all right? The way she described it, at least, it's called Stampede, and it puts her in an uncontrollable state. You're free to trigger that and die if you like, but try not to take me with you."

The words were enough to restore Clayman's composure. He resentfully groaned. "Psh. What a bastard of a demon lord this is. Very well. Using her *should* give my words a little more presence among us all. And you, Frey; you're a coconspirator as well. I'll expect you to work for me."

"Oh? I thought we were equals."

"Fool! I'm the one who came up with this plan. You're already one of my pawns. Or would you like to engage Milim in battle?"

"...Are you threatening me?"

"Ha-ha-ha-ha! You can take that any way you like. But if you don't want to die, I'd suggest not angering me."

It was classic Clayman—sometimes offering the carrot, other times the stick, but always with a heaping helping of arrogance. And it's true; this *was* Clayman's plan all along. That, and it was his hint to Frey that Milim had a weakness for the word *friend*. How he managed to learn *that* little tidbit, she didn't know, but all Frey did was keep her promise—although she only did so because of one she firmly believed in.

"...All right."

"Good. Just don't think about doing anything to betray me. As long as you listen to my requests a bit, I will personally guarantee your position as ruler of the skies."

The escape route was cut off. Now Frey was Clayman's business associate—a fancy name for his puppet. All of this happened several weeks before the Day of Ruin that visited Tempest.

....

......

...

Thinking it all over again, Frey sighed.

With Milim under his wing, Clayman was using her overwhelming potential violence as a cudgel to coerce her with. Now Frey was simply following orders, forced to do his bidding.

She couldn't help but laugh at how much she deserved this. She felt like such a fool for believing him. But she also had another thought. Clayman was a sly, conniving demon lord, never one to play down, but he also tended to overestimate his own powers. That's why he never had a perspective on the true essence of things. Frey, luckily, was blessed with exactly those observational skills—not a "skill" like breathing fire, but something she naturally picked up in her relations with other people. The ability to see the kind of truth that someone like Clayman, who treated people as nothing more than useful tools, could never notice.

So, trusting her instincts, she made a bet. And no matter how it turned out:

I don't think you'll be alive for much longer, Clayman.

She began going over the procedure to come. The "promise" came to mind once again. It made her smile.

●

The frigid land was encased in howling snow and ice, surrounded by frozen tundra. Temperatures stayed at well below zero degrees Fahrenheit, driving away nearly all life.

In the middle of it all stood a tall, looming castle, a beautiful, fantastical palace. A demon castle, one materialized from an unimaginable amount of magical force. It was called Icefayr Castle, and it was the domain of the demon lord Guy Crimson.

A calm, collected man strode along a corridor inside the castle, his hair of platinum blond, eyes long and narrow. Those blue eyes were a prominent feature of his chiseled visage. His skin was fair, practically translucent, and his beauty would almost make some assume he was female.

This was the demon lord Leon Cromwell, known alternately as either the Platinum Devil or the Platinum Saber, and he stalked the halls of this castle like he owned them.

Ahead of him was a large door, decorated ornately by a master woodsmith. It led to the audience chamber where the master of this domain awaited. Leon was here to see Guy Crimson, and as he stood before the door, two large, heavy magic-born grunted and strained to open it up.

"The demon lord Leon Cromwell has arrived!"

A beautiful female magic-born beyond the door shouted Leon's name as he entered. There, he saw two lines of powerful Greater Demons lining the way ahead on both sides. Each one was a named demon, and each had been granted physical corpuses for use in this world. All of them were powerful beyond the definition of a Greater Demon, easily surpassing what a high-level magic-born could manage. They were also bedecked in a fine array of magical equipment, each having evolved in their own unique ways. They numbered two hundred or more in all, and some were even calamity-class threats, rated Special A on the scale.

But not even these demons could defy the figures beyond—the sheer overpowering awe exuded by the six demons that surrounded the throne in the chamber's midpoint, under the watchful eye of Guy Crimson.

These were named Arch Demons, capable of subduing even calamity-class monsters. If anything, they could be defined as demon lords themselves.

Amazingly, not even *these* demon kings were allowed to speak freely in this chamber—for there was a wall, an impregnable force, that none of them could ever conquer.

The green-haired demon that heralded Leon's arrival was soon joined by a demon with blue hair that guided him down the aisle. She was gorgeous, the personification of all human desires. Her graceful, wispy arms were hidden in the sleeves of a dark-red maid's dress.

The green-haired one was Mizeri, the blue-haired one Raine, and they were the two pillars who stood on both sides of the absolute ruler Guy Crimson, doing the speaking for him. They were both Demon Peers, superpowered creatures that each rated a disaster classification—the equal of a demon lord.

Now Leon was at the throne. Mizeri and Raine nodded at him, then took their posts beside Guy as the man on the throne stood up. The only people in this room allowed to move a muscle were the two demon lords.

"It gladdens me to see you, Leon," he said in a clear voice that carried across the chamber. "Doing well, I hope? I appreciate your answering my invitation."

His bloodred eyes had stars of gold and silver dancing in them, and his wavy, burning hair was a deep shade of rouge. He was about as tall as Leon, and while Leon was feminine in his beauty, Guy's was more prideful and distant. He had an alluring sort of attractiveness, the look of one born to lead—and conquer.

He walked down the steps from his throne as he greeted Leon, bringing an arm to his chest and embracing him. Then, without hesitation, he placed his hand upon Leon's face and kissed his lips.

Leon pushed him away, wincing. "Leave me," he complained, like he always did. He glared at Guy, looking genuinely peeved. "I am not interested in other men. How many times have I told you?"

"Ah-ha-ha-ha! Oh, you never were any fun like that," Guy gleefully replied. "I'd be happy to become a woman for you, if you like. But very well. Let us change locations."

He walked off, without waiting for a response. This, too, was how it happened every time.

Considering the arctic region he lived in, Guy's clothing was quite unusual. He mostly had his clothes draped over him, revealing a great deal of bare skin. To Guy, who never felt the cold anyway, that was never an issue. He wore a near-mystical smile to complement his bewitching beauty, perhaps recalling the sensation of Leon's lips

against his—and then a snakelike tongue licked his bright-red lips, creating an eerie sort of irresistible allure.

For Guy, who could adjust his gender at will, men and women were both targets of his sexual appetite. He—or she, depending—was Guy Crimson, demon lord, master of this castle, and the oldest and strongest of demon lords. As the Lord of Darkness, he was the sole and absolute ruler of this blindingly cold continent.

Guy pressed on ahead, not bothering to guide Leon. Leon followed behind, as if this was normal to him. No one else in the audience chamber moved until they were both gone. It was forbidden. They all bowed their heads to them, waiting for their ruler and his guest to leave.

Once all were sure they were gone, Mizeri and Raine stood before the rows of demons. And then, a single word from Raine:

"Disperse."

Then the two Demon Peers left, setting off to prepare tea for their guest. They were the highest-ranked among all the demons in this castle, but their sole occupation was to take care of Guy Crimson. This work was prioritized above all else in this domain—and so they quickly set off, not wanting to attract their master's ire.

. . . .

. . . . . .

. . .

Following Guy, Leon stepped into the ice terrace on the highest floor of the castle. Despite being open to the elements, not a single snowflake made its way inside. It was a comfortable, fully air-conditioned environment, and since Guy was wholly unaffected by the temperature around him, he had set this up exclusively for Leon's sake. He might have been arrogant, but when it came to his friends or those who recognized his authority, he took care of them down to the last detail.

Musing about how little Guy had changed, Leon gruffly threw himself down in his seat. It was made of ice but didn't feel cold at all. That didn't faze him, nor did the way the ice bent pliably under him, providing a soft cushion.

"So," he asked, "what did you call me here for?"

An ice table appeared out of nowhere. Raine lined up two cups of tea on it, as Mizeri soundlessly stood by the terrace entrance. They were not to interfere with their masters' speech, unable to speak themselves without permission. This was not at all an equal relationship. Until ordered, they could not even allow their emotions to be shown in public. If they ever acted on their own without their master's orders, they would be provided with nothing but a quick death.

Even Demon Peers as powerful as them both were mere tools before the demon lord. That was how strong Guy was, and that was why they wouldn't move even if Leon attacked Guy right there. His rule was absolute, and worrying for his safety was the height of disrespect. Their presences were thus ignored as the conversation continued.

"Well, as you know, a Walpurgis Council is coming soon. I thought I should implore you to attend, no matter how inconvenient it was."

"Oh? Rare of you to force anything upon me like that."

"I know. Even if it means I owe you a favor, I want you to participate."

"...Why is that?"

"Ha!" Guy smiled, enjoying this. "Wary as always, I see. Very well. Let me explain. It was Clayman who proposed this one. A little man. But for some reason, Milim's name was among the cosigners. Milim is one of the oldest demon lords, up there with me. She wouldn't lift a finger for someone the likes of Clayman. So I believe..."

"You believe that reports of Carillon's death might not be entirely true?"

"Oh, you know, do you?" Guy resented having his thoughts guessed so easily.

Leon paid it no mind. "Clayman went too far," he continued. "He tried to harass me without leaving any evidence behind, but I'm not letting it pass this time. Whether Carillon lives or not, if Milim is taking action, that is bad news."

Guy gave this a relieved nod. "Hmm. I agree with you. This might be just another game to Milim, but I don't like to see anyone tipping the balance of power among the demon lords. It just gives me more work."

Waiting to make sure Guy was no longer peeved, Leon decided to tackle the question that interested him the most.

"So, Guy, do you think Milim is being controlled by Clayman?"

"Thinking about Milim is pointless," came the blunt reply. "Someone like me is too intelligent to read the behavior of a moron. That is one of my very few weaknesses." He shrugged and gave Leon a broad grin, then went back to his first question. "But if you worry about it that much, Leon, should I assume you will be participating?"

Leon could tell that dancing around each other like this would lead them nowhere. "Yes, I intend to. I hate working with others, but this time, I suppose I have no choice."

"Oh? Well, very good. Before then, I was hoping we could embrace each other in bed later this evening—"

"I have no interest in men. *Or* in women, unless they strike my fancy. Besides, what benefit would embracing you, as you put it, have for me?"

"You don't have to start with *that*. If you wish, I would happily take on a woman's body for you..."

Guy slithered in for a hug. Leon, seeing it a mile away, dodged it beautifully. One saw this little exchange between them on regular occasions.

"By the way," he said after it was clear Leon wasn't putting up with it, "it's rather rare for Ramiris to provide feedback to us one way or the other, but do you know anything about this 'Rimuru' person?"

This was another topic of the next Walpurgis, something everyone had an interest in since it'd mark the first new demon lord after Leon.

"The way Clayman puts it," Leon replied, "he's just a self-styled demon lord. Personally, if he has the strength to back it up, I have no problem with him."

"Ah. So you think Rimuru is qualified to be a demon lord? I was just wondering, since Ramiris, of all people, is involved. If someone's piqued her interest *that* much, it should be a lot of fun for me."

Although this Walpurgis was convened by Clayman, Ramiris had made the additional proposal of having Rimuru himself attend. By Guy's estimate, Ramiris must've had something to say about Clayman's actions here.

"...Ramiris? I have trouble dealing with that fairy. She makes fun of me every time we meet. I've thought about strangling her to death countless times..."

...But if it was Ramiris making this request, Leon had to agree with it. He couldn't help but feel like he owed that much to her.

"Ah-ha-ha-ha! Better not. If you kill her, you'd be making me your enemy, you realize."

"I'm sure. I wasn't being serious. Besides, there's no way I'd win in a fight against you."

That was no lie. Leon was no fan of Ramiris and her big mouth, but he didn't actually mean her harm. And to be honest, he had no hope of beating Guy. They were both equal in demon lord rank, but the difference in strength was like night and day. Leon was closer to Mizeri and Raine than Guy on that score. There was just no comparison.

"Mm? I wouldn't be so sure. Maybe you'd kill me one in a million times?"

"Don't be ridiculous. I'm not interested in a fight I'm not guaranteed to win."

"Quit being so modest. There aren't many people who could wound me. The mere fact that you have a chance of killing me makes you more than strong enough, Leon."

"Pfft. The truth's the truth. You and Milim are on a different echelon from us. And speaking of that..."

Leon was reminded of something—the reported resurrection of Veldora, the Storm Dragon. And when he told that story, Leon managed to honestly shock Guy for the first time in his life.

*   *   *

Just then, an icy, shrill voice echoed across the terrace, cutting them off.

"Oh my. I am *very* interested in that topic."

The voice was a perfect match for the beautiful woman it belonged to. Her skin was like porcelain, her eyes a fascinating sort of cold, glowing blue diamond in color. Her pearl-white hair cascaded past her cheeks, where the light-green shade of her lips drew the eye.

She was allowed to move and speak without Guy's permission, shining more beautifully than any crown jewel. She was praised as the Ice Empress by some, but to the rest of the world, she was known as Velzard, the Ice Dragon—one of only four dragon types to exist, and the demon lord Guy Crimson's friend and partner. Just like Leon, she was on equal footing with Guy.

"Ah, Velzard," Leon said, dripping with sarcasm. "I suppose there *was* a dragon type here, wasn't there?"

"My, cold as always, aren't we? But I'm glad to have the chance to see you."

"Are you? Well, it's a great honor to have a glimpse at your face."

There was little real emotion behind this exchange.

"You never did get along with each other," Guy observed with a groan. Not that he had any interest in mediating. Normally, this would kick off a series of back-and-forth put-downs, but today Velzard changed the subject.

"So the topic you were discussing? Sir Leon, my younger brother has awoken?" Her blue eyes were shining as she asked for details on Leon's big news. "You are sure of that, Leon?"

"I stopped feeling his presence two years ago, so I assumed he had met his end, but...?"

If Veldora had resurrected himself, it would've been obvious. His massive, out-of-control aura would've changed the world's weather patterns. But none of that happened. Guy and Velzard could be excused for their shock.

"It's no mistake. A spy I sent to the Western Nations reported as much to me."

"Oh...? So why is that evil dragon acting so obedient? Has he weakened to the point that he can no longer replenish his magicule stores?"

"And who would've undone the seal placed upon him? I don't think he could've broken out by himself..."

The Hero had sealed Veldora away—and Velzard had done nothing to save him from it. To her, this was a good way to teach Veldora a lesson for all that selfish rioting. She figured she would spring him out before he disappeared for good, once he was a bit more mature. But then he really *did* disappear, which perplexed her. It happened much quicker than she anticipated.

"As the spy put it, Clayman's scheming was the cause. He had impressed upon the Western Nations, and the larger kingdom of Farmus in particular, to defeat and destroy the Great Forest of Jura Alliance this Rimuru character has established. The results cost Farmus its entire military force and caused Rimuru to place his hat in the demon lord ring."

"You know much about this, Leon."

"Of course I do. I'm a former human, unlike you. I've also just recently learned that Veldora was apparently sleeping right in the middle of the most intense combat. Just before his soul disappeared for good, he was exposed to vast amounts of blood, and it awoke him. That is the truth."

The Farmus troops were subsequently massacred by his rage, he went on to explain, although Rimuru escaped injury.

"So *that's* it? The seal just undid itself?"

"That much, I can't tell you."

Velzard nodded at this. Leon could be right, but a single spy's report wasn't enough to make a policy decision from. The Hero's unique skill Unlimited Imprisonment encased its target in a dimension of an imaginary number, shutting out any access or interaction with the real world. But now Veldora was exercising his presence here, once more?

"Perhaps the Hero's seal wasn't so complete after all..."

This made sense to her...before Leon corrected her.

"That's possible, yes, but I have another theory. What if someone swallowed Veldora up, seal and all, and placed him in another sub-space of their own making?"

Guy smiled giddily at this. "Ooh, I like that! So someone did undo the Hero's seal, then! The seal's too interwoven with the Hero's own abilities to be undone by any normal skill. Perhaps you or I could do it…but if this person exists, then he must be as power-ful as us. How fun!"

"It is just a possibility, keep in mind."

"And you think this person might be Rimuru, Leon?"

"…Exactly."

"I see, I see. Then we definitely *do* need to size this person up."

Now it made sense to Guy. No wonder Leon wasn't showing his typical reluctance to attend a Council. Clayman was engaged in reckless violence; Milim was acting unusually strange; Rimuru undid Veldora's seal and declared himself demon lord. What if all these events were actually connected? At the very least, it'd make this Walpurgis a hell of a lot of fun.

A longing smile erupted across Guy's face. "You know," he whis-pered, "why Veldora is acting so obedient, then?"

"…I think he's been weakened," replied Velzard. "I'm receiving only the tiniest of reactions from his presence. Nothing like before."

Even as a fellow dragon type, Velzard had to concentrate to receive even a weak blip from her younger brother. If his energy had been drained, that would explain that.

"Strange that he hasn't acted out at all, though. With his person-ality, violence is practically what he lives for."

Velzard was having trouble making sense of all this, too.

"Well, be that as it may," Leon matter-of-factly replied, "I'm not terribly interested in Veldora. If you want to try to drag an old friend of yours back here, be my guest."

While Velzard was family, and Guy had torn his hair out figuring out what to do with Veldora in the past, Leon had no connection to Veldora. As long as this dragon didn't mess with his domain, he had no intention of being involved. That's how dangerous Veldora was to him.

"Are you leaving?"

"Yeah. That's all you needed from me, right?"

"Well, one moment. No need for all the rush. I wanted to ask: Have you made any progress in pursuing your real goal? You know, targeted summoning?"

Guy was referring to the experimentation Leon had spent much of his life working on. He was just as interested in the subject as Leon.

"...Not quite yet on that, no. I changed up my plan and tried having them perform summons at random, but that ended in failure as well. It just attracted too much attention, you see. I brought the theory of 'incomplete summons' to the Western Nations, but the Free Guild interfered with me. It's already a horribly inefficient way of going about this business, and it'll face another obstacle in the future. Once it does, I'll just have to find another way."

To put it in an extreme way, Leon really didn't care about the Council or the new demon lord. He was simply trying to pick out young weeds before they grew and got in his way.

"Obstacle?"

"Yeah. This one apparently saved the lives of some kids who were just waiting to die. Before I could pick them up, no less."

"Ah. So they were forced into rescue before you saw any results? And you're sure you'll continue being interfered with?"

"Seems likely. He got angry about all these nations summoning children, so he may start applying pressure to each of them. So it's time to clear out that experiment. If we go any further with it, he'll find out that I'm there, behind the scenes."

"Hmm. Could you perhaps rub out this hindrance?"

Guy hinted with his eyes that it'd be all too easy for Leon. But his friend simply sighed.

"Well, this 'hindrance' is the exact Rimuru we were just discussing."

"What?! That's no coincidence, is it?"

"Funny, isn't it?" Leon nodded, face dead serious. "That's why I wanted to meet him for myself sometime."

Of course, he still could've afforded to ignore this Rimuru person, if only Ramiris hadn't chosen to stick her nose in...

"All right. This seems to be getting more curious all the time.

Perhaps Milim is thinking along similar lines, too. She may be a moron, but she's got quite the instinct for this kind of thing."

"Perhaps. Tonight's Walpurgis could be a rather raucous occasion."

"Hee-hee! No doubt about it."

Leon and Guy exchanged smiles as the gentle blue eyes of Velzard watched over them. They proceeded to chitchat a little more before Guy changed the subject.

"By the way, I had been wondering about something else. Who is this collaborator of yours providing your information?"

"I don't know much about him. He seems to be a human from the Empire, and he calls himself a merchant."

Summoning an otherworlder required vast amounts of magical energy, exacting conditions, and convoluted rituals to work. The pickier you were about who you summoned, the longer you had to wait before you could attempt the summon again. To get around this, Leon did some business with this merchant, who then conducted the summons for him.

"And this merchant can be trusted?"

"Trusted? Trust never needs to be involved. All I'm doing is using him."

"Ah. Well, if that's fine with you, I have no complaints. But be careful, all right? I don't want you dying on me."

"Heh. You, worried about me? That's a rare sight from you, Guy. But don't worry. I have no plans to die until I'm finished with my goals."

"Again with those 'goals.' It's that important to you?"

"It sure is. I'd put them ahead of well near everything else in this world."

"Hmm. I'm starting to feel jealous."

"Don't give me that nonsense. But I will accept your warning. See you tonight."

With that, Leon left the terrace. Guy refrained from stopping him this time, as Leon left a single shining crystal and used Spatial Motion to set off.

A pair of eyes watched him go.

"Talk about impatient. I know that's how Leon is..."

Guy grinned a little as he spoke softly.

"It feels to me that Leon is leaving himself uncharacteristically open to attack," Velzard observed in her icy voice. "He's working with people without even knowing who they are. Should I investigate for him?"

"Nah," Guy replied, unconcerned. "Meddling in Leon's affairs would just offend him. I don't want my friends to hate me."

To him, Leon was a trusted friend, someone whose personality he was keenly aware of by now. He knew about Leon's talent more than anyone else. If Leon wasn't looking into his cohorts' backgrounds, it must have been because he saw no great need to.

"If he asks us for a favor, you can help him out then."

"All right."

And that was the end of their conversation.

Now the attendees of tonight's Walpurgis were set in stone.

Clayman proposed the Council; Frey and Milim signed on to it. Ramiris, with her additional proposal, was also attending, as was the homebody Leon.

Speaking of homebodies, there was another demon lord whose location was a complete enigma. Guy had reached out via their specialized demon lord connection, all but demanding that one's attendance.

Beyond that, there was his old friend Daggrull, along with... Hmm. What about that other guy? He *should* be coming. Daggrull promised to bring him along. And that just left Guy himself. It'd mark the first Walpurgis in a while to have all the demon lords show up, except for the missing Carillon.

"It should be a fun one, for sure. You want to join me?"

"Hmm..." Velzard reflected on this. "No, I think I won't. Perhaps if my brother were there, but otherwise, I have no interest in demon lords."

"No? All right. Keep the lights on for me."

"I would be glad to. Now, time to prepare."

Velzard stood up, leaving Guy to brood over the upcoming Walpurgis as he gazed at the aurora covering the frigid land.

A demon lord working behind the scenes, head full of schemes.

A newer demon lord, but one that could crumble at any time.

An old friend who was starting to get surprisingly active, considering he hardly left the house.

And then the potential birth of a new demon lord.

So exciting! His heart hadn't sung like this for hundreds of years.

He needed real change like this. Demon lords weren't friends; they were supposed to be competing with one another. There was no artificial limit placed on their number—there were times when a dozen existed at once, even more. Whether it's ten or a hundred, anything was fine. If they weren't strong enough, they'd get pushed out of the picture the next time a Temma War came around, every five hundred years.

It's just that each time that happened, this new crop would fight for a piece of the pie, and to combat this, the maximum number of demon lords was finally set at ten. The human world, once they became aware of this, started calling them the Ten Great Demon Lords. Guy was firmly against it, but it became a sort of tacit agreement among them. The humans didn't mind the demon lords picking one another off until they were a more manageable number. Ten was enough.

But Guy figured it was time to put an end to that. The weak didn't deserve the title demon lord. Perhaps it was time for a new era of rule to unfold—one, he thought, where *real* demon lords held sway.

Guy was one of the seven Primal Demons, and the first demon lord to be summoned to this world as an Arch Demon. Each of these demons had a primary color associated with them, and his was Rouge.

He was an unnamed demon unleashed upon the world, fulfilling the wishes of the powerless human who summoned him and destroying a nation that the human was apparently at war with.

He followed that up by destroying his human's own nation as well. That earned him his name—Guy, pronounced "ghee." An unpleasant-sounding name, like the shrieks of the doomed and desperate as he crushed them.

Upon being named, Guy realized he had awakened into his new class of "true" demon lord. He thought it needless at first, given that he believed he was already the strongest out there—but this evolution also affected the Primal Demons Vert and Bleu, summoned alongside him as errand girls. They, too, were given physical bodies to work with, as well as the brand-new class of Demon Peer.

On a whim, Guy decided to make them his servants and gave them names. For Vert, Mizeri, reflecting the misery of mankind. For Bleu, Raine, the rains of blood that fell wherever he strode. They had been faithful to him ever since.

Just after Guy awakened to demon lord-dom, another one did the same. That was Milim, a girl conceived by a human in this world and the first of the four dragon types that ever threatened it. That dragon had paid for its strange dalliance by losing the majority of his power to his own child. The act had been reviled as taboo ever since.

Upon losing his power, the dragon type dispersed his body, came to the surface to attain a physical form, and became the founder of the dragons as they existed in this world. This led to dragon types as being defined as the self-sentient propagations of natural spirits, the prototypes, and all the dragons that existed and thrived in the world came from this first father—Veldanava, the Star-King Dragon.

One day, the Star-King Dragon gave his daughter a pet, a young dragon that would serve as his next incarnation someday. This "pet" was killed by a certain foolish kingdom that ignited Milim's rage, causing the very heavens to tremble as the nation was destroyed. This made Milim awaken, and the resulting new force sent her wholly out of control, almost wiping all life away from the world.

It was Guy who stopped her. The battle took place over seven days and seven nights, the most severe anyone had ever seen, turning the bountiful fields of the west into an utter wasteland.

In the end, no winner could be crowned. The battle ended once

Milim regained her senses. It was Ramiris who did this, back then a leader of spirits who sacrificed her own power to neutralize Milim's rage. She paid a heavy price for this. Being exposed to the auras of demons and dragons sapped her force and made her fall to the world's surface, becoming a continually self-resurrecting fairy.

But it did the trick. It prevented the end of the world and allowed Guy and Milim to come to an agreement.

These were the first three demon lords, and each had their own goals.

One wanted to find the farthest reaches of power.
One wanted to live free from all barriers.
One wanted to promote balance in the world.

But that was fine. These differing goals were exactly why they could see one another as equals.

The demon lord ranks were soon swelled by a giant protecting the gates to heaven, as well as a vampire from ancient times. A figure fallen from heaven became number six. This was the second generation—not as strong as the oldest but more than strong enough to rule over the world.

The giant's body was too imbued with the holy element to allow the seeds of demon lord-dom to take root, but he was still so blindingly strong that he got in anyway—an unusual path to take. The old vampire was shrewd, sly, and more conniving than any of the others—although someone else was currently occupying her seat at the Council for her.

The sixth one was interesting. Definitely strong, but completely uninterested in the world. Laziness was the watchword here. No doubt had the ability to rule the land but probably still living just as "fallen" as ever somewhere.

Four out of the six demon lords at this point had "awakened" to the job, apart from the giant and the fairy. They had survived multiple Great Wars, polishing their skills with each one—enough so to earn ultimate skills, like Guy's and Milim's.

In addition to them, there was Guy's friend, Leon. Leon was a human and a former Hero. A unique upbringing led to him picking up an ultimate skill, making him strong enough even to satisfy Guy's strict standards.

That made seven. And how many of this next Walpurgis's attendees would live up to the standard of these seven? Guy couldn't wait to see.

And then there was Clayman.

That fool thought he could rule over Milim. It was just too hilarious. Guy could barely contain his laughter. *That* was impossible. If Guy couldn't do it, there was no way someone like Clayman could. Lower-level skills simply didn't work on those who possessed ultimate skills. All the natural laws that ruled this world were nothing more than unique cases to them; they could easily nullify any magical attempt to cloud their minds.

An elemental attack that struck at their weak points might have some effect, yes. But mind-domination magic? Out of the question. Anyone spineless enough to be ruled over by conditions like *that* would never be able to obtain an ultimate skill in the first place.

Ultimate skills, as the name implied, gave the wielder ultimate power to control the very laws of nature. The only way to counter an ultimate skill was with another ultimate skill. That was the absolute, unbendable rule of this world.

Clayman couldn't do a thing against Milim. Milim was just having him dance on the palm of her hand.

What a fool...

Guy flashed a weak smile as he watched the events unfold.

The era of weaklings styling themselves as demon lords had come to an end. The fakers would get sifted out; the generation of true demon lords would begin. Guy was sure of it. He smiled.

And thus he set off for what was bound to be the most chaotic Walpurgis in recent memory.

CHAPTER
4

IN THE LAND OF
DESTINY

That Time I Got Reincarnated as a Slime

So everything was set. After giving my final instructions to Veldora, I waited for an envoy to direct me to the Council site. I didn't know where it was, so I'd be going along with Ramiris—who, by the way, also didn't know.

I asked why, and she had replied, "Because someone always comes to *take* me there!" Which made sense, I suppose, in its own way. The way she always got lost, wherever she went, I guess it's just a given that she had a guide. If someone doesn't really feel like memorizing a route, they never will, no matter how many times they repeat it.

Either way, I figured someone would be teleporting in to guide us, so I decided to wait for that.

It was almost an hour before midnight when I was contacted—not by an envoy, but by Benimaru.

"What's up? Some kind of problem?"

I was expecting the worst, but Benimaru instead had a request for me. Battle had just begun with the enemy, and we already had a full gauge of their capacity.

The gifts Benimaru earned from my awakening had upgraded his class to Oni. This was a type of spiritual life-form, along the lines of the dryads—Benimaru, in other words, had reached the same lofty heights as Treyni. Shuna, Soei, and Hakuro were all Onis as well, which put them about as high up on that ladder as you can go.

This was wonderful, but the issue was the skill Benimaru obtained. The unique skill Born Leader was geared toward granting enhanced control over his powers, as befitting the naturally aggressive Benimaru. No matter how much of it he unleashed, he could keep himself from rampaging out of control. Its secret lay in Compute Prediction, which could fully read the flow of power in his body and prevent bursts of waste.

It was also useful in battles between large armies, not just in duels. He could sense the flow of power among his forces, reading his chances for victory like a prophet. If things were looking bad for his side, he could instantly send orders to his forces and change his strategy. It was almost like cheating. In a battlefield, the correct conveyance of information meant everything, and this allowed him to command his full army without a single miscommunication.

Right now, the combined forces of thirty thousand were under Benimaru's command, and he could move them as smoothly and easily as his own limbs. These thirty thousand elites were no also-ran army, that's for sure.

What's more, the Born Leader skill also came with the Inspire Forces effect, adding bonuses to the forces he led that boosted their power by some 30 percent or more. That meant the entire army was nearly a third stronger. We weren't losing out in troop numbers; we had better-quality fighters... We weren't disadvantaged in any way. If we could get *that* bonus, too, then hell, all the better.

And with all of that, Benimaru could see from the start that victory was ours. Once he did, he had a bright idea for a new strategy.

(...So that's why I wish to attack the main enemy force. Soei's ready to go as well, and so I thought that, if Clayman's castle is indeed beyond that cloud, we might as well lay waste to it, too.)

That Benimaru. Brimming with confidence.

(Isn't that dangerous? You've only barely begun fighting. We don't know how this'll turn out yet...)

(We're fine. I am stationed over here. It would be Soei and Hakuro striking the castle...)

(Wait, my brother!!)

Shuna had interrupted our Thought Communication as she was preparing some tea. Um, this was supposed to be a secure line? She broke in there a little *too* easily for my tastes.

(Er, hello, Shuna. What did you want?)

I could hear Benimaru's voice jump several octaves.

(Don't ask me what I want, my brother! The demon lord Clayman is dangerous! He has the power to bend people's minds! If Soei or Hakuro fell victim to that...)

(No, they'd be perfectly fine against—)

(You can't!! If you insist on sending them in, then I'll join them!)

Whoa, whoa. Shuna's usually a lot more chill than this. What's gotten into her?

Benimaru and Shuna continued to argue as I sat there in shock. As my friend in my previous life put it, there's no way a man can ever win against his younger sister. Benimaru was no longer brimming with confidence at all. The all-out assault from Shuna sent him reeling.

The next thing I knew, Shuna was beaming at me. "All right, Sir Rimuru! Give me your orders to move out!"

Um, how do I respond to that...?

I didn't want to send Shuna anywhere lethal, but she did have a point. No matter how unlikely, I'd never want Soei to be thought controlled. I wanted to keep them from doing anything dangerous, but taking a castle to rob the enemy of an escape point was a classic strategy. With Clayman gone for the Walpurgis Council, now would be the perfect opportunity.

Still... I mean, as long as I made sure Clayman didn't get away, we're good, right? And it's not like I wanted to kill every single one of the magic-born working for him.

(...You have nothing to worry about, Sir Rimuru,) Soei chimed in. (I promise I will keep Lady Shuna safe.)

(And with me around,) Hakuro added, (it will be no problem to at least peek into the enemy's stronghold. They might be holding Lord Carillon there. I feel we need to investigate.)

My Thought Communication was getting worryingly busy. Shuna must've recruited them both to convince me. It was rare for her to act so selfishly, so I could understand why they wanted her to have her way this time. The fact Carillon was last seen being taken in the direction of Clayman's castle also intrigued me.

"I am terribly angered by all this, Sir Rimuru. It is hard for me to contain my feelings. What Clayman has done is unforgivable!"

Dahh... Yeah, I get that. I know I'm not the only one who felt a little helpless against him, back there. And I can see how Shuna would resent being left waiting around on the home front.

(All right. I'll let Shuna join in. But Soei and Hakuro, I want her safety to be job one for you. And if their HQ has more defenders than you predicted, put safety first and just bring back intelligence for me. Even if you discover Carillon, don't reach out to him unless you're sure it's safe. Got it?)

(Thank you for accepting her request.)

(I will be fine,) Shuna replied. (I can simply teleport out if something happens.)

(Indeed.) Hakuro laughed. (If anyone might be taking their sweet time in there, I imagine it would be me.)

(All of us have resistances to spirit-based attacks,) pointed out Soei, (so I imagine we will not waste much time. And with Lady Shuna there, there is nothing to be concerned about. If we do discover Lord Carillon, we will think over matters then.)

That put my mind at ease a little. Certainly, with Shuna's unique skill Parser, she'd be able to identify any attacks aimed for her mind—and with Spatial Motion also in her arsenal, I didn't see that much to worry about. She didn't have that much magical energy to tap, but the skills in her quiver were excellent.

Soei was right about Carillon as well. He might not be there at all, so there was no point harping on the issue.

(All right. You have my permission, then, but always make sure you're on top of the situation over there. Just in case, I'll have you begin operations at midnight, just after the Walpurgis Council begins.)

(((Yes sir!)))

✳

So now I had a three-member team attempting to infiltrate Clayman's base of operations.

It was just before midnight now, so I decided to take a moment to ask Veldora about the demon lords. "I have no interest in such little gnats," he began (of course), but he still had a fair amount to say about them all—except for Leon, who ascended to the role after he was sealed away.

Given his penchant for violent rages across the countryside, Veldora had fought against a demon lord or two in his time. Around two thousand years ago, he attacked and destroyed a city of vampires, which naturally earned him the anger of legions of those creatures—a chase he apparently loved. One of them, a female vampire, was particularly beautiful (and beautifully dressed) and boasted strength beyond all her peers. When the dust finally settled, her cadre of vampires disappeared from the scene, and Veldora didn't know what had happened to them.

"What was her name…? I believe it was Lu, erm, Lurus? Or Milus? Regardless, I never treated her that seriously, but she was a rather challenging plaything for me, so I would be wary around her. She can't take a joke, do you see?"

I think that was more Veldora's fault than hers. Anyone would be a little pissed off after their homeland was burned to embers. Of course, that was millennia ago; maybe she's mellowed.

"Ooh," interjected Ramiris from adjacent to me, "didja know that guy Valentine's a demon lord now, too?"

This Valentine had apparently taken over the original one's role about 1,500 years ago. I can only hope time's healed wounds between these vampires and Veldora.

Daggrull, the demon lord giant, was another keen rival of the dragon's. They had tussled several times, with no clear victor ever being crowned, and if Veldora bothered to remember his name, he must've been a pretty mean match. This guy had the power—or the guts, at least—to take on a dragon type. Probably a standout among the demon lords. Better watch for him.

Our conversation moved on to the topic of demons. Veldora had apparently dispatched several groups of demons in his time—a practice he found fun, since even if you incinerated them, they always resurrected to an even stronger form over time. A bunch of great playmates for him, really.

Not even he had fought the lord of these demons, however. This king held his domain in a castle on the frozen tundra of the northern continent, a place so frigid that he never bothered to make the trip.

"It is far too cold up there! What's the need for me to pay a visit? Kwah-ha-ha-ha-ha!"

That sounded pretty evasive to me, but he refused to give up any more details. No need to think about that now, though. It *would* be going pretty far out of his way to storm the place.

"Yes, well, Guy isn't any pushover," Ramiris observed. "Me, him, and Milim are the oldest demon lords you'll ever find!"

That's doesn't mean much coming from Ramiris. Suddenly Guy sounds like nothing special at all. But ah well. I'll back-burner this guy.

So how many demon lords does that leave remaining? I had already met Milim, Ramiris, and Carillon; we had just discussed Valentine, Daggrull, and Guy. There was Frey, the one who Phobio said had dealt the decisive blow to Carillon. There was Leon to think about, along with my current target, Clayman. So one more…

"Mm? I couldn't say." The allegedly sage Veldora was useless.

"Oh, you must mean Deeno!" Ramiris cried. "He's even more of a goof-off demon lord than I am!"

I suppose he and Ramiris were two peas in a pod, then.

"We are *not!*"

I'll just ignore that.

So that's ten, some of whom had a bone to pick with Veldora. I'd need to keep that in mind as we discussed matters. Many seemed far more capable of defending themselves than I thought. Using this wimp Ramiris as a baseline could land me in deep trouble—maybe it was better to assume Milim was par for the course with them. Even after my evolution, I was leery about my chances of beating her in battle. We had sparred a few times, but she wasn't being at all serious about it. I needed more data. In sparring mode, I could totally take her on now, but I couldn't be cocky until I knew what she was more fully capable of.

I still couldn't believe that Milim de facto approved of rubbing me out. There's got to be something behind that. She's not the type to backstab her friends or be mind controlled like that, and there was never gonna be any negotiating with her. There had to be some reason—a reason of her devising, too.

…*Well, no point dwelling on it. I'll figure it out when I see her.*

As we talked, I felt a wrinkle in space erupt out of nowhere. *Here comes our ride*, I thought as this huge, bombastic, ominous-looking gate appeared. Pretty fancy. Me, I usually just kind of ripped a hole in time and space, so maybe I could learn from this. Once I had a concrete image in mind, it'd be easier for me to whip up a gate like this next time and teleport through it.

Regardless, the door opened, revealing a green-haired woman in a dark-red maid's outfit. She bowed her head toward Ramiris. "I have come to take you, Lady Ramiris. And is this your guest? I'll be happy to guide you together."

Then she stood by the gate and lowered her eyes, eliminating her presence as much as possible. A well-trained pro at the servant biz, it felt like.

But something concerned me. She was exuding just as much over-powering force as Diablo at his best. She was a demon, a high-level one. Regular demons could only climb so high up the latter. No matter how long-lived they were, an Arch Demon was about the most they could hope for. Anything beyond that required a certain trigger…which, in the case of Diablo, was me naming him. This let him break out of the base demon framework entirely, evolving him from an Arch Demon to a so-called Demon Peer.

"Heh-heh-heh-heh-heh. I have no interest in strength," he had said at the time, *"but now I see there is always something higher to strive for. Perhaps I should try to make more of an effort at this?"*

He had "no interest" in strength, but he had a hell of a lot of interest in fighting. As he put it, he had been too content with himself before, since becoming *too* strong would squeeze all the fun out of battle. Was he kidding with me? Because if he wasn't, that's just scary.

And now I had this other Demon Peer here, this maid. Or more like a maiden messenger from the underworld, I suppose. With the kind of anime and manga I consumed way back when, a maid was more a type of battle unit than anything—and with her being a Demon Peer and all, she was clearly one deadly woman.

"Oh, hey! Haven't seen *you* in an age, Mizeri! How's Guy doing?"

Ramiris clearly wasn't afraid of her. In some ways, it made *her* even scarier.

"…It is not upon me to worry about the condition of my master…"

"Ah. Haven't changed a bit, have you? Well, that's fine."

She fluttered her way into the gate, the rest of us following behind. We had to hurry, or else we'd get shut out. If I wasted any more time here steeling my resolve and wound up missing my ride there, I don't know how I'd ever explain that to Benimaru and the rest.

So this maid Mizeri works for the demon lord Guy? The lord of the demons, and one of the oldest demon lords to boot. If he recruited Demon Peers as doormen, that said a lot about his power. Probably shouldn't try riling him, then…unless the times called for it.

But having someone as strong as Mizeri do this kind of low-end work? Talk about arrogance. Here I thought the demon lords were all I had to worry about. So much for that. Maybe I should've taken Diablo along after all, even if he and Shion would've gone out of control with each other…

Well, it's too late for second-guessing. Time to put up or shut up. The world's rulers are waiting for me beyond—but I didn't feel scared. That's because I was one of them. One of the strongest in the world. If anything, I felt cool as a cucumber as I crossed the door.

Benimaru grinned broadly as he surveyed the battle unfolding below him.

It was all going according to plan. The enemy had been lured, like clockwork, right into the traps Geld set—which could have been predicted, given how lightly they had treated the Tempest side.

"Sir Rimuru was right," he said to himself, pitying his foes. "If they've set the table *this* kindly for us, it would almost be more difficult to lose."

They could pull this off thanks to the perfect control he had over his armies, but Benimaru didn't think it that impressive of a feat. As he said, they had caught Clayman's forces comically off guard—they expected their numbers to overwhelm Tempest, after all. They had pursued the fleet-footed beastman fighters that had posed as refugees, and now they were completely cornered.

Alvis flew up to the point in the air Benimaru chose to watch events from. "It appears to be decided," she observed, quietly flapping her wings so as not to break Benimaru's train of thought. "By this point, I see no way for the enemy to recover itself."

"Ah, Lady Alvis." He turned his crimson eyes to her. "Enough of that blather. We haven't won anything yet."

"Please, Sir Benimaru, Alvis is fine…"

"You are not subordinate to me," he coldly refused.

"No, perhaps I am not, but we beastmen have given up our command to you for the moment."

Benimaru nodded his understanding. "Very well. For this battle, at least, I will appoint you as my aide."

"I appreciate it, Sir Benimaru."

Now—in name, at least—Benimaru had command of this combined force. With the supervisor of all Eurazania's armies officially declaring herself below him, Benimaru was now officially supreme leader of the entire show. There was no defying the supreme leader; in the world of monsters, the strongest called the shots.

"…But despite appointing you my aide, I'm not sure there is

much left to do, is there? I am keeping a steady watch on matters, but victory is imminent."

"I agree with you. However, I do sense the presence of several strong members on their side."

"True," the unwavering Benimaru replied. "Once the outcome is set in stone, I will send Geld's troops their way."

"Hold on," Sufia interjected. "I want to join in on that!"

"Yeah," Phobio added. "I don't want you hoarding all the action, Commander. This is the land of beastmen—our land. If we leave it all to you, Lord Carillon'll chew us out for it."

"He's right! If you've left us to ensure everyone is safe, you could at least let us handle this battle."

"Sir Benimaru," said Alvis, "I leave command of the armies to you. Please allow us to target and defeat the ringleader of the enemy force!"

All three bowed their heads to him. Benimaru greeted this with a clicking of the tongue.

"So *that's* why you made me commander?"

"Oh, how do you mean?" Alvis replied, playing dumb.

"…Very well. I was planning to have you join the fight anyway. However, if you feel you are about to lose, retreat at once. With some of their fighters, arrogance could be your downfall."

He had a point. Several members of Clayman's force remained question marks. Depending on who was paired with whom, things could become dicey in the battle ahead.

But, Benimaru thought as he boldly smiled to himself, *I'm always here. As long as I can detect when we're in danger, we will not lose.*

Each of the Lycanthropeers already had their targeted prey in mind, sharpening their claws and letting their proud animal instincts run wild in pursuit of these loathsome interlopers.

The trap would go off in another few minutes.

"…I wanted to ask you something else," Alvis said as she waited. "What will we do with those caught in our trap?"

"Kill them all, is what I would like to say…" Benimaru thought for a moment. "But I would like to leave judgment on that to you beastmen."

"Meaning?"

"Take anyone willing to cooperate with us prisoner. Sir Rimuru is a generous leader, despite appearances. He is not a great proponent of genocide, although he'll gladly carry it out if they take any of our lives."

"...I see. In that case, let us decide how to deal with the prisoners later."

"Certainly. That is fine. I imagine Sir Rimuru probably pictures them as a potential source of labor."

"...Oh?"

"You are going to rebuild your capital, aren't you?" Benimaru casually asked. "The more able workers, the better."

"You'll do *that* much for us?!"

Alvis, along with her two cohorts, was shocked. Rimuru not only took victory almost as a given; he already had the script written for what came next.

Where does that confidence come from?! We're fighting the closest companions to the cunning, deceitful Clayman, and yet...

The biggest surprise of all, though, was fighting this on the assumption that they'd take prisoners. In this world, it was far easier for most people to kill in battle rather than capture. You would never find a commander who'd care whether a force was partially surrendering before doing them all in with ranged magic. The idea of using prisoners as a labor force had never occurred to anyone before.

This shook the Three Lycanthropeers to the core. It meant that the magic-born working under Rimuru never even considered the possibility of defeat. They went into this fight backed by an absolute confidence in their victory.

"Well," Benimaru added with a laugh, "assuming our strategy goes to plan." It only terrified the beastmen more.

And then the battle began.

(Everything to plan, Soka.)

(Understood, Sir Benimaru.)

With that short exchange, the Clayman force experienced its

first casualties. They were about a hundred magic-born, led by a named one of some renown, but they all died at once, their magical cores plucked out by Soka when she appeared out of nowhere. The four team members working under him were already busy taking down the other squad captains of Clayman's army, only striking those targets they were absolutely sure they could defeat. That was Benimaru's order, and they followed it to the letter.

The result: The enemy's chain of command was pulverized. Orders from above were no longer making it to the foot soldiers.

"This is a trap! The beastmen have surrounded us!"

"That's crazy! How could they—?"

"Retreat! We have to regroup our forces!"

By the time they noticed, it was too late. Unlike a human army, monsters tended to over-rely on their own strength and bravery; a leader to guide their instincts was indispensable. Without them, Clayman's army was doomed to fall to pieces.

(Geld, you may begin.)

(Yes sir!)

His orders given, Geld called out the signal.

"Start it now!"

""""Rahhh!!""""

The next moment, the ground caved in, swallowing up the enemy forces. Tempestians gifted in controlling the earth had unleashed their magic. This natural-looking stretch of land was actually pock-marked with pit traps, an illusion created by their skills.

Only monsters with the power of flight could escape, and even those were quickly picked off by avian beastmen and Gabil's Team Hiryu. The ones who were caught found themselves in a cavernous underground hollow, the soil liquefied beneath. They were unhurt but buried up to their waists, unable to move.

These *were* monsters, of course; some used magic or skills to wriggle out of this mousetrap, falling over their weaker companions to reach solid ground again. But the plan accounted for this, too. It helped thin out the crowd. The stronger ones among the force were killed without any chance to resist; the weaker, seeing this, had their hearts crushed. The survivors would know all too well where they stood strength-wise, likely losing their will to fight. The pit trap was set up entirely to procure pliable prisoners, willing to follow orders.

Ten or so minutes after the plan was launched, the battle was already far too one-sided to offer any hope for a turnaround.

"This... This many?"

Benimaru had a bird's-eye view of over ten thousand Clayman soldiers, cut off and plunged into the pitfalls. Geld's Yellow Numbers were patrolling the edges, surrounding all the holes at regular intervals and taking out the magic-born who managed to claw their way up. The enemy forces were outnumbered, and any unexpected shows of strength were handled with Tempest's superior numbers and equipment. Even the most powerful magic-born could be taken out by a handful of beastmen or Team Kurenai. Most of Clayman's force had marched into what appeared be a flat field; the remaining several thousand were holed up in the rear, but they weren't enough to change anything.

"We won," Benimaru matter-of-factly whispered.

"Truly, an amazing show," marveled Alvis.

"Heh. We were bound to win. That was why we couldn't afford to let our guard down. I have my own work to do now. Alvis, Lycanthropeers, you are free to do as you like. Take the heads of the enemy leaders!"

"That's what I've been waiting for, man! I'll be back!"

"Now we can finally have some fun! I can smell the bastard who defied me before. Think I'll go after him first!"

"I suppose I will join them, too. The rest is up to you, Sir Benimaru."

The commander nodded, face pointed straight ahead.

"Go!"

""""Yes sir!!""""

With that, the three warriors sprang into action.

Sufia tore across the sky, faster than wings could take her. This was Skywalk at work, an Art only a small handful of magical creatures could wield, but Sufia used it like second nature.

She was headed for a small group at the very far end of the battle-field, unarmed and looking out of place. They were priests, led by Middray of the Dragon Faithful. She didn't know them, but Sufia's animal instincts told her that these were the strongest forces the enemy boasted.

As she sped forth, she heard the voice of Gabil, commander of the skies. He, and the hundred members of Team Hiryu, were following her.

"Gah-ha-ha-ha! Let me give you a hand, Lady Sufia!"

"Ah, Gabil." She smiled a beautiful, heroic smile. "Sorry, but you might be left with the short end of the stick here."

"Wah-ha-ha! Not a problem for me. We've taken care of most of the aerial forces, and I wouldn't want to take any more work from the flying beastmen. Where are the enemies that lie between us and victory?"

"Ha! Victory is ours, yes, but I think we have to put down the people in the back, just in case things go haywire on us."

"Right. I hear you loud and clear! You get that, men?!"

"Understood, General!"

"As long as you don't screw up, either, General!"

Gabil snarled at his dragonewts. Their exchanges usually went something like this. Sufia chuckled at it a bit before focusing her lethal energies on the target ahead.

Middray had set up camp in a safe spot toward the rear...although it wasn't a "camp" so much as a completely different location, a medic facility built by the supply team. He hadn't asked for this battle, but being so belittled by the force all this time made him feel too embarrassed to face Milim again.

Lady Milim will surely deride me for this, too...

The thought concerned him enough that he demanded to be stationed on the front lines. That request was turned down by Yamza, who certainly didn't do it out of concern for Middray's safety—he just didn't want anyone else horning in on his upcoming glory.

Still, victory was all but guaranteed today. Their force was three times the size of the enemy's, which was not at all a coherent fighting unit. They were being forced to retreat while guarding a large crowd of refugees, rendering them incapable of any counterattack.

It's more dishonorable, if anything, to attack an opposing force like this...

Such was the thought in Middray's mind in the days leading up to this clash. Things, however, did not quite work out that way.

"We might be in trouble, Father. The battle's all but lost, isn't it?"

"Mm... They are weak, Hermes, too weak. I had no idea the demon lord Clayman's soldiers were this incapable..."

"They aren't, Father! The enemy just had the superior strategy!"

"What? Don't be stupid. We should have the power to force our way right through any of their silly tricks! If that's the weak excuse you have for this, I'm disappointed in you, Hermes!"

"Look, if this was just a one-on-one duel, that's one matter, but in mass combat like this, the quality of your army's command is what decides the day! That, and how well you can catch the enemy unawares. Today, that was the opposing side. They hid their war power until the last moment and even sprang a trap on us."

"Pfft. I can see that much!"

Middray was never one to use his head very much. Hermes had a habit of bringing up all these meddlesome, annoying topics with him, just because he happened to be a little smarter, and he never liked that much. Now, however, even Middray could see that there was nothing he could retort with. The scene presented to him was all the evidence Hermes needed.

"But, Father Middray—"

"I know. The fighters headed our way... They're powerful. As much as I hate to say it, we are standing in the midst of a battle-field. If they're coming for us, I say we come for them!"

"So it goes, does it? Very well, then..."

Hermes reluctantly agreed as Middray next to him began to burn with a desire to fight.

Here, in the rear of Clayman's forces, was fought the most intense and ferocious of the day's conflicts.

Landing on solid ground, Phobio silently ran forward. Discovering a group hiding in the shadows behind the battlefield, he stopped right in front of them.

There stood a man wearing a mask of anger and a girl wearing a mask of tears. This strange duo was Footman, the Angry Jester, and Teare, the Teardrop Jester; both members of the Moderate Jesters and both here observing the battle by Clayman's request.

"Hey," Phobio quietly said, holding back his rage. "I owe you one from last time."

Footman's eyes twinkled ominously beneath his mask. "Oh-ho? Well, well, if it isn't Sir Phobio!"

"Sir Phobio," Teare said in a chiding, singsong voice as she traipsed around him. "The beastman who could never quite become a demon lord! Sir Phobio, the one who lost to Milim! Thank you *so* much for helping us out then!"

"Heh. Glad you still remember me. It'd be a shame if I killed you when you had no idea why you deserved it!"

"Ooooh? What're you angry about?"

"How odd. What could this fool be so livid for? Those raging emotions are so delectable, but there's no reason for us to die here."

"Oh, not at all, not at all!"

"Shut up! Maybe I was a fool for letting you trick me, but a fool like me doesn't need a reason to ask for a little payback from you guys!"

Phobio broke out his sharp claws. Teare and Footman were unmoved.

"Hmm? You want to go with us? You shouldn't push yourself like that. You're too weak for that!"

"Hohhh-hoh-hoh-hoh! None of that, Teare. Sir Phobio here is trying to make us laugh with this little joke of his."

Neither could successfully rile up Phobio. More than anything, he regretted letting his short temper steer him straight to failure in the past. So, once the greetings were over, he quickly stepped forward and instantly closed the gap between them.

"Ngh...!!"

"Tch!"

Realizing their mind games had no effect against him, Footman and Teare changed their approach. Things began to move quickly. The air twisted around them, opening a portal through which a man with the head of a wild boar appeared.

"Long time no see, Footman. Remember me?"

"Hoh? Hmmmmm? Ah, the orc general? My, look at how impressive you've become!"

Footman attempted to sound playful with the sarcastic taunt, but the expression on his face indicated he was in trouble.

Despite appearances, Footman was a coolheaded, calculating type—a trait Geld was fully aware of. The jester was with the forces that laid waste to the ogre village that Benimaru and the others called home, and Geld knew his powers were difficult to ignore. Footman was on a different level from other magic-born, as far as Geld was concerned.

Plus, there was Teare. Footman's peer in many ways. The extent of her powers was an unknown, but she wasn't one to be underestimated. Phobio might have been the Black Leopard Fang of the Beast Master's Warrior Alliance, but even with his strength, taking on Footman and Teare by himself would spell trouble.

The beastman let the rage bubble within. *Heh-heh… Well done, Sir Benimaru. Not a disagreeable piece of prey at all!*

The commander, overseeing the battle from the skies, had ordered Geld to assist Phobio. He wondered why at first, seeing as it meant Geld would abandon his command post, but now he saw that Benimaru was right. The rest of the battle had already been decided, to the point that even Geld's aides could handle it well enough. Only the top leaders among the magic-born under Rimuru's command could handle two Moderate Jesters like this.

"Allow us to assist, Sir Phobio."

"Ah, Geld. Thank you!"

Phobio wasn't turning him down. Even here, he could sense the difference in combat ability between him and this pair. To him, the best path to victory was worth choosing more than his own pride.

So began a smaller battle between two duos, in the shadow of a small hill away from the battlefield.

The reports Yamza received from this battlefield bewildered him. The overwhelming advantage he thought he had was just an enemy trap all along.

He didn't want to consider the thought of defeat. It would obviously enrage Clayman. He had to find a way to turn this around, to snatch victory from the jaws of defeat—but he doubted he had the man power left to achieve it. He still had enough of his wits to realize that, and now he had to think of other forces he might be able to stir into action.

The five fingers, Clayman's inner circle of associates, was led by the middle finger, Yamza, the strongest magic-born out of them all. Only Adalmann, the pointer finger, and Nine-Head, the thumb, could compare with him.

Adalmann, head of the defense forces in Clayman's castle, began life as a wight, a deathly spirit who resided in the Great Forest of Jura. He was a well-known bishop during his *living* years, but that meant nothing now. Clayman's accursed magic had greatly boosted his power as a monster, transforming him into a wight king that ruled over the undead. The holy force he wielded when he was alive had transformed into impure demonic power that he used to curse the living.

But despite his vast strength, Adalmann had one weakness—his lack of intellect. The only thing he could do was follow his orders to destroy any intruders; that's why he wasn't involved in this war.

Nine-Head, meanwhile, was a fox spirit, an extreme rarity in her field. She was still young, just three hundred years old, and only three of her tails had grown out. Her magicule energy, however, was already well past Yamza's, up to the level of Clayman himself. She was with him now at the Walpurgis Council, serving as his bodyguard, so Yamza couldn't tap her for backup, either.

It'll have to be Adalmann, then...

The problem was how to call him over. Actually, no, it wasn't a problem. It would be simple to have him show up right this instant.

Yamza would have to then gather up his surviving troops, flee back into Milim's domain, meet with him there, and go back on the offensive. *That's the best approach*, he thought. Walpurgis Councils had lasted upward of a month in the past—if all went well, he could wrap this whole thing up before Clayman came back. It wouldn't exactly be simple to make Adalmann move, but it wasn't impossible.

Either way, if he stood down and accepted defeat right now, it was clear Yamza would be purged. *Lord Clayman is a vicious man. He would do away with me in no time—I am sure of it… And even if I were lucky enough to survive, I don't want to turn into a soulless puppet. As much as it vexes me, I must admit defeat here—but I will reign victorious in the end!*

Yamza turned his gaze toward the battlefield—and there, he witnessed a sight that made him doubt his eyes.

In the front was a bewitchingly beautiful woman, her hair a mix of blond and black. She held a golden staff and was boldly racing across the land, as if no one was around her at all.

Protecting her was a group of Carillon's finest, the Beast Master's Warrior Alliance. They numbered only a few dozen, but almost no one could defy them in combat, each one bearing the strength of a thousand. There was Zol, an elephant beastman; Talos, a bear beastman… They couldn't beat the Three Lycanthropeers, but they were all stout fighters, worthy of serving under the great Beast Master.

They were also accompanied by a group in crimson garb, using searing flame spells to burn away the supplemental forces kept in the rear. They meant little to Yamza, but there was no doubting they were ranked above the magic-born around them.

Things had suddenly become very bad for him.

The unbelievable visitors deepened Yamza's gloom.

"It can't be… Why are the Three Lycanthropeers here?! Have they abandoned their troops and come to provide reinforcements themselves? But how could that…?"

He could hear the trusted magic-born around him shouting. Agitation was in the air.

"They're pointing their greatest force toward our main army?! What are the lookouts doing?!"

"Allow me to interrupt, sir! We can't make contact with our lookouts. Someone has killed them all!"

"What?!"

The enemy was moving so fast, they were completely behind on dealing with them. By the time Yamza noticed that, they were already lethally late. The realization made the blood drain from his head. There would be no regrouping now—even escape would be fiendishly difficult.

No. No, no, no, no, no!! I may not even be able to escape here with my life!

Yamza began to panic. If this was one-on-one, he might be able to deal with that, but he wasn't self-absorbed enough to think he stood a chance against a squadron like this.

"Buy me some time! I will return to our homeland and bring Adalmann back here. He can summon the dead to restore our forces!"

It was just a pretext. He already knew all was lost, and he had decided to run away, as fast as possible. Luckily, he had only volunteered his fealty to Clayman, so his behavior was not restricted the way it was with the other four fingers. Following him any farther would be suicide, and that made it easy for Yamza to sever all ties.

"Yes sir!"

"We can give you three hours, sir!"

His men each gave him stern, resolved looks that did nothing to move his heart. All he could think about was how stupid they were. The next moment, he chanted a teleportation spell. But something was off.

"It's...not working? Is this a...Spatial Blockade?!"

Yes. He was already too late. The moment Yamza and his men saw Alvis, Alvis's gaze landed on them as well, thanks to the power of her skill Snake Eyes. It was an extra skill, one that applied a large variety of ailments—paralysis, poison, insanity, and so forth—and worked on anyone caught in her line of vision. A tremendously useful skill, the only way to escape it was by either successfully resisting it or simply weathering it out.

And Alvis had another card up her sleeve—the unique skill Oppressor. This spatial skill gave her the effects of Mind Accelerate, Spatial Control, and Spatial Motion, letting her impede enemy movement and give her allies superior positioning.

A single motion from her was enough to neutralize all the masses surrounding Yamza. The more weakhearted of them were instantly driven mad; the stronger ones were still paralyzed long enough for the poison to kill them off. Some had even been turned to stone. Less than a hundred managed to emerge unscathed. Before they could put up any resistance, the unworthy had been denied even the right to stand before Alvis.

Her Spatial Control had snuffed out Yamza's magic, having the power to both obstruct spells and fix their spatial coordinates in place to prevent them from affecting the air around the caster at all. No magical escape from this area was possible now—"this area" being the range of Alvis's vision. The entire battlefield was now in her total control. Such was the power of the Golden Snakehorn.

Realizing escape was impossible, Yamza gritted his teeth.

He still had a last resort. But it was a forbidden one, one that he'd prefer not to use. Beyond that, the only path to survival involved winning this.

"...So be it. Let's show them what we've got."

"Ah, Sir Yamza!"

"Sir Yamza at his finest could overwhelm even the Three Lycanthropeers!"

"Let me join you, sir! Our fighting will surely please Sir Clayman!"

His men were elated for the fight. Yamza found it boundlessly foolish. The demon lord Clayman sought only two things: victory and profit. He would never accept this performance—wasteful attrition, followed up by total defeat.

The only thing he believes in is pure, unadulterated power...

No matter how faithful Yamza was to him, Clayman never saw him as one of his own. He was just a useful pawn, a talented minion; that was as far as the lord's affection went. The Ice Blade had been a gift, yes, but it was simply provided in an effort to strengthen him. It was all for Clayman's sake.

Still, Yamza provided him with respect and reverence, and the gifts he received in return helped. They both had a common interest. But Yamza had no intention of offering his life to Clayman.

...About time to head out. I have to survive this and bounce back!

This failure would force him to go into hiding for a while. But a Special-A talent like him, a giant among high-level magic-born, would no doubt be picked up by another demon lord before long, he thought.

(I like this,) he Thought Communicated to Alvis. (One of the greatest magic-born under the Beast Master's command, part of the valorous Three Lycanthropeers. Are you willing to duel with me?)

It was a risky bet. He wanted to defeat Alvis, the strongest figure in the group, and crush the enemy's will to fight. Perhaps that would be enough to change the script—and even if it didn't end well, he thought it could give him a chance to escape.

(Very well, Sir Yamza—head of the five fingers beneath the demon lord Clayman. I will show you how far out of your element you are!)

This, Alvis thought, would prove once and for all where Clayman and Lord Carillon stood with each other. She promptly transported herself before him with Spatial Motion, and in an instant, Clayman's surviving servants swarmed over her.

It was not what one would normally call a strategy. Beastmen are mostly simple folk, easily provoked, and this cowardly approach took full advantage of that. If they can exhaust Alvis, even a little bit, that'll make it easier for Yamza to win—such was the reasoning behind this kamikaze strike.

"You think those tricks will work?!" Alvis shouted as she turned up the intensity on her Snake Eyes. To Yamza, though, they had already done more than enough. That single instant, when Alvis used her power, was the exact thing Yamza needed for his assured victory.

"...Got you!!"

In a flash, he was upon her, slashing his sword at her exposed back. And just before the tip of his blade reached her body—

"Nuh-uh! Backstabbing someone like that's not manly at all!"

Someone had leaped straight out from Alvis's shadow, babbling to himself as he deflected Yamza's sword.

"Dehh! Who're you?!"

"I'm Gobta! We were hiding out just in case this happened!"

As he explained that, more and more figures popped out from the shadow. They were, of course, the Unified, four-legged goblin riders, tapping their physical agility to attack the magic-born that were still moving.

"And you didn't tell me?" Alvis said. "I was wondering why something didn't feel quite right."

She had actually noticed them all along. That was why she was unafraid to go plunging in like this.

"Heh-heh! Benimaru ordered us to," Gobta casually replied as he fired off a Case Cannon bolt at Yamza. He could tell the moment he crossed blades with him that this wasn't a battle for him to win. So while the commander was distracted by his short sword, he thought now would be his best chance. Gobta's definition of *fair and square* differed a bit from the norm—it was something he asked of his foes but never followed himself.

Still, Yamza managed to deflect the blast with his sword.

"Out of my way, weakling!"

He pointed the tip of his blade at Gobta and cast a spell, sending an Icicle Lance hurtling his way. Gobta simply used his dagger to fire an Icicle Lance of his own—not to fire back, but because he had planned for this follow-up strike from the start. It wound up saving Gobta's life, as the two magic bolts met in the air and dissipated.

"That... That had as much force as this magic sword?! And without casting? Cheeky little weakling, are we...?"

Now Yamza recognized Gobta as his foe—but Gobta had already pretty well exhausted his arsenal. *Uh-oh. I couldn't follow that counter of his at all. That ice just happened to save me, but if he stabs me with that thing, I'm a goner. Probably oughtta start runnin', huh?*

Fortunately, the goblin riders had already made their contribution to this fight. No one would complain if they retreated now. Gobta made up his mind.

"All right, let's pull—"

But just as he began to make the order, Yamza's sword sailed right past his nose.

"Pyah?!"

In another stroke of luck, he had taken a timid step back just in the nick of time. It made Yamza almost lose his nerve. *This little sneak made it past my attack three times?* Three in a row couldn't be any coincidence, as he saw it—that supersonic swipe he just made proved that the hobgoblin before him was no also-ran.

"Heh-heh-heh... Oh, how the Lycanthropeers have fallen! Sneaking their minions into a one-on-one duel!"

The boast, made with wide-open, bloodshot eyes, was part of Yamza's strategy. By his estimation, dealing with both a Lycanthropeer and this mystery intruder at once was dangerous.

Gobta seized the opportunity. *Woo-hoo! That means I don't have to fight this crazy-dangerous magic-born, right?*

He suppressed his joy just long enough to declare "All right, I'll serve as an observer for this duel, then!" Yep. Definitely an observer. With all his tactics exhausted, that beat just standing there and getting in the way. Rimuru could accept defeat, but he could never accept his people getting killed in action. Gobta wasn't stupid enough to volunteer to be war casualty number one for Tempest.

"Oh, you can have him if you want," Alvis playfully said.

"If I take your prey," Gobta wittily replied, "wouldn't that hurt your honor as a beastman, ma'am? I don't need it that bad, so go ahead and fight all you want! Sorry I got in the way!"

Alvis accepted the inane excuse without a word. If anything, it was the luckiest thing to happen to Gobta all day. He had dodged a bullet with this total unknown before him. Alvis had no intention of letting anyone else score this kill anyway, and he had wriggled out of a battle against a foe that completely outclassed him.

Whew. That's the end of my work!

At the very far end of the rear guard, the group of priests led by Middray was clashing with Gabil's Team Hiryu.

Of course, only a few were standing by now. Nearly two hundred fighters on both sides were lying on the ground. But Middray was unhurt, his white robes free of dirt and grime, and it was clear he was still going strong.

"Waaah-ha-ha-ha! Not too shabby, you guys. I see you *are* the descendants of dragons!"

Middray flashed a contented smile, surveying the fallen and pretending the panting and exhausted Sufia in front of him didn't exist.

"Don't you ignore me!"

Sufia, half Transformed into her beast form, had used her vastly strengthened physical skills to attack Middray. But the head priest, perhaps sensing this, had simply leaned over to one side, preventing her from landing a lethal blow. The effort had left her wide open.

"Hyah!"

Taking the clawed arm extended out to him, he tripped up Sufia's legs, picked up her body, and sharply slammed her against the ground. The judo-like throw was unique to the Dragon Faithful.

"I wasn't ignoring you at all," Middray happily explained. "I don't have much opportunity to use this against monsters, so this is rather fun for me. It's been ages since I had a foe so worthy of that throw."

This was more than Sufia was willing to bear.

"D-dammit! You, you made me…"

She was being treated like a plaything, her face red with humiliation. But she had to admit it. Middray, this man standing before her, was more powerful than she ever imagined. Now he was surveying the landscape once again, waiting for her to stand up and ignoring her until that happened.

Curse him, he's treating me like a second-class fighter! And how could my Self-Regeneration fail me like this…?

It was true. Sufia's skill was not healing any damage, because her physical body hadn't sustained any wounds. She was exhausted simply because her stamina was tapping out on her, and the force of each slam added to the burden. He was wounding her internally, where the damage wouldn't be visible.

But Sufia stood up anyway. As the Snowy Tigerclaw, she could not let this affront continue to stand.

"Imagine, a bastard like you serving Clayman. I thought Yamza was the best around here, but I suppose my instincts were correct all along."

"Yamza? Ah yes, sir. Yamza. He is rather capable, I'll admit, but not enough to serve as a playmate for me. I may not look it, but I've sparred with Lady Milim on regular occasions, you see."

"Milim... The demon lord Milim?! So you're the Dragon Faithful?!"

No wonder, Sufia thought. They seemed so different in disposition from the rest of Clayman's troops. They seemed to enjoy fighting for the sake of fighting, not at all concerned with actually killing their enemies. And compared to the other magic-born, they were all overwhelmingly strong—and enjoying every minute of it.

"Ooh? Say, that dragonewt just felled Hermes! Wah-ha-ha-ha-ha, that was quite a performance!"

Hermes was tangling with Gabil, and Gabil had just knocked him down with his spear.

"F-Father, stop laughing and help me, please!"

"You lost, fool! Just sit there and think about what you could've done better!"

He laughed at his associate, lying there on his back and pleading for assistance. He could tell that Hermes wasn't as bad off as he claimed and that Gabil had no intention of taking his life.

"All right. Counting me, that leaves three remaining. You command a truly wonderful set of fighters, given how evenly we are matched. It proves you've honed your bodies *and* your minds, instead of relying on skills."

"I suppose I should appreciate the compliment. My name is Gabil. And you are with Lady Milim...?"

"Indeed! I am Middray of the Dragon Faithful."

"And I am Sufia. Sufia of the Three Lycanthropeers! I have no ear to lend to the servants of Clayman, but if you worship Lady Milim, that is another story."

"Mm. Lady Sufia, is it? I will make sure to remember that. So what'll it be now? I could take on the both of you at once, if you like?"

Middray calmly folded his arms, implying that he liked his chances.

"Can I ask you a question before that?"

"Mm? What is it?"

"I... I just mean, how can a mere human be so strong? Or are the Dragon Faithful human at all? Something seems strange about you."

Middray nodded at this, his curiosity piqued. "What do you mean by human?" he asked. "That's the crux of it. If you are inquiring about our species, however, the answer is simple. We are dragone-wts, like Sir Gabil over there."

"What?! The same as us?"

"Yes, precisely. The difference is that instead of evolving from lizardmen, we are the descendants of dragons that 'humanized' themselves and mated with the human race. But in essence," he closed with a smile, "we are the same."

"Ah... And come to think of it, my sister Soka turned wholly human in appearance."

"Yes. But almost none of us can bring ourselves back to our original shape. The priests you see strewn around us don't have any skills like Dragon Change or Dragon Body. There is hardly any difference between them and human beings."

Middray turned his eyes toward Sufia.

"But that power is still handed down. Our worship of the dragon does not allow us to forget the blood within us. Any more questions, Lady Sufia?"

"No. Human, monster, it doesn't matter. I just wanted to know if your skills were the result of a weak human building himself up to perfection. You say you are little different from humans, and if so, I must pay respect to your efforts."

"Wah-ha-ha-ha-ha! You think the same way I do. One may be born with strength, or one may acquire it. Magic-born are so weak because they rely too much on the strength they've always had. That's why they compare their strengths based on magicule capacity and so on. True strength can't be seen with the eye. The level of your skills is the only solid, trustworthy index there is."

Sufia was born strong. She had more fighting skill than most monsters, through no special effort of her own. Her massive well of energy, and the surging aura it created, made even magic-born go out of their way to avoid her. Her battle senses made full use of this, and her instincts alone had brought her to where she was. Now, Middray's words made her realize how little time she had spent polishing her Arts, her learned skills.

"So you mean I can become stronger?"

"Wah-ha-ha-ha-ha! Precisely. There is no such thing as an experience that can win over being in actual battle. Here, come at me! I'd be happy to spar with you."

He remained where he stood, arms crossed and standing high.

"Lady Sufia and me at the same time?" a dubious Gabil asked. "Are you sure you aren't being a little too conceited?"

Middray just grinned at him. "Hmph! I could take you on without even using my arms, little man!"

Gabil wasn't about to take that sitting down.

"Lady Sufia…"

"We'll tackle him together. We have to admit it. He's a strong one!"

The battle between Alvis and Yamza was about to reach its raging climax.

The two were evenly matched, but Yamza had finally used his ace in the hole.

"Ha-ha-ha! Well performed, Lycanthropeer! Your ability to keep up with me is astounding. But now, my victory is assured!!"

"What?"

"Pfft! Did you think this magic sword was my only secret weapon? Yes, you may be strong—strong enough to hold me back. I will freely admit that. However! What if there were two of me?"

With that shouted question, he unleashed the magic inside the bracelet on his left wrist. This was a Doppelganger Bracelet, an incredibly valuable Artifact capable of producing a perfect copy of the wearer, right down to their clothing and equipment. Now Alvis had to fend off two Yamzas at the same time—and if one was an even fight for her, she would have to be at a severe disadvantage.

"Well? If you capitulate to me now, I could be convinced to spare you—"

"So what?"

"...What did you say?"

"You think that parlor trick will outclass me? You really are nothing more than a lackey of Clayman's. Quite the would-be finisher, there."

Alvis didn't give an inch, openly ridiculing her foe.

"Then die!"

And even before Yamza could scream that at her, Alvis played her own final card.

Now the top half of her body was a beautiful woman, the bottom half that of a large, black snake. This was Alvis's true, Animalized form, and now she was ready to use its full force.

Unlike Phobio and Sufia with their focus on close-quarters fighting, Alvis was usually thought to be a long-range specialist, lobbing her magic attacks from afar. In truth, however, she was a dyed-in-the-wool fighter, masterful at short range in the way anyone serving the Beast Master needed to be.

Her fighting style, however, ventured from the beaten path. Alvis brought her staff up to her forehead—and in the next instant, it disappeared, as she grew a golden horn from above her eyes. Finally free, her aura surged outward from her, greatly amplifying her power. This was her second Transformation and her most secret of abilities.

She stood there, her entire body protected by dragon scales. The whole space around them belonged to her, her aura producing streaks of lightning in the air.

"Wha?!" Gobta spat out, sensing danger. There was no way Alvis could remain coolheaded enough to tell friend from foe like that.

"You said your name was Gobta? You have my permission to move out immediately."

"Ohhh, you don't need to tell me twice, ma'am! Riders, retreat!"

One shout from him was all it took to make the goblin riders flee the scene. The surviving magic-born took the opportunity to quickly surround Alvis.

"You fool! You intend to take us on alone?"

It was nothing for her to worry about.

"Is that how little you think of me? Ah-ha-ha-ha-ha-ha-ha! Die, you mob of idiots!!"

By the time Yamza saw it unfolding, it was already too late. One magic-born before him fell to the ground, spewing blood. One turned to stone and shattered against the earth. One had his body literally rot away on the spot, until nothing but a pile of dust remained. His army was being killed, struck by ailments by one degree or another, and Yamza had no way to stop it.

"Yoouuuuuu!!"

Alvis was, in the end, best suited for close-quarters combat. The Golden Snakehorn's lone horn on her forehead became a symbol of the death that permeated the atmosphere—and then Yamza realized that his defeat was total.

"Surrender, and I will take you prisoner and guarantee you your life."

Her offer was the only method of survival he had. A quick stare with her Snake Eyes had completely shattered his Doppelganger's body. It even had the power to destroy equipment, apparently, leaving Yamza's partner to fade away before battle even began.

...My limbs are starting to go numb. I won't be able to defend myself before long... What kind of sheer strength do these Lycanthropeers enjoy?!

It was bad luck that Yamza had to be paired with the strongest of that trio. He chose the wrong woman to pick a fight with, and he had no idea. Alvis rarely had the chance to fully exercise her power, since she was often picked to serve a commanding role. As a result, she was seen as the de facto manager of the Lycanthropeers, not as a formidable warrior in her own right.

That was Yamza's appraisal as well, and he had totally underrated her.

The war was won. But it was not over. Clayman was a sly demon lord, one who would never forgive betrayal among his own armies. And just when Yamza prepared to nod his agreement to Alvis's offer:

(—You know I would never permit that, yes?)

It was Clayman's voice, booming within Yamza's mind. "Uh?" he instinctively grunted. Then his body began moving, beyond his own control.

"S-stop! Stop that! Please, Sir Clayman, stop this at once!"

A hand took a bluish-purple orb out from his pocket, then brought it to his mouth.

"Mmghh!!"

He locked his jaw as tightly as he could, trying to scramble away from it. It was a pointless act of resistance, and it didn't last long. Struck by Clayman's Marionette takeover, Yamza's body was no longer his own to control.

"...What are you doing?" a suspicious Alvis asked. But by the time she did, Yamza was busy swallowing the orb in his hand—a section from Charybdis's body.

"Hah? Harbhh, nnhhh... Graghaghaaaahhh!!"

"What on—?!"

Alvis tensed up, confused—as long, thin tendrils shot out from his body toward the dead lying around him, taking in the corpses. He ballooned in size, turning into a vast, grotesque ball of flesh. Uncontrollable magical energy flowed within the Alvis-dominated air, forming a hurricane-class blizzard.

The creature before her consumed, expanded, and burst. Having no monster core of its own, it was a self-destructing being, rampaging across the land before meeting its demise. But its temporary power was every bit as strong as Yamza's—and the nature of it was deadly. Its insatiable desire to eat everything in its path was just the same as well.

This was the "forbidden" tactic Yamza was reluctant to use, the intricate trap Clayman had laid. Charybdis had now appeared once more.

✳

Alvis's face tightened as she threw her full force into an attack. It didn't work. No regular strike would ever pierce this constantly expanding Charybdis. Its Ultraspeed Regeneration took in the corpses around it, rapidly reforming it into a temporary body for itself.

"Ngh! This monster…!"

All Alvis could do was gnash her teeth, her Snake Eyes and lightning having no effect. This monster was disaster-class, on a level far, far above her. Even the strongest of the Three Lycanthropeers could do little about it by herself. The only saving grace was that this was a distance away from the main battlefield; there was time before this could start to affect her allies but only until Charybdis could finish creating its body.

Desperation flew in like a violent storm. The worst part was how this monster wasn't satisfied enough using Yamza as its substitute core—it had taken in his Ice Blade as well, sucking up all the heat around it and making the local temperature plummet. The monster was destroying all in its path, turning its aura into an Ice Blizzard, pummeling the area with icy snow and intense wind. That was scary enough, but what Alvis feared even more was the moment when it released all the heat energy it had taken in.

Those who can teleport out might be fine, but everyone else…

…would die.

"I hate this! May all the gods curse that bastard Clayman!!"

Letting her true nature take hold, Alvis screamed as she continually attacked—again and again, no time in between to breathe. It was all in vain. Even if she scarred Charybdis's exterior, any damage to the monster itself was light. It just healed itself too quickly.

"Dammit! I've just got to get everyone out that I can—"

Even through the desperation, Alvis tried to take the best measures she could. To her, this meant trying to relay a plea to Benimaru to retreat everyone from the battlefield.

In the end, however, this never happened. It didn't need to.

"You're ignoring orders, Alvis. I told you to get out if you faced a battle you cannot win."

There, with no previous warning, Benimaru himself appeared.

"...Sir Benimaru?!"

"Oh, Charybdis, eh? My offense did little against it last time, but how about now?"

He gave her a defiant smile.

"Sir Benimaru, this monster is just too—"

"I know. It's perfect for testing my current powers."

Benimaru raised his right hand and grasped it—both Charybdis and his own strength. The fight was over in an instant. His feet planted on the ground, his sword, covered in jet-black flames, slashed the monster's flesh, although it did not fully slice through its freshly constructed body. But something was different from before. Unlike with Alvis's efforts, the Self-Regeneration never started. Dark flames were dancing across the gash, rapidly engulfing its entire body.

"Tch. Not quite there yet. We have no time to play with here, so I'll sadly have to end this."

He turned back toward Alvis, leaning his sword against his shoulder, seemingly unconcerned with Charybdis.

"My apologies. I was hoping we could spar once it had achieved its complete form, but..."

The gigantic beast had not taken to the air yet, but its body was already nearly the length of half a football field. Now, however, it had been fully encased in a black dome.

"Away with you," he whispered, and then a percussive *boom!* shook the land.

It was Hellflare, his wide-range razing attack, this time far more powerful than ever before.

Benimaru's Dominate Flame gave him a full grasp of the flow of magical energy, stabbing right through Charybdis's Magic Interference and rendering its body into ash. It proved to the world that Benimaru's control over magicules completely overpowered this monster's.

"You're kidding me!"

Alvis's surprise was understandable. If his attacks worked on Charybdis, it meant Benimaru's magic force surpassed the monster's. This meant that Benimaru himself was disaster class, on the same level as Alvis's master, the demon lord Carillon.

"I have some business to take care of, Alvis. Effective immediately, I hereby appoint you as my aide to command our entire force."

"...Yes, Sir Benimaru."

She undid her Transformation to kneel down and take the post. She had more than a few questions for Benimaru, but now was not the time for them. Calming her frenzied mind, she meekly accepted her orders.

Charybdis was an unprecedented, unexpected threat, but when faced with that irresistible force, it fell without a moment's delay.

"Hoh, hoh-hoh-hoh... This is quite a surprise. I was expecting Yamza to turn tail and flee. But imagine, dispatching Charybdis that easily..."

"Mm-hmm! I kind of have an affinity for it, but not even we could pull off a kill like that."

"Clayman's forces are destroyed. The mission's a failure—the losses immense. He should have just sat there and played nice, the way our fellow jester told him to."

"Yes, yes. Well, Laplace warned him. Clayman can't blame anyone for it but himself."

Footman and Teare exchanged looks as they spoke. Before them was a heavily wounded Phobio, kept on his feet by the attending Geld.

"We'll need to brief *him* about this, so I'm afraid playtime is over."

Footman himself was unhurt. Teare wasn't, but she was still healthy enough to fight. Judging by their injuries, Geld and Phobio appeared to have lost the day.

"You think you can leave?" Phobio groaned, staggering as he tried to keep himself up. "I knew you guys were bad news. If we can keep you here, Alvis and Sufia will show up before long. Plus, we've got Sir Benimaru. It'll be the end for you."

He was scarred from head to toe, but his wounds had already closed up. The speed at which they healed was mind-boggling, going well beyond the Self-Regeneration most beastmen had and almost reaching the realm of Ultraspeed Regeneration. Phobio had inherited that skill to some extent after the previous Charybdis swallowed him up.

"Just give it up already, kitty!" Teare shouted as she gave Phobio a punch that sent him reeling. It didn't leave Phobio down for long. In a few moments, he was back on his feet.

Teare was the quicker of the two, but she could never quite land a lethal blow. Phobio, on the other hand, was slowly but surely damaging Teare's body. He might have appeared defeated at first glance, but the longer the fight lasted, the more likely it was that it'd end otherwise.

Footman, meanwhile, was rolled up like a meatball, bounding around at hyper-speed and trying to run Geld down. Geld used his great shield to deflect his trajectory, swinging his Meat Cleaver to try to smash him up. His attempts were blocked by Footman's thickened skin, preventing him from dealing decisive damage.

On offense and defense, it was safe to call them perfectly even—but only because Footman hadn't begun seriously fighting yet. And now, with Charybdis defeated, Footman's recess time was over.

"Mgh?!"

Geld, realizing this, positioned himself in front of Phobio.

"What is it, Geld?"

Before he could answer, Footman began raining attacks on the both of them. These were balls of magic, each one enormous and

230

stuffed with energy—a simple attack but one with enough force to alter the landscape around them. One of the magic orbs was enough to shatter Geld's shield and even smash up the armor covering his body. It damaged Phobio in the process, and he no doubt had Ultraspeed Regeneration to thank for still being alive.

(Hooooooh-hoh-hoh-hoh! We weren't tasked with taking care of you two, so we'll extend you the honor of letting you go.)

(I hope you're grateful! If we were serious about this, neither of you would be in this world any longer!)

Neither Geld nor Phobio could stand up any longer to contest them. When the dust from the explosions finally settled, Footman and Teare were gone.

"...This was a total defeat," Geld groused. "I thought I had some strength, but I suppose there's always someone better than you."

"No, Geld. If you hadn't been here, I'd probably be dead right now. Sorry to drag you down..."

"Not at all. We may have lost the battle, but we're still alive. As long as we win next time, we're good."

"Yeah. Yeah, you're right!"

Phobio was not a weak beastman. Footman and Teare were just too strong. Strong enough that you could even call them demon lords. Perhaps Geld had more magical energy at his fingertips, but without the ability to use it shrewdly, that power meant nothing. Geld focused entirely on defense against Footman, but even he knew that he'd never win in a serious fight opposite him. For now, though, that was fine.

(Sir Benimaru, the jesters have fled.)

(I saw,) came the Thought Communication reply. (They might think they're letting us live. How naïve of them.)

Benimaru's orders for Geld were to discover what the enemy was capable of and keep Phobio safe. *I couldn't just sit there and watch things unfold*, he thought, *but not killing me was a bad mistake. Sir Benimaru has recorded how that battle worked out—and then Rimuru will analyze it and break open the secret to their strength.*

Thus, this was a defeat with some benefits to them. Mission accomplished. And if he can't win now, he can close the gap with his future training. He had hoped to settle the score with these guys for using and abusing him, but Geld simply didn't have what it took.

But next time, I'm winning, he silently resolved.

(I'll go back to my command, then.)

(Please do. There's one more dangerous element on the field right now, so I'd better tackle that.)

Sir Benimaru sure has it tough, Geld thought as he closed the link. This battlefield was full of dangerous elements, and since they had to deal with them all at once, he was forced to divvy up his army's assets and scatter them around. Benimaru intended to sort these conflicts by priority and step in himself to handle any rescues needed, but one misstep along the line could lead to serious danger. He seemed to be handling his post well, however. One would think he'd focus on finding and killing Footman first, but he successfully managed to put overall victory above his own vendettas.

This isn't some general with a thirst for blood, I suppose. Compared to when we fought him, the growth he's shown has been amazing...

It made Geld trust in Benimaru all the more.

It was several minutes into the battle—minutes that, to Gabil and Sufia, felt like hours. But it ended unceremoniously.

"Mgh?!"

"What on...?!"

"Huff...huff... What...what is the matter...?"

After the second or third repetition, Sufia had learned how to roll with Middray's throws, helping recover her energy. Gabil, meanwhile, had flung his spear wildly around at this attack he wasn't used to, completely exhausting him. Middray, dealing with them both, appeared completely unhindered by fatigue—compared to sparring with Milim, this wouldn't even make him break a sweat.

And Middray was the first to notice it.

"All forces, use your healing magics!" he shouted, the casual ease disappearing from his face. "Stand up! Stand up and rouse everyone around here!"

"This is bad, Father Middray," Hermes said, apparently feeling much better now. "This guy… The reading I'm getting is huge."

"I know that! This is Charybdis, the beast Lady Milim dispatched just the other day. Or is it its remains?"

"Yeah… It looks unstable to me. I imagine it'll disintegrate before the day is through…"

"But this is a battlefield. If things go wrong, it could rapidly evolve. Better not to give a monster like that the food it craves."

The fallen priests around him cast healing spells to revive both themselves and Team Hiryu under Gabil's command.

"Charybdis?" Sufia asked. "The monster that used Phobio as a core to revive itself with?! I thought Lady Milim had already destroyed it!"

"Yes," Gabil added, realizing this current match was over. "If it was Charybdis, Lady Milim definitely killed it…"

"Calm down. It's not the real thing; just a fragment of its force. I think it used Yamza as its replacement core…"

Middray was using Dragon's Glance to analyze the innards of the creature. It was not as strong as Milim's own Dragon's Eye, but it still provided him with ample enough vision and analysis skills.

Hermes, meanwhile, was surveying the area for any other potential threats. "Looks like you're right, sir. That ass Yamza was trying to kill us, but his soul's already been consumed. With how he is now, we'll just have to keep damage to a minimum and wait for him to fall apart," he coldly concluded.

"Did you hear that? Keep your weapons at the ready, people. And don't get greedy! If buying time is all we need, that won't be a tall order."

"Let us help you out," Gabil added, in sync with Middray as if they were old friends. "We are more used to high-altitude flight since last time. If we can catch those scale attacks before they strike, they cannot hurt us."

Even a crazed, twisting beast like Charybdis had a tendency to chase after anything moving. A flying target, Gabil reasoned, would make the perfect lure. Sufia was also thinking unusually lucidly, trying to execute on what she could do here.

"Right," Middray began, "I'll aid in the retreat so it can't feed off any of our ground forces and—"

But before he could finish, things took an abrupt turn as Benimaru all but vaporized Charybdis.

"What...on...?! He just pulled off the most unbelievable thing!"

"...Who is that guy? A demon lord? Unless you're Lady Milim, how could some regular magic-born do *that*? He has to be some kind of monster..."

Only Middray and Hermes had an accurate bead on the situation. Sufia and Gabil saw it at the same time but couldn't parse what just happened. All they could see was that the evil aura of Charybdis had been snuffed in an instant.

"Hey, what's going on? Tell me!"

"Yes. We seek an explanation as well."

"Yeah, um, I'd want to explain," Hermes said, "but..."

"I don't think we need to," Middray finished.

Before either of them could, the air in front of them twisted and warped, revealing a magic-born with hair as red as roaring flames. It was Benimaru, sword rested on his shoulder, and he was here to take on Middray, the last threat on the battlefield.

"Well," he said with a sneer, "I see you've been entertaining my friends?" Then he realized something wasn't quite right about this picture. There was evidence of combat around him, but there were no injuries—and by the looks of things, no hard feelings on either side.

"Sir Benimaru, wait! These are Lady Milim's fighters, the priests of the Dragon Faithful!"

"What? Lady Milim's?! In that case..."

"Yes! They healed our wounds with magic!"

"...I see. It seems I've jumped to conclusions. You seemed like such a threat in this theater, I couldn't help but be alarmed."

"Wah-ha-ha-ha-ha! You didn't jump to conclusions at all. We *were* actually fighting, yes. And we did perform some healing, but that was to prepare for what we thought was an oncoming disaster. Now I suppose all that wasn't necessary."

"…Ah. So what now? Are you taking us on?"

"Well, what *should* we do…?"

"Because personally speaking, I would prefer not to engage in combat with Lady Milim's forces."

"No, I suppose not. I can understand wanting to try it, but there is no quarrel between us. I would simply want to compare our powers."

"Yes… I can see that."

The two gave each other knowing grins.

"Whoooa!" Hermes interjected. "Not good, Father!"

"Yes, Sir Benimaru! If you hurt one of the Dragon Faithful, there's no telling what kind of calamity that would bring upon us!"

"You heard her, Father Middray! Sir Rimuru is Lady Milim's friend. It would all end in tragedy, I am sure of it!"

Sufia silently resented Hermes and Gabil for stepping in.

"Fair enough," Benimaru said. "Besides, if I don't come at him trying to kill him, I expect it'll result in nothing but defeat for me—and I don't like engaging in losing battles."

"Wah-ha-ha-ha-ha! Quite so. And I'm not sure even I could withstand a blow like the one that buried Charybdis!"

Middray might have laughed the concept off, but he had a suspicion that he could win the battle before Benimaru had a chance to bust that out. That would result in a life-and-death duel, however, going well beyond the boundaries of a friendly sparring session. A battlefield was the wrong place for this, and it no longer meant anything anyway.

Thus ended the battle in the former kingdom of Orbic, while the unified forces enjoyed a near-total victory. But this wasn't the only battlefield.

At the stroke of midnight, Shuna, Soei, and Hakuro sprang into action. They quickly discovered Clayman's headquarters within the wetlands covered by the mysterious mist and began to stealthily make their way there.

Beyond these wetlands were several murky swamps, gas bubbling out from the surface. This was what created the cloud of mist, making things seem eerier than they already were. The moment they waded in, visibility plummeted to nearly nothing.

"Uh-oh. This mist is blocking our Magic Sense."

"It is," confirmed Soei. "That was why we called off our investigation. With this poor visibility, anyone inside would have to rely on their own five senses to 'see' around them. That's what the enemy must use to keep track of what goes on in here."

"Mm, I see. So we face a brutal disadvantage."

"Indeed, Sir Hakuro. You and I can use Covert Agent to hide our presences, but Lady Shuna..."

"I should be fine."

It was true. Hakuro could use his Haze concealing skill to all but disappear to the external observer, as could Soei. You could be standing right next to them and never realize it. Shuna, despite not having this exact Art, could still perfectly heal herself.

"Hmm... A combination of illusory and mystical magic? It doesn't work like Haze, but it has the same effect. Well done, Lady Shuna."

Hakuro was right—this approach was Shuna's original creation. While she wasn't quite as gifted at it as Rimuru, her Creator unique skill allowed her to conjure up her own magic spells without a recipe.

"Then we should be fine," Soei said. "But I want you all to remember that Thought Communication won't work in this fog. Visibility is low, it is hard to stay in contact, and we all need to proceed carefully and cautiously. Also..."

Even with Soei's Replications, Thought Communication–based conversation would be impossible. Instead, he provided a length of Sticky Steel Thread around each of their wrists for emergency contacts. Focusing on this thread would allow them to maintain at least a modicum of communication, but if the string broke, that would be the end of the contact. Using it required a great deal of caution.

Shuna and Hakuro nodded and wrapped it around their wrists.

They were ready now. "Let's get going," Shuna said, and the three ran off.

✳

Then, after several minutes of walking, Shuna stopped.

"...Oh no," she whispered. "We seem to have fallen into a trap."

"A trap?"

"I can feel my senses going haywire on me, yes, but I don't feel any enemies around the— *What?!*"

Before he could finish speaking, Soei felt multiple presences nearby appear from out of nowhere, virtually surrounding them.

"How on...? Where were so many of these enemies hiding, such that we couldn't notice them?"

"No, Hakuro! They weren't hiding. We were lured right to them!"

"Ah... This fog. The cloud's doing more than confusing our sense of direction. It's concealing the enemy and inviting us right to the middle of their circle..."

"I see. That explains the odd feeling I had just now."

"You're right. The mist is triggering Spatial Interference to lure intruders from any direction to a specific place—"

Before Shuna finished explaining this, one of the presences appeared. Soei and Hakuro steeled themselves toward it, keeping a watchful eye out for the still-unseen monsters in the mist, as Shuna closed her mouth and focused on it—a skeleton dressed in a vestment of pure white.

"Such massive magical force," she whispered, beads of sweat on her forehead. For a moment, she thought it might have been Clayman himself, although she banished the thought quickly. It was past midnight; the demon lord should be over at the Walpurgis Council. Perhaps it was one of Clayman's five fingers, then—but the figure before them exuded pure presence, beyond that of the Lycanthropeers and approaching demon lord level. The power of this magic-born was overwhelming; it was a wonder that it was subservient to anyone else.

She recalled what Mjurran told her about Clayman's most senior leaders—and that one of them was geared strictly toward defending their base.

"...You must be Adalmann, then. The ruler of this land—the wight king with power over countless undead..."

Hakuro had just used Heavengaze to reach the same conclusion. But this figure was more ominous than how Mjurran described it, its force far more massive. The guardian of this wetland was a wight king on the level of a demon lord.

Soei accepted Shuna and Hakuro's appraisal, finding no reason to doubt it. Then, quietly, he sharpened his bladelike mind. No matter who the enemy is, he *will* kill him—that was his credo.

But just as Soei was about to move, the wight king spoke.

"Indeed, I am Adalmann. I have been ordered to protect this land by the great demon lord Clayman. Lowly intruders like you may do nothing but humbly submit your lives to me. Do it, and I will kill you without pain."

This was the command of a kingly figure, not the words of a foe who saw Shuna and her companions as equals. Considering the massive, overwhelming amount of Adalmann's magic energy, anything else would almost seem improper.

Now, all around the area, a legion of over ten thousand undead were writhing, as if attracted to the seemingly inexhaustible supply of magicules. Cracking, wrenching sounds filled the air as they moved to encircle the trio.

"We are fully surrounded," Shuna breathlessly reported. "This mist is working alongside a directional barrier to prevent teleportation outside. All our means of communication are blocked. The only way to get out of here is to defeat this Adalmann foe."

"Then we must strike their leader at once."

"No disagreement here. A blow from me can even kill the dead."

Hakuro and Soei had no interest in following Adalmann's advice. As Shuna explained the situation, they both went on the attack. But Adalmann simply laughed in their faces.

"Heh-heh-heh... You appear not to know your place. I generously provided you mercy, and yet, you remain foolish to the end. You will regret refusing that offer shortly."

He breezily swung an arm. The next moment, the most surprising thing happened—the white blade of Hakuro, instantly zooming within range of Adalmann, was blocked by the knight who had appeared in front of him.

Hakuro stepped back in shock, failing to believe that this killer blow could be parried. This was a death knight, ranked A-minus in the Guild system, but from that clash, Hakuro could sense something was off. It was a powerful monster, yes, but no garden-variety death knight could ever block a slash from him.

"You are no normal adversary. Very well. Let me give you my full attention."

He had an accurate bead on this death knight and the threat it carried for him. Its strength relied not on physical toughness but on the built-up level of its skills—which meant Heavengaze would tell him nothing about it. So he used his own physical might to confront it.

"......"

The death knight was silent; the corpse serving as the shell of its body was incapable of speech. But there was a blistering blue flame in its sunken eyes. The light of consciousness was in there, the pride of a former human being, and it told Hakuro that his challenge was accepted.

Even after abandoning life, this death knight was a proud, noble warrior. The difference in magical energy between the two was negligible, as was their physical muscle. It marked the beginning of a clash between built-up skills, one that quickly made sparks fly.

Before Soei, meanwhile, was Adalmann himself, an enormous shadow from out of nowhere blocking all attempts to attack him.

"Deh!" Soei glared at the towering shade. "No... A dragon zombie?"

"No, Soei!" Shuna could see it more fully, through the muck. "Nothing that weak! Its magicules outnumber yours; it stands at the peak of the undead—it's a death dragon!"

Soei's face tensed upon hearing this. He could manage this solo, but fighting this foe while guarding Shuna was a different story.

The usually reliable Hakuro was too busy with the death knight. He had to dispatch this death dragon as soon as possible, or else Shuna would be overrun by the thousands of undead lumbering their way in from all sides. Now, Soei realized, was no time to hold back.

"Then, die! Mystic Thread Strike!"

Without delay, Soei dealt out the most powerful attack he could, a killer move that fricasseed the enemy with thousands of branching strings of Sticky Steel Thread, each granted the Insta-Kill effect from his Shadow Striker unique skill. They created a virtual garden of beautiful, bloody blooms, like a kaleidoscope. Even a half-spiritual life-form like an undead would be snuffed out by this spiritual body-slicing move—or so it should have.

"No! It's regenerating?!"

Soei could feel himself begin to sweat. The sixty-foot-long beast's body was ripped apart, seemingly ending the battle. But then, as if nothing was amiss, the death dragon's body reassembled itself. It went so fast, even faster than Ultraspeed Regeneration, that it seemed like nothing less than immortality.

"Then let me destroy you, soul and all…"

"Soei," Shuna shouted out as he steeled himself, "calm down! You know how to analyze your foe's strengths. You should know that you can't beat a death dragon!"

"But…"

"That dragon's soul is within the magic-born Adalmann," she quietly declared. "Don't worry about me; just work on keeping that dragon where it is. I'll defeat Adalmann!"

"That's too dangerous!"

"No, Soei. Listen to me. I'm angry."

A cold smile stretched across Shuna's face to dispel Soei's worries. They shined a piercing light, exhibiting her raging emotions. The sight made Soei clam up, unable to speak.

As the former princess of the ogre tribe, Shuna's words had the power to make others do her bidding—and now, that power was stronger than even the otherworlder Kirara Mizutani's Bewilder unique skill. Besides, Shuna wasn't some precious cargo that required constant protection. Soei knew that. So there was only one answer.

"Yes, Lady Shuna. Best of luck."

She contentedly smiled. "You too, Soei. That dragon's all yours."

Soei nodded back, giving Shuna his full trust, then threw himself back into his own fight.

✳

Shuna, left alone, didn't waver at all as she confronted Adalmann. The wight king rewarded this by glaring at her.

"Hoh? And what do you intend to do, little girl? What could *you* do without anyone to defend you? How are you going to engage ten thousand foes at once?"

There was an odd sort of joy in Adalmann's voice. He *was* enjoying this, in fact. The demon lord Clayman's orders were absolute, but Adalmann was still afforded his own sense of free will, although his activities were limited in every other way. The only thing he was allowed full rein to do was wipe out intruders.

Clayman's other minions derided him for having so much power but so little brains to back that up—and it was only because he was not allowed to leave this land or do anything on his own volition. And it was perhaps the way that he wasn't even allowed to provide excuses to them that made people fail to realize it.

Adalmann was less a magic-born and more a weapon, a base-defense mechanism bound to this land. His soul remained unbound, but his behavior was now automatic, following the orders input into him. He spoke of his loyalty to Clayman, but that was just an act. He had been preset to pay his formal respects to the owner of this device.

In his heart of hearts, Adalmann wanted to be released from these bonds. That was why he enjoyed talking with Shuna. The defense mechanisms worked automatically; he had no authority to alter them in any way. The chats he had with intruders were his only hobby to speak of, the only thing no one else could interfere with. The demon lord Kazalim, creator of this structure, offered him that much mercy. Or maybe not. But Adalmann wanted to think so. That gesture, after all, was what had allowed him to live all this time, a thousand years or so, without succumbing to insanity.

Even if it was just a measure to keep this system running longer, I have to thank him for that, at least.

And he meant it. That was why he never spared any effort to hammer down intruders, regardless of what he thought about it. But at least he prayed, as he imagined an army of ten thousand undead preying upon Shuna, that it could be done painlessly.

But then her voice rang out sharply once more.

"No need to worry about me. Alignment Field!!"

At that instant, the area within a three-hundred-foot radius of Shuna became holy ground, where nothing of evil alignment could tread. It was another original product of Shuna's mind, using her experience to Analyze the Anti-Magic Area and Holy Field, then Fuse them together. This barrier obstructed all magicules, but it could also be set to block fire, wind, or any one of the other four major elements, making it a shockingly formidable defensive spell.

"Now we won't be distracted. If I defeat you, that will destroy the defense system with you at its core, right?"

"…Hmm. Impressive. And you've seen through my secret as well. What is your name, girl?"

Shuna was absolutely right. If Adalmann died, the whole base-defense system would crumble. It was structured to bind Adalmann's soul down, using it to circulate the large amounts of magicules it required. That would no doubt free the death dragon serving him—as well as the death knight, Alberto, who was once Adalmann's friend and confidant. Shuna had seen all that at a glance, and Adalmann offered her his honest respect for that. Respect and the ever-so-slight hope that she might be able to release him from this pain.

"My name is Shuna."

"Shuna… Lady Shuna. Then let us settle this for good. If you can defeat me, I will follow your wishes."

"My, thank you for the polite request. However, all I seek is the destruction of the demon lord Clayman. If you stay out of my way, I could leave you alone to live on this land, perhaps?"

"Heh-heh-heh. I'm not sure that's possible, I'm afraid."

"No? I thought you might be capable of conquering the ties that bind you, but perhaps I was wrong. Oh, well. In that case," she said without a moment's hesitation, "I will kill you as I intended to."

If I could conquer them, thought Adalmann, *I would have done it eons ago. Kazalim is a man to be feared, a foe no one can hold a candle to. The nickname Curse Lord is not just bravado. And she makes it all sound so easy...*

"Then the time for talk is over," he declared, still having no ill will toward her. "Try to resist me with everything you've got!"

....

......

...

Adalmann was born a prince in one of the small nations under the jurisdiction of the Holy Empire of Lubelius. These lands were all too weak to have their own standing militaries, instead relying on the Temple Knights sent from the Church's central headquarters. In exchange, they were required to adopt Luminism as the state religion and provide money and qualified personnel for their knight corps.

The Western Holy Church of the time didn't enjoy the influence they wielded now; this was before the advent of their Crusader groups. Practitioners who showed talent could be granted the name of "acolyte," a nonhereditary title, but that was it. In the midst of that, Adalmann was an exceptional performer—and with his elder brother taking over the country and quickly giving birth to an heir, he was free to devote himself deeply to spreading the faith, joining the Church's missionary corps and quickly making a name for himself.

He was devout to the faith, constantly fascinated by the divine works of Luminus. Never once did he doubt the existence of this lone, true, powerful goddess. That devotion eventually led him to learn the "divine miracles" of the Church's archbishop class, making him the greatest master of holy magic in his era.

In time, he advanced to the rank of cardinal, the loftiest in the Western Holy Church. In the Lubelius noble hierarchy, he was no one particularly special. But he redoubled his efforts, extending his interests to magic beyond the holy spells he was familiar with. He would hold long discussions about magic with Gadora, one of his best friends at the time, as he incessantly polished his skills. The effort eventually paid off—he became an Enlightened, transcending the bounds of humanity itself.

An Enlightened was a person who retained their human form but on the inside was a demi-spiritual being, similar to a higher-level elemental. Their powers were leaps and bounds above those of a regular human, and they were often seen as defenders of the human cause. This power quickly put Adalmann in a position of immense central authority.

Time passed. Adalmann's intensive study continued. And eventually, he took the next step forward, to the highest peak of mankind—a Sage. As he did, he was greeted with wondrous news: He would be called to the Inner Cloister, at the top of the Church's holy mountain.

The offer filled him with joy.

Finally, an audience with Luminus herself!

He always believed that Luminus was real, an unwavering belief that served as the source for all his faith. So he promptly set off for the holy mount, not believing for a moment that it would lead to tragedy. That belief, sadly, would ultimately betray him.

....

......

...

The intense magical battle continued.

"Melt all and wear it away—Acid Shell!"

The aspectual spell Adalmann had just cast conjured balls of liquid in the air, each capable of melting flesh to the bone. They rained down upon Shuna.

She didn't miss a beat.

"Flame Wall."

The barrier of fire deflected and vaporized all the magic-infused droplets. Between accelerating her mind to a thousand times normal, possessing superior Analyze and Assess skills, and changing the rules with Cast Cancel and Control Laws, Shuna's unique skill Parser was made for a clash of magic like this. From the moment Adalmann began constructing a spell, she had a way to deal with it.

"Then how about this? Malicious dead, accept this sacrifice—Curse Bind!!"

This was necromancy, an offshoot of elemental magic that took advantage of the negative energies from ghouls and the undead. Curse Bind was a particularly nasty one, summoning zombies that latched on to anything living—human or magic-born—and drained away their life energy.

Even that wasn't enough.

"Holy Bell."

Shuna's refreshingly clear voice reached Adalmann's ears, and right after came the tolling of bells he was once well used to hearing. That was all it took to send the grudgeful zombies to the afterlife.

"...It can't be! Why? Why is a monster wielding elemental magic?!"

Adalmann's eyes shot open at the divine miracle playing out before him. The magic was deployed all too beautifully, reminding him of his youthful days spent studying.

This was holy magic in the air, something a monster girl should never be able to weave. The unbelievable sight made him scream without thinking.

Shuna smiled as she decided to answer Adalmann's question, even though she had no obligation to. "Do you find it strange? Perhaps you need a little more imagination. Holy magic is not the exclusive domain of humans; it will work with anyone who believes in the power of miracles, based on the strength of their belief."

Conventional wisdom in this world stated that holy magic worked by forging a pact with an elemental spirit. This was both right and wrong. The fact that magic-born could cast healing spells indicated that "holy" magic was possible for them without any pact with a holy being. Most humans, and even monsters, didn't understand that.

The sole condition for acquiring holy magic was having faith—believing in miracles, to put it another way. Good, or evil, didn't

factor into it; the strength of one's emotions was directly converted into power. That was how this family of magic worked. (This was also the reason why the Dragon Faithful that worshipped Milim could access holy magic.)

Hearing this terse explanation was staggering to Adalmann. *I—I was wrong the whole time? I was betrayed. I lost my faith in the goddess Luminus. I thought I would never be able to wield holy magic again...*

Luminus betrayed Adalmann—or to be precise, he had been trapped by the supreme leaders of Luminism. He still didn't know why. Perhaps they feared his rise in power; perhaps it was another reason. All he knew was that Luminus, his goddess, offered him no helping hand.

It's almost comical, in a way. The Seven Days Clergy tricked me into setting off to quell a large army of undead attacking our people... I never could've guessed it was a trap. And thanks to that Gadora conducting magical experiments on me, I've been revived as this twisted, reviled figure...

Unaware that he was being led to his grave, he waltzed right into the far edge of the Great Forest of Jura, where he still dwelled today. He was awaited by a legion of undead, led by a dragon zombie. He was accompanied by Alberto, acolyte and his closest friend, along with four knights and an expeditionary force that loved him, and they fought with all their might. It wasn't enough.

Adalmann fell to the ground—and died once. But then Reincarnation, a Mysterious Art placed upon him by his other friend Gadora, activated and resurrected his soul—a soul that had already been poisoned by the miasma across the land, the malice of the dead around him. He was reborn not as a man but as a wight, transformed into a skeleton. The metamorphosis had caught the attention of the demon lord Kazalim, and now here he was today.

"Thus, if you are incapable of handling holy magic, then I am positive you are incapable of beating me."

Shuna's words hit home like a knockout punch, reminding Adalmann that he was still in battle. "Wh-why?" he instinctively asked. "Why did you think I was a master of holy magic?"

"Because of how you look," came the cold reply. "That white

vestment, which only high-level bishops and above are permitted to wear. You were worthy of such fine robes, and yet, you whine and carry on about being unable to conquer such a basic bind like this. I hardly needed to examine you closely to see that you wore that robe simply out of blind attachment to your former holy magic."

She had him pegged the entire time. He could hear it in her voice.

"Nnnhh... I have let you spout far too much nonsense!!"

Adalmann flew into a rage—not at Shuna but at himself. Seeing his true heart now, something he couldn't notice until it was pointed out to him, made him both exasperated and enraged at his own spinelessness. But he could also feel an inexplicably refreshing comfort in his heart, like the fog of a thousand years had finally lifted from him. He let his raging emotions drive him to cast another spell.

"I offer this prayer to my god. I seek your divine powers. May my request reach your ears safely—"

Yes. I simply lacked the resolve. Having my beloved friends turn into undead, I couldn't let myself die and leave them behind... I wasn't good enough. Necromancy and aspectual magic cannot cleanse the undead. Who could say how many times I wished I could tap into holy magic...

Those "friends" were one reason why Adalmann was bound to this area. He couldn't abandon the fine men and women who died here but lived on as accursed zombies. And that intent was the bond that tied them to this land. Finally, just now, Adalmann realized the mistake he had made.

So he connected together a complex seal with the bones that were his hands and boldly declared his prayer to the lands above. It was an incantation, as shown by the complicated geometrical shapes that appeared in the air before him.

This girl, Shuna... I have no grudge against her. If anything, I owe her a great debt for opening my eyes. But suicide is forbidden to me. I apologize, but I will need to have you join me—

That apology came from the heart.

The checks placed upon him by Kazalim ranged far and wide, holding Adalmann down—but if he was caught up in the fallout from an attack on the enemy, that was hardly his fault. He planned to destroy himself, taking Shuna along him, for only then could he free the people who unwittingly joined him.

A layered circle of magic spread out, covering Shuna and Adalmann.

"—and render all to dust! Disintegration!!"

"I was waiting for that! Overdrive!!"

Just before Adalmann could complete his spell, Shuna used Parser for a Control Laws rewrite. The results wrested control of the local spiritual elements away from Adalmann, driving them haywire.

"Wh-what…? You have less than a tenth of my magical energy! How could you possibly overwrite my magic?!"

Magicules and spiritual particles were controlled by magical force. Having his magic overwritten could only mean that Adalmann's force was overpowered by Shuna's. To him, Shuna looked hopelessly outclassed, but now, at long last, Adalmann realized he was wrong on that score as well.

"Impressive. Let me reward you by releasing you from this land!"

The wight was swallowed up by a flood of light, unable to hear Shuna's words to the end. She had used magic on him, realizing that someone like Adalmann—at least her equal in terms of holy magic—could collect the energy required to purify the local area. She wasn't expecting him to break out the most powerful of all holy spells, but luckily for her, she knew how that one worked. That was what made it so easy to overwrite.

The light now permeated the land, enveloping not just Adalmann but all the other undead—cleansing them.

∗

Hakuro and Soei ran up to Shuna.

"I tell you, I wanted to end this sooner, but that death knight was far more capable than I estimated. You saved my life there, Lady Shuna."

With the land fully cleansed, the death knight reverted all the way down to a lowly skeletal fighter and fell to the ground. Following Adalmann's will, it had lost any further desire to fight. The sight was enough to make Hakuro realize the battle was over. He regretted losing such a challenging opponent, but protecting Shuna took priority over everything else, and she required his attention right now.

"No, Hakuro, you were a great help to me. You too, Soei, distracting that death dragon's attention and buying me so much time. If it had fallen out of our control, I doubt we could have won."

"It shames me that I could not defeat it."

As Soei implied, the death dragon was a powerful foe, capable of healing light damage instantly and boasting an aura that infected the mind of anyone who touched it. It took someone like him, capable of controlling multiple Replications at once, to emerge from that unscathed. If anything, he deserved praise for holding out so long against a foe that shut down his decisive weapon.

The death dragon, too, vanished upon Adalmann's defeat, unable to maintain its existence after the magicule supply that powered it was shut off. Soei didn't much like how it ended, but anything you can walk away from is a victory.

A victory, yes, but one with regrets. The three looked at one another and sighed.

"Still," muttered Shuna, "if Adalmann had engaged me seriously from the beginning, none of us would be alive, would we? I think I let my anger drive me to be a little too reckless."

Adalmann never let up on her at all during the fight, but he also never attempted anything underhanded to snare her. If he really intended to kill them all, he could've done so in many other ways. Shuna could see that, and it filled her with regret.

"Quite true," Hakuro commented. "Perhaps our new strengths have made us grow a tad conceited."

"Certainly. It is just as Sir Rimuru fretted about. There is no telling what may happen in battle. I should have gathered more intelligence."

In the end, however, a win was a win. Clayman's domain had lost its main line of defense. But that didn't end things. The trio had a job to do—seize Clayman's castle and fully neutralize the threat inside.

Noncombatants comprised the majority of the people remaining in the castle, none of whom signed any oath of loyalty to Clayman.

The more quick-witted among them, or those who took the employment simply for money's sake, surrendered without a hint of resistance. There were also many who were restrained in the castle by mental or spiritual bonds, but a combination of persuasion and magical de-cursing on Shuna's part allowed them to capture the entire castle in short order.

With the occupants neutralized, it was time to start searching. They had already confirmed that the demon lord Carillon wasn't being held here, but they wanted to seek out anything they might be able to use against Clayman.

As they did, a figure approached them.

"...Please, one moment."

"Mm? You're still alive? Did you need me to finish you off?"

"Wait, Hakuro. He has no will to fight left."

It was Adalmann, and Shuna had to calmly keep Hakuro from drawing his sword. The wight fell to his knees, accompanied by a single skeletal fighter.

"Please, allow me to call you Lady Shuna. Thanks to your magic, all of us have been released from the bonds that tied us here. Perhaps it was fate that kept us alive without being cleansed. I have a request that I hope you will let me propose."

"...What is that?" a quizzical Shuna asked, fearing this would be yet more trouble for them.

"Thank you for hearing me out. I was hoping I would be able to meet the figure that you have devoted your faith to, Lady Shuna. When I lost my faith, I also lost the chance to ever reach the heights of my power ever again. My faith in my goddess Luminus is dead—and I need to find a new god for myself."

""".....""" The three each gave Adalmann incredulous looks.

"I... Well, we have a great respect for Sir Rimuru, yes, but we don't worship him," Shuna stammered in reply.

"Sir Rimuru, you say?" Adalmann was unfazed, still eager to sell himself. "Truly a wonderful name, one fully worthy of describing the glories of my new god. We may merely be a pair of fragile undead, but I believe we may be able to offer you assistance. Lady

Shuna, would it be possible to arrange an audience with this Sir Rimuru?"

Shuna wanted to remind Adalmann of the difference between blindly, unconditionally worshipping someone and treating them with respect while dealing with your problems by yourself. But she didn't. It seemed like too much to get into. Instead, she conjured up a mental image of Rimuru, the boingy slime she knew.

Well, why not? Once he sees Sir Rimuru in the flesh, that might be enough to make him give up.

Adalmann seemed to be the type who got the wrong impression of people easily. It would take time to persuade him to think otherwise, so Shuna figured it'd be expeditious for everyone involved if she just nodded and said yes.

Once the dust settled, Shuna was in command of Adalmann and the several thousand undead that "survived" the battle (or whatever it was that undead did). Clayman's castle was now fully conquered.

That Time I Got Reincarnated as a Slime

The impossibly ornate door connected right to the meeting hall.

A large, round table was positioned in the center, with twelve evenly spaced chairs surrounding it. Ten demon lords were on the invite list (with Carillon absent), so two of these seats would be empty even if I took up one. Attendees sat in chronological order of their demon lord appointment, and so I was placed right in front of the door—not that I minded. My attention was focused in the room around me anyway.

On an occasion like this, I wanted to observe my new colleagues as much as possible. Of course, there were only two people here right now. One was Ramiris, at the seat of honor way on the other side. She was seated and kicking her legs around, having a whale of a time, like a kid on a car trip. I figured I could ignore her.

No, my attention was on her right, at the seat directly facing me. There I saw a man with bewitchingly attractive red hair. A man, definitely, but there was more than a touch of femininity to his dashing good looks. His eyes were shut, but I doubted he was napping.

One look was all I needed to know: This dude was trouble. Analyze and Assess seemed to suggest that he wasn't any big deal, but my sixth sense was giving me the eeriest vibes with him. At first glance, he seemed like an inexperienced kid, kind of magically strong but unable to control his aura. Without the Great Sage's analytical skills, I might've been tricked—that was how crafty he was at hiding his true self, feeding the people around him misinformation and making them underestimate his true skills. We hadn't even started fighting yet, and the battle was already under way.

It made me recall the mind-reading skills of Gazel, the dwarf king. Kind of like my Great Sage, nobody would know you had that skill unless you told them. It wouldn't be until someone tried it on you that you'd notice it, I think, unless it was a mind reading that went really deep into your psyche to avoid that. As long as my latent resistance didn't fail me, I was pretty sure I'd be okay.

As a result of this, hiding your skills was very important. You could also bluff people into thinking you had certain skills or deliberately mess up a skill to make them think you were inept to wield it. There were all kinds of ways to play with your opponents' minds, and that was exactly what this pretty boy was doing—tricking other people's Analyze and Assess skills to mess around with them.

My idea had always been to hide my powers, keep my aura turned down as long as possible, and give the enemy zero information to work with. This guy, meanwhile, was using his rivals' data-gathering skills against them. It was a sort of screening process. He was, in effect, asking his foes "Do you have the power to read me?" If they didn't, they were out of the picture; if they did, he'd gauge their response. If the fake info he planted into their minds was enough to scare them off, they weren't worth dealing with in the first place—but if you *did* notice his trick, that glance at the sheer depths of his powers would make you unable to resist him.

But think of it like this. Even the data he *wanted* you to know about indicated that he had as much magical force as Carillon. There was no way to guess how much he actually had. Even if you understood his game, it was hard not to let it unnerve you a bit.

This was Guy, and he was clearly on a whole other level.

By the time I was done examining Guy, a large man lumbered into the room, bringing only one guest with him. This was Daggrull, the demon lord giant whose overwhelming presence dominated any room he was in. He immediately walked up and slammed himself into a seat at Guy's right, kicking back and putting his feet up. The empty space between them must've belonged to Milim, indicating that the table divided demon lords into two halves based on their order, with Guy on one end and me on the other.

I turned my eyes to him. Guy was a tall figure himself, but Daggrull was enormous, not to mention comfy-looking in his specially made chair. Even something like this chair was an opulent-looking magical item. This was Veldora's favorite rival, and the magic with which he presented himself definitely signaled to me that he could take on a dragon type.

Plus, the amount of magicule energy on him was just ridiculous. Was that higher or lower than Veldora's? It seemed bottomless to me, but it'd be hard to accurately measure unless I fought him for real. Still, quality beat quantity. Just because he had a bunch of magicules on hand didn't make him seem that scary to me. The key was how well he used them. Differences in skill level were a vital aspect of any fight, of course, and a demon lord like Daggrull couldn't be *that* unskilled. *I suppose I'll need to watch out for him, too.*

Now another one came in, a handsome, muscle-bound man decked out in some real fancy-looking threads. He was tall, if not as tall as Daggrull, and his facial features looked like they'd been chiseled. His short, curly blond hair looked wild on his scalp, perhaps representing his violent personality. To put it simply, he had Hollywood good looks, and he knew how to charm people.

I suppose, of course, the thing that stuck out the most were the two fangs visible from his lips. He must've been the demon lord Valentine, the vampire. He sat to Ramiris's left, so in terms of the seat order, he must've been about as old as Daggrull—that, or perhaps he just took over for whoever he replaced. Not that seat assignments mattered that much.

What struck me more were the pair Valentine brought with him. One was an elderly man, kind of a manservant type. Definitely well-trained, unmoving and statuesque. His aura was restrained, revealing nothing—the same strategy I used. The second one, meanwhile, was an eye-catchingly beautiful silver-haired girl who seemed to shine like the sun. Her skin was pale, and she had one red eye and one blue. There was something oddly eerie about this girl, who appeared to be on the cusp of adulthood and was clad in a maid-style dress. Maid dresses are like battle uniforms, as they say, and it wouldn't be odd for this girl to be pretty strong.

And these two were both working for this guy? That's a surprise. The girl, in particular, was just letting her gigantic aura out all over the place. *But—hang on.* When our eyes met, I was struck by the most uncomfortable feeling. Maybe I was imagining it, but it seemed like she was changing the nature of her aura at random.

Understood. Analyze and Assess indicates that the target likely bears more magicules than the demon lord Valentine.

Ah, I knew it. I couldn't read her overall energy count, but it's higher than Valentine's, the guy she's serving. It was very cleverly concealed—if you didn't have an ultimate skill like mine, you'd never spot it. But again, they weren't really intent on hiding it—like Guy, they wanted to assess you, see whether you spotted it or not.

Could this girl be the *real* demon lord? Or perhaps the previous holder of this seat, the demon lord that retired out. Maybe this is that "Milus," the vampiress that even Veldora had high praise for. The changeover happened more than 1,500 years ago, so perhaps not too many demon lords knew about that—or did but were keeping mum about it. Or didn't care. Either way, better be careful.

Valentine, the current demon lord, was no pushover himself. He had a heroic sort of ambition, even more than an untransformed Carillon, so there was no reason to doubt his strength. And if that wasn't enough, he had that freaky girl with her. If it was her domain that got burned to ash, it wouldn't be strange for her to despise Veldora at all. I resisted the urge to yell "Why'd you have to piss *that* lady off?!"

At least there was one saving grace—who wouldn't mind dying by the hand of such a beautiful figure? (Quite a few people, I imagine, but…) *I'll just have to hope she doesn't learn about Veldora and me—or if she does, that I don't have to clean up the mess.*

After a little while, the fifth person showed up—this one a loner, almost sleepwalking to his post. He had two swords on his belt, but that's it. Not much of an arsenal. I got a quick glance at his eyes; they were light blue. His hair was a very dark shade of purple with silver streaks in it. He still looked young to me, maybe even high-school age, and he had well-defined facial features, although they were spoiled by his sleepy eyes and general listlessness.

He stopped by Ramiris's seat to say hello. "Yo. Man, you're still, like, the size of a bug, huh?"

"Oh, you trying to start a fight with me? Like you could even handle me, Deeno."

So person number five was Deeno. He definitely seemed cut from the same cloth as her. Neither was seriously riled; they seemed to just be screwing with each other.

"Why would I need to, dumbass? Like, it's totally obvious who would win."

"Pfft! I didn't realize you were in *that* much of a hurry to die. I'm in perfect physical form today, I'll have you know!"

"Uh-huh. Hey, haven't you shrunk since last time I saw you?"

"What do you *want* from me?! I only just got reborn recently!"

When I asked her about it, Ramiris said she had been resurrected around five hundred years ago. It would apparently take her several centuries to fully mature. This seemed to convince Deeno.

"Ohhh, that's why? That's kinda a pain for you, isn't it? But you kept all your memories, right?"

"My memories, yes. But my spirit's degenerated along with my body… Ooh, but I'm still the strongest outta all of you! I need a handicap like this, or it's no fun!"

"Guy, I think Ramiris is sayin' something? Did you hear her just now?"

"Bahhh?! What are you, stupid? I know how to pick my enemies, all right? I'm not saying I could KO Guy in one punch or anything!"

A bigmouth like her changed her stripes all too quickly. I guess that red-haired guy really was Guy, too, and judging by Ramiris's freak-out, he really was a menace. *I'll just write "Guy = dangerous" in my internal notepad. It's little notes like these that have saved me from peril more than once. You can't underestimate the power of that.*

The two kept on talking in hushed voices so as not to rile Guy. They were discussing Beretta and Treyni, Ramiris's guests, and of course Ramiris was bragging up and down about them.

"Wha? Why's a total loner like you got attendants here?" Deeno complained. "You're making me look like a dweeb for showing up alone!"

"Hee-heeeee! Now I can get back at everyone for calling me a little shrimp and a loner, *you* in particular! Wait'll you see how powerless you are against these guys!"

"Oh, you want us to fight? Is it okay if I rip 'em up?"

"Huh? Of *course* it's not okay! If you break them, I'm seriously going to tell on you to Guy and make him make *you* pay for it!"

It's like Guy was her big brother or something. It was breathtaking how quickly she let other people do the dirty work for her.

"...But really, *man*, these guys are the real deal. Like, I looked at 'em for real just now, and it's like, *damn*!"

Beretta and Treyni silently nodded at Deeno. They were far too good for Ramiris, really.

"Right! You see? You see, you see? Now I've got some muscle to back up my words, know what I mean?" Ramiris stuck out her chest (not that she had much of one) to show up Deeno. *Their upgrades were entirely my doing, but ah well.*

Beretta and Treyni remained silent. They were the perfect attendants. They didn't speak, and the dozing Shion behind me could definitely learn a thing or two from them.

Once he finished saying his hellos, Deeno stumbled over to his seat. It was next to Valentine's, making him another member of the old guard. Deeno ignored Valentine entirely as he sat down...and immediately put his head on the table and started sleeping. *That* seemed kind of rude. Maybe demon lords didn't make it a habit to say hi to one another, and all those put-downs with Ramiris were the exception to the rule.

Deeno couldn't have acted less interested in being here. Showing up was enough for him, it seemed, but falling asleep without even bothering to read the room was, in a way, incredibly self-centered. Fearless, too.

I suppose that act had to be backed up with some actual ability. Hopefully. Let's go with that. He *was* jamming my skills a bit, so I couldn't be sure of what he had. He stared at me with his half-open eyes whenever I tried analyzing him, so he had to have noticed. That banter with Ramiris made me think he was pretty chill, but I definitely shouldn't put my guard down. Given the rapport he seemed to have with Ramiris, though, I hoped I didn't have to make him my enemy.

The next one through the door was the empress of the harpies, the demon lord Frey. Milim told me about her, and let me tell you, she was *explosively* erotic. I wondered how she flew with those breasts; they must generate a ton of wind resistance.

…Oops. My mind's going off track. But can you blame me? That was just the sheer impact of her appearance.

Once she stepped inside, her eyes turned first to Milim's empty seat and then to me. Even the way she turned her head was mesmerizing. I mean, come on… And when she passed by, oh, what a wonderful aroma she had on her.

As I basked in this, I felt something sinister behind my back. Shion was clearly peeved. Must've noticed I was letting that perfume get the best of me. *Well spotted, Shion.* Riling her any further was too scary a concept to entertain, so I reset my mind and got back to business.

Her magicule count wasn't anything to write home about—maybe smaller than Shion's or Benimaru's. Of course, Shion could probably line up well with Valentine at this point, so I'm not saying it was *that* tiny. Quality, not quantity. It'd be foolish to judge on this alone. In terms of chest size, meanwhile, it was really hard to pick a winner— *Oops. Better not think about that.*

If I had to guess, maybe she had a lot of hidden skills? That was the kind of concerning vibe I got.

What *was* worth noting were her attendants. One was another big-breasted harpy, on the same level as Frey. She was young, and her body was about as lascivious as they come. The other was a large man, his magical energy on par with Frey's. He had huge, eagle-like wings sprouting from his back, so he must've been a male harpy. He was a measure smaller than Daggrull but otherwise could give Valentine a run for his money in muscles and good looks, although the lion mask on his face made the latter part unclear.

Wait. Lion?

Report. According to my analysis and assessment—

Yeah. No way, right? I mean, this guy felt totally different from Carillon. It had to be some other guy. I didn't need Raphael to spell it out for me. I'm not *that* dumb.

......

There was no way the AWOL Carillon would attend Walpurgis with such an obvious ploy. He'd be more careful with it, taking pains to act prudently. They say there are at least three people in the world who look exactly like you, and I'm sure that's the story with this guy, too.

As I observed them, I was struck by the odd feeling that a chilly wind was blowing over me. I turned to find a blond-haired beauty coming in, blessed with looks that only the gods themselves could have given her. She walked right up to me.

"...You are Rimuru?"

"Yeah, but—"

I thought about saying "Yeah, but who're you?" at first. I definitely didn't know her—but then it dawned on me. There were four demon lords left. Carillon was missing, and that just left Clayman, Milim, and Leon. *Leon was blond-haired, I think, and beautiful enough that people called him the Platinum Devil... Hmm...*

"...Oh, you're Leon? Did you need something?"

"Yes, I am Leon. And no, I need nothing from you. The sight of you brought back some memories, is all."

It *was* him. He was beautiful, so much so that you could easily mistake him for a woman. In my past life, I probably would've been jealous enough to wish for him to get hit by a truck. He was formerly human, I was told, but kept a majestic presence about him—the majesty of a demon lord.

And I brought back "memories"? I suppose my face was essentially Shizu's at a young age. So Leon must have—

"Shizu's dead, Leon."

Seeing me simply conjured up old memories of Shizu in his mind.

"I know," he coldly stated. "And of course she would be. She took in Ifrit but refused to become a magic-born."

"She asked me to punch you out for her. Mind letting me do that?"

I just kind of blurted it out. I wasn't trying to start stuff; I just didn't like how Leon was talking about her. It was maybe a little too direct, but Leon handled it with calm composure.

"No, thank you. I wanted her to live as a human being. I even gave her Ifrit as a farewell gift. I see no reason why I deserve a beating for it."

What a disappointment. I figured he'd be enraged, but he just calmly fired back at me.

"...But I *do* have a bit of an interest in you. If you have an issue with me, I'll happily invite you to come visit. You can turn down the offer, of course, if you think it's a trap."

Talk about a one-sided deal. He was basically daring me to chicken out. I had to accept it.

"All right. I'll do that. Feel free to send an invitation, if you get around to it."

I didn't say anything more after that.

Leon nodded, looking a little annoyed. "I will. Assuming you walk out of this meeting hall alive, that is."

With that blunt rejoinder, Leon settled down in the seat just to my left. It was his way of saying our conversation was over. For now, I was fine with that. I got to tell him about Shizu, and I now knew that Leon wasn't out to antagonize me. At least not here at the Council. He wouldn't have said yes to that invitation thing if he was.

Maybe it was just postponing the dispute for later, but right now, I wanted to focus on Clayman as my enemy.

*

These proceedings all unfolded in the hour after we reached the meeting hall at midnight. It looked like the older demon lords had been guided in first, with me getting a head start because I happened to be traveling with Ramiris. It wasn't any official rule, though, given that people like Leon could travel here themselves.

All that remained were Clayman and Milim. And just when I thought the Council was about to begin, Benimaru tossed a Thought Communication my way.

(Sir Rimuru, may I brief you for a moment?)

This hall seemed like it was in another dimension of sorts, but I guess this link with Benimaru still worked?

Understood. A soul circuit has been established with the monsters under your command. The link is using this to allow your conscious to interact with them.

Oh. That sort of thing?

I guess this soul circuit got hooked up with the gifts I handed out to everyone for my evolution. It didn't seem as robust as the connection I had with Veldora, but it was good enough for talking, at least.

So I asked what was up. Apparently, the battle ended less than an hour after it began—incredibly lopsided and pretty much as we planned it. Our side had numerous casualties but no deaths. Clayman's forces had at least a thousand killed in action and over three thousand wounded. That was fewer deaths than I expected, but in this world where you can always get healed as long as you stayed alive, that much was a given.

Still, that was a massive, overwhelming victory. We managed to take some prisoners as well, so I couldn't ask for much more.

Yamza, the enemy commander, had turned into Charybdis for some strange reason, but Benimaru was kind enough to vaporize the guy for me. Apparently. I'm not really sure what all that meant, so I just kind of glossed over it for now.

...Or I wanted to. But how did he deal with Charybdis's Magic Interference?

Understood. A number of Arts and skills combined with the unique skill Born Leader allowed him full control over Hellflare.

Aha. So he used control beyond what Magic Interference could handle to hit it with a direct, massive wave of heat. Easy for me to say, but that has to require a hell of a lot of talent. Benimaru's gotten stronger than I even imagined. Pretty hot stuff.

One factor we didn't expect was the Dragon Faithful. They were reportedly a pretty formidable fighting force, as you'd expect from Milim's followers. We didn't lose anyone to them because they weren't really out there seeking to kill...but I guess it was my bad for not thinking about them. I figured a force of a hundred-odd was no big deal, but I was wrong. Wars in this world depended more on the powers of a few than the many, but my conventional wisdom from my old world was making me forget that.

Lucky thing that didn't result in any major breakdowns. I'd have to be more careful next time.

Based on Benimaru's report, we had a general idea of Clayman's story.

The force led by Yamza was marching on the pretext of investigating Carillon's betrayal. They wanted to collect evidence that he backstabbed the other demon lords, killed one of Clayman's top leaders, and was connected to me. Well, not *collect*. More like *concoct*.

With our victory today, that line was cut off. I didn't know what kind of excuses he would come up with here, but I didn't imagine they would be well received by any other demon lord. Of course, I intended to kill off Clayman in the end, and I was prepared to do the same to anyone who got in my way. *Let's just try to steer this so I'd secure victory here in the easiest way possible.*

I'll be counting on you, Raphael!

......

Raphael's rarin' to go, too. That's a relief.

Whoops, here's another report from Soei. Sounds like they've captured Clayman's headquarters. Man, there is just no mercy with that guy. Hakuro pitched in a hell of an effort, too, but apparently Shuna shined the brightest in the fight.

Also, it turns out that I now have an army of undead for some reason? I sort of missed the plot on that, and Soei was being oddly vague about the whole thing, simply stating "Lady Shuna will explain the details later."

The most important thing, though, was that Carillon wasn't being held in Clayman's castle. Plus:

(—We discovered the castle's treasury, so we've called upon Geld to begin the transport process. The room included some evidence linking Clayman to the Moderate Jesters, which I think should help your case.)

Wow. No mercy. We're even pillaging Clayman's treasure vault. That doesn't count as theft, does it? Oh, well. No point sweating the small stuff. We'll just call it collecting damages for all the trouble Clayman gave us. There's reportedly a lot, which should help our own budget out greatly.

More important, however, was that dossier of evidence. Benimaru had sent some over for me, and Soei had discovered some more. All of it was now safely received in my Stomach, and with it, I should be able to shut down the basis for any excuse he comes up with. It'd be important to make myself look good around here.

So, much quicker than I expected, we had thoroughly and completely crushed Clayman's force. It'd remain to be seen how he'd approach this Council, but let's try using these developments to my advantage.

...And then, just as I finished reading the reports, Clayman finally appeared before me.

✳

He was more handsome than I pictured him—and high-strung. His clothing looked expensive, and I suppose he placed a lot of importance on his appearance, because he was sporting a whole array of Unique equipment that would make him a more-than-decent fighter. It certainly befitted his image as a demon lord not to be trifled with.

What struck me the most, however, was the fox he was carrying in his arms. It was packed to the gills with magicules and mystical force, maybe even up to demon lord levels. That was one of his attendants, and I suppose a demon lord's servants had to be pretty damn powerful, too.

That, and I tried running an Analyze and Assess on him, and something interesting caught my eye there. I didn't want to coast on this just because we had occupied his HQ. It was important to finish him off *right*.

Anyway, Milim followed behind him, completing the night's attendee list.

All were real monsters, ready to burn you at a moment's notice. Doing the A and A once-over on Leon produced nothing useful, either. It was kind of funny, seeing Raphael say that it couldn't analyze something. It meant he had an ultimate skill of his own, something on the same level as mine.

Then I made a realization. Guy had let me read fake info, but was that his way of fending off ultimate skills? If I couldn't use my ultimate to analyze something, it meant the target had an ultimate, too. That may be why he was feeding me a bunch of nonsense instead—I just happened to know it was fake nonsense because

Raphael was smart enough to see that. If it hadn't noticed, I could easily have been tricked.

This meant, of course, that Guy had an ultimate skill as well. I suspected Milus (?) did, too, and Leon definitely did. An ultimate was several orders of magnitude more powerful than a unique skill requiring an intersection of one's attributes, luck, and a plethora of incidental conditions. They were rare—uncommon enough that even a true, awakened demon lord may not have one, and all were great as a last-resort ace in the hole.

That was why I needed to be extra careful here. That, and—*ugh*—it was safe to assume Guy knew I possessed an ultimate now. Big mistake. My lack of experience playing this game screwed me there. I was dealing with some of the orneriest demon lords out there; I should've been more on the alert.

Still, what's done is done. It wasn't a lethal mistake, either. I just needed to figure out how to deal with it. It's easy to hide mind-reading skills, just as Gazel did. Guy still didn't know what *type* of skill I had, so I probably didn't need to be too hung up about it. Hell, I could even use this to make them think I'm a fool. To be exact, I would direct Raphael to hide everything at all costs, but maybe show off one ultimate skill that was okay to reveal as my trump card. That way, I could still keep a few cards hidden at all times, right?

It was a gutsy bit of subterfuge, but I was safe in pulling it off with the four ultimate skills I enjoyed. I was planning on kicking up one hell of a storm in the upcoming battle against Clayman anyway, which would make the debut of—

Suggestion. Hiding Belzebuth, Lord of Gluttony would be difficult.

Yeah, I think you're right. It was a great offensive and defensive weapon, capable of consuming and destroying nearly any attack thrown at it. Predation was a pretty core battle tactic for me, so revealing Belzebuth seemed like a good idea. Let's go with that as my main battle weapon, keeping my other skills hidden until otherwise needed.

I suppose I'm glad that I noticed the need for something like this early on. If I got out of here safely, I'd need to rethink my battle tactics a little. No point being reluctant to use my skills if it wound up killing me.

After that moment of regret, I saw one of the most amazing sights of my life.

"Move it, you half-wit!"

Out of nowhere, Clayman closed-fist *punched* Milim. *That* Milim.

"Sit yourself down, you stupid dunce," he said, ruthlessly bossing her around. I thought I'd explode in anger, but I held it in. *Not yet. Just a bit longer. I have to hold back until I have the chance to declare it all, following the rules.*

But what on earth happened to Milim? Milim the Destroyer? If it was Clayman being punched, well, that'd just be Milim being Milim. But this? *Oh, man, I fear for his safety…*

…and yet, despite this bout of violence, Clayman didn't look like he'd be decapitated anytime soon. Milim did nothing to resist or complain about his treatment. She just followed his orders and sat at her seat.

This is weird. *Is she under his control after all? I may have to consider the worst-case scenario here.* And to add insult to injury, some of the other demon lords, Daggrull and Deeno included, were looking similarly flummoxed at this. Guy was stone-faced; I don't know what he was thinking.

Clayman, meanwhile, was looking like he was king of the world, his superiority complex written all over his face. It made my anger burn all over again… *Don't expect your death to be an easy one, Clayman. You'll pay for hitting my friend.*

And with that oath to myself, Clayman's death was now set in stone. I had no intention of forgiving him, no matter the excuse. But there was no need for panic. The Council had only just begun.

The event was attended by a total of nine people, minus Carillon:

"Lord of Darkness" Guy Crimson (demon)
"Destroyer" Milim Nava (dragonoid)

"Labyrinth Master" Ramiris (pixie)
"Earthquake" Daggrull (giant)
"Bloody Lord" Roy Valentine (vampire)
"Sleeping Ruler" Deeno (fallen)
"Sky Queen" Frey (harpy)
"Marionette Master" Clayman (walking dead)
"Platinum Saber" Leon Cromwell (ex-human)

...And then, me—the subject of this Council, the slime who'd dare call himself demon lord.

Raine, the maid in Guy's service, made all the above introductions in her clear, loud voice.

Leon was the one who piqued my interest the most. I seem to remember his nickname being the Platinum Devil, but now he was acting all cool and calling himself the Platinum Saber. He certainly looked more the part of a dashing swordsman, but who thought up these nicknames anyway? They didn't make them up themselves, did they? ...*Well, I probably shouldn't comment, given my track record for naming things. Let's let that topic die on the vine.*

After the intros ended, Clayman stood up as the host.

"All right. First, thanks to all of you for answering my invitation and coming here. It is now time to begin our festival! I hereby declare this Walpurgis Council convened!"

Thus, with the chance for cataclysmic events electrifying the air around us, the event kicked off.

*

Taking advantage of his position as chairman, Clayman started things off by going into a speech, eyeing all of us in order and looking supremely satisfied with himself. His eyes stopped for just a moment when they reached Valentine, but maybe I imagined it—that's got nothing to do with me anyway.

Leon was seated to my left; the chair on my right was empty, and to its right were Clayman's and the absent Carillon's seats.

Clayman went on for a while, explaining matters with an obvious sense of pride, and I diligently listened to all of it. Here's the executive summary:

- The demon lord Carillon enticed me into declaring myself a demon lord. This allegation is backed up by the fact that Carillon's armies are stationed in our town.
- He then incited the kingdom of Farmus into attacking the Great Forest of Jura, requesting my cooperation to fend them off and using that as an excuse to meddle with human nations.
- After defeating Farmus, I assumed the title of demon lord, enjoying Carillon's support behind the scenes.

This kind of unauthorized collusion violated the demon lords' agreements.

He was better prepared to make this argument than I gave him credit for. It was all a bunch of nonsense, totally ignoring the actual timeline of events, but proving that would be difficult. All of this happened at the same time as the demon lords withdrew from their mutual nonaggression agreement for the Forest of Jura, and (as he bluntly put it) there was no excusing that. As if, you know, I cared about that.

"...That is the testimony I have received from Mjurran, one of my advisers. However, upon briefing me about this, she was murdered— by that fool over there, Rimuru. Thus, I decided to exact my revenge."

What is he, a thespian? If not, he missed his calling. He almost convinced me, even... Almost. I mean, Mjurran's pretty alive right now.

"Rimuru was conspiring with Carillon to make an attempt upon my life. And with her last gasps of breath, Mjurran sent me a magical missive to inform me of the plot."

He paused a moment, pretending to be overcome with emotion. His handsome looks certainly made it a moving sight, but it mostly served to rankle my nerves.

So he's saying I tried to kill him to claw my way into a demon lord's seat? And it was Carillon who engineered it all? I have to say, that's a pretty impressive story to make up. If you actually knew Carillon and how relentlessly in your face and warlike he was, it'd be enough to make you blurt out laughing.

Clayman's tales continued, meandering here and there, but basically, he was accusing Carillon of betraying the Council. This enraged Milim enough to destroy the Beast Kingdom of Eurazania, and Carillon was now dead. *Hmm. Dead? Not missing?* That seemed unnatural enough to worry me, but I kept on listening.

Milim had taken action out of concern for Clayman, but he had rebuked her, since wrecking nations without any evidence was generally frowned upon. Ever since, she had fostered an affinity for Clayman, relying on and trusting in him—and with his adviser Mjurran dead, Clayman decided to send out a force to secure evidence linking me to Carillon. In addition, he wished to use this Council to discuss how to handle me, after I tried to kill him and declare my rights as demon lord.

The tale he wove couldn't have possibly painted him in a better light. I was impressed.

But, man, he just kept on talking forever. I wanted to counter his excuses with a little logic of my own. My intention was to show my innocence, prove that my actions were justifiable, and then crush Clayman, after all. That was why I was sitting here politely and hearing him out, but my patience was reaching its limits.

Could we maybe get started soon?

Listening to his tale, I had noticed a pretty decisive hole in his logic—his evidence. His entire dossier of evidence was made up of testimony, all from a single witness—Mjurran, the ring finger, who had sworn absolute loyalty to Clayman. It made me laugh. Not only was she alive, but the Mjurran-related evidence he presented was as flimsy as a plastic bag. I suppose he ran out of time to fabricate anything more substantial than that.

All in all, it seemed like I could build a pretty credible case for myself. I already had all the evidence I needed.

"...That concludes my case," Clayman bellowed, looking all self-important. "Hopefully, everybody in the room now fully understands that Rimuru, that trifling magic-born over there, is nothing more than a charlatan posing as a demon lord. I believe that a purge is in order here..."

The other demon lords must have been pretty darn patient if they were willing to put up with all this prattling. Some of them had already nodded off, it seemed. I guess it was okay, as long as you didn't bother anyone. The only rule, I surmised, was that you had to shut up and listen to the guy who convened the Council to start with.

Now we were all free to state our own opinions—and I was ready for it. Raine, who must've been taking the emcee post, turned her eyes to me.

"We will now listen to testimony from our visitor."

Ugh, finally. I had been patient long enough. No more of this clowning around.

"So, um, Clayman, right? You're a liar."

"What?"

"I mean, honestly speaking, I don't give a crap about demon lords. That story about Carillon luring me into this is a load of BS, and Farmus attacked us out of their own greed. Those two things aren't related to each other at all."

Clayman gave me an irritated sneer. "Ha! Who would ever believe trite excuses like that? One of my most senior advisers has been killed!"

Here we go. Just what I've been waiting for.

"Yeah, Mjurran, right? Well, I didn't kill her. In fact, she's alive."

"Pah! Of all the ludicrous—"

"Whoa, whoa, hear me out. Pretty much all of that speech was based off verbal testimony and your own conjecturing. And maybe that'd be enough to deal with some rank and filer, but it won't work on me. Mjurran, your supposed tipster, is under my protection. That's why I'm not letting you mess with me, and that's why your testimony has absolutely no credibility whatsoever."

Going into that much detail made even Clayman go a bit pale. But he had no intention of ceding his point.

"Heh-heh. You're willing to stoop to such lows, then? Did you meddle with her corpse and install some evil spirit inside?"

It was a spur-of-the-moment accusation but not an insane one. In a world as rich with magic as this one, you could even make the dead seem alive if you wanted. Talk about freaky—and another reason why you couldn't trust oral testimony like that.

"Well," I said, "I wasn't planning to believe anything you said anyway. That's why I figured I'd come over there and beat you up myself, but I wound up changing my mind. Before this Council began, my forces gathered some evidence of their own."

I flashed a smile as I attempted to show him up. This enraged him, I could tell. He was easier to toy with than I thought.

"What are you trying to say? If you want to die that badly, just come out and say it—"

"Calm down a sec," I said, cutting him off. "I told you, I have evidence."

I then produced several crystal balls from my pocket, teleporting them to the center of the round table and magically triggering them one after the other. Each one contained its own video image, including one featuring me fighting the orc general and another shot from Gelmud's point of view. Shuna had found them all in the ancient castle Clayman called home.

One of them, meanwhile, contained footage from the battle fought just today. It was taken by Benimaru, from his vantage point overseeing the entire landscape, and it contained some really juicy stuff.

"S-stop! Stop that! Please, Sir Clayman, stop this at once!"

Right there, in the ball, Clayman's field general was screaming and being transformed into an incomplete Charybdis. And that wasn't all.

"...This is quite a surprise. I was expecting Yamza to turn tail and flee. But imagine..."

"Clayman's forces are destroyed. The mission's a failure—the losses immense..."

"*...Well, Laplace warned him. Clayman can't blame anyone for it but himself. We'll need to brief him about this...*"

That conversation between the two weird jesters Geld and Phobio had witnessed was all on video. Probably Footman and Teare from the Moderate Jesters, I assumed. With Laplace's name popping up, it had to be them. That and "him"—I thought Clayman was behind all this, but it seemed like there was someone else. Maybe...

Understood. It is estimated that all of this is connected.

...I thought so. Whoever it was that tried to make me fight Hinata was also controlling Clayman. That explains the timing—while I was busy fighting the Western Holy Church, this figure had Clayman spur Farmus into combat, and then that whole tragedy unfolded.

Maybe I could understand all this, even if I didn't appreciate it much. But you went too far, Clayman. So I'm taking you down. Don't resent me for it. In this world, it's survival of the fittest.

I proudly beamed at him. "*This* is what real evidence looks like, Clayman."

Having this stuff with me definitely made things proceed more quickly, but even if I didn't have it, it would've turned out the same way. I was gonna crush him with my own force anyway, so all I really needed was something to shoot down his lame excuses with. It wasn't a matter of good or evil—it was all about keeping up appearances. Besides, I had *real* evidence here, and I saw no reason for anyone to complain about that.

"You, you *couldn't*! All of this was fabricated! Fake images, built with magic, to prop up your lies! How could you be so *base*, you slime?!"

"Lies? They aren't lies, you dummy. Your army's all done. And you're joining them next."

Clayman turned toward me, face scrunched up in anger.

"Ev... Everyone, you can't listen to this trickster! This slime, Rimuru, is a notorious bluffer. He undoes the seal on Veldora to destroy the Farmus force, and then he parades around pretending he did the act himself. He's just a little slime, all bark and no bite! And it is simply outrageous that he dares to deceive us all in the proud demon lord family!"

It was an impassioned speech. As if *he* wasn't the one relying on others to save his ass. As if *he* wasn't the little one. If he was acting right now, like I said, he was a pretty good actor.

"Look, Clayman…"

This was Daggrull, his voice just as grounded and dignified as his appearance. Wasn't expecting *him* to speak up.

"Didn't you say just now that Rimuru goaded the kingdom of Farmus into attacking? If the news of Veldora's resurrection is true, why would he execute it in such a roundabout fashion?"

"…All right. Allow me to explain."

Clayman looked lost for a moment but then opened his mouth again, ready to commit to this tale—the story of the attempt to collect people's souls to awaken into a true demon lord. I suppose he wanted to keep that under his hat so that the other demon lords wouldn't get the jump on him, but Daggrull had forced him to fess up.

"…This low-class, unwitting slime must have had the incredible good fortune to acquire the traits of a demon lord. But he must have let it go to his head, for he then traveled to the human realms to investigate the truth behind what he obtained. That drove him to set off a war with the humans on a whim, using the banished Veldora to stage a brutal genocide."

He was doing his best to convince the table, complete with overblown, theatrical hand motions.

"Leaving someone like this free to maraud again would damage our very reputations as demon lords. I believe he must be purged, but what is your opinion?"

"So cough up some evidence," I retorted. "Not that you have any, do you? Everything you said was just a bunch of 'wouldn't it be nice if…' junk, and you still think they're all gonna swallow it?"

Clayman gave me another unamused glare. It didn't bother me. I was already sick of putting up with his pathetic accusations.

"Ngh… Why does some slime claiming the might of a dragon

for himself think he has the right to defy us?! There is no way you could ever become a demon lord!"

"Whether I'm a slime or not doesn't matter, and besides, Veldora's my friend. I'm not here to listen to you go on with your bullshit, all right? Can we get to the point, please? Just admit it. Phobio, the magic-born in that video, just showed us how Charybdis was resurrected at your demand, right? As those jesters guided him to. And now one of your own men transformed into Charybdis and went insane. That's what I'm talking about when I say solid evidence. If you think I'm bluffing, go right ahead, 'cause you'll be thinking that all the way to the grave."

I shot to my feet, kicking up the adjacent seat as I did, and tried to look as threatening as possible. Casually, I placed my hand on part of the round table in front of me—and in an instant, the large table disappeared. Nothing to be surprised about. I just stored it in my Belzebuth. Now we had a decent-size space to work with.

The chair I kicked up sailed in the direction of Clayman, smashing against the wall behind him with a loud crash. This didn't faze the demon lords, either. Only Clayman was unnerved by it.

"All of you are willing to put up with this reckless violence?! He is making light of us all. Should we not be exacting our judgment upon him at once?!"

What, all of them? I always knew he was a wimp. I walked to the middle of where the table used to be.

"Yeah, maybe you're right. Like I said, I don't care about you demon lords at all. All I want is to build a nation that I can enjoy living in. I need the humans' cooperation for that, so I decided to offer my protection to them. Anyone who gets in the way of that, whether a person or a demon lord or the Holy Church, is my enemy. Just like *you* are, Clayman."

I explained my ideals to the group with far more passion than Clayman could ever manage.

"What?!"

"And if you call *that* reckless violence," I said as I sized him up, "what would you call taking over someone's mind while we're all chatting at Walpurgis?"

Did he think I wouldn't notice? In the midst of that whole speech, that little sneak was launching mind-control attacks at me. If I had to guess, he was trying to dominate my consciousness. Too bad it didn't work; Raphael was guarding me the whole time, so I had it fully taken care of.

At least I had a justifiable cause on the table, so to speak. That was now in the ears of all the demon lords, and Clayman had already started trying to strike me. If any of them wanted to oppose me, it was now or never.

Time to switch over to *real* action.

I had asked the question to Clayman, but it was answered by someone else—Guy, the red-haired demon lord seated on the far side of the chamber.

"Indeed," he said with a charmingly attractive smile. "In order to keep things fair, we are only allowed to appeal to others through our own voices."

"But, Guy, he is insulting us all—"

"Shut up," I interrupted. "If you don't like it, then it's between you and me, isn't it?"

"He is correct, Clayman. If you call yourself a demon lord, then use your powers to defeat that magic-born. And you—" Guy looked straight at me. "Do you intend to declare yourself a demon lord?"

"Yep. I'm already leader of the Great Forest of Jura, and as far as anyone on the ground's concerned, I *am* one."

No matter the path we had to take to get there, I imagined they would all accept that I'd teamed with the Storm Dragon to rule the forest. There was no point denying that Tempestians were already calling me demon lord.

"Very well. And we have an array of witnesses here as well. If you can win against Clayman before us, I will allow you to adopt the title."

So beating Clayman ties up all these little strings, huh? This was *exactly* the development I hoped for.

*

Clayman began to laugh, just as suddenly as he regained his composure a moment ago.

"Heh-heh-heh... How exasperating. I simply attempted a little trick because I didn't want to dirty my own hands, and now look at the storm I've unleashed. What a mistake."

He was smiling the whole time. Did he have a screw loose? His thin, almost inhuman smile was still clinging to life as he looked at me. And then, quietly:

"You're up, Milim."

Tension raced across the chamber. Even the demon lords were nervous, although some were maintaining perfect calm as always.

My eyes turned to Milim. There was the source of Clayman's confidence—the belief that he had her under his control. Control that he exercised right at that moment.

So she *was*...?

"Wow. What a bigmouth. After everything you said, you're relying on someone else? And bringing in Milim after you punched her out to make her do your bidding?"

I tried provoking him a little, but not even Clayman was stupid enough to bite.

"Don't be ridiculous. I will be fighting, too, of course. Is there any issue with that, Guy?"

"Not at all, Clayman. If Milim is aiding you on her own free will, I will not stop her."

This...wasn't good. Clayman I had a handle on, but Milim was *deadly*. With Guy so readily granting permission, there was no way I could dodge having to fight her. Even with what I could do by now, I didn't like my prospects against her—and besides, I wanted to help her out. *No, I will help her out!*

Just then, the unmoving, doll-like Milim made two fists and struck an overwrought, triumphant pose...or so it looked like to me. Maybe not. It was just for an instant; I dunno.

Man. Poor lady. *Don't worry, Milim*, I swore in my heart. *I'll get you out of there.*

"Well, all right. I was planning to rescue Milim anyway, so I think I'll just undo that brainwashing trick you pulled on her—by force, if I need to."

"Enough of your prattle! You will die in despair."

"The only one dyin' here is you, Clayman. I think one of my officers would make a better match against the likes of you. Fighting you myself would just make me a bully."

Clayman's face stiffened. A thick, black aura began to float out of him, perhaps generated by his anger. You can't be a demon lord unless you know how to intimidate your foe, I guess. Not that it was *that* impressive—but between his rage and panic, that should open up some weak points to exploit. Shion would be fighting him in my place, and I was sure she'd be able to take advantage of that.

I motioned with my eyes to Shion. She immediately sprang into action. In a moment, she was upon Clayman, launching an attack. Concentrating her aura around her fist, she used that single instant to land a good thirty or so blows on him. Then she turned back at me with a look of relief and asked, "Is this all right?"

…Um, aren't you supposed to ask before you start clobbering? All I did was give you a sidelong glance. That was supposed to be a "You get it, right? Clayman's all pissed off, so get 'im while he's off guard" kind of glance. I wasn't expecting you to beat the crap out of him before I blinked again. Does the expression off guard mean anything to you?

Well…so be it. What's done is done. The force of the strikes propelled Clayman right in front of me, in the middle of the circle. "You, you, you *bastard*!" he shouted as he stood up. He was tougher than I thought.

That black aura around him thickened, instantly healing his injuries. It was far faster than what the orc lord could do, but that was pretty much normal for a demon lord. Either way, it made Clayman accept Shion as an enemy, so we were still more or less sticking to the script.

"If that's what you want," he said, "then I'll kill both of you." Then the fox that had jumped down to his feet swelled up in size.

Report. This is believed to be the Nine-Head mentioned by Mjurran.

*   *   *

Oh yeah, she *did* say that, huh? So it was another servant of his, not some pet. Then another figure emerged from Clayman's shadow, wrapped in a black robe. He had two servants, and I had Shion in battle mode. Ranga was similarly enlarged now, ready to pounce.

Wait. Hang on. We're outnumbered if Milim is joining in… Nah. No need to panic yet. That's what Beretta is for— Huuhh?!

The moment we all stepped into the circle where the table used to be, it was shut away from the audience by a barrier. The area within it exploded in size, the surrounding chairs seemingly far away and distant. They must have installed some kind of enclosing barrier to protect the other demon lords.

I kind of expected this, given that they created that whole fancy event space and everything…but Beretta, one of my supports, didn't make it in.

Oh, crap, I didn't see that pitfall coming— But just as I thought it, Clayman started screaming.

"Milim, kill him!!"

And she was ready to do just that.

There was no doubting the fist coming my way. The force behind it was deadly. But after expanding my senses a million times over with Mind Accelerate, there was a chance I could avoid it. It wasn't impossible, but I didn't have much leeway to mess up.

A white-hot ball of energy scraped past my cheek. The speed amazed me. Even with Raphael running at full speed, I still couldn't fully avoid it. If I even thought about a counter, it'd leave me open enough for a lethal strike.

The only thing I could do, then, was try my hardest to keep up with Milim while I concentrated on breaking her mind control. Even so, my Detect Magic was telling me about events in the circle. It was almost scary, the way I could juggle all of that. Too bad I couldn't bask in it right now.

Shion was fighting Clayman, but it was two on one with that black-robed figure in the mix, so I couldn't say she had the advantage. Ranga, meanwhile, was pitted against Nine-Head, and I thought he was winning, but then those three tails on the fox spirit transformed into two magical beasts. All of a sudden, it was three on one.

I, meanwhile, had Milim to deal with. There really was nothing I could do. Nothing, besides pray that everyone stayed alive until I could finish running Analyze and Assess on her.

So, uh, you guys take care of yourselves! Got it?

●

Beretta quickly set to action, asking Ramiris if it could join the battle. Ramiris, for her part, wasn't about to turn her toy down.

"Whoa, Guy! I'm with Rimuru, all right? So I want my Beretta to be part of that, too."

"No," he coldly replied, paying her as little attention as possible.

"Why not?!"

"Mm? Mere attendants aren't allowed to join a battle between demon lords. This is a dispute between that slime and Clayman, is it not? You have no reason to join in."

"What're you *talking* about?! Milim's in there, ain't she?"

"Oh, she's fine."

"So what's with that? Why's she fine, and I'm not?!"

Guy rolled his eyes, tiring of this. Ramiris was always something of a loudmouth. Once she got started, it was hard to make her stop.

She had never brought attendants to a Council before, so Guy realized she must've had some reason to do it this time. Considering Milim's involvement, letting Ramiris join in would just add to the chaos. He had isolated the battle zone in part to prevent this.

"Because Milim likely has her own motivations for this. Now will you shut up?"

"Oh, so you think there's not a thought in *my* mind about it at all?"

"Is there? Besides…" Guy gave Beretta a look. "Who has your attendant sworn its loyalties to? Your other companion seems ready to devote her all to protecting you, but I'm not so sure about this Beretta. It's faithful to you, but not completely so. You want me to trust someone so suspicious?"

He had spotted the truth. Beretta's loyalties weren't only to Ramiris. And as one of Ramiris's closest friends, he wasn't willing to allow an attendant who was weighing its master on the scales against someone else.

"My master is on the balance, yes," Beretta freely admitted.

There was Rimuru, its master. Rimuru, its creator, but also Ramiris, its current leader. She was a ridiculously optimistic, rash, curious, even cowardly demon lord, but Beretta had grown to love her. It didn't even mind all that abusive manipulation. Rimuru had wished for Ramiris to be protected and for Beretta to serve her as well. There was no contradiction at all in its mind.

There was just one thing: Beretta wanted to repay the favor to Rimuru. It was once a demon, and Rimuru had granted it both a new life and a new mission. It felt a need to make up for that.

"And if Lady Ramiris wishes to save that figure as much as I do..." It spoke to Guy without any fear.

"Hoh? Audacious enough to address me, are you? Interesting. May I trust this golem at its word, Ramiris?"

The fairy gave him a look that indicated no answer was needed, but she gave one anyway. "Oooh yeah, yeah, of course! So you go help out Rimuru in my place, all right, Beretta?!"

"Hmm. So it will take action if you wish it to, then? You've obtained quite a good attendant for yourself, Ramiris."

"Nah, nah, not obtained. We're friends! Me, and Beretta, and Treyni, and Rimuru, too!" She smiled contentedly. "Like, everyone, a whole, whole lot!"

Guy wasn't quite sure what Ramiris was trying to say, but if she was fine with that, so was he.

"Well, all right..." He reluctantly extended a hand to open a hole in the barrier.

"...I thank you, Rouge," Beretta said.

"Sure. Don't call me that. I'll allow you to call me Guy. But I *refuse* to allow you to recognize another master apart from Ramiris from now on. Is that all right?"

Granting this honor meant Guy saw Beretta as strong enough to live up to his own standards. Now, he was asking it to pick a master.

If it attempted to weasel out of the question, he intended to smash it up on the spot. But it immediately agreed.

"In that case, Guy, I will swear my loyalty to Lady Ramiris exclusively from now on. So please allow me to be of service to Sir Rimuru at least once."

Guy was a tad surprised. Demons, as a rule, wanted to be recognized by their masters for their strength. Beretta, meanwhile, didn't seem to see strength as too important. Its standards had gone all haywire. It was a nonconformist.

"You are fine with that?"

"Yes. Sir Rimuru has servants stronger than myself."

That made sense to Guy. But it also confused him, someone this powerful admitting to not being the strongest out there.

"I also enjoy conducting research," Beretta continued. "The research I do with Lady Ramiris on a daily basis is truly like a dream... Oh, pardon me. My serving Lady Ramiris is part of Sir Rimuru's request. There is no need to worry about that."

The words reminded Guy of a demon he knew, the very definition of strange, one who pursued only what personally interested him. If they were part of the same lineage, perhaps demons with dispositions like Beretta's shouldn't be so unexpected—but the demon in Guy's mind rarely birthed other family members. Only an elite few were aware of him at all.

"Let me ask—what is your lineage like?"

Beretta winced underneath its mask and laughed.

"...I was one of the least of the greater demons. However, I think you will find very few demons in the same family tree as I."

A small lineage. That has to be it, then. Beretta's hair was gray, the color gone from it, but once upon a time...

"I see. No wonder you didn't fear me. That family always was self-centered, curious. So someone like you admits there are stronger creatures than yourself?"

Guy shot a passing glance at Shion and Ranga fighting away, then turned back toward Beretta. Yes, Shion and Ranga were powerful—but he didn't think Beretta was at all behind them.

"I thank you for the honor, but I still have far to go. As long as the two of them serve Sir Rimuru, if I miss this opportunity, I may never have another one."

"Yes, true. I understand how you feel. You may go."

The barrier already had a hole large enough to wriggle through.

"Excuse me, then."

With an elegant salute, Beretta plunged in. Guy cracked a smile as he watched it go. He had an idea who this would be.

...So that's it. You're on the move as well, Noir?!

This was an old friend, one who went away from him ages ago. If *this* was the type of people he was serving now, the slime fighting Milim in front of him must be quite the fascinating figure. A nonconformist serving a nonconformist.

He basked in joy as he watched the battle, even as he thought he could see its conclusion already.

Rimuru was his name? I will have to remember it.

●

Oh, crap. I'm screwed.

Who's screwing me? Milim, of course.

Dealing with Milim as a foe made Clayman's anger seem like a toddler's tantrum. She hadn't taken the battle form Phobio saw yet, so she still wasn't going all out...but her strength went beyond all common sense. I was already exercising everything I had. Raphael, at least, was really humming along for me—seriously, if I didn't have that skill, I would've been dead already.

So I was fully booked with Milim, but my fighting companions were working hard as well. I had thought being outnumbered might sink us, but now I wasn't so sure.

Ranga had summoned two star leaders, fellow commander-level starwolves, boosting his team so it was three on three. I guess it was possible for him to summon up to three at once, but Gobta was using the third one right now, so that was all we had on hand. Still, I think it was enough.

Nine-Head boasted a massive amount of magical energy, but

it didn't seem too experienced in battle. Ranga held the upper hand from start to finish. The two magical beasts Nine-Head summoned, however, were trickier than I thought. Analyze and Assess told me they were a White Monkey and a Moon Rabbit, respectively. They were both intelligent and capable of attacking in tandem, which made them fiendish in battle. The Moon Rabbit could control gravity, weighing down everyone in the battle zone. It allowed the White Monkey to pummel their foes and Nine-Head to finish them off.

That was their standard path to victory, but Ranga saw right through it, breaking down their teamwork. If he used one of his stronger finishers, he could've wiped them out instantly, but he was hesitating since Shion might be caught in the cross fire. He had the upper hand, but landing a decisive blow was proving elusive.

Shion, meanwhile... Well, she was hanging in there, out of pure fighting spirit more than anything. The black robe was hiding an elaborately built magical puppet, and I'm not kidding when I say it looked stronger than Clayman.

"Ha-ha-ha-ha! How do you like Viola, my greatest work of art? Beautiful, is she not?"

Clayman was boundlessly confident, and I could see why. A real tour de force, although *beautiful* wouldn't be my choice of words if asked. Not with, you know, all those swords and spears flying out of her. Each one of those projectiles was a Unique-grade weapon, as was her armor, but this kind of kitchen-sink approach wasn't what I would call beauty, really. Whether it was heat, electricity, blizzards, crushing, resonation, or anything else, she had a seemingly limit-less supply of every attack type in the world, and she was lobbing it all at her foe.

It was nothing to Shion, however. That was thanks to Ultraspeed Regeneration, which sucks if you're fighting someone who has it. No matter how much damage she took, Shion could instantly heal back up. Clayman and Viola working together prevented her from going on the attack, but that was just helping fill up Shion's anger gauge. Once that blew up, things were gonna get *scary*.

As I thought about that, Shion had someone join her.

"I apologize for making you wait. Sir Rimuru, please utilize my power."

Whoa, it's Beretta! I don't know how, but it must've broken into this battle zone.

"I've been waiting for you, Beretta!"

"Yes sir!"

"This needless meddling... I was just about to turn these fools into a pair of bloody husks!"

Shion was acting like a sore loser, but I'll just ignore that.

"Well, don't let up. Smash them!"

""""Yes sir!!""""

We were now fully back to the original script.

✳

No losing now. The path we took here got a little hairy midway, but with things as they were, our victory was unshakable.

The only problem was Milim. She still wasn't going all out. If I could free her, we'd win for sure. My qualms about the future settled, I focused my full consciousness on her. The noise surrounding me disappeared. I sharpened my mind, looking at nothing but Milim. Now, much more clearly than before, I could see the path her fist traced in the air.

I focused, using every cell in my body for my calculations. If I lose this, it'd all be meaningless. I had to do whatever it took to release the curse Clayman placed on her. *Come on, Raphael. Analyze and Assess every inch of her for me!*

What was that? I'm berating my foes for relying on other people, but using Raphael to solve all my own problems? I don't know where you're getting the wrong idea. Raphael *is* my power.

There isn't a single iota of guilt in my mind!

So, uh, yeah, go ahead.

Understood. Conducting Analyze and Assess... No results.

*   *   *

Huh? *Huhhhh?!*

Um, what do you mean by that? You can't seriously mean that you can't figure out the silly curses Clayman placed on her?

No curse-oriented magic found. This is—

Dude, how useless can you get?!

Whenever this happened before, I figured it was because I wasn't concentrating hard enough, but after all that effort, nothing. It couldn't even discover any curse at all. Guess I can't trust Raphael in a pinch.

This was bad. Really, really bad. Not to sound all depressed, but the chances of me winning in a knock-down, drag-out brawl with Milim were laughably poor. *Well, so be it—I'll just have to hold out until Shion and the rest defeat Clayman.*

My mind made up, I confronted Milim. I *had* gotten stronger. She might be both under someone's control and not *really* trying yet, but I was certainly holding my own against Milim. In the past, I'd be eating dirt before a minute elapsed. Right now, we were at minute thirteen or so, and I was still fighting at a full clip.

Hey, maybe she'd snap out of it if I just gave her a good sock on the noggin?

The thought crossed my mind for just a moment, but I dunno... Striking Milim kind of goes against my personal rules...

Suggestion. An energy absorption attack using Belzebuth.

Oh? Ohhhh! That could work!!

I immediately tried it out. Any direct strike on my body would cause damage, so I was mainly parrying her moves. I would be applying just a little bit of force from the side, enough to adjust the paths of her punches and kicks. As I did, I'd use Belzebuth to vacuum up her magicules.

This turned out to be pretty effective. Milim reared away from

me, a scowl on her face. It was a teeny-tiny amount of damage, but it worked. All of Milim's attacks were protected by her own draconic aura; if I could take that out of the picture just by touching it, I'd gradually be able to sap her stamina.

Would I win with this, though? That was another story. If I was focused on "winning," I'd need to bust out my full strength, leaving nothing behind, and even then there was no guarantee. Even if I pulled it off, I'd wind up revealing all my hidden abilities to the demon lords watching us. In the big picture, that'd be a defeat.

Right now, all I could do was chip away at her like this as I waited for her curse to be undone. *Let's hope that Shion can finish off Clayman sooner rather than later.*

I couldn't say how many back-and-forth exchanges we went through.

I say *exchanges*, but it was entirely me defending. The rules were intense—one mistake, and you're out—but I was still fending her off.

A roaring fist from Milim surged past my right cheek. If I didn't focus, I'd never be able to dodge it. A single hit would shatter my body, no doubt. I had Infinite Regeneration, a healing skill more powerful than even its Ultraspeed cousin, but abusing it would drain my magicules too quickly. I could probably regenerate myself after being reduced to goo, but keep that up long enough, and I'd run out of stamina first.

So focus. Focus. Read ahead of Milim's moves.

Her right fist had changed in shape. A dragon-fang lash disguised as a punch. It'd glance past my cheek once again, then decapitate me with the nails on her fingers, like the teeth of a dragon. The correct way to deal with it was not to dodge but to take it from the side.

So I took it, pushing myself with my left hand from the inside out. I could feel a burning pain sear through that hand, an explosion of energy that left it heavily damaged. And that was me *avoiding* the attack. Trying to take a full-frontal blow from her would've been crazy. Absolute power, on this level, was a kind of finisher in itself, crushing its opponent. I had just learned that the hard way, but if I didn't sacrifice my left hand, I would've been mortally wounded. I was fine with that, but I was really starting to resent the sheer unfairness of this.

Then, as if reading my mind, I had an unexpected chance. Right there, as Milim lost her balance, she forced her remaining left hand to snap off a punch.

Here we go!

Report. It is believed to be a trap—

Huh?! I thought, but it was too late.

Leaving Raphael's composed guidance in the dust, I began my attack, grabbing Milim's left hand and attempting to throw her. If she was off-balance, I thought I should be able to pick her up on my back and slam her down.

But if that was Milim's trap...?

Her hand stopped dead in the air, a carefree grin on her face—a total "gotcha now!" smile.

Oh, craaaaaaaaaap?!

I was attempting to twist my body in front of Milim, both hands reaching out for her left arm. I could see all of that with Detect Magic as if watching it on TV, but it left me totally open. Cornered. Game over.

Her fist moved again—and just before she smashed it right against my head, something cut in between us. A dull *thud* rang out.

"Gnhh?! Where did that come from? That was just mean."

I was greeted by a dark-skinned man with blond hair. Looked a little bit like me, actually... *Wait, Veldora?!*

He was curled up on the floor, grabbing at his head and looking like he was in at least some pain. But if taking a punch from Milim only did that to him, I didn't see much need to worry. I took the moment's delay to rebalance and steel myself toward Milim.

"Hey, Veldora, why are *you* in here?!"

"Grrnnn, what a cruel blow..."

"You'll be fine, all right? What's happening in town?"

"Nothing. That man, Diablo or whatever it was, came back, so our defense is as strong as ever."

Huhhh? Diablo was back? There's no way they could've captured Farmus that quickly…but let's focus on Veldora for now.

"So what are you here for? If it's to whine at me, then go away."

"Why are *you* being cruel, too, Rimuru…? Ugh. Look, it's about this!"

He thrust his hands out at me, as if a *ta-daa!* sound effect should have been playing behind him. He was holding one of the volumes of manga I gave him—the final volume of a long-running series.

"What about this?" I asked, confused.

He looked at me, positively indignant. "What do you *mean*, what about this? The story in here's completely different from the rest of the series! Were you playing some kind of trick, taking the ending away from me?"

Ahhhhh! Yes! Now I remember. Yes, it was a trick. I kind of pulled a prank on him, the idea being that I'd give him the rest of the manga if he followed my orders. Kind of like training a pet, really. I had no idea *that* was the series I left for him.

So he traveled all the way here just because he wanted to read the ending? In this enclosed space in an alternate dimension? I knew I could summon Unlimited Imprisonment with my ultimate skill Veldora, Lord of the Storm, but I guess *he* could, too. That'll learn me, I guess.

But that didn't matter. Diablo was already back in town. Might as well make lemonade out of this.

"All right. Before I give you the real ending, I need you to do me a favor."

"Mm? What?"

"Play with Milim over there for a while. But don't hurt her."

"Milim? Ahhh, yes, my brother's only daughter. I haven't met her before, but she's still just a child, isn't she? Very well. I am on my way!"

I didn't know whether it was the manga or Milim that captured his interest the most, but either way, he agreed. The "my brother's only daughter" bit captured *my* interest, but again, everything in due time.

Milim herself was looking our way, steeled for anything, and Veldora seemed to be capturing her interest. I could see it in the twinkle in her eyes. Hopefully that meant I was safe leaving for now. Which one was stronger anyway? I was kind of interested to see, but if Veldora was stronger than me, I was sure he could buy me enough time.

There's just no way I can't take advantage of this chance—so with my newfound freedom, I wanted to defeat Clayman and settle the score for good.

$$*$$

So how had things gone while I was occupied with Milim?

Leaving her and Veldora behind, I turned toward Ranga first, since things seemed the most intense with him.

"Ranga, you all right?"

"Ah, Sir Rimuru! I am fine, but I have a little situation here."

Something was up? There didn't seem to be much life to his attacks, and I didn't think it was because he was losing interest.

Just as I was about to ask what was up, I picked up on the cause.

(—lp me. Help me. Help me!!)

This childlike wailing was leaking out to us, via Thought Communication, from Nine-Head. The White Monkey and Moon Rabbit were merely trying to protect their shivering master, hence why they kept resisting without admitting defeat. *Now I see. Let's help him out.*

"Ranga, hold back the Monkey and the Rabbit. Don't let them get in my way."

"Right."

He took the Monkey, while his two star leaders handled the Rabbit, and I walked toward the snarling Nine-Head—this poor young child, controlled by Clayman.

Report. Analysis indicates a Demon Dominate curse. Remove?
        Yes
        No

*   *   *

This time, at least, the curse was discovered and removed quickly. Wish I could've seen some of that talent when I was dealing with Milim. Ah well.

The moment I undid the magic, Nine-Head gave a joyous yelp, then settled down to sleep, no doubt exhausted. It was as cute as any baby-animal video I had ever seen; apart from the three tails and the golden color to its fur, it looked exactly like a little fox cub. Ranga was right next to me, growling as menacingly as he could, and—all right, that was pretty cute, too. In a cool way.

"Keep this cub safe."

"Yes, my master."

I gave the cub over to Ranga as I petted him. That took care of his foe.

Next, I turned to Beretta, and that confrontation was already over. It was lining up all the Unique weapons and armor on the floor, practically beside itself with excitement.

"Hey! Heyyyy! What're you doing?!"

"Oh yes, hello, Sir Rimuru!" It gave me a joyful salute. "It is a pity I could not show myself in action to you, but I have prepared some spoils of war for you."

Spoils...?

Viola, Clayman's greatest work of art, had been taken apart, its pieces strewn all over the place, and now this was Beretta's gift to me. I knew it was pretty strong, but it took down that arsenal-like magic-born without suffering a scratch...?

And that wasn't even all.

"Uh, Beretta, no offense, but are you imitating all of Ramiris's bad habits or what?"

"Huh...?!"

It looked at me—surprised, I think. Its face was hidden behind that mask, so that was only my impression. I thought a word of advice was in order. *If this keeps up, Beretta's going to pick up on nothing but her negative traits.*

"I mean, hopefully this is just my imagination, but what are you going to do with all that booty?"

"Well, this... I thought I would present it to you, Sir Rimuru... and I thought you would accept it and, in exchange, provide a place for Lady Ramiris and me to live."

Um? A place to live...? I knew Ramiris had an urge to live in our town, but why Beretta?

"What...made you worry about that?"

"Actually..."

Beretta's explanation floored me—and not in a good way. It sounded like Guy cornered it into choosing a master before allowing him to enter the battle zone. Beretta responded that it would serve Ramiris after helping me out in here—but clever demon that it is, it thought about a way to wiggle out of that. If Ramiris were to move to our town, Beretta would be obliged to follow her—and then it could go through Ramiris to serve me as well; that was its plan.

It was one of the flimsiest excuses I ever heard, and it was laying this out like supreme gospel. The word *demon* couldn't have described him more accurately.

"Uh... Look, I'm serious, you're *really* starting to resemble Ramiris."

"It is an honor to hear, although it feels rather little like a compliment."

That's 'cause it's not! I swear, I take my eyes off you for a second, and you've grown incredibly shameless. Kind of neat to see this maturation take place, though.

"Well, we can save that for later. I'll have to think about it. I can't set up something for you guys *that* easily."

"Understood, sir."

It seemed happy enough with that. I figured we were good for now.

That left only Shion to check up on, and that confrontation was right on the cusp of its climax.

∗

Clayman was panting for breath as he glared at her, a loathsome look on his face. Shion had all but made him admit to her strength.

It might've appeared like they were locked in an intense competition for superiority, but that would be a dreadful mistake. That was because Shion had Ultraspeed Regeneration, that undefeatable X factor, on her side. They were equals in strength, but Shion could keep up the fight for far longer. While they seemed an even match in each exchange of blows, Clayman's fatigue had begun to stand out while I was fighting Milim.

Shion probably didn't need my aid to win this. And now that her advantage was clear to all, Clayman was starting to panic.

"Is that all you've got? You are far too weak to call yourself a demon lord!"

Wow, Shion. No mercy, huh? She was totally dissing Clayman.

"You—you—you'll pay for that! Come to me, Marionette Dance!!"

The demon lord unleashed five puppets, each transforming into a magic-born that lunged at Shion. Each one was high in level, formed from a soul Clayman had put in a doll for deployment at any time. It was part of his hidden arsenal, I suppose—now was no time for him to hold back, no doubt, so he was busting out everything he had.

This was more than enough firepower to take out your average magic-born. But with that massive sword she loved so much, she mowed down all five with a single swipe.

"Pathetic," she said, not a hint of fatigue on her face. "You never were anything special, were you?" She had been fighting and fighting, and there wasn't a scratch on her. *She* was starting to look and act more like a demon lord now.

Clayman, meanwhile, was visibly quivering. "Don't—don't give me that, you!" he shouted out of humiliation. "It's too early to boast of your victory yet! My Marionette Dance will recover itself in moments, striking at you again. The *real* show begins now!"

He probably wasn't making that up out of spite. They really *could* do that. Shion waited for them, a thoughtful look on her face—but the dolls showed no sign of getting back up. There was a good reason for that.

Panic crossed Clayman's face again. "N-no," he whispered. "Why aren't they reviving?"

I could understand the shock of having your beloved tools of battle fail you like this. I decided to provide a little color commentary.

"Hmm, how about I just reveal it to you? Shion's greatsword is a type called a Soul Eater. Those puppets didn't have any physical and spiritual defensive spells applied to them, right? You cheaped out on creating them, so she broke them in one hit."

That much wasn't worth keeping under wraps to me. Clayman was going to be my prey anyway; if he wanted to know, then let him know.

"A, a sword with spirit-based attacks?!"

"It's not that rare. There's a human with one out there, y'know."

"N-no! That's one of the least common traits, even with Uniques!"

"Ohhh? Well, what's it matter? One of my friends forged it for us."

Shion's sword was a modified blade created using Hinata's as a reference. It had the power to attack the spiritual body itself—not literally eat souls or anything but deal damage to spirit-based life-forms. There were no restrictions like that "seven hits" thing with Hinata; depending on the force applied, it could kill instantly unless successfully resisted. It wasn't guaranteed to kill all the time, but Shion wasn't exactly a delicate fighter, so it didn't matter. Since it dealt both spiritual and physical damage, she didn't need seven hits to finish foes anyway.

"Oh, I see. So this is Goriki-maru Version 2!"

She didn't know...? I, um, I'm pretty sure we went over all this when I gave it to her? Ah, whatever. Shion was never one to sweat the small stuff, so setting her up with this was the right idea.

"Heh...heh-heh-heh. I see. It was the power of that sword that allowed you to fight against me. Then allow me to add that dirty little blade to my collection! Take this—Demon Marionette!!"

Sounds like Clayman had misread her.

The ominous strings of black light that streamed from both his hands wrapped themselves completely around Shion's body. She didn't move. Kinda wish she tried to dodge it or, you know, *something*, but I guess she didn't need to.

Clayman, assuming Shion didn't react in time, found this much to his liking. "Heh-heh-heh-heh-heh... Behold, the ultimate cursing magic, with the power to rule over demon lords themselves! It seems a waste to squander it on magic-born like you, but so be it. I have some slots to fill in my five fingers, and you would be wonderful to take under my wing."

He *totally* had the wrong idea—if that's what he was saying, poor guy. It wasn't that Shion *couldn't* move—she just *didn't* move. Despite all of Clayman's lofty words, he was probably freaking out over why it wasn't working at all.

Complete Memory, one of Shion's skills, was the power to record memories into her astral body. In layman's terms, it let her retain her memories even if her brain was destroyed. Combine a conscious soul with a set of memories, and you could regenerate the physical body even if it was vaporized. This made Shion into a special sort of race—call her a demi-spiritual life-form if you want—but essentially, it allowed her to think with her soul, and that meant any effect that tried to take over her spirit was neutralized. Against Shion, no mind-takeover curses could ever work.

"Hey," an annoyed-sounding Shion called out from within her cocoon of black string, "what are you trying to do with this? It's not hurting me at all, but should I wait a little longer?"

You know—and this has been something I've been thinking for a while now, but—I really wish she'd stop acting like this was a pro-wrestling bout. This was supposed to be a duel to the death. Why was she deliberately letting herself get hit by her enemy's moves? Shion, Sufia...and Milim, too. I just didn't understand how these war-loving freaks thought sometimes. Gimme a break.

Raphael confirmed to me that Shion wasn't being affected at all, though. There wasn't any need to even beware of Clayman's secret techniques.

"That—that's ridiculous... My Demon Marionette doesn't work? It has to! This cannot even be possible! It's the ultimate in demon domination! It can exact its rule over demon lords!"

It had ruled over Nine-Head a moment ago. Certainly, you could take over the mind of a calamity-level monster with it easily enough. But would it work on the disaster-class demon lords? I think Clayman overestimated his own strength.

Apparently sick of waiting any longer, Shion used his aura to rip her cocoon apart. "So ridiculous," she scornfully muttered. "Relying on such cheap tricks as this... You don't deserve your title at all."

Clayman just stood there, finally succumbing to the panic.

...Or not. What Shion said must've flipped a switch somewhere inside of him.

"Heh-heh-heh... Ha-ha-ha-ha-haaaaaaa!! I don't deserve my title? You'll regret saying that, you maggot! Yes, you'll regret extracting my full strength from me!"

His shoulders were shaking as he shrieked with laughter. Off went his fancy-looking suit jacket and shirt, leaving him topless. It also left assorted other items he had hidden on his body to clank against the floor, no longer of use to him. I had thought this was over, but Clayman still had something left to rely on.

Suddenly, two pairs of arms grew out from his uncovered back—long, thin, and protected by a black exoskeleton. This was his true character. Not the dolled-up form from before, but this form that evoked wild, crazed insanity.

"But yes... Yes, you're right. A demon lord... I am a demon lord. I focused on ease and elegance in the way I go about matters, dispatching my foes with style. But enough of that. It doesn't matter. I had forgotten about how this feels, for so long...and now I'm going to crush you in my hands!!"

The true nature of his rage came to the surface. All he had on him was something he kept preciously protected in his hand. A mask. A jester's mask, decorated with a smile. Without a moment's pause, he put it on.

"Hoh? Looks like you've grown worthier," a happy-sounding Shion said. "I'm glad to see that. I am Shion, secretary and personal guard to the demon lord Rimuru, and I will be happy to fight you!"

"And I am the demon lord...no, the 'Crazed Clown' Clayman. You are *dead*, Shion the magic-born!"

The introductions were made. The two moved at the same moment.

∗

Clayman, in his "real" form, was a powerhouse, laying out the full extent of his demon lord–worthy magical force against Shion. His normal arms wielded those ominous black beams of light. The upper arms from his back wielded an ax and a hammer; the lower ones, a sword and shield.

Dealing with both magical and melee attacks at once baffled Shion for a moment. But she was stronger. Swinging the sword she called Goriki-maru Version 2, she clanged the sword out of his hand and crushed his shield. A simple, tactless roundhouse slash from above smashed through the ax and hammer Clayman crossed in front of him.

That freakish force came courtesy of Shion's intrinsic skill Ogre Berserker, and her frenzy of weapon breaking was the work of Guarantee Results and Optimal Action, both part of her Master Chef unique skill. In other words, Clayman was still no match for her. Even with all his might, she was just pummeling him.

Now he was crossing his two pairs of steellike arms to block Shion's fists—but they, too, were smashed to ribbons. Her next punch landed squarely in the pit of his stomach.

"Orrgghhh…"

He fell in agony, foaming at the mouth. *There it is. The end.*

Not that it's for me to say, but Shion really had gotten overwhelmingly stronger. Dying and getting resurrected like that gave her power on a scale like nothing she ever had before.

"Gerrhhaaahh?!!"

She planted a follow-up kick on him, making him roll around on the ground in agony. The mask was cracked now, revealing bloodshot eyes.

"N… N-no… This can't be. How could…could I…I, a demon lord, Clayman…?!"

Now Clayman understood the difference in power. But he still refused to accept this reality. It was devastating to him.

"May I put him out of his misery, Sir Rimuru?"

Hmm. There were a few things I could ask him, but I could predict most of the answers. Beyond that, I wanted to know about whose bidding he was doing, but was he gonna be honest with that?

"D-dammit all!! Milim! What is Milim doing?! Destroy that magic-born at once—"

Clayman was screaming out the words now, realizing that his death was near. But Veldora was holding Milim back. Clayman looked at him with disbelief.

"Wh-who…? What—what is this? His power is off the charts…!"

He must've just realized that Veldora wasn't just another magic-born.

"Well, he's in human form right now, but that's Veldora. I told you, remember? He's my friend."

This silenced Clayman. I'm sure he wanted to deny it, but seeing him spar evenly with Milim forced him to admit it. The two had been fighting for a while now, and it was turning into quite the fireworks show. Skill names flew back and forth, many of which I think I remembered hearing before, and Milim had an honest look of surprise on her face.

Hey, is she really being controlled? Because I'm starting to wonder.

……

Raphael's reaction made me ponder the idea for a bit, but it was no big deal at the moment. Besides, this would be the first time she'd met Veldora as a person, and it seemed like she was having a blast.

Thus, Clayman gave up on having Milim to rely on. Even in his panicked confusion, he managed to flee to the edge of our isolated battle zone, shouting at the audience outside.

"F-Frey! Frey, what are you doing?! You and I share a common fate! Get in here and lend a hand!"

The pleading fell on cold, dead ears.

"Oh, I'm sorry, Clayman. Nobody can go through this barrier unless Guy lets them. Such a pity."

He resentfully groaned at this heartless reply, then turned back toward Milim, his eyes twitching and revealing the insanity inside. He must've gotten another wild idea in his mind. A crazed laugh crossed his lips as he looked at her once more.

"Kah! Kah-ha-ha-ha-ha! Milim! Milim! Follow my orders and execute a Stampede! Kill everybody you see in here!!"

Well, *that* sounds awful. Clayman just wanted to survive now, and he didn't care how bad he looked along the way. *This is bad, I have to admit. Now isn't the time to sit around and watch things unfold. Back into the battle I go.*

But just as I started to run, I heard the most unbelievable thing.

"Why do I need to do that? Rimuru and his people are my friends!"

Surprised, I turned around—only to find Milim chilling out there, a wide grin on her face.

"Milim?! Whoa, you—weren't you being controlled…?"

"Waaah-ha-ha-ha! Thanks a lot for getting tricked by that, Rimuru! You know someone like Clayman would never take over my mind!"

Wh-what?!

……

I can't articulate why, but I had the strangest feeling Raphael had been angry at me for a while. But back to Milim.

"So Clayman *didn't* seize your mind?"

Um, what's going on here? I felt obliged to check one more time—but Milim just gave me a proud smile. I could hear at least one demon lord in the audience say, "Huh? But she didn't react at all when he punched her!"

The most surprised of all, of course, was Clayman.

"Y-yes. Yes! I used the Orb of Domination *he* gave me to put you completely at my beck and call… You killed Carillon under my orders, did you not?!"

Ohhh, Clayman. So shocked by these events that he has no idea what he just said. That oughtta make my video evidence more believable. After all, he just revealed that not only was he the culprit, but there was someone else pulling *his* strings, too.

"Yes! That! That's what I wanted to hear," exclaimed Milim. "Answer me, Clayman. Who's this *he* you're talking about?"

She asked the question casually enough, but she backed it up with sharp, seeking eyes. She had totally ignored Clayman's question, which was so like her.

Right. So Milim wasn't being controlled, and she had her doubts about Clayman from the beginning? For what?

Before I could get an answer, another voice butted in.

"Whoa, whoa, who's been killed here?"

It came from the other end of the battle zone, this low, heavy voice—belonging to the man with the eagle wings that Frey brought along with her.

Wait, no way... Like, with that obvious a costume...?! And if I didn't pick up on that, does that make me...?

......

Whoa, why does it feel like Raphael's exasperated with me? And wasn't it about to say something to me back then? Or maybe not? Ah, maybe I was just hearing things. Let's forget about it and, um, pay more attention in the future.

The man, Carillon, ripped the mask off his face, his awe-inspiring aura shooting out with it. With a moment's concentration, he was instantly back to his original appearance. *Yep. That's the Beast Master, all right. No doubt about it.*

"Wow, you were all right, Carillon?"

"Yo, Rimuru. 'All right' ain't how I would describe it, but that's fine. Thank you for taking care of my forces."

"Oh, not a problem."

After thanking me, Carillon gave Clayman a knowing grin. Now it was obvious that Milim was under no one's control.

"Wha—? How...? So it's true...? But Frey told me... No, Frey, too? You betrayed me as well, didn't you?!"

Finally getting the whole picture, Clayman gave Frey a half-crazed glare. She responded by pretending he wasn't there.

By the looks of things, I wouldn't call this a betrayal, per se...

"Hmm?" Frey nonchalantly replied. "Since when were you laboring under the assumption that I was your ally?"

Yikes. I knew it. Women can be so scary sometimes.

Frey was tricking Clayman from the get-go.

"You, you have to be kidding me! All, all of you... You'll pay; I'll make you all pay for this!"

The scream of the pitiful clown echoed across the field, and...

"Shion, do it."

"You got it!"

Like a hungry dog released from the command to stay, Shion bounded off, using both hands to swing down her blade as quickly as she possibly could. It was a single blow from her sword, a judging strike. Clayman did his best to block it, but his three pairs of arms were all sliced off, his body slashed diagonally down from head to toe. It was unsurvivable—and that one stroke from Shion's spirit-crushing blade made Clayman fall wordlessly to the ground.

✳

It was over for Clayman. Carillon was alive, and we had all the testimony in order. I'm pretty sure I could avoid being branded the enemy of the demon lords now.

Clayman was barely clinging to life. He was no longer a threat; there was no way left for him to turn the tables. Things were already set in stone, and there would be no more excuses. So, before the demon lords, he had revealed everything. And each of them might take the news differently, but regardless, their trust in him had vanished, none willing to cover for him.

The barrier covering us was removed, and Frey quickly ran up and approached Milim.

"I believed you were still of sound mind, but I truly had my doubts at times, Milim! And you kept our promise anyway. I appreciate that."

"Wah-ha-ha-ha-sha! Of course I did. We're friends. But you've been taking care of that for me, right? Didja bring it over?"

"Yes, yes, you mean this, right? I have to say, though, withstanding the Orb of Domination was simply amazing..."

As they spoke, Frey took something out of her pocket and handed it to Milim. It was the Dragon Knuckle I gave her as a present.

Milim accepted it like a kid on her birthday and immediately put it on, beaming ear to ear.

The rest of the demon lords, seeing this, finally put two and two together, and I could hear whispers all around the room.

"Such a cheap performance."

"I—I saw through it the whole time!"

"Yes, I assumed as much."

"Yeah, I figured…"

I don't think I was the only one Milim tricked, but everyone else found the results just as plausible as I did.

Then I heard a groan from below, like the sound of blood being coughed up.

"…When? Since when were you deceiving me…?"

It was Clayman. He was still breathing, still incapable of grasping the unbelievable reality before him. And it was Milim who revealed the cruel truth.

"Y'know, I had a real hard time doing it! With that promise I made with Frey, I had to pretend you tricked me. Then I put on that pendant and made you think it was working on me."

"You… You couldn't… I put my full power into it, with the Orb of Domination… The perfect…ultimate Demon Dominate…?! And you…you…"

"Uh-huh! Most magic like that bounces off me pretty easily, so… First I had to remove all my barriers, then hold back my force so I didn't passively resist it. I had to convince you that the curse was working before your own eyes, or else you'd be far too wary to believe me. So I had to work really hard!"

"Wh…? What…? You… You accepted it on purpose?! My most valuable Artifact… My hidden gem, the ability to control demon lords…"

"Oh, was that what it was? Well, too bad you could never control me!"

She stuck her chest out, looking relentlessly proud of herself.

"Yeah, really," I commented. "I feel stupid for worrying about you. And between that two-fisted sports pose and the smile you had on your face, your acting abilities really suck."

"What do you want from me? I was just glad to see you were all angry for me, Rimuru."

Frey just shrugged at this. "Still," she said, "when Clayman punched you, I thought I was going to lose my composure. If you decided to fight back against him, you would've destroyed my home. Great job putting up with him. That, at least, I have to compliment you for."

An interesting revelation. So that wasn't the first time Clayman physically abused her? What a nutcase. Was he actively trying to get himself killed?

"Mm-hmm! I'm all grown up now, too, y'know. So I can deal with stuff like that!"

That obsession with being grown up indicated all too well how childish she still was.

"Oh, *how?*" Frey protested. "...Well, that's fine, but you couldn't have dealt with all that just because of our promise, could you? What did you really want?"

"Hmm? Well, you know, I remember Clayman talking to me about some weird stuff before. Like, about making Rimuru into an enemy of mankind and triggering a war between humans and monsters. If he did that, that wouldn't be too fun for me, so I thought I'd meddle a bit!"

"Heavens. Imagine, you lifting a finger for somebody else."

"Wah-ha-ha-ha-ha! I told you—I'm all grown up now!"

"Yes, yes, let's just call it that."

Well, huh... I suppose Milim was sharp enough to realize Clayman was doing someone else's bidding. So she pretended to be brainwashed in order to find out who it was? She had some kind of promise or deal with Frey, too. Let's just ignore the fact that she totally tricked me.

The thing to focus on was: That orb didn't hypnotize her at all. She didn't struggle out of it midway; it never worked once. It was all an award-winning performance. As she later explained to me, she had been consuming bell peppers to maintain her poker face. The blank expression that resulted from eating this detested food of hers made everyone think her mind had been erased. It wasn't enough to trick Veldora, but he played along, enjoying the combat session as a way to get limber in his new body. Maybe he was a lot more adaptable to things than I thought.

Like, seriously, Raphael, you never saw it?

......

Oh, um, okay. Guess you did try to tell me something.

I suppose it telling me "No results" should've been pretty bleed-ingly obvious, looking back. Of course it couldn't find any curse effects on her. I was just jumping to conclusions. I should really adopt the habit of listening more carefully to people—that and hearing them out until the end.

I wasn't about to tell anyone about it, but, yes, I had my personal regrets.

"By the way," Carillon asked as he strode up to Milim, "if I could ask you something?"

She smiled back with the Dragon Knuckle eased into her fingers. "Mm? Sure! Anything!"

"I just wanted to be sure... You weren't under anyone's control? So that was all *you* when you were whipping the life out of me?"

Carillon was smiling, too, but I could see the veins on his fore-head bulging. Yeah, I'd be wondering about that, too.

"Huh?! That, um..."

"It's fine, it's fine. It just means I'm weaker than you. But," he added, no longer hiding his anger, "you willfully blew up my entire nation, didn't you?"

Milim was caught off guard for a moment—before immediately raging back at him.

"Oh, come on, Carillon! That's the kind of small stuff you're preoccupied with? What's it matter?!"

Yep, that's the real Milim, all right.

"It's *not* small stuff! You know I could have died back there?!"

"Oh, don't give me that. Just shut up! I was so passionate about my performance— Um, I mean, passionate about deceiving Clayman that I was trying really, really hard! It's all *Clayman's* fault!!"

"*His* fault? Ugh… Well, whatever. Not that you'll ever listen to anyone else's complaints…"

I was starting to feel a little bad for Carillon. Seeing those tears appear on his rugged, masculine eyes, I wanted to console him as best I could. She tricked *me*, too, so I thought we had something in common.

"Now, now, Carillon. Your Lycanthropeers and everyone else are safe—and they all put in a hell of an effort, fighting for your revenge. It wasn't all bad, was it?"

"Ah, Rimuru… Thanks for the thought."

"Yeah, so don't worry about it. Besides, you can always build another town. I even had our forces capture Clayman's magic-born to serve as your labor force."

"Huh? Whoa, are you serious…?!"

"Yep. I'll provide any technical expertise you need, and all of us at Tempest will help you out as best we can, too. So let's make it a better, happier Eurazania than ever before!"

We had time for it. Time—and funds kindly provided by Clayman. Considering our future trade prospects, it'd be strategically beneficial for us to have Carillon owe us a favor. It seemed like a great opportunity to exploit, and I wanted to maybe make friends with more beastmen through the work, too.

"Wahhh-ha-ha-ha! Isn't that great, Carillon? You have me to thank for that, too!"

Her to thank for *what*, I wondered. Maybe for completely flattening the land around the capital and thus saving us the trouble of hauling away the rubble?

"I'll really owe you one," the surprised yet thankful Carillon replied. "And you know, Rimuru—or maybe Sir Rimuru? I promise to you that the Beast Kingdom will never hesitate to help you out if you need it. We'll be allied nations forever! …And I wish *you* would at least pretend to regret this a little more," he didn't forget to add, turning to Milim.

To her credit, she was back to her usual self—if Carillon and I were cool, she was cool. That's Milim for you. Always looking out for number one—and I didn't mind, if Carillon was feeling better.

It appeared that my promises surprised a lot more people than just Carillon. They were a shock to the demon lords assembled around us, too.

"So *that* was it!" observed the smiling red-haired Guy. "I thought leaving those magic-born alive was a sign of weakness...but I see you're a rather creative thinker! Hardly any wonder that Noir's taken a liking to you."

Noir? Who's that? Ah well.

Frey was back to focusing on Clayman, a quiet anger enveloping her. "So, Clayman," she said. "You always were the sort to domineer over weaker people, or those who couldn't resist you. I don't think you have any right to call yourself a demon lord. I didn't intervene since Milim was trying so hard...but you know what? I was kind of angry at you, too."

It made it clear that Frey had no interest in rescuing him.

"Yeah, I know it's survival of the fittest, but you took a step too far, I'd say. You wrecked my country, and I wanna see you pay for that, okay?"

Carillon *did* have a lot of damage to deal with. Damage technically inflicted by Milim, yes, but he was willing to shift the blame to Clayman here—and make him suffer the consequences.

None of the other demon lords voiced any opposition to this. I suppose Clayman wasn't too popular a guy in this clique. He was already cornered—and now, the final moment was approaching.

Time to finish him off.

Feeling the life ebb away from him, Clayman's heart was filled with regret. Regret and the words of his friends and advisers, flashing before his eyes.

"Now's not the time to be too reckless. Whatever ya do, don't letcher guard down..."

—Ah… You were absolutely right, Laplace…

He thought he was being careful, but he let power drown him. When he beheld Milim's overwhelming strength, he made the erroneous assumption that it was all his to wield.

It's just as you felt it. In the end, I was the one being controlled by Milim. I thought I was paying attention…but she tricked me. You trusted in me, left me to rule as your demon lord, but I suppose this is the end for me…

He had ignored his friend's warning. And that set these results in stone.

"You're weaker than us, Clayman, all right? So no trying to pull anything weird by yourself, if you could."

"Hohh-hoh-hoh-hoh! Teare is right. Feel free to depend on us instead."

Ah, Teare. Ah, Footman. You're right. I forgot…

He was too focused on himself to feel it right to rely on his friends. He *did* file the promise in his mind, actually, but he forgot about that when it counted—one of the most inexcusable things he could have done.

I just wanted to get as close as I could to them. Of course I'd take risks to achieve that. Why wouldn't I? I was part of the Moderate Jesters, too…

It was true. Clayman wanted the respect of his peers. He wanted his powers to be recognized, so he never revealed his Moderate Jesters' side to the public. Now he realized that was a mistake.

But it was too late…

…He recalled when he first met the mysterious patron that led him to this.

"Hey. You're Clayman, right?"

"Who are you? Someone in a hurry to die, apparently, if you address me that casually."

"Whoa, whoa, no need to act so alarmed. We have a common acquaintance who pointed me here."

"An acquaintance?"

"Yeah. The demon lord Kazalim. Your creator, of sorts."

"What?"

He had intended to kill this boy with haste, but then he mentioned a name from his distant past. Now Clayman was interested in hearing him out. And when he did, he discovered the truth about him. His ambitions and his power.

"I'm going to take over this world, Clayman, and I want you to help me."

"Heh... Ha-ha-ha-ha-ha! I like it. So that's your request?"

"Yes. A job for the Moderate Jesters."

"And what are your terms?"

"How does resurrecting Kazalim sound to you?"

It was beyond all expectations. There was no reason to refuse. The powers the boy displayed to him made it clear beyond doubt. He immediately accepted the job.

"I thought you'd agree to it. Now the world can be ours together. It's gonna be one crazy place for us to live in!"

Seeing this boy, living life as if it was all some kind of wonderful game, Clayman honestly thought he could pull it off. There were obstacles in their way, massive ones, but that made it seem all the more fun. It *seemed* that way, but now, his mistakes had crumbled the foundation of their whole strategy. And after the boy had fulfilled his part of the bargain and revived Kazalim...

My thoughtlessness led to this. There is no defending me to him now...

Kazalim was alive and well, and he had no way to congratulate him. More just deserts for him. He had been ordered to sit tight and watch how things unfolded, and he ignored those orders for his own petty reasons.

The last thing he recalled were the words of the man himself—the advice his beloved demon lord Kazalim gave him.

"...Clayman. I see much of myself in you. And you may imitate me if you like, but do not imitate my negative aspects."

It was wise, all too wise, and something he should have recalled quicker.

Ah... Sir Kazalim... I apologize. I forgot your advice, and I committed the gravest mistake possible...

Yes, it was Clayman's mistake, made in the worst possible

fashion. And just like Kazalim, he was defeated in the most shameful way—by a freshly born demon lord. Karma in action, one could say—but to Clayman, it hurt more than anything else.

And I even lost the army you granted me through my mistakes... I cannot die. No, I cannot die yet. If I die here without atoning for this at all, I'll never be able to forgive myself...

If it had come to this, he at least wanted to pass on what he knew. The thought kindled the light of life in Clayman before he could completely resign himself to his fate.

"You are a walking dead, created by me from a dead body, but I have placed special weight upon your brainpower. You are not geared for combat, unlike Footman and Teare, but no one can use strategy and artifice to command armies the way that you can. That, Clayman, is why you shall become a demon lord..."

Kazalim had high hopes for him, and he betrayed them all. But if it was power he lacked, all he needed was to obtain some. Then he could stand tall with Footman and Teare—surpass them, even. If only Clayman had some power to back up his intelligence, he could've sprung past them all with ease.

Yes... Yes, indeed. There was no need to awaken to a "true" demon lord at all. So give it to me. Give me power... Give me the overwhelming power I need!!

Confirmed. Converting the soul into magical energy... Successful. Disassembling and reconstructing the receptacle body...

Clayman wasn't expecting the internally shouted wish to come true. But the World Language had other plans for him. Right here, at the last moment, his wish had been granted.

So heaven hasn't forsaken me yet!

In which case, Clayman's answer was obvious.

Heh...heh-heh-heh... So you treat me like a fool? Well, I'll repay you for all that. For now, though, I've got to get out of here...

He was weak, too weak to even use his voice, but Clayman's soul was burning bright—his life was a raging flame. And now, with a coolness that was quite the opposite of what was in his heart, Clayman resolved to retreat. The older demon lords—Guy, Milim, and Daggrull, in particular—were too much to handle. Simply awakening wouldn't give him the winning edge against them, and now was no time for recklessness.

First, he would report back to the boy. That took precedence over everything. The despicable slime he looked down upon was still a question mark, but even the magic-born that served him were stronger than Clayman—and he was on good terms with a revived Veldora, a point he couldn't afford to ignore. Anyone who survived a confrontation with Hinata couldn't have done so out of sheer luck.

He needed to abandon his rose-colored glasses and analyze things for what they were. And that was why he had to take the information he learned here and bring it back.

Quickly, he assembled a plan. His idea: to release a massive ball of magical force, as much as he could manage, and slip out of this chamber in the chaos.

I will need to watch out for Guy...

Guy had no time to deal with weaklings. He probably wasn't even paying attention to Clayman any longer.

...It's all right. I'll get out of here, I promise.

And if he could take out a few demon lords along the way, he thought as he scrambled to his feet, all the better.

Among the demon lords watching, I was probably the first one to notice. I had my eyes on Clayman the entire time, never giving up the watch.

"Shion, get back!"

Quickly heeding my command, Shion fell back to my side. Immediately after she did, the area around Clayman—including the spot she stood on—was swept over by a huge quantity of magicules. The storm gathered even more energy from the chamber, focusing itself squarely upon Clayman. If I had yelled out a moment later, Shion would've been caught up in it.

"Looks like it's really happening."

"Sir Rimuru? What is…?"

The sight of me keeping my cool appeared to relieve Shion. There was no reason to panic. And I wasn't panicking, *buuuut…*

"Clayman's awakened. Just as planned."

"Just as planned? Well, great!"

I was glad to earn Shion's full trust, but I wasn't quite so assured myself. *This is all according to Raphael's plan, but are we really okay with this? 'Cause if we lose, it's gonna stop being funny real fast…*

When I first laid eyes on Clayman earlier, I could see a large number of rifts in the air around him, as if they were attached to his soul. It was malice personified, the remains of the souls from the people he had killed up to now. But I couldn't just take them from him. They couldn't go on to the afterlife, and they couldn't dissolve into the air. If I killed Clayman, they'd go down with him.

As I thought over what I could do about this, Raphael suggested a plan of action: force Clayman into a corner and make him awaken to a "true" demon lord.

Suggestion. If you use Belzebuth to consume the energy Clayman releases upon awakening, it will be possible to restore your magicules.

It was easy for Raphael to say, but there was a litany of problems with that. I didn't know if Clayman would awaken, and if he did, he'd undoubtedly be powered up. But hey, um, wouldn't he just fall asleep, like with my Harvest Festival?

Understood. Since Clayman's evolution did not follow the standard procedure, the process will not be fully complete. As a result, it is believed that he will not require sleep.

So sort of a limited power-up, then. *I guess I'll just have to defeat an awakened Clayman, then.*

According to Raphael's predictive calculations, defeating him would be a breeze no matter how much he was enhanced. That was based on everything from his core strength to the power he could earn and the skills he was likely to acquire. Even at the maximum threat level, its answers indicated I was still on top of him.

No point worrying about it, then. Just gotta do it.

Besides, it was kind of true that my magical energy was just about ready to bottom out. I could replenish it really fast, so it'd bounce right back after deploying a large-scale spell, but restoring it to full actually took a while. Although I had more energy than my awakening took, I was also using Veldora this whole time as a fuel tank to restore it. With him no longer part of me, it was natural to want to keep my own magicules topped off.

It'd also earn me some street cred with the other demon lords. As the new recruit, I needed to seize a seat at the round table with my own power. Showing off my battlefield skill was the best way to earn their acceptance without stirring up trouble in the future. If I didn't want 'em wheedling me later, I wanted them to think that *I* shouldn't be messed with.

Let's use this awakened Clayman to show off my power. It'll save everyone a lot of trouble as time goes on. And the power to show off? The ultimate skill Belzebuth, Lord of Gluttony, of course.

"Hey! Rimuru! Clayman's awakened? I can't believe it, but look at all that force! Let me help with—"

"You're fine, Carillon. I'll take him on. I'm calling myself a demon lord, and I want to earn my way into the club. I'm gonna dispatch him and make them all accept me!"

Carillon shrugged and stepped aside. "Well, don't blow it," he said, and I definitely didn't intend to. The enemy had to be crushed—that was the only reason I needed. I was more pissed off at Clayman than anyone else. It was time to settle this.

So I walked toward Clayman, now fully on his feet. The other demon lords were content with watching, seemingly all right with me fighting alone. I was sure they wanted to gauge what I had, so I assumed they wouldn't complain. Milim was brightly smiling at me, and Ramiris was happily humming to herself. Nobody was doubting my chances—which I took as them believing in me.

"Shion, Ranga, step back."

"But…!"

"I've got this."

"Y-yes sir!"

"Good luck, Sir Rimuru."

The other lords gave them enough distance to retreat away so that I wouldn't unwittingly hurt anyone else.

Now I was alone, and Clayman gave me his sickly little laugh. "Heh-heh-heh, ha-ha-ha-ha-haaaah! Look at me! I've obtained the power! *You* thought I was finished, you worm! Now prepare to be crushed!!"

The laughter grew louder as he looked down at me. But it was all an act. It was sad, how well Raphael had predicted all his moves.

As it described matters, there were two potential strategies Clayman could take. One was a desperate bull rush to kill me; the other was to sneer at me, make me lose my cool, and search for a path of escape. Evidently, he chose the latter, and that meant I knew what he'd do next.

I grimaced at him, keeping my eyes firmly on every move he made. Clayman was looking for an opening. So I played along with his performance.

"I told you, you're cornered. I'm stronger than you. Give it up and tell me whose bidding you're doing."

Of course, in my case, it wasn't a performance—it was what I really wanted from him. Perhaps that was why Clayman so easily took the bait.

"Heh-heh-heh… Impertinent to the end, I see. Once I release my—"

He kept up the act as he suddenly took action. He must've figured I was off my guard, because he fired a massive ball of magical energy from out of nowhere. Must've been building it up as we talked. It was a huge, superpowered blast, one that contained all the energy he had just awakened into, and it was hurtling straight my way.

Clayman assumed I would dodge it. That or maybe fire off a blast of my own to neutralize it, although a spur-of-the-moment

spell like that from me wouldn't be enough. If I jumped away, it'd explode in midair; if I tried blowing it up, he'd be able to escape in the resulting gigantic explosion. That, I imagine, were his thoughts.

Too bad, though.

"Didn't I just tell you? You're cornered. That attack won't do a thing. Projectiles don't work on me."

Belzebuth gobbled up that massive energy blast, leaving our surroundings completely unaffected. Clayman's scheme bit the dust hard.

"...Whaaaa?!"

It surprised Clayman enough to leave himself open—just long enough for me to snap my fingers. At that instant, a Barrier erected itself over the two of us, a kind of imitation of the one Guy built.

"So he's stealing my skills?" a bemused but unangered Guy asked. "Talk about shameless."

Now, I calmly thought, *I can consume Clayman with confidence. Man, my thought processes are getting more and more evil by the day, aren't they? Because I'm a monster, maybe?* I wasn't shirking the idea of eating him up at all. *Or was it because I'm a demon lord now? Ah, it doesn't matter.*

"Wh-what? What happened...?"

Clayman could no longer hide his confusion. The biggest, proudest attack he had was wiped away in an instant, and his brain hadn't caught up to that yet. *Like, how many times do I have to say it? You're already cornered. The moment someone with your level of talent took me on, your future was cast in stone. It's so important, isn't it, to fully gauge your abilities against those of your opponent?*

"Look, if you're gonna be serious about this, make it fast. I'll wait for you. Or were you thinking about ducking out of this chamber while that attack exploded all over us?"

It was a fully rhetorical question I was cornering him with. Talk about disrespecting your fellow man. Well, I'm a slime now, so it's all right.

I mean, Clayman was still screwing with me. He was on high alert, watching for what I'd do next, but he was still a wimp about it.

Just as Raphael expected, getting awakened didn't do all that much to change him. He had a ton more magical energy, but that was it. Apparently, he hadn't obtained any ability to control it or new skills to take advantage of it with. His "awakening" was a far different thing from mine. Me, I could use Mind Accelerate to speed up my brain a million times until it felt like time stopped. I could even cast spells in that state, making it look like I could just *think* of a magic spell to set it off.

Kneading together a big ball of magic was a terribly inefficient use of my time, so I didn't opt for that here. Unlike a full spell, which could be conceived and cast through one's will (or knowledge, in other words), controlling one's aura always led to a time lag. Of course, I could handle that because I had Cast Cancel and All of Creation. No matter how long and intricate a spell was, living life a million times slower than normal made it simple. One second, after all, now felt like two hundred and seventy-seven hours. Even the fanciest of spells could be pulled off in less than a day, so that meant I could trigger them in less than a tenth of a second. With regular magic, it was simple for me to set off multiples at the same time, even.

Thus, if I were in Clayman's shoes, I'd use multiple layers of magic to throw the chamber into confusion, then attempt to run as fast as I could. He didn't choose that, which meant he didn't have the strength for it. He hadn't even noticed that I built a barrier around us—one that cut off any escape route. If he wanted to get out, he'd have to do it over my dead body.

Whether he was aware of this or not, the atmosphere around Clayman began to change.

"Heh...heh-heh-heh... A mere slime with a big mouth, I see. You are strong, I will admit that much. But I am capable of far more than this!!"

He had changed tactics to the first scenario—a desperate bull rush to kill me. Giving up the escape, revealing his full force to the demon lords... A risky bet, to be sure, but it gave him a winning chance. Surrounded by a bunch of lords who believed that strength was everything, it'd even be a chance to write off all his previous crimes.

Assuming, of course, he could beat me.

"You seem confident in your aura-control abilities, but do you think you could deal with this? Here we go—my most powerful hidden skill! Demon Blaster!!"

After that long speech to throw off my game, he put his feelers to the ground, stretching them out around me, and then released.

The attack harnessed the ley lines under the ground, stacking them together and mixing in his own magicules to amplify them, then released it as a destabilizing ray of light. That was the long and short of it, and anyone caught in it would have their arrangement of magicules thrown into chaos, destroying them from the inside. Physical resistance would be useless, and even a magical Barrier would be instantly smashed.

This was the natural enemy of any monster, and I had to hand it to him—this was real demon lord stuff. But it didn't work on me.

"Swallow it all down, Belzebuth…"

The Demon Blaster light beam looked like a herd of dragons rising up from the ground—but now they were caught up in a rift before they could reach me, screaming their last as they were sucked inside. There was no escape, almost like a black hole that consumed all light around it.

"Forget it, Clayman. You're weaker than me."

I had to crush him. Crush him and hopefully make him reveal something about his patron. The best way to do that was via terror.

"No… That, that's not possible!! That—that was my secret weapon!"

Secret or not, projectiles just didn't work on me. Maybe if he used his head and did something to land a direct hit on me, things would be different.

"Do you see that you can't win now? So let me ask you. Tell me what you know and who you're cooperating with. Be honest with me, and I'll give you a painless death."

"Ha-ha-ha-ha-haaa! I am a walking dead! Kill me all you want; I'll just resurrect myself and come back later to kill— *Ounngh?!*"

I punched him. Then again, and again and again, without a word. I also applied Mind Accelerate, speeding it up a million times for him. Raphael could influence not just my perspective but those of people around me.

In the real world, it lasted several seconds. But in Clayman's mind, I was continually punching him, tormenting him with pain and terror, for several dozen days. So I could carve that pain and terror into his soul. And in those few seconds, the terror made Clayman's hair fall out, transforming his visage into the ghastly, bony gaze of the actual dead.

"Clayman," I quietly called out.

His body convulsed, then froze out of terror.

"I'm going to ask you one more time. Who are you getting your information from, and how is this person related to you? Tell me, and I'll make it easy on you."

But Clayman had more backbone than I thought.

"Don't... Don't treat me like a child. I would never betray my friends—and especially not my clients. That, and that alone, is the ironclad rule of the Moderate Jesters!"

Huh. So even villains had certain unbreakable rules.

"All right. Well, so be it." I casually changed my tone. "Oh, right, I should probably tell you—you realize you aren't gonna be resurrected, right?"

He had talked about doing that a few seconds—or days?—ago, but it wasn't gonna happen. Being consumed by Belzebuth was an even more tragic fate than being caught in the inescapable Unlimited Imprisonment Veldora was locked in.

"Wh-what? What are you talking about?"

Was he keeping up that macho act because he was counting on a new life later on, then? The moment he heard me, Clayman began to quiver.

"Look, um, what you told me earlier? About how walking dead can come alive again after they die? And that's why you wanted me to focus on killing you, so you could pluck out your astral body and try to run away. Right?"

He was an underhanded sneak, but I had to applaud him for his single-minded devotion to his cause. But my observation made his face pale.

"Wh-what did you…?"

He tried to cover it, but I could tell I was right. Not even I needed Raphael to figure it out—but Raphael had even more amazing stuff for me.

"Ummm, so you can connect your astral body to the ley lines here to keep your consciousness and memories protected, yeah? So even if you lose your physical body, you'll never truly die. That's why you were pretending to die there?"

Ahhh. Now I see. And just parroting out what Raphael told me made Clayman convulse before me. I was absolutely correct.

"W-wait, wait…"

I knew his game. And now it was time to end it. I turned toward the demon lords surrounding us, ignoring the gibbering Clayman.

"Well! I guess I won't extract anything else from Clayman, so I'm going to execute him shortly. Anyone have any objections? 'Cause if you do, I'll be happy to take *you* on, too."

It would *suck* if someone did, but I doubted it.

"Do as you please," Guy answered, speaking for the Council like I thought he would. No one else voiced any complaint.

"Stop! Wait, stop it!!"

Now Clayman was loudly pleading for his life, finally realizing there was no escape.

"After all the grief you gave me, I'm absolutely sick of you. Don't expect your death to be all sunshine and rainbows, all right?"

With that, I placed my hand on his head. I thought I'd make it quick 'n' easy on him if he coughed up some info on his master, but Clayman never sang. I really wanted him to, considering what I'd have to deal with in the future, but hey, I'd probably manage without it. There might be some more leads in his castle to explore, and given the testimony I had that the Modest Jesters weren't a monster ring, it was obvious that Clayman had worked with humans. I didn't know if that meant the Eastern Empire or the Western Nations, but either way, if he knew about my own movements, he had to have connections in the west. Track those down, and I should find a trail to follow before long. In a way, relying on the not-too-credible Clayman's testimony might just lead to more confusion.

So. Clayman.

"...I hope you'll spend the last few moments before your soul vanishes regretting what you've done."

"No! Wait, wait! Stop!! Stooooopppp!! Help, help me, Footman! Teare, help me! I can't die yet. I can't die heeeerrrreee!!"

It was pathetic, watching him try to flee. But I wasn't about to allow it. No matter how much he carried on, none of it would ever touch my heart. Leaving someone like this alive would just be planting the seed of disaster.

Plus, thanks to you, the naïveté in me just died. There was no way I could let that get one of my companions killed again.

"P-please, Lord Kazalim, help me—"

He reached out to his broken mask, clutching at it as if in prayer—

Crunch.

In an instant, the wailing, howling, resisting Clayman disappeared from sight. Body, soul, and all were greedily consumed by Belzebuth. And now it was converted into pure magicules inside me, where he would get to experience the torments of hell.

And whether a dirtied soul like his—a tainted, evil soul—or a sensible, good soul, death treated them all equally.

And for a moment, I thought I heard his voice:

—Ah, Laplace. You were exactly right. I think I went a little too far. I should have waited and bade my time, like you warned me to... You always were right...

Was that regret? I suppose even a villain like him feels regret. Let's hope that the "death" I gave him helps him get more familiar with that emotion.

GUY
CRIMSON

DAGGRULL

LEON

CHAPTER
6

THE OCTAGRAM

That Time I Got Reincarnated as a Slime

The moment I consumed Clayman, the red-haired demon lord Guy stood up.

"An impressive feat," he solemnly intoned. "I hereby recognize your right, from this day forward, to call yourself a demon lord. Does anyone disagree?"

Nobody appeared to. I had passed the exam. That's a relief, because—to be frank—goading the other demon lords into combat with me felt like suicide. I guess I never had much to worry about.

I undid the Barrier, allowing Ramiris to fly right up to my face, like she always did. "Ha-*ha*! I always knew you delivered the goods when the time came for it, Rimuru! In fact, I'd be happy to hire you as my apprentice!"

"Uh, I'm good, thanks. Find yourself another one."

"Why?!" she grumped. "What's the big deal? Why won'tcha just say yes like a good kid?"

"Hmph!" Milim proudly sniffed. "Rimuru's *my* friend. I heard he doesn't even want to get along with you!"

"What? No way! Hey! That's a lie, right, Rimuru?"

"Wah-ha-ha-ha-ha! Sorry, Ramiris, you aren't part of our team!"

"Whaaaat? Hyah!"

Taking the bait, Ramiris launched a flying kick at Milim's face.

She leaned to the side to dodge it and laughed even harder at her. *Huh. These guys are better friends than I thought.*

Meanwhile, I noticed Veldora engrossed in friendly-looking conversation with the demon lord Daggrull, bragging about how he was training to keep his aura hidden. "You see him, Daggrull?" he said, pointing at me. "*That's* how you do it."

"Indeed," the giant replied, nodding. "It was just for a moment, but I felt an explosive amount of magicules from him. Amazing he can hide it so well."

Veldora had apparently been providing color commentary for my battle against Clayman. I really wish he'd knock that stuff off. That was exactly why I told him to keep watch in town for me.

Deeno, meanwhile, yawned at me, his attention span already waning now that the action was over. "Well," he moaned, "it's fine by me." *Weirdo. And a hard one to pin, too. I'm never sure what he's thinking about.*

To Leon, however, none of this mattered. "Heh. I don't care who becomes a demon lord. Do whatever you want." Talk about cold.

Frey and Carillon had no objections to my new title. Which left one person.

Valentine, who had remained silent until now, lumbered up to his feet.

"Mmmm. Personally, I would never want to allow a low-born slime to ever become a demon lord, but..."

Dressed as gaudily as a mighty emperor, Valentine sneered down at me. Guess he was a no, even if I was guaranteed to win by majority vote. *No worries, then*, I thought as I was about to turn my attention elsewhere, when:

"Kwaaaaah-ha-ha-ha! Are you insulting my friend, you lackey?"

Veldora turned his casual attention on the maid next to Valentine.

"Come on, Milus, you really need to train your servants better. Want me to provide a little education?"

Whoa! Hey! What the hell, man?!

"What are you talking about?" Milus returned Veldora's gaze, her voice frigid and her expression icy. "I am simply a faithful attendant of Sir Valentine's."

"Heyyyy, don't do that! Valentine's hiding the truth, Veldora. You can't say that!"

Um, Milim? Did you just kind of blow the door open on that, or what?!

I had a suspicion something fishy was going on with him, but I suppose I was right. This fetching young maid Milus was the *actual* demon lord, and now she glared at Milim, attempting to stab her in the chest with her eyes.

"Ah!"

Finally realizing her error, Milim began whistling a tune to divert everyone's attention away from her.

Maybe it would've worked better if she could actually whistle, but no sound was coming out, and I doubted it'd make much difference. Milus didn't seem the type to take a joke, and these antics weren't about to calm her down.

She looked around the chamber, thoroughly annoyed, her eyes making her look like she planned to kill us all and hide the evidence. She looked hostile and dangerous, but luckily, she decided not to take on the entire rest of the room.

"Tch. Such a bothersome, villainous dragon. How long will he insist upon meddling with me...? And you've forgotten my very name, no less. How can anyone have such a gift for aggravating me?"

Now the atmosphere was very different as Milus—well, the demon lord Valentine, that is—spoke. It seems that Veldora was dunderheaded enough to misremember her name entirely, which did a lot to push her buttons.

"Enough of this," she huffed. "You may call me Valentine." Then, with a massive outburst of magical force, her appearance transformed, her maid outfit turning into a fancy Gothic-style dress. It was Change Dress in action, a neat trick Milim was adept at as well.

Yep. *This* was the real thing. The stand-in Valentine was a remarkable specimen himself, but his "maid" was on another dimension. Now we were greeted by a demon lord among demon lords, the ultimate personification of strength and beauty.

"You can leave ahead of me, Roy," she ordered the kingly ex-Valentine.

"But Lady Valentine—"

"If I've been unmasked in front of *this* many people, there's no point keeping up the charade."

She glared at Veldora yet again. "It...it's not my fault—I didn't know," he stammered, feeling out of sorts and trying to avoid her gaze. To Milim, meanwhile, it was already someone else's problem. The topic was over in her mind. Selfish as always, I could see.

Perhaps understanding that more than most, Valentine seemed ready to drop the subject, as peeved as she was about all this. Shaking off her anger, she stood before Roy, now comfortably back in the servant role.

"Anyway," she intoned, "there is something that concerns me. When Clayman looked at you, his eyes stopped for a moment, did they not? He might be involved with those cockroaches that invaded my domain earlier. I want you to return home and inform my people to step up our security."

Guess Carillon and I weren't the only guys Clayman picked a fight with. No wonder everybody hated him. Maybe he was just trying to discover where Valentine's domain was—it was still a secret—but even for a data-gathering fiend like him, sometimes it was all too easy to step over the line.

"...Yes, my lady."

Roy left the chamber alone, not questioning Valentine's order for a moment. No, he had no business being on the throne at all. He really *was* just a political stand-in. It was, I suppose, a sign of Valentine's power and influence.

✳

Time to switch gears. I plucked the round table out from my Stomach and set it back in place. Good thing I thought about storing it before I smashed it up. If battle had broken out before the barrier was in place, I'm sure it would've been a mess. The thing looked *far* too fancy for restitution to be cheap.

All the demon lords sat back down at the table, while Guy's two maids prepared some tea for us.

"Ah," Leon suddenly said next to me, "I just remembered. I

thought I had heard the name Kazalim somewhere before, but that's the demon lord I killed, isn't it?"

I thought I was gonna spit the tea out right there. How could he be so nonchalant with that?

"You know him, Leon?"

And how could Milim not know that? The other demon lords seemed similarly unfazed, many apparently clueless about the guy. Even Ramiris had completely forgotten. I thought she kept her memories whenever she was reborn? I wanted to poke fun at her about it, but that'd just be mean.

...So what's Kazalim got to do with this?

...Understood. The word Kazalim was uttered by Clayman as he called for help.

Oh, right, right! Now I remember. He *did* scream something like that. I totally remember that, so hopefully nobody's putting me on the same boat with Milim and Ramiris.

"So how is this Kazalim related to Clayman?" I asked.

"Kazalim is the Curse Lord," Carillon explained. "You and he recommended me to this post, didn't you, Milim?"

"Ohhhh, *him*! The Curse Lord, I remember. Huh. So that's the demon lord Leon killed?"

So she knew him by his nickname? That made a little sense. But really, it's not like Leon killed any *other* demon lords. If I had to guess, she probably almost forgot since it was just all too boring to her.

"Right. Kazalim was a walking dead like Clayman," said Carillon, his voice a tad nostalgic. "A unique monster, he said, evolved by himself from an elf. I was kinda friendly with him, so that's what he told me. The two of them must've been connected behind the scenes. Clayman took over Kazalim's old seat, besides."

Unlike Clayman, Carillon didn't seem to have any bad blood for this guy. *But hang on a minute. I almost let it pass, but if Kazalim's a walking dead, too...*

"Is Kazalim still alive? Maybe he just pretended Leon killed him, and he's hiding out somewhere?"

"Yeah," agreed Carillon, "that might be the case. He was a really sharp guy, you know? You had to be even more careful with him than Clayman."

So maybe I was right.

"Well," Leon naturally objected, "I don't much like you phrasing it like I let him get away. He invited me to join his force, claiming he would help me become a demon lord. Turning him down would have led to assorted annoyances, so I decided to defeat him and seize his position. Whether he's alive or dead, it doesn't matter to me."

Certainly, I could see it if Leon just wanted to stage a display of power without actually wanting to kill him.

"Whoa there, Leon. That's exactly why Clayman hated you, you realize."

"Hmph. Do you think I care?"

Yeah, to Leon, the whole subject was just an annoyance, no doubt. I didn't realize Clayman was trying to put the screws to Leon, too, though. He was just trying to hit everyone up, wasn't he? I was starting to wonder just how smart he really was.

Still, I was starting to gain a picture of what Kazalim and Clayman were up to. Leon had taken his seat here around two centuries ago, so maybe Kazalim got Carillon and Clayman into the club, then tried to earn a few more friends for himself. Clayman's earlier scheme to turn an orc lord into a demon lord seemed like kind of a rehash of that—he wanted more people friendly to him, so he could wield more power at Walpurgis. Trying to build blocs of voters, like in an Earth government, was a surprisingly sneaky and non-demon-lord-like move, I thought. A pretty powerful one, too.

"Among Clayman's allies were a group called the Moderate Jesters," I said. "Those Jesters hinted that they had connections among the human world, so perhaps the resurrected Kazalim has taken human form, you know?"

According to Leon, Kazalim's body disappeared after he was defeated. If he was alive again, it'd be in his spiritual-body form at first. It made sense that he'd then install himself into the physical body of something else. Reviving himself within the realm of a demon lord would lead to being instantly discovered, and considering nobody had found him yet, that theory could be safely discounted.

"You might be correct," Guy unexpectedly stated. "Leon's attacks have the power to destroy your spirit. If anything, I would mightily praise Kazalim for surviving. Plus, even for demons like ourselves, a full resurrection from our souls alone takes hundreds of years. I doubt a walking dead could ever perform it alone. Not without assistance."

Walking dead, unlike demons, were dependent on their physical bodies. Full resurrection from the astral body took time, and if anything, Kazalim being alive would be a small miracle. So did Guy mean to imply that Kazalim had help? It all seemed connected, but for now, we had no further evidence to go on.

"Well, either way, I'll just assume he's alive and stay on my guard for him. If I just killed Clayman, he might be out for revenge."

"Wah-ha-ha-ha-ha! Why worry, Rimuru? You're a lot stronger than him now!"

"Milim," I shouted, "that's the exact kind of cockiness that leads to getting killed!"

Thanks to my victory today, Clayman's forces were out of the picture. I didn't think our foes would make any moves for a while, but we still had to keep a sharp watch out. Me alone was one thing, but I now had legions of friends to keep safe. We'd have to devote more resources to our defense and think up ways to handle the threats ahead.

After some more chatting, the Council continued. With the one who called it out of the meeting, Guy took over in his place.

"The main subject of this Council was Carillon's betrayal and the rise of Rimuru over there, but those issues have been settled. Carillon has betrayed no one, and Rimuru has demonstrated ample power to join our ranks. Personally, I'd be happy to adjourn this session here, but an opportunity like this doesn't come along every day. Does anyone have something they'd like to say to the other demon lords?"

"Could I, perhaps? Since we're in the middle of this Council, I have a suggestion to give, or really, more a request," Frey said.

"Certainly. Go ahead."

Frey nodded at Guy. "Starting today, I've decided to serve Milim. As a result, I want to abdicate from my seat as a demon lord."

Well. *That* was a bombshell.

"Whoa, that's kind of sudden, isn't it?"

"Wait, Frey! I didn't hear anything about that!"

"No, because I didn't say anything about it. But I've been thinking about it for a while, do you see?"

She squinted, as if looking at some faraway point. Then she laughed, like she was recalling something amusing.

Frey recalled a conversation she had with Milim, the one that made her decide to place her trust in the girl.

"Hey, Frey, you wanna be friends with me?"

"…Why are you asking me that?"

"Well, Rimuru and I just made friends! Friends are really great. If you ever have any trouble, you both help out each other!"

"Oh, really? Well, Milim…if you're willing to help me out, then all right, I can be your friend."

"Really?! Oh, I totally promise, of course!"

"You do? I'm glad to hear that. But I'm a pretty wary woman, so I'll trust you only if you keep that promise."

"All right! Hooray, we're friends now!"

Frey had no trust in Clayman. That was why she believed in Milim, putting her own safety in the balance as she pretended to accept his terms.

What if Milim broke that promise? What if Milim's mind really was under his control? The questions worried her, but Frey still placed her chips on Milim—and they paid off, big time.

That was the reason. The reason why Frey put all her trust in Milim, volunteering to become her servant. At that moment, a lofty queen who had never trusted anyone before in her life finally found it in her to believe.

●

"Well," she resolutely stated, "I have my reasons. But the most important one is that I think I'm too weak to be a demon lord. I realized that for sure watching that battle just now; if I fought against Clayman, I'd be lucky to even match him. As for an awakened Clayman, I don't see how I could win…"

"But, Frey," Daggrull interrupted, "you specialize in high-speed aerial combat, do you not? I see no reason to depreciate yourself like this."

"You're right. If it was in the air, I would have the advantage. But demon lords don't have the right to make excuses. Besides, I know quite well how having an advantage doesn't mean anything, at times."

She paused to give me a look, her voice resolute.

"So I've decided to become one of Milim's followers instead. Plus, Milim can't afford to be as selfish as she is forever, can she? She needs to think about managing her domain, sooner or later."

In other words, Frey wasn't just thinking for herself. Milim was a wild child, and you couldn't just let her off the leash. Someone to both support and keep an eye on her was definitely needed.

Despite Frey's own admission, I really couldn't see her as being that weak. If anything, she was a strategist in a different way from Clayman, a strange, eerie leader who never let you see what she thought about you. The type that reminded you just how formidable her sex could be.

What would happen, though, if this actually happened? Thinking of Frey in terms of a servant, not as a demon lord, she definitely had enough power to be an aid to Milim. She didn't really have a nation of her own, but if Frey joined her, they'd no doubt have a formal territory in place before long. We'd have to think about building political relations soon after, and with Frey handling them, I bet the negotiations would get pretty thorny. Thorny, but still fun.

Frey turned toward Milim. "What do you think? Will you accept my suggestion?"

"Ooh, I don't really like to keep a citizenry to rule over—"

"Wait a second," Carillon said. "I got something to say about that, too. Y'know, I've already lost to Milim in a one-on-one match. I'm honestly startin' to think now's a pretty good time to hang up my cap as a military leader. On paper, all us demon lords are equal. If we're all facin' a Hero, that's one thing, but if I lost to another demon lord, I really oughtta do away with the title, y'know? So, I dunno, it just felt absurd for me to keep calling myself a demon lord. So I think I'll join Milim's faction starting today. Great to be on the team, boss!"

He wasn't asking for feedback.

I could understand the logic. With these guys, might always makes right. Still, though… I mean, Milim didn't have anyone under her, no advisers or officers to go out against this, but was it really okay for two demon lords to step down and join her side?

"Wait a minute, Carillon! That one-on-one was all Clayman's fault! I was under mind control. I don't know anything about it!"

Eesh. I really don't think that excuse is gonna work, Milim. I could see the other demon lords rolling their eyes at her.

"Don't play dumb with me, you. You just declared a minute ago that 'Oooh, nobody can take over *my* mind, no!'"

It was a remarkably good impression on Carillon's part. He had quite a talent for acting.

"Mgh?! I, um, that…"

"Well, that muscle-bound idiot can wait. What about me, Milim?"

"You—you aren't all saying this to trick me, are you? If you start 'serving' me, that means we can't talk all casually any longer, yeah? You won't play with me, and we won't come up with any more fun schemes, yeah?!"

Frey shook her head. "No. I'll get to be together with you all the time. We'll get to have more fun than ever."

I could see the brainwashing— Er, the *temptation* take hold. See? This is why you gotta watch out for her.

Carillon, meanwhile, was taking the fastball-down-the-middle approach. "Besides," he complained, "you're the one who blew my entire damn country away! Rimuru said he'll help me out with that, but *you've* got a duty to support us, too!"

I didn't think she did, really, but Milim was always weak with complicated concepts like this. Man, he was smarter than I thought. Milim's eyes were bouncing to and fro; he almost had her—and then, growing weary of thinking at all, she exploded.

"Daaahhhh! All right! Just do whatever you guys feel like!"

Smoke flew from her head like an erupting volcano as she abandoned all sentient thought. That's Milim for you. She acted all smart, but she really sucked at critical thinking.

"Are you really sure about this, Carillon?" Guy asked.

"I am. I've been thinking, too. Not about abdicating the throne of the Beast Kingdom, but about maybe building some kind of new structure with Milim at the top of it."

Guy scoffed at this, looking disappointed. "I liked you, though. In another hundred years, I was expecting *you* to awaken, too." Then he grinned at him. "But very well! From this moment, Frey and Carillon are no longer demon lords. You are free to serve Milim in any manner you please."

Now the abdication was official, and nobody voiced any further complaint. Myself included, of course.

So now I was officially deemed a demon lord, one had dropped out due to brutal death, and two had stepped down to become vassals answering directly to Milim. The Ten Great Demon Lords were now eight.

∗

I thought this would mark the end of the Council, but there was one problem left.

"Huh, so we aren't the Ten Great Demon Lords any longer?"

It was just a sidelong observation on my part, but it generated a much greater reaction than expected.

"That *is* a concern," Daggrull rumbled. "In terms of our dignity, we will need to consider a new name."

Huh? It's really that important?

"Fortunately, Walpurgis is still under way. We have all our demon lords here. Now would be a wonderful time to brainstorm."

Even Valentine, the demon lord who *definitely* couldn't take a joke, was unironically up for it. *Does this really matter, guys? I think the humans are gonna come up with one for us either way, right?*

"Oooh yes, it was a real mess the last go-round. Our numbers kept going up and down, and we had to hold so many darn Councils to settle on a new name each time!"

Wha?! They trigger Walpurgises on something that unimportant?! Ramiris described them as this grand, stately event, a special meeting of the minds... *Oh, but didn't she call it a "chat over tea" at first?* I was really starting not to care.

"You're right," said Daggrull. "The Ten Great Demon Lords thing stuck after the humans came up with that, didn't it? After we wasted all that time thinking something up. Well, I'm through with it. I don't have the wherewithal to think about it."

You just wanted to stop using your brain for a while, didn't you? Don't act like you were such a helpful participant up to now.

"Silence, you! All you did was complain. I don't remember a single constructive suggestion from your end!" Valentine knew exactly what I was thinking.

"What're you talking about, Valentine? You left that whole process to Roy, did you not?!" Deeno shot her down.

Unlike Milim and Ramiris, their erudition was mainly utilized to avoid work as much as possible. Why were they spending all this time thinking up names anyway? Like, they appeared dead serious about this. Did all demon lords have this much free time to work with?

Upon further query, I learned that the name Ten Great Demon Lords from the human realms stuck because they had spent *years* trying to devise something themselves. That was due to fluctuations in the number of demon lords—just when they thought they had something nailed down, they'd go up or down a head. So they wound up just going with the Ten Great Demon Lords, even though some were less than happy with it. It was all some of the most useless trivia I ever heard.

"All right. People. Calm down. We need to show some coopera-tion for a change. We can overcome this!" Guy had just admitted that his fellow demon lords were usually pretty damn uncooperative.

"Um, but… Should we, um…? The Eight Great—"

Ramiris's suggestion was met with such deafening silence that she couldn't even get it fully out.

"R-right," she stammered, trying to deflect it. "Guy's got a good point! Let's work on this together!"

Enthusiasm for the Eight Great Demon Lords was at an all-time low. Everyone was in agreement on that, but it didn't mean we were being any more cooperative with one another.

"Wah-ha-ha-ha-ha-ha! I'll let you guys take care of that stuff!"

"I'm tired. I'm gonna go to sleep."

It took less than a minute for us all to fall apart. I expected it from these guys, and I sure got it. I wasn't expecting one big happy family, but it was exactly as I predicted.

But one among us was able to cut through the awkward atmosphere—someone behind me who wasn't picking up on our impasse at all.

"Oh? If that's the problem, then my Rimuru's a real professional!"

It was Veldora, no doubt growing bored and pining to go home already. Ugh. Now all their eyes were on me. *I really wish he had some manga to read instead. Wait. Did he already finish reading the last volume?*

And now I could see Milim's eyes fixated upon him—or actually, that manga volume in his hand, like a hawk sizing up its prey. I had a bad feeling about that, but there were more pressing issues at hand.

"You know," Ramiris said with a nod, "when he named Beretta, he came up with *that* name in no time flat, too!"

Great. They were delegating everything to me. That bum… She's treating me with less and less respect over time, I swear. I could tell she was gradually going to push more and more on my plate. Look-ing around, I could see expectant expressions all around the table. *Crap. They've already fully surrounded me?!*

The demon lords looked at one another, then Guy stood up. "Rimuru, today you stand as a new demon lord. I wish to grant you a wonderful new privilege—"

"Oh, um, I don't need it, thanks."

I tried cutting him off before he could finish. He wasn't gonna let it happen. With a heavy *wham*, the shiny, obsidian-like, horribly valuable table was chopped right in half.

"Yes," he said as he gracefully walked right up to me, running a hand past my cheek, "I will grant you the right to provide us with a new name. A very honorable position, I should say. You will accept it, yes?"

He was totally wheedling me. The gesture might have made it look like kindness at first, but his voice made it clear that no insubordination would be allowed. I looked at him, neither nodding nor shaking my head, attempting to plead the fifth.

"And you *know*," he whispered, half biting at my ears. His fingernails were practically screeching as they dug into my cheek. "This all happened because *you* culled our numbers, did it not? You'll be kind enough to take responsibility and come up with a name, yes?"

An impartial observer might wonder if we were lovers sharing a special moment. We weren't. He was threatening me—but if things had gone this far, I had nothing to refute him with. It's really *that* much of a pain...?

Well, whatever.

"All right! Sheesh. You don't have to whine so much just because you don't like it."

Resigning myself to my fate, I grudgingly took up the post. The looks of relief on my colleagues' faces spoke volumes. Some were even kicking back and accepting refills on their tea, like this was already over. Well, screw them.

Really, I didn't mind the Eight Great Demon Lords much...but yeah, maybe it's a little *too* obvious. I figured that was what Ramiris was about to suggest, so let's just trash that right off. The pressure to drop the idea immediately was palpable in the air. No way *I* wanted to have those frowning faces upon me.

Which left... Hmm. Come to think of it, it's a new moon tonight, isn't it? A night sky, full of beautiful twinkling stars...

"Hey, how about the Octagram? You know, like an eight-pointed star?"

It was greeted by silence, the demon lords closing their eyes and scrutinizing the word. Then they all reopened them in unison.

"Settled, then. Quite lovely."

"See? I toldja! I just knew Rimuru would pull it off for us!"

"Impressive. I can see Veldora's recommendation was an apt one."

"Hmph. Well, so be it. Perhaps you are *slightly* talented."

"Dang! Just like that! Wow. Like, what was with all the trouble we had last time anyway?"

"...Mm."

No negative feedback. Well, great. If anyone *did* voice a complaint, I was thinking I'd throw the job over to them instead. *I don't know why Milim's acting like she engineered all this, though—and that's the question I'd want to ask you, Deeno. What were you talking about all those times before?*

I had a lot of questions, but as a mature adult, I had the composure to just pretend my problems didn't exist. From this point forward, we would be feared and revered under a new name.

We were called the Octagram:

> "Lord of Darkness" Guy Crimson (demon)
> "Destroyer" Milim Nava (dragonoid)
> "Labyrinth Master" Ramiris (pixie)
> "Earthquake" Daggrull (giant)
> "Queen of Nightmares" Valentine (vampire)
> "Sleeping Ruler" Deeno (Fallen)
> "Platinum Saber" Leon Cromwell (demonoid)

...and me:

> "Newbie" Rimuru Tempest (slime)

We numbered eight in all, and with those eight, we had just opened the curtain on a new era of demon lords.

The first order of business was how we distributed our domains.

I was granted the entirety of the Great Forest of Jura, which was a hell of a bargain, but Milim got an even better deal—the unified domains of Frey, Carillon, *and* Clayman under her rule. "Rule," of course, in name only. Carillon and Frey would be handling the day-to-day management, alongside the Dragon Faithful directly serving Milim.

Clayman's old domain was also something of a buffer zone bordering the Eastern Empire. We'd have to investigate how he administrated it and build defense lines as needed. Kind of a pain in the ass; someone would need to devote a lot of detail-oriented work to it. But that was something for Milim and her new government to think about. I had my own priorities to manage.

The rest of the demon lords saw no change in territorial land. Some simply wandered around with no home to call their own; some kept their exact location hidden; some set up fortresses on far-flung continents. It was rare for any of them to have precisely defined borders, so even if there *was* any change, it'd be hard to decipher.

These demon lords tended not to sweat the details, no, but they did have ways of keeping in touch. That was the function of the ring granted to each one, as a symbol of their post. Not only did they identify the wearer; they also provided for interdimensional calls between demon lords, either secret ones between two people or party lines with multiple participants.

A pretty useful bit of magic jewelry, this so-called Demon's Ring. With it, I could get into contact with them even if I was stuck inside an Unlimited Imprisonment. I'd have to consider running Analyze and Assess on it for mass-manufacturing purposes, not that I was about tell *these* guys about that.

Clayman's schemes, and the chaos he spread around the forest, were a thing of the past. I had been accepted as a new demon lord. Kazalim, Clayman's apparent master, was a worry to me, but the demon lord drama I dealt with was now all taken care of.

Now, I was a full-fledged vertex on the Octagram.

ROUGH SKETCHES

DEENO

LUMINUS—
MAID VER.

VALENTINE

EPILOGUE

IN THE HOLY LAND

That Time I Got Reincarnated as a Slime

Dang, Laplace thought as he ran as fast as his legs could take him, *I thought I was gonna die!*

Just as they had discussed, he had attempted to break into the holy domain once more, the moment the Walpurgis Council began. He was on his way to the cathedral inside the Holy Temple, headed for the Inner Cloister where he ran into a demon lord last time... only to run into the worst person possible.

She was none other than the epitome of strength and beauty—Hinata Sakaguchi, captain of the Chief Knights of the Holy Imperial Guard and leader of the Church's paladin forces.

Whoaaa! What the hell? This ain't how the promise went!

Laplace cursed his absent client. The "promise" was that said client would lure Hinata out of there for him. He could already hear the guy laughing and saying "Oops! Sorry, sorry" to him. The mere thought of it irritated him gravely.

But now was no time for grousing.

"I do so detest insects like you. Burrowing into a holy place such as this..."

The sound of Hinata's cold voice made him feel like the life was ebbing out of him. Without another moment's hesitation, Laplace decided to run—and he made it out, alive and well.

*　　*　　*

His mission was a failure. The Inner Cloister might as well have been on another planet. But none of it was Laplace's fault.

Whether the demon lord Valentine's absent or not, if she's *around, it doesn't bloody matter...*

"You expect me to beat that monster?" he whispered to himself as he gave up the job. *Still*, he thought, *I've been doin' nothin' but run lately, huh?*

He wanted to give himself a well-deserved pat on the back for getting away from Hinata at all, but that didn't mean he liked it much. Given the terrible hand fate had been dealing him lately, it didn't seem smart to assume he'd make it all the way—

Then he felt a rift appear, on the outskirts of the holy city, erupting into a massive wave of magical energy.

"Whoa... For real...?"

Laplace could barely stand this any longer. That wasn't just a high-level magic-born—it was something even stronger than that. Plus, Laplace was familiar with its magical wavelength.

"You little worm! Show yourself before me, now!!"

The voice of the demon lord Valentine thundered angrily, like a maelstrom of purging fire.

"Dammit! Now it's a demon lord?!"

Laplace wanted to wail out loud at the completeness of his sheer bad luck. But now wasn't the time for that. He attempted to run off once more—

"Hmph! You're just as lowly as him, I see. Do you just enjoy inching around?"

—then he stopped, sensing something in Valentine's choice of words.

"What do you mean?"

"Pfft! It does not involve you." Valentine scornfully laughed. "But very well. Just a moment ago, the demon lord Clayman lost his life. That foolish, sniveling little maggot fled for *his* life, too, just like you, mewling pathetically the whole time."

"What?"

"Ha-ha-ha! What, are you angry? What does it matter to you?"

"Shut up! Are you fer real? Clayman's dead?"

"Haaaaah-ha-ha-ha! So the maggot's let the cat out of the bag, has he? I *thought* you two might be connected. By the will of the goddess Luminus!!"

Laplace stood there, dazed, before Valentine's loud laughter. Clayman's death was too much for him to believe. Not that he *couldn't* believe it, he just didn't *want* to. To him, Clayman was a good friend and companion, if restless and nervous.

"What're you laughin' about, ya pile of garbage?!"

"Who do you think you're talking to, you—*gnnngh*?!"

"Dumbass! I *told* you not to laugh at my friend!"

Laplace's fists never stopped swinging. They were literally killer, both of them.

"Gnhh, don't—don't you start on me, maggot!!"

His face reddened with anger and humiliation, Valentine glared at Laplace. No matter how much this insect hit him, Ultraspeed Regeneration made it all pointless. Death was the only way to give fools like these a lesson, as he thought it. He didn't even stop to wipe the blood sprays—sprays that even now turned into a fine, crimson mist that descended around them both:

"Die! Bloodray!!" Valentine cried.

Amid this absolute barrier of gore, a torrent of visceral blood particles hurtled at the speed of a bullet toward—nowhere.

"Uh-uh. You're a dead man."

"Wha...?!" Valentine had no idea what happened. He bore overwhelming power, and this little maggot was toying with him. He had tried to kill him with his most powerful of skills, but for some reason, it never went off. Tonight *was* a new moon, the period when his powers were at their lowest point, but to a demon lord, the difference was trivial.

There could be only one explanation: Laplace was strong. And this turned out to be correct. In Laplace's hand, there was something throbbing.

"...!!"

"Yep. That's yer core, there, your heart. Can't move, can't speak, am I right? That's what I do."

As Laplace gave him the cruel news, Valentine's body began to unconsciously shiver, little by little. It almost felt like...

...*Fear? Am I feeling fear?!*

"You were juuuust a little late on the uptake there. But you got it now, yeah? I'm a strong one."

Valentine's face turned pale, wincing in desperation. He realized that Laplace really did have his core in his hand. All was lost.

The expression made Laplace whoop in crazed laughter as he crushed it with his fingers. The battle was decided in a single moment.

Laplace didn't stop smiling for a while after.

...*Oooh, Footman's not gonna like this...*

He had massacred all the guards who spotted him.

...*Ooh, and Teare's probably gonna cry, too...*

He had attempted to flee straight out of there.

...*And that's exactly why I'm laughing. Laughing at you, Clayman. For being such a perfect idiot.*

The Crazed Clown, in his estimation, had experienced exactly the death he deserved. Laplace wasn't angry; he wasn't crying; he was just laughing, in commemoration of a friend who would no longer laugh with him.

ROUGH SKETCHES

AFTERWORD

Hey! It's been a while! About five months since the previous volume. Yes, it's Volume 6 of *That Time I Got Reincarnated as a Slime*, and it's time for the traditional afterword.

This volume is the result of yet another epic battle between my editor, Mr. I, and me over what to write and what to cut out.

Mr. I was a lot nicer to me back in Volume 1, you know. I remember one conversation:

"You know, if you really don't like writing an afterword, it's okay if you don't!"

"Really? Thanks a lot! I don't know what I should write in it. I'm just not very good at that kind of thing, so I really appreciate you saying that!"

HOWEVER!

Flash forward to this volume:

"I'm putting the pages together, and it looks like we're gonna need about eight pages of afterword."

"Huh? Eight? Isn't that a lot?"

I mean, seriously, eight pages is a *crazy* amount of afterword. You can see why I was aghast.

"Well, there's just no getting around it, I'm afraid. With the binding we're using, if we cut out all the blank pages, we won't have space for an afterword at all."

"Oh, okay, let's go with that—"

"No! What're you talking about?! I really need an afterword from you!"

Once upon a time, he gently whispered to me that he didn't need any afterword for Volume 1. Where did that kindly Mr. I go? Sure, I look forward to the afterwords of novel series I have a thing for, but once *you're* the one writing them, you quickly defect to the "don't need 'em" crowd. That's one of my special (if distressingly awful) skills, the ability to freely change my mind based on my current perspective.

I tried using that superpower to have Mr. I see things my way, but:

"Whether it means more pages or not, I've got to have you write it! The 'no afterword' choice is *not* on the table!!"

With a single roar from the editorial office, the option of skipping the afterword was crushed to oblivion. So I gave up, and after several more rounds of negotiation, we successfully managed to cut a couple pages.

I tell you, though, it's starting to become a regular exchange between us.

"I think the page count's gonna go up a little this time, too…"

"That's fine! Don't worry about it! Just keep on writing!"

And then there's the afterword on top of *that*. And here I was worried about the manuscript ballooning too much. This volume's already thicker than normal, and now I had to cough up more afterword pages. Mr. I must be nuts.

By the way, when I submitted my first draft, Mr. I's first piece of feedback was:

"The scene with [censored] isn't there, but what's up with that?"

"Ooh, well, the page count was going up too much, so I very reluctantly had to cut it out."

"You can't do that, can you? That's a really vital scene!"

"Yeah, but there's nothing else I can cut out..."

"Seriously, man, I don't want you worrying about cutting your own content! Just write it! When it comes to *Slime*, we've decided to just let you write as much as you've got!"

Thanks to that, despite the first draft already being the longest manuscript in *Slime* history, it wound up being expanded a good several thousand words more.

In Japan, this series is published by GC Novels in the *shinsho* format, which features two separate columns of text per page instead of one so more can be crammed in. Thanks to that, I had already published the novel with the highest word count in GC history, but with *this* volume, I am now number-one in page count, too. "It's a new record!" Mr. I crowed. I have no idea what he's aiming for with that.

But anyway, the result of all that silly back-and-forth is Volume 6. It's thicker than anything that came before it, and I hope you've enjoyed it for a lot more than just its size.

Now let's cover a bit of the content. As I mentioned in Volume 2, I'm the kind of guy who peruses the afterword first, so I just want to warn you that I'm not gonna be shy with spoilers ahead. Proceed at your own risk!

∗

I mentioned this topic in the afterword to Volume 5, but number six is full of original content not in the web version, too. It should be quite obvious from the table of contents, but this is the volume where Rimuru is recognized as a demon lord in name and deed and the term *Octagram* is coined for the whole gang.

Volumes 5 and 6 cover everything in Chapter 4 of the web series, the Birth of a Demon Lord arc, and given how Birth of a Demon Lord's events wouldn't even fill up all of Volume 5, you can see how almost everything in this book is new material. The exchanges Mr. I and I had about this were discussed in Volume 5, and I tried my best not to have the results read like a watered-down bottle of Calpis.

Speaking of that content... Well, as always, I'm running a large cast of characters. Perhaps readers of the web version have a head start, but if you're following the printed novels alone, it might be pretty tough going. If you think about it, though, this book has over twice the word count of your typical paperback light novel, so maybe it's not *that* bad, proportionally speaking.

I wanted to fill it in with some illustrations, of course, so Mitz Vah's put in a hell of an effort for me this time, too! All ten demon lords (What? There's eleven? Well, *that's* weird.) show up in this volume, and I think they're all looking really cool. There was another heated battle between Mitz Vah and Mr. I over how large to make the female characters' breasts, but that wasn't anything for me to get involved with. I'll have to wait for the final illustrations to see how the results of that debate turned out.

Oops. Getting off track here. Thanks to those wonderful illustrations, though, I think they make it a lot easier to picture the cast in your mind.

Regarding conflicts between the web and print versions—well, I think we're somehow managing to keep the overall story arc identical, you could say. Of course, you've got at least one character with completely different motivations, others whose backstory itself has changed, and if you examine the smaller details, there are differences all over the place. It might be harder to find unedited passages that're exactly as they were written on the web, maybe.

Going forward, all these changes might pile up to the point that it turns into a completely different story. I'm intending to stick to the same general plotline, but really, I can't truly know until I start writing. That's the philosophy of *Slime*, I suppose, and I hope you'll keep reading.

＊

I'd like to close this afterword with a few words of thanks.

First, to Mitz Vah, who provides such excellent artwork. Seeing some of the rough drafts has made me completely rethink my image of certain characters. It's great to receive this kind of stimulus! We've still got a bunch of new characters to introduce, so keep up the good work.

Next, Taiki Kawakami, author of the manga version, along with his editor, Mr. U. I can't say enough about how they answer all my petty requests for each chapter. I asked him for a couple of bonus pages for this volume, too, and he very kindly accepted. Thanks so much! (Huh? You think I just wanted to reduce the number of afterword pages I had to write? I have no idea what you're talking about.)

My editor, Mr. I, has always been there to discuss things with me. His opinions and feedback are truly a treasure. If an editor doesn't understand your work, I doubt there's any way you'll ever convince a larger audience to like it. Keep that feedback coming. Don't hold back!

Thanks also go out to everyone involved with proofreading, design, and production. I'm sure the proofreaders in particular had a hard time checking such a huge quantity of words. Thanks so much for your hard work!

Finally, I just want to tell the readers kind enough to purchase this book that I'll continue to strive to make *That Time I Got Reincarnated as a Slime* the most enjoyable read it can possibly be.

See you in the next volume!

PSST.
The next two pages
reflect the original
Japanese orientation,
so read backward!

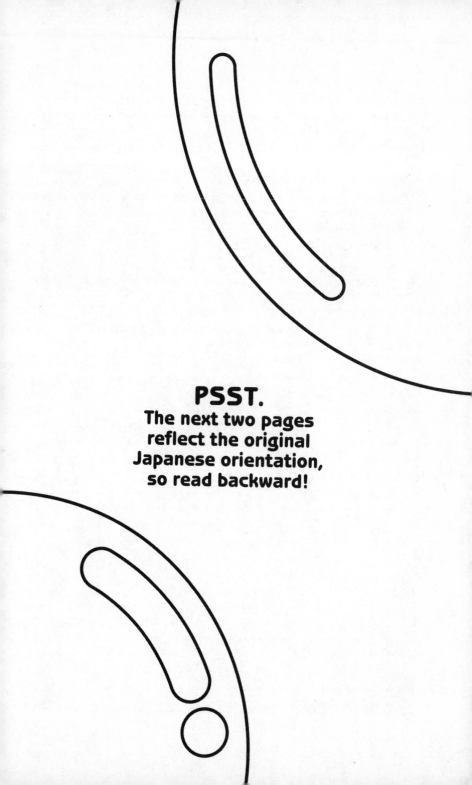

HEADPIECE

STRIKE A POSE!

THIS IS STILL PRETTY CUTE TOO ...!!

RIMURU'S GIVEN UP...!

Celebratory Comic Simu-Launch
SPECIAL MANGA

Art: Taiki Kawakami

You've read the novel, now pick up the manga!

With gorgeous, detailed, and hilarious art by Taiki Kawakami!

Manga vols. 1-10 are available now from Kodansha Comics!

Plus: Each volume includes an exclusive prose side story by creator Fuse!

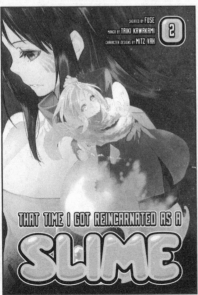

"Pushes manga in new directions." –Adventures in Poor Taste